PRAISE FOR CHRISTINE MICHELS'S *ASCENT TO THE STARS*

BURNING DESIRE

"What...what are you planning to do with me?"

Trace glanced at Coventry quizzically. "Now that is an interesting question," he murmured absently. "It brings so many prospects to mind. Let's just say that, like it or not, you and I will be spending time together." He raised his head from his task to rake her body from head to toe with an intense stare. "We could get to know each other well."

Stunned, Coventry watched his lean-fingered hands caress the smooth nylon of the bag. His blatantly suggestive statement paralyzed her. A picture of his strong fingers caressing her body insinuated itself into her mind. She trembled at the sudden heat the image invoked.

ASCENT TO THE STARS

CHRISTINE MICHELS

LOVE SPELL NEW YORK CITY

*To Brandon, for being a son a mother can be proud of—
most of the time.*

*And to my husband, Don, for having faith in me—
most of the time.*

I love you both. Keep dreaming with me.

LOVE SPELL®

February 1994

Published by

Dorchester Publishing Co., Inc.
276 Fifth Avenue
New York, NY 10001

Cover Art by John Ennis

The name "Love Spell" and its logo are trademarks of Dorchester Publishing Co., Inc.

Printed in the United States of America.

ASCENT TO THE STARS

Chapter One

Production music flowed eerily around her. The pale, disembodied faces of the hushed audience swam in a sea of shadowy obscurity beyond the brilliantly lighted circular stage. Tonight, Coventry Pearce found the familiar setting of the theatre sinister and frightening. "They" could be out there watching her, and she would never know it. She didn't even know who "they" were. A sudden starred coruscation of light flashing from the darkness slashed at her frayed nerves. Someone taking a picture? Pulse pounding in her throat, she performed on autopilot. Thank the stars, this was the final act of the show and she had no lines to deliver. The words of the message that she had received in her dressing room during the last break echoed in her mind.

Coventry. I need a disguise. When your show is over, please bring something I can use to the Honeymoon Suite. Conceal it in the bag I'm sending. It's important, Cov, or I wouldn't ask. They will probably be watching you, so make certain you're not followed. Trust nobody. Love, Dalton.

Who would be watching her? Why did her brother need a disguise? And, why the Honeymoon Suite? Coventry's parents had conferred the name "Honeymoon Suite" on the apartment they'd kept in the city prior to their deaths in a public transit accident. When Rina and Colin Pearce had passed away eight months ago, Coventry and Dalton had been unable to decide what to do with their parents effects and had agreed to simply maintain the apartment for a time. But why would Dalton want her to meet him *there*? It just didn't make sense.

It had been weeks since she'd last seen Dalton, but to her knowledge, his position as a strategist for the Global Intelligence Network did not involve field operations. Although the G.I.N. was administered by the United Nations and competing factions sometimes conducted "policing investigations" to ensure the integrity of their allies, Coventry could not perceive how any of Dalton's work could have involved him in a situation where he needed a disguise. Yet, whether she could conceive of it or not, it was the only explanation she could come up with. Dalton's life outside the network had been all but nonexistent since the day he'd joined the organization. Perhaps he did do some simple fieldwork on occasion. In which case, he must have a need to remain incognito due to the surveillance of some foreign division. But why wouldn't the network supply the necessary disguise? And why would "they" be observing her?

The performance began to come to a close and Coventry forced her mind to focus. Hell! She'd almost missed her cue. As she danced nearer the edge of the stage, executing her performance by rote, her eyes settled on two men in the audience who did not seem to belong. Garbed in unrelieved black street clothing, they stood out like Fringers at a society assembly. And they seemed to be observing her closely.

Paranoid idiot! Of course they watched her; she

was delivering a performance. She mustn't allow Dalton's melodramatic message to affect her.

Nevertheless, she breathed a sigh of relief when the curtain fell and she could make her exit. She strode quickly in the direction of the small cube-like room that served as her dressing room.

"Hey, Cov." A pert blonde actress grasped her arm to slow her down. "You okay? You seem a bit preoccupied tonight."

"I'm fine, Vickie." Coventry forced a smile. "Just a slight headache."

"Well, let me know if you need anything."

Coventry nodded absently, her eyes already roaming ahead. "I will. Thanks." She began to maneuver her way through a group of fellow actors; the dense fog insulating her thoughts made the cacophony of their post-production chatter seem distant and dreamlike.

Completing the walk to her dressing room without further delay, she closed the door firmly and triggered the latch. Expelling her breath in a long sigh, she felt the nervous tension begin to leave her rigid muscles. She always suffered a certain amount of tension before and after a performance but tonight it was worse. Leaning against the door, she took several deep breaths, releasing each successive one as slowly as possible.

Then, somewhat more relaxed, she sat at her dressing table to remove the pins and clips which held her hair in an elaborate style which, Coventry swore, had been designed with the express purpose of torturing the wearer. As her golden-blonde tresses tumbled free, flowing in thick lustrous waves to her hips, she used her fingers to hastily knead her aching scalp.

As she set about removing her makeup, she began to consider the type of costume she could

11

supply for Dalton. Facial makeup was no problem. She possessed an ample supply because she often preferred to apply it herself and just have a makeup artist do the finishing touches. She even had a couple of masks. But apparel was another matter. She would have to appropriate an old ensemble and hope that it wouldn't be required for a production.

She completed removing the layers of cosmetics from her face, and automatically studied the emerging picture of her own features. Her flawless ivory skin was her greatest asset. A permanent peach flush which she'd had introduced to her lips and cheekbones granted her an image of health and vitality. But her eyes . . . Dull, brown eyes framed by a thick tangle of black lashes, they were completely at odds with her blonde hair and fair skin.

Reflexively, she reached for her shoulder bag. Extracting a small gray case, she opened it to reveal an array of tinted contact lenses. Briskly selecting a mauve pair without any real consideration, she dipped them in solution and placed them in her eyes. After taking another swift glance at herself in the mirror, she rose to change into her own clothing.

As she adjusted her garments she looked thoughtfully at the costume she'd flung haphazardly over the back of the chair. It had a small rent beneath the arm which, she had no doubt, the wardrobe people would find and repair when they came to collect the ensembles. But, if she took it with her to wardrobe . . . if anybody asked why she was there . . . she could say she wanted to point out the tear. Unconsciously she gave a quick, sharp nod as she came to the decision.

She picked up the capacious blue nylon bag

provided by Dalton and, for the first time, thought to wonder why he'd sent it. She could have found something in which to carry the disguise he'd requested. Oh well, since he had sent it, she might as well make use of it. She carefully placed some makeup, a couple of masks, and a reversible wig into it. Then, flinging the costume over one shoulder, her shoulder bag over the other, and carrying Dalton's bag she strode from the closet-like room.

Less than fifteen minutes later, Coventry left the studio by a back door. She paused, studying the area hesitantly. The bright, full-spectrum city lighting—installed within the atmospheric-dome of Providence City to provide even night workers with the opportunity to soak up the benefits of natural illumination—dispelled any pretense toward darkness even though it was late evening. There was no sign of the two men in black. She looked longingly toward the almost deserted promenade walk with its carousel-like lighting overhead. Should she risk taking it, or choose an alternate route? Despite her determination not to allow herself to be affected by the melodramatic tone of Dalton's message, she was nervous. She observed the few people in the area. None of them appeared to be watching her. She gnawed her lip indecisively.

Her weariness hit her abruptly, as it always did, and she realized she'd worked twelve hours that day. That decided the matter. Strolling the few yards to the promenade, she stepped onto its endlessly rolling surface and chose a seat on one of its benches.

As she summoned hidden energy reserves to stave off her weariness, her eyes and thoughts merely drifted for a time. Her gaze skimmed the surfaces of the towering buildings of glass and steel that lined the avenues, but there was nothing to be seen behind the mirrorlike surfaces and her attention switched to the street. Although hundreds of sleek, silent computerized vehicles still traversed the gleaming surface of the thoroughfare, she didn't think it was as busy as usual.

A sudden movement on the periphery of her vision startled her. Adrenaline surged into her system as her head snapped around to identify the source of the abrupt motion. She sighed in relief. Heavens, she was more apprehensive than she had realized. It was just somebody trying to negotiate his way through traffic on foot. No . . . She frowned as she observed the figure of the young man as he wove his way frantically through the street traffic. Stars! Another Fringer had broken into the city seeking paradise within the dome. No, on second thought, his clothing looked slightly more stylish than that of a Fringer. And a Fringer would be pursued by dome-guards in wailing vehicles. Must be a Probie outside authorized territory. She wondered how long it would take before Central caught the violation. Even as the question occurred to her, the young man clutched his head in twitching fingers, opened his mouth in a silent scream, and collapsed. The crime deterrent capsule embedded within his brain stem had been automatically detonated by Central.

Shuddering, Coventry turned her eyes away from his convulsing body. What crime had he committed to have been placed on probation in the first place? And why had he committed suicide? No one ever escaped Central's probationary monitors.

On the opposite side of the six-lane street, she could see people walking along the surface of another promenade. No one paid the slightest attention to the small drama unfolding on the street. *Familiarity breeds dispassion. So, why do I always wonder about them? Feel for them?* But she knew the answer. Dalton.

Years of listening to him doubt the honesty of the media's version of events; hours of listening to his theories on how the Fringers and Probies could be reintroduced into productive society. She frowned. It was strange how he'd just stopped talking about it within months of joining the Network.

Her gaze was drawn once more to the body of the young Probie as it was scooped up by the coroner's van. She wondered if he had a family who'd miss him. Then, forcibly tearing her eyes away, she attempted to shrug off her morbidity.

She observed a young couple holding hands and felt a twinge of wistfulness. At twenty-eight years old, Coventry had all but relinquished hope of finding love. Had it not been for the example she'd seen in her parents' marriage she would have doubted its existence all together.

Disgusted by her persistent gloom, Coventry reflexively pressed a button on the arm of the bench. It was time to look ahead, not behind. Immediately the seat pivoted, halting automatically after a half turn that allowed her to see in both directions along the promenade. She was about to press the button to complete the turn when she paused in deference to a pair of ladies strolling by her bench as they walked along the rolling promenade. Watching them as they moved away, Coventry's eyes happened to fall on the portion of the promenade walk that traveled in the other direction. She tensed.

Two men approached. Two men who could have been the twins of those she'd seen during her performance . . . or the same men. They'd had plenty of time to get ahead of her and backtrack.

Make certain you're not followed. "Damn you, Dalton," she muttered under her breath as her heart began to race. She was not cut out for this. Cursing herself for taking the time to sit, Coventry nibbled the inside of her cheek. Now what?

She forced herself to remain seated. Casually, she watched the men through the curtain of her lashes as they came opposite her and continued to move in the direction from which she'd come.

How far was it to the next taxi stand? She lifted her gaze to study the backlit map on the ceiling of the promenade. Not far. As soon as the men on the opposite promenade rolled out of sight . . . They were gone!

She'd taken her eyes off of them for barely a minute. Where were they? Frantically her eyes searched up and down the reverse promenade. They had not seated themselves. Had they switched promenades? Were they now behind her? Almost fearfully, she turned her head a little. Her throat closed.

Less than thirty feet from her, just beyond a man reclining on a bench working with a notebook-size computer, one of the men openly watched her while the other regarded the street. The man looking at her bared his teeth in the semblance of a smile before turning his head to survey some people passing on the other promenade. Since he seemed to know that Coventry was observing him from the corner of her eye anyway, she decided to discard subtlety and inspect him and his companion openly.

They both wore black bodysuits—relatively common street clothing, designed for active people, which no longer looked out of place—and conventional dark glasses concealed their eyes. In fact, neither man looked anything but ordinary except that they were dressed virtually identically. The man observing the street with unfailing attentiveness appeared to be about five feet ten inches tall and had thick brown hair combed straight back. The other man had black hair worn in the same style and, although about the same height, he was slightly heavier which made him seem a little shorter. They each wore wrist computers. No, the units had a slightly different appearance. Terminals probably.

Wrist terminals! They'd be on-line to Central! If she took a taxi and they happened to observe the license number of the vehicle, they could track her easily. The entire city transportation system was computerized. Coventry looked away, staring sightlessly at the opposite promenade, as she struggled to come up with some course of action. Thanks to her darling brother's ambiguous message, she didn't even understand why she was being followed. Who were these men? How could she escape them?

She nipped at the inner flesh of her bottom lip. Precious seconds slipped by as her mind groped for answers. They were probably very determined and, depending on their motivation, potentially very dangerous people. And she, untrained and completely unenlightened as to the nature of the situation, was no match for them. How was she, an actress, supposed to elude men who were trained trackers?

Act! Coventry glanced back at the men. They hadn't moved. The promenade approached a restaurant and she eyed it speculatively. Grasping the handle of the tote bag firmly, she risked one last peek at the men. Wait . . . wait. Now! In one continuous, fluid motion, she rose, jumped from the promenade, took six giant steps, and entered the crowded restaurant. The merest pause allowed her to locate the public rest room, and race toward it. As she entered it, she risked a glance at the entrance. Two men in black stood there.

If she'd had any doubts that she was actually being followed, they were erased now. Quickly secluding herself in the only vacant cubicle, Coventry extracted her large makeup mirror from her shoulder bag and affixed it to the wall. Then, removing a mask from the tote, she put it on. The masks always appeared wrinkled until the desired features were created with the accompanying syringe. After extricating the cylindrical instrument from the tangle of items within the tote, she studied the mask. Inserting the tip of the syringe into one of the tiny holes she injected air into the pocket and observed the transformation as wrinkles smoothed out.

Coventry had decided to play the part of a woman slightly past her prime, despite the fact that the costume she carried was designed for a man. She simply did not have the accessories to convincingly transform her curvaceous frame into that of a male.

Seconds later, finished with the alteration of the mask features, she removed her contacts and replaced them in their case before donning the wig. The short dark brown curls concealed her own blonde hair and she adjusted the wavy fringe around her face to hide any facial flaws which might exist due to her hasty application of the mask. Then she extracted the costume and studied it critically.

A mere seven minutes from the time Coventry had entered the rest room, a wide-hipped mature woman with a slight fanning of creases around her brown eyes emerged, still patting the curls of her short brown hair into place. She walked firmly, but casually, past two men standing near the door, through the restaurant and out the door in the direction of the taxi stand. Although she didn't appear to bear a purse of any kind, she carried a large black carryall beneath one arm.

Arriving at the taxi stand, she paused to look back the way she'd come before stepping beneath the open winged-door of a taxi with the word *Southside* emblazoned on a backlit sign on its roof. So far, so good. They'd have no reason to check with Central as long as they didn't suspect she'd gotten past them and taken a cab. Moving quickly now, all the time keeping her eyes trained on the restaurant from which she'd come, she removed a card from the pocket of her voluminous slacks and slid it into the slot on the dash of the taxi.

"Where to?" a pleasant computerized male voice queried.

"Riverton Centre. Quickly please."

"Certainly," the computer responded. The vehicle began to move just as two men emerged from the restaurant. She ducked her head in the hope that the men would think that the cab had been summoned from its station unoccupied.

Arriving at Riverton Centre, Coventry departed the taxi, which quite naturally had halted at the entrance to the Riverton complex, and strode quickly in the direction of the Riverton taxi stand. This time she chose a taxi heralding the *Eastside* district.

"Phoenix Towers, please," she stated in response to the computer's request for a destination. As far as Coventry could tell she was no longer being followed.

Using her identification card to unlock the main doors of the central tower, Coventry walked swiftly across the brightly illuminated lobby to the security panel and placed her hand, palm down, on the scanner.

"Good evening, Ms. Pearce. Will you be visiting long?"

"No." Coventry responded automatically to the programmed computer query as she glanced over her shoulder before walking quickly in the direction of the elevators. The doors slid open spontaneously as floor sensors registered her approach. Leaning against the rear wall, she closed her eyes in relief as the lift sealed.

Disregarding the flashing blue light signaling that it awaited instructions, Coventry triggered the door lock and stripped out of her disguise. Removing her shoulder bag and other paraphernalia from the bottom of the tote, she turned the nylon bag right-side-out exposing its distinctive blue color again. Then squirming out of her oversized clothing, she shoved it haphazardly into the carryall.

"Floor thirty-two," she instructed the waiting blue light as she removed the wig, raked her fingers hastily through the tangled abundance of her hair, and began peeling off the uncomfortable mask. Now that the adrenaline reaction engendered by flight had begun to wear off, she discovered she was trembling. Thank heavens elevator computers weren't programmed for mundane conversation. She didn't think she could manage even that much right now.

As she sensed the momentum of the elevator slowing, Coventry opened her eyes to watch the floor numbers flashing by on the digital display. At thirty-two, the doors slid silently open and she stepped through them onto the soft, blue air-carpet of the wide hall. Although normally she would have walked to her parents' apartment, tonight, tired and lugging the unwieldy tote, she simply chose one of the seats along the wall and entered the apartment number. The chair, attached to the wall by means of the track along which it moved, immediately began to slide along the corridor.

Feeling safe for the moment, Coventry allowed her mind to turn once more to Dalton and his note. The piece of pseudo-paper was still in her shoulder bag. The way things had been progressing she thought that perhaps she should destroy it.

A group of people, conversing loudly and merrily, passed her and she smiled absently at them. She hoped Dalton was at the apartment. If she had to wait much longer to find out what was going on, she would cheerfully decapitate him when she caught up with him.

The chair slowed and came to a stop. Rising and crossing the corridor to the door, Coventry placed her palm against the identification panel. A musical series of beeps sounded as it verified that she was one of those authorized for entry. There was an audible click as the lock mechanism disengaged itself and the door opened a crack.

21

The apartment beyond lay shrouded in darkness. Dalton hadn't arrived yet.

Cursing under her breath, Coventry opened the door with her foot as she maneuvered the bulky tote through the opening and stepped into the darkness. "Lights please, Magna," she demanded rather grumpily of the maintenance computer as she dropped the carryall unceremoniously beside the entrance. Soft illumination partially dispelled the gloom and her eyes fell on the inviting shape of the soft sofa.

A sigh emerged. She lifted a foot to take a step toward it. The hair on the back of her neck rose. Off balance she tried to turn. A powerful hand clamped over her mouth, jerking her upright and back against a massive and decidedly solid body that her senses told her was most definitely male.

They'd caught her!

Chapter Two

Coventry struggled desperately against the constraint of the muscle-corded arm encircling her waist. Her fingers clawed at the hand which seemed about to crush her jaw in its viselike grip as it forced her head back against an unyielding shoulder. Was there only one of them? The coarseness of a man's abrasive chin scraped her temple as her eyes raked the softly lit apartment searching for his cohort. He *was* alone. Perhaps she'd have a chance.

Slamming an elbow back into his body, she encountered an abdomen of solid granite. Her blow didn't even elicit a grunt. Squirming doggedly against the strength of his grasp, she drove her foot back in the hope of incapacitating a knee but misjudged and hit a shinbone as solid as a tree trunk, succeeding only in hurting her own ankle.

"It might be prudent of you to refrain from grinding that charming little backside against me, lady."

Coventry froze. The husky baritone of his softly accented voice emerging on a warm breath next to her ear sent shivers down her spine. What had he said?

As the meaning behind his words slowly penetrated her fear-numbed brain, the reason for his comment suddenly became disconcertingly apparent. Moaning in panic against his palm, she attempted to arch her lower body away from his, but her effort was curtailed by the sheer power of the arm binding her waist.

"If you calm yourself, and promise not to scream, I will release you. Agreed?"

Hastily, Coventry nodded although the constraint of his hand made the movement all but imperceptible.

Slowly, as though doubting the honesty of her agreement, he removed his hand from her mouth. Apparently encouraged by her docility, he loosened his hold on her waist. As soon as she felt the constriction of his hold ease, Coventry shoved herself away from him and raced across the small room, instinctively wanting to put as much distance as possible between them. Then, crossing her arms over her chest to grip her shoulders, she turned to face him.

Her mouth opened in wordless surprise. This was not one of the men in black. She confronted a complete stranger. A sinister looking stranger, cloaked in shadow, with a small rectangular object directed unwaveringly at her. A stunner! She swallowed.

Dressed in a loose-fitting medium blue shirt, its sleeves folded up to his elbows, and dark pants that hugged his powerful body like a sheath, he stood well over six feet tall. Remembering the feeling of that rocklike abdomen, she was certain that his body housed not one molecule of fat, yet she would not call him lean. She tried to see his face, to read an expression there that would help her understand the situation she found herself in, but the subdued lighting of the apartment eclipsed his features. "Increase lighting intensity,

Magna," she ordered hoarsely.

The maintenance computer complied instantly and she almost wished it hadn't. The man standing before her radiated menace and violence from every pore. Her brain screamed *danger* and shot a bolstering dose of adrenaline into her system that had her trembling like a hypothermia victim. Fear raced through her with each frantic beat of her heart. Yet, despite it, the man's incredible presence engraved itself upon her mind. If he were to disappear in the next instant, she knew that she would remember him the rest of her life.

Thick black hair, combed straight back, fell in shining waves to his shoulders—slightly longer than was fashionable—framing bronzed features that would rarely be termed handsome. Although possessed of a rugged magnetism, there was little attractive about them. Dark eyes glittered like obsidian from beneath thick ebony brows, one of which curved upward at the outer corner due to a small scar that extended into the hair at his temple. His nose, straight and narrow, definitely possessed some patrician aspects, but the intractable set of his square jaw negated the influence.

"Who are you? What are you doing here?" The growled query distracted her from her perusal. As the meaning of his words penetrated, Coventry was struck momentarily dumb with incredulity.

"Who . . . who am *I*?" Her voice emerged on a squeak of surprise. "Who are *you*?"

"You are trying my patience." He emphasized his statement with a small but explicit motion of the stunner. "Who are you?"

Coventry gritted her teeth in an attempt to control their tendency to chatter before responding. "Coventry Pearce. This apartment belongs to me . . . me and my brother." She was silently amazed at the evenness of her tone. "Now, will you tell me who . . . who *you* are?"

"Ah," he responded as black brows winged upward, arching over unreadable eyes. A slight nod seemed to indicate she had just solved some sort of puzzle for·him. "Where is Dalton?"

Coventry's eyes narrowed. Everyone wanted to find Dalton. At least she could answer truthfully. "I haven't the faintest idea. He asked me to meet him here." She eyed the stunner apprehensively. "Could you please put that thing away? I promise I won't hurt you." The inflammatory comment was intentional, designed to prick his male vanity, shaming him into lowering the weapon. But it didn't work. He continued to stare at her appraisingly.

Coventry decided to ignore the weapon. "Will you *please* tell me who you are and what you're doing here?" She waited but he still didn't seem inclined to respond and she began to get angry. Angry at Dalton for getting her into this, whatever *this* was. Angry at this man for frightening the wits out of her. And angry at herself for her distinct lack of courage.

"Look! Since I don't remember meeting you at the last family reunion, I think you owe me an explanation. How exactly did you manage to get into a security apartment?"

"Mmmm." He gazed intently at the seascape mural covering the wall behind her before shifting his piercing eyes to her, examining her from head to toe. Coventry found his scrutiny unnerving; the penetrating perceptiveness of his look raised gooseflesh on her arms.

"Would you like a picture for posterity?" she asked caustically, without forethought, and immediately wished that she'd bitten her tongue.

He grinned, giving her a fleeting glimpse of even white teeth, totally transforming his appearance. "No, that will not be necessary." The grin disappeared. A small furrow etched itself between his brows as he put his hands behind his back to tuck the stunner into the waistband of his trousers. Then, turning his eyes to the floor, he began to pace the small room with a smooth distance-eating stride. His feet, shod in thick-soled black boots that laced to his knees, were absolutely soundless. He no longer seemed inclined to use the stunner. In fact, he seemed to be totally ignoring her existence.

Coventry's fear began to diminish rapidly in the face of her increasing outrage at his refusal to communicate. His infernal pacing made her edgy. She was scared to death and getting angrier by the second. Impatience gripped her. "What the hell is the matter with you? Will you please tell me who you are and what you're doing here?"

Her words had an instant effect. He stopped, raised his head, and looked at her with an expression of extreme annoyance. "You will not use profanity. Such words coming from a woman's mouth are distasteful."

Coventry was shocked speechless. What had she said? Oh yeah, *hell*. The word was such an integral part of her vocabulary that she rarely was aware of using it. But what had *he* said? A woman's mouth? A *woman's* mouth?

"As for your questions: I will answer them in a moment. First, you will let me think." Without waiting for a response he resumed pacing, his eyes on the floor. Thus it was that he missed the effect of his words on Coventry and was totally unprepared for the repercussion which followed.

"You unmitigated boor. You arrogant cotton-headed—" Coventry floundered as she searched her mind for another descriptive simile. Failing, she continued her harangue undaunted after the merest pause. "If I want to *use profanity*, I damn well will. Compared to some people I've met, I hardly swear at all. Where the hell did you come from? The seventeenth century? A woman's mouth, my ass! I've memorized worse language in scripts than I ever use offstage. And don't you dare tell me what I *will* or *won't* do. You—" Coventry broke off abruptly as the subject of her statement began to walk toward her with a very dangerous glint in his eye.

Warily backing up a couple of paces, Coventry came up against the wall. Her eyes widened as she realized he didn't appear to have any intention of stopping. Oh, hell! Why couldn't she ever control her temper? In her outrage, she'd completely forgotten the possible danger this man represented. The door, her only means of escape, was on the other side of the room, and he was between it and her. She took a step to the left and came up against the unyielding column of his arm as he blocked her passage.

"Don't—" Her statement was cut off by a large calloused hand closing over her mouth once more while the other hand clasped her neck, effectively preventing any possibility of twisting free. She raised her hands to tug ineffectively at his forearms, steadfastly ignoring the not-unpleasant sensation of silky black hair against her palms.

"Your employer must be very pleased. You seem to have an excellent memory for distinctive, if somewhat tasteless, profanities." His calm, even tone seemed all the more ominous.

He moved closer, his big body a scant hand's-breadth from hers. She could feel the heat of him and, despite the fear that was once again rising in her throat, she was stunned by the realization that her body responded to his proximity, not as a threat, but as a man. An incredibly sexy man!

"My name is Rainon . . . Tiern Rainon. On Earth I am called Trace." The warm breath expelled by his quietly spoken words caressed Coventry's face, stirring a tendril of her hair to tickle her forehead. "No, I am not from the seventeenth century. I am from Thadonia."

Coventry's eyes widened. Thadonia! It explained the slight accent she'd detected. Although, she'd heard something of their world from Dalton—he'd developed quite an interest in comparing Thadonian and Earth cultures—she'd never met a Thadonian. But what would a Thadonian be doing here? Did Dalton's strange request for a disguise have something to do with his presence?

Tiern Rainon, apparently having paused to let her assimilate his abrupt statement, continued. "*On Thadonia*, well-bred women do not soil their pretty mouths with language fit only for the taverns.

"As to how I got into this apartment: Dalton Pearce—your brother, I believe—transferred my identity authorization to the apartment computer. We were to meet here to . . . discuss a matter of some importance." He paused to study the expression in her wide eyes. "Satisfied?"

Without hesitation Coventry nodded, avoiding his eyes. His explanation made a certain amount of sense and, although she wasn't a hundred percent certain that she believed him, she had to put some distance between them. She could have sworn that her stomach had been invaded by a swarm of amphibious creatures known for their propensity for hopping. But even more potentially embarrassing, her nipples were screaming *male alert* with tingling intensity, while her brain responded to the message by sending waves of prickling heat to her lower body with mortifying persistence. That her body should react this way *now*, in this situation, when it had unfailingly ignored most of the male acquaintances to whom she felt she should have been attracted, alarmed her.

To her chagrin, Tiern did not release her instantly. Coventry held her breath in the hope that his gaze would not be drawn to the telltale buttons which, scorning her conscious mind, pressed in eager anticipation against the thin fabric of her peach-colored blouse.

Unable to bear the tension any longer and desperately in need of air, Coventry tried to hasten her release by twisting her head against the restraint of his hands. It didn't work. She took a shallow breath and raised her eyes from the thick column of his bronzed neck to his jaw. The density of the whiskers beneath the surface imparted a blue-gray tinge to his tanned flesh. She raised her gaze to meet his. Faint lines fanned out from eyes which, rather than being black as she'd first assumed, were an incredibly dark blue. Suddenly, she realized his gaze was not even focused on her.

His eyes distant, the slight frown once again between his brows, he was merely gagging her, quite effectively, while he withdrew into thought. Fury choked her. Here she was, fighting her body's awareness of him with every fiber of her being—and failing—while he simply dismissed her from his mind as though she didn't exist. Before she could consider the consequences of her action, she lifted her foot and brought it down with all the force she could muster on his instep, simultaneously twisting her head in his grasp.

He winced. His grip on her head tensed. His eyes focused. Coventry, her breath coming in short quick gasps of rage, tried again to wrench her head free as she dug her nails into his arms. His nostrils flared like those of an animal with a scent. In anger?

His eyes began to drop from her face and Coventry panicked, attempting to talk against the relentless pressure of his palm while her nails clawed at his arms. He ignored her. His gaze began to fall toward her chest where her breasts, heaving in rhythm with her enraged-panicked-fearful breathing, pressed against the front of her blouse. Coventry exhaled and froze, trying to make herself as small as possible, her gaze never leaving his face. His eyes continued to drop, passed over her torso, her legs, until they reached her feet, or rather her foot. The offending foot. Coventry began to breathe again.

"Would you like to know what it feels like to have someone stamp on your foot?" He didn't even raise his eyes to her face, merely waiting to feel her response to his deceptively calm query through his hands.

Coventry's eyes widened as her imagination provided a graphic image of one of his enormous feet coming down on hers. He'd smash her foot into bits! She shook her head.

"I did not think so." His eyes began to travel up her body once again.

Why did he do everything in slow motion? Was it some type of intimidation tactic? The lingering perusal of his penetrating eyes inflamed her fear.

He was terrorizing her deliberately. She knew it. And yet, she couldn't repress her escalating alarm. Her breath froze in her throat as his gaze began to skim her upper body again.

The hand that held the back of her neck moved almost imperceptibly and his thumb caressed the hollow beneath her ear. A shock-wave of sensation shot through her to the very tips of her toes. She gasped. Something flickered in the depths of his eyes. No! The specter of rape rose in her mind. Despite the inexplicable reaction his proximity generated in her body, her intellect rejected him. He was simply not the kind of man she could ever care for; he was . . . uncivilized. She could sense ruthlessness in him, just below the surface, an integral part of him.

His eyes rose to search hers. "Do I frighten you?" The question was quiet, silky; his face devoid of expression.

Coventry didn't know how to respond. Nothing in his countenance directed her. She nodded.

"Good. At the moment, I do not have the time to deal with a rebellious woman. So perhaps you will now do as you are told, hmmm?" His lips quirked in a predatory and self-satisfied manner. She didn't respond. "Yes?" he coached, his eyebrows raising satirically.

Slowly, Coventry nodded.

His smile deepened and he released her. "You will sit down . . . please." He gestured at the sofa.

Tiern watched her as she eyed him warily before moving to take a seat. So this was the woman. She was quite beautiful and—his lips twitched—not indifferent to him either which might have presented . . . interesting possibilities . . . had *Sotah* regulations not expressly forbidden sexual relations while on foreign territory.

She was quite tall for a woman—probably no more than ten inches shorter than his own six feet six inches—and possessed of a fine bone structure that added elegance to her instinctive grace. Yet she was not one of those slim, polished, but virtually formless women so common to Earth. Her legs were long and slender beneath the snug fabric of her leggings, but very shapely. Although her waist was small enough that he felt certain he could span it with his hands, firm rounded hips flared from it in a manner that drew a man's eyes as surely as the sight of a tavern at the edge of a desert. She took her seat and his eyes were drawn once more to her chest as the soft fabric of her blouse briefly tautened over it. He had rarely seen a woman so generously, yet proportionally, endowed by nature. But despite her physical attributes, she simply was not the type of woman who appealed to him—too independent and argumentative. And, he had much more important things to consider.

Dalton Pearce had failed to appear with the data he had promised. Yet, even though he had only had one meeting with the man, Tiern knew that Pearce would never have placed his sister in danger had he still been capable of preventing it. Therefore, his next move had to be based on the assumption that Pearce would not materialize. Magar! He never should have allowed the Thadonian government to contract him to Earth's G.I.N.

Frustrated and angry, Tiern shot another glance at Coventry. He had to discover what had happened to Pearce, find the report, and return it to Thadonia. Any other course of action was unacceptable. He studied Coventry's tense form speculatively. Pearce had obviously never informed her of the situation. Still . . . he must have contacted her in order to have her come to the apartment.

If Tiern told her the truth, could he count on her cooperation? Somehow, he didn't think so. She had no reason to trust him, and their alliance had not gotten off to a particularly auspicious start. He received the distinct impression that she didn't like him.

And also, Pearce, in describing his sister, had hinted at a self-reliant, if somewhat fragile, disposition. Even if, against all odds, she did believe him, he couldn't rely on her obedience. Tiern knew women. He was almost certain Coventry was the type who'd either try to release him from his contract with her brother—which of course she could not do—or insist on debating every course of action he chose.

No, he'd have to try to find out exactly what Dalton had told her without revealing too much about his own position. Would she lie? Probably. But Trace was well-trained in spotting dishonesty and perhaps she would give herself away in some manner. Besides, her fear of him might induce her to cooperate.

He frowned. But it wouldn't take her long to determine that he meant her no real physical harm. He felt a twinge of discomfort in the foot she'd stamped on. Well, no *lasting* physical harm anyway. And when she deduced that, his edge would be gone. He would have to do his utmost to maintain her fear of him a while longer.

He moved to take a seat opposite her, where he could watch her reactions closely. "When your brother contacted you to meet him here, what did he say?"

His knees, when he sat on the edge of the chair

facing her, were a scant foot from hers. Instinctively, Coventry shifted back on the sofa as she racked her brain for a plausible response. She couldn't risk placing Dalton in danger. Her mind remained blank, her eyes fixed on the shiny fabric of Tiern's trousers. Leather? If he could afford leather he . . . He what? He had credit, and lots of it. But, she didn't have a clue who she was dealing with. It was possible he had told the truth about Dalton arranging to meet him here. But it was also possible that he was just a polished liar. Dalton, where are you? Suddenly her chin was grasped in a large, calloused palm. Her eyes flew to meet those of her captor.

"Answer me." He frowned, his brows lowering menacingly over his eyes so that they once more appeared black.

"He . . . he just asked me to meet him here."

"He didn't give you a reason?"

Coventry shook her head.

Tiern released her chin, leaned back in the chair clasping his hands over his flat belly, and stretched out his long legs as much as space allowed. "How did he contact you?"

"He sent . . . He phoned me."

Tiern's lips tightened. "He would not have phoned. He would not have used any form of computerized communication. The risk of eavesdropping is too great. So where is it?"

"Where's what?" Coventry hedged.

He sat forward in his chair again, drilling her with his eyes. "What he sent you. A note I presume."

"I . . . I destroyed it." At least that was what she was going to do as soon as possible. Where had her shoulder bag gotten to? Had it fallen by the door?

His abrupt movement as he rose and strode toward the door startled her. What was he doing? Oh, no! He'd begun rooting through the blue carryall removing the articles and placing them on the floor. How was she going to explain the costume? But he didn't even ask. Having emptied it of its contents, he surveyed the floor area surrounding him and spotted her purse where it lay half beneath a cabinet.

Coventry's heart leapt into her throat. *Dalton, what kind of situation are you in? Is there anything in that note that could . . . ?* She jumped to her feet as Tiern began to open her bag. "You can't do that! It's private."

He looked at her with eyes that could freeze the blood of a far braver individual than her, raised a single mocking brow and said, "Sit," as though he were speaking to a recalcitrant pet.

Coventry's backbone stiffened in outrage as she stood staring at him defiantly.

"Do you require a repeat demonstration of the advantages of cooperation?"

"I promise you that you will regret this." Coventry spoke through gritted teeth as she resumed her seat, casting one longing glance at the door in front of which he knelt.

Ignoring her threat he began emptying her bag. Within a moment he had the note Dalton had sent her in his hand. He cast her a taunting glance before he began to read.

Coventry watched his brows contract as he read. Then, crumpling the note he picked up the blue carryall, resumed his seat opposite her and began to study the empty bag intently.

"What . . . what are you planning to do with me?"

He glanced at her quizzically. "Now that is an

interestingly phrased question," he murmured absently. "It brings so many prospects to mind. Let's just say that, like it or not, you and I will be spending time together." He raised his head from his task to rake her body from head to toe with an intense stare. "We could get to know each other well."

Stunned, Coventry watched his lean-fingered hands caress the smooth nylon of the bag. His blatantly suggestive statement paralyzed her. A picture of his strong fingers caressing her body insinuated itself into her mind. Stars! What was the matter with her? When had this strange masochistic tendency become part of her psyche? Perhaps, she'd merely enforced abstinence on herself for too long. Despite the fact that she'd always thought sex to be slightly overrated, it did serve to release certain tensions. She had to escape this man, find Dalton and get this mess sorted out, and then . . . then she was going to actively seek another companion. Somebody civilized!

So intent was Tiern on his examination that Coventry began to measure the distance to the door with eager eyes. She had to get away from him while he was occupied. She didn't think he would try to kill her. If he was going to do that, he would have done it already. Wouldn't he?

Before she could put her plan into action, a triumphant "Ah-hah" drew her eyes back to her jailer. He withdrew a small silver disk, the size of a large coin, from beneath the lining of the bag. "A computer disk. Right?" His eyes pinned her.

Puzzled, Coventry nodded. "For a palm-size or wrist computer."

"Do you have one?"

"No–o. Why—?" Coventry shut her mouth, completing the question in silence. Why would

Dalton have concealed a computer disk in the bag he'd sent when he had planned on being here himself?

He studied the tiny piece of silver plastic. "Is there a small computer here?" His eyes swept the apartment.

Although Coventry's curiosity had surfaced as she watched Tiern peer at the disk as if to extract its secrets by vision alone, she remained obstinately silent.

His hard gaze pinned her. "See if you can find one."

Coventry glowered as his tone once again communicated his expectation that she would not dare refuse. "Find it yourself."

He rose and, to her surprise, grasped her arm almost gently as he pulled her to her feet. "We will look together. Agreed?"

Jerking her arm away from his burning touch, Coventry nodded and proceeded to search. Had Tiern been telling the truth? Had Dalton really transferred his identification to the apartment computer so that they could meet here? Perhaps Dalton *was* involved in some sort of field operation which required him to meet this man. She didn't *think* he acted like an enemy of Dalton's. Although his appearance alone frightened the wits out of her, he hadn't been really vicious. And any relationship between Dalton and Tiern would *have* to be based on a business alliance because Tiern clearly was not the type of person Dalton would associate with socially.

At least as far as she knew, he wasn't. She and Dalton really hadn't been all that close since . . . since he had begun working for the G.I.N. No, that wasn't totally fair. She, too, had been wrapped up in her career. They'd both grown more distant as they let their personal ambitions dominate their lives. Still, how much could he have changed?

So . . . assume that Tiern told the truth. He and Dalton had arranged to meet here—a place of relative safety because few people knew that she and Dalton had retained possession of the apartment. Tiern had obviously expected Dalton to give him something—the computer disk?—or he wouldn't have searched her bag. The information would have to be something pertaining to or of interest to the Thadonians. But, who were the men in black? Perhaps, members of a foreign division who regarded the Thadonians as enemies? Who? Why would Dalton need a disguise *after* giving the data to the Thadonian? Yet, that was obviously his plan because he'd requested that she meet him here at the same time that he'd arranged to meet the Thadonian. And Dalton hadn't shown up. Was he in hiding? Hurt? She had to find him! But the Thadonian insisted that they would be spending a lot of time together. Why? Where did she come into this?

Within five minutes, they found the compact computer stashed in a drawer in her father's office. Since *he* insisted on dragging her from room to room, she was glad she'd found it before they'd had to explore the bedchamber. The thought of sharing that room, even briefly, with someone as potently masculine as her captor induced near panic; she couldn't have handled the strain. "Here—" She caught herself as she turned, realizing that she'd thus far not spoken his name aloud, although she'd been thinking of him as Tiern. "What do you want me to call you anyway?"

He looked at her suspiciously as he took the computer from her hand. "I told you my name."

"You gave me two names. Three if I count your surname. You said you're known as Trace by most people on Earth. How are you known on Thadonia?"

"Rainon." His reply was abrupt, as though her pickiness concerning something so trivial irritated him. Good! It was about time somebody returned him a measure of irritation.

"Who calls you Tiern?"

"My mother."

That stopped Coventry dead. Somehow she just hadn't pictured this big hunk of bone and muscle as having a mother. But of course he would have to, wouldn't he? Unless he wasn't quite as human as Thadonians were supposed to be. "She must be a very tolerant woman."

"Now why would you say that?" He looked up in definite exasperation now as her chatter seemed to be interfering with his operation of the tiny computer.

"She allowed you to reach adulthood without putting you out of her misery."

His lips quirked in what might have been the beginning of a smile. *Don't tell me he actually has a sense of humor.*

"I seem to remember hearing a similar sentiment not too long ago from my sister."

"I don't wonder." Coventry fell silent for a moment as she watched him get the small disk installed in a slot and activate the apparatus. "So, what do you want me to call you?"

"In time, I am certain you will come up with an assortment of different, if somewhat disparaging, labels. However, until your imagination mobilizes, Trace will do."

Sarcastic boor! "Fine." She refused to give him the satisfaction of provoking her. Moving into the living room once more, Coventry picked up the abandoned carryall and headed for the costume left lying in a heap on the floor.

"What are you doing?" He'd immediately followed her, of course.

"Picking up this mess."

"Leave it and come and sit down."

Ahhh, he didn't trust her so close to the door. Tough! "It'll just take a minute."

"I said, leave it."

"Go to hell." Coventry managed to keep her voice even despite the nervousness that began to tie her stomach in knots again. She had a plan, and part of that plan involved making certain she could grab the disguise, all at once, and be out the door. His booted feet moved into view where she knelt stuffing the articles back into the bag. Steadfastly, she ignored him, expecting to feel his large hands close over her shoulders and haul her to her feet at any moment. But, it didn't happen. Finished, she took a deep breath and rose to face him.

"You will return to your chair. Now!"

"Certainly." Coventry responded as smoothly as though he'd kindly offered her a seat rather than issuing another order. Although his face remained as inscrutable as ever, she was certain that there was a slight hesitation in his manner as he followed her.

Coventry went into acting mode, relaxing casually on the sofa as though she were watching her favorite holo program. She waited until he relaxed his vigilance somewhat as he studied the information displayed on the tiny screen of the computer.

"*Magar!*" His outburst startled the wits out of her, throwing her act completely off-stride for

41

a moment. If she thought he'd looked menacing before, he looked positively malevolent now, as though he could cheerfully tear her up into tiny bits.

"What? What is it?" Rising, she moved to stand beside his chair, out of his direct line of sight. Slowly, ever so slowly, she reached her hand to caress the edge of what had been her mother's favorite vase.

"I must get this information back to Thadonia immediately."

"Oh." Coventry raised the vase over her head and brought it down with all her might on top of a head of midnight black hair.

Expecting a somewhat satisfying clunk, she stared in dismay at the remnant of the shattered vase that remained in her hand. "Sorry, mother," she whispered, staring at her unmoving victim. The palm computer fell to the floor with a dull thud as Trace's head fell forward a few inches to rest against his chest. She glanced at the stunner lodged in the waistband of his pants, but decided against attempting to abscond with it. She didn't know how to use the damned thing anyway.

Moving in front of him, but staying well out of reach of those strong hands of his, she examined him. He had remained sitting upright due to the positioning of his elbows on his knees. A trickle of blood worked its way down his temple. His eyes were closed. Stars, she hadn't killed him, had she? Tentatively, she prodded one hard shoulder. He sprawled back in the chair with a moan. He was alive!

Dropping the piece of vase clenched in her shaking hand, she raced for the door. Grabbing the carryall and her shoulder bag required the slightest pause, and then she was scrambling with the lock. A groan sounded behind her. Flinging open the door, she didn't delay to close it behind her. She raced down the corridor. A roar of wrath resounded behind her, spurring her on.

Chapter Three

Coventry made one last sharp examination of the people in the vicinity before moving swiftly to the entrance of the Parisian Building. She knew that the fact that Dalton had not requested that she meet him at his apartment signified that, for some reason, he hadn't felt it safe. Yet, she had no other place to begin her search for him.

As a precaution, after making certain the Thadonian wasn't in sight, she'd taken a cab ride and a bus trip to differing areas of the city before coming here. Of course, if the men in black still sought her and really wanted to locate her, they could track her simply by accessing Central to find out where she'd used her debit card. But Central was busy and such methods required priority coding and were highly expensive—more so than manpower—so she really didn't think they'd go to such lengths.

She wondered how much transportation credit she had left. When she'd completed her last biyearly banking report, she'd only requested an allotment from her salary credit of enough transportation allowance to see her to and from work, with little left over.

Entering the lobby of the building, she took a swift glance around before entering the elevator. Realizing that if Dalton's apartment was being watched, there would most certainly be surveillance on the elevator too, she requested floor twenty-two. The one above Dalton's.

As the elevator arrived at the requested floor, Coventry scanned the corridor. Empty. She located the door to the stairs before exiting the lift. Hopefully they wouldn't be watching the stairs; few ever used them. She moved quickly to the door, opened it a crack, and peered into the dimly lighted stairwell. Vacant. Entering, she hugged the wall, making certain she moved as quietly as possible on the hard concrete, as she descended one floor.

Her pulse pounded in her ears; more from fear of the unknown and worry for Dalton than from any overt sign of danger. She opened the stairwell door. The corridor on Dalton's floor appeared unoccupied as well. If they *were* watching, they were using a means that she was unaware of because there were no cameras in Dalton's building. Warily, she progressed down the hall to her brother's apartment. Taking another nervous glance over her shoulder, she used her palm I.D. to gain access.

The lights were on! Dalton never left the lights on. And then she saw it. Chaos! She stood surveying the destruction of his suite uncomprehendingly. "Stars above!" No wonder no one had been watching the apartment. They'd broken in and torn the place apart. What had they been looking for?

Dalton! She hadn't expected to find him here. Her thought had been that perhaps she'd find something pointing to where he'd gone. But now, fear for him clamored in her brain like a gong. "Dalton?" Dropping the carryall, she ran frantically from room to room. "Dalton?"

She didn't find him. Calming herself with an effort, she tried to look at the situation objectively. Whoever had destroyed the apartment had been looking for something. If Dalton had been there, they'd have had no reason to resort to such extensive damage. Therefore they must have been looking for something other than Dalton himself. And, they'd either found it and left satisfied; or, they hadn't found it and had concluded that neither it nor Dalton was likely to put in an appearance. Either way they wouldn't waste valuable manpower to keep the place under surveillance. But what had they been after?

The computer disk! Of course. Suddenly the small disk that Trace had found concealed within the carryall achieved enormous significance. The thought that Dalton might be giving away information that he was not entitled to pass on occurred to Coventry for the first time. Her brother was the most honest person she knew. She'd assumed that he'd concealed the disk in his carryall for safekeeping and requested a disguise to avoid being detected due to some minor misunderstanding with a foreign contingent, someone whose diplomatic ties with the G.I.N. were wavering. But, if *his own* superiors hadn't wanted that particular information leaked—then the situation made more sense. Horrible, terrifying sense. And Dalton was in a perilous predicament.

Righting an overturned chair, Coventry sank onto it with a sigh. "Damn you to hell, Dalton," she murmured, tears sparkling in her eyes. "What do I do now?" She was so tired. Almost five hours had passed since she'd left the theatre. She'd been awake for eighteen and a half hours. Laying down on the floor she used relaxation techniques to release some of the tension engendered during the last few hours. She had to think clearly.

Minutes later, a new glint of determination in her eyes, Coventry decided to go through with her original plan to go to Dalton's office if she found no clues to his whereabouts in the apartment. Provided the duplicate identification card Dalton had told her about hadn't been discovered and appropriated, of course.

Searching the apartment, she looked for anything that could have been a communiqué. Nothing. Not even a To-Do list that could have been a subtle message. Of course, if there had been something, it might have been taken.

Moving into the kitchenette, she studied the positioning of the refrigerator. It had been moved but, unless they'd shoved it partially back into position, it looked unlikely that they'd found Dalton's hiding spot. Tugging at the wheeled appliance she maneuvered it until she could squeeze behind it.

There in the corner, she could see the loose tile. Bending down in the cramped space, she pried at it with her fingernails until it lifted. Beneath it lay Dalton's I.D. card and the security code she'd have to punch in for access to the inner office. "Thank you," she whispered. She refused to think about how she'd get past the palm-print identifier. She'd find a way when the time came. Now, for the disguise.

Well, Cov, what are you going to do now? Coventry stood outside the G.I.N. office building wearing virtually the same disguise she'd worn earlier—for want of an alternative—layered rather uncomfortably over her own clothing.

47

Although she'd been forced to abandon the carryall, she'd refused to do likewise with her apparel or shoulder bag. The mask features formed a slightly younger countenance, while some of the padding in the hips of the trousers had been removed to give her a marginally slimmer profile. She'd reversed the wig, using black hair to conceal her own blonde coloring.

She didn't know how much good the transformation would do though. She wasn't authorized for access to the G.I.N. building with or without a disguise. In fact, she'd almost abandoned the idea of wearing it at all. But the thought that they'd followed her earlier, as herself, made her decide against it. The disguise could keep them guessing her identity long enough for her to escape again if necessary.

The city lighting dispelled any pretense toward a shadow that she might use to conceal herself and as she sidled up to the building she realized her stomach had somehow become lodged beneath her ribs, crowding her lungs and making breathing difficult. There didn't appear to be anyone around, but appearances could be deceptive. Dalton had rarely discussed the security measures the organization used on its own territory. She'd simply have to go on instinct when knowledge failed her. A buzzer sounded briefly from within the building and her pulse leapt chaotically in reply.

For an instant, she considered abandoning the whole idea. Maybe she should go home. Let Dalton contact her. But, if Dalton had been able, he would have met her at the Honeymoon Suite. And judging by the shambles she'd discovered in his apartment, he was in serious difficulty.

She, having only suspicions as to what that difficulty might be, had no resource but to trust her own intuition. Her instincts told her she had to find Dalton. If only she didn't feel so terribly frightened and alone. *Trust nobody*. She almost wished she had that insufferable Thadonian with her. Almost, but not quite.

She studied the lobby through the glass doors. She'd have no problem getting into *this* door with Dalton's I.D. card. It was the next door that gave her pause. But she couldn't do anything from out here. She'd have to go into the lobby, hide, and wait for the opportunity to arise. Her eyes lit on the enormous planter in the center of the foyer.

Quickly checking to make certain that the antechamber remained empty of personnel, Coventry inserted Dalton's card and opened the outer door. Pulling the card free she slipped it securely into her pocket as she moved swiftly to the planter. A bench and a garbage disposal unit placed in close proximity to the planter formed a reasonably secure spot. Ducking into it, Coventry sat down to consider what she knew about the inner door.

Embedded into the wall beside it was a standard palm identification panel. On the other side of the door there was a motion sensing device which counted the number of bodies passing through on a single identification. No one entered without palm-print verification; if they tried, the computer provided a warning and a one-minute delay before sounding an alarm. She knew this because the security device had been a bone of contention with Dalton. When a number of colleagues arrived together the safety measure was time consuming and irritating. The only means of fooling the device, Dalton and a coworker had discovered, was to deceive the computer eye into thinking there was only one person by close physical proximity.

Coventry bit her lip. She'd have to wait until somebody else gained access, then attach herself to them without them becoming aware of her. Which was, of course, impossible. Hell! She frowned thoughtfully. She'd seen computer observation devices in operation in the business sector. The mechanisms were usually installed at six-inch intervals that started about eighteen inches off the floor and stopped about the same distance from the ceiling. Perhaps, after someone entered, she'd be able to roll or slide under the eye. It was the only possibility she could come up with. Now she'd just have to wait for opportunity to present itself. Heaving a sigh, she closed her eyes to relax for a moment.

Coventry opened her eyes with a start. Stars! She'd been asleep. She checked her watch. Two hours! She'd lost two hours! Two hours and how many opportunities? Furious with herself for succumbing to the lure of sleep, Coventry bit her lip.

What had awakened her? Listening carefully, she raised her head from her hiding spot enough to peek over the rim of the planter. A sudden clatter lodged her heart securely in her throat as she ducked back. A maintenance droid! And it was heading right for the garbage bin which provided part of her cover. Quickly, she scanned the lobby to ensure there were no human eyes to evade. Then, abandoning the relative security of her hiding spot, she squirmed beneath the bench and froze, hoping against hope that her immobility would prevent the droid from seeing her.

It did. The droid emptied the bin and turned

to other duties. Heaving a silent sigh of relief, Coventry wormed back into the shelter of her previous position. Then, realization penetrated the residue of anxiety and she grinned. The droid would open the inner door when jt was finished. And, it pulled a large wheeled bin behind it which could feasibly provide a small measure of cover when she initiated her plan. It was the best chance she was likely to get.

Critically she studied her apparel. She didn't think the added padding in the clothing would cause any problem. But, her shoulder bag was another matter. The bag, designed like a small backpack except that the strap was worn over only one shoulder, would add a good six inches to the depth of her body in an area which, due to her generous chest, didn't need any added depth. It was six inches she didn't want to risk. Yet, she was loath to abandon the bag. Keeping an ear on the droid, she went through it, redistributing its contents to flatten it as much as possible. Then, after performing some minor alterations on the strap, she attached the bag firmly to her narrow waist. It would have to do.

Fifteen minutes later, by which time Coventry had gnawed her lips almost to the point of bleeding, she saw the droid swing in the direction of the door. She began rising to her feet only to discover that her cramped position had left her legs numb. Rubbing them with her hands, she attempted to return some circulation to them. The doors began to slide aside. The droid moved forward. Numb legs or not, Coventry began to follow.

The droid was through. The bin was in the doorway, and the door had already begun to close. She ran the last few steps, hoping against hope that the droid wouldn't turn around and sound a warning. Dropping to the floor immediately behind the ambulatory container, she pressed her body to the floor and began to slide. She expected at any second to hear the discordant note of an alarm or feel the agony of losing some part of her anatomy to the door. But, she didn't.

Three feet inside the corridor, Coventry rose and paused to still the frantic beating of her pulse in her ears as she looked around. The maintenance droid was already disappearing around a corner ahead. There was a camera affixed to the ceiling at the end of the hall, but it didn't appear to be operating. At least the light wasn't on. She could only hope.

Moving down the hall, Coventry began to read the plates on the doors. Knowing from Dalton that the elevators were equipped with cameras which worked on an intermittent timer, she decided to use the stairs. There it was, *STAIRWELL*. Dalton had described the location of his office to her once. Third level, sixth door on the right from the elevator. The higher you advanced within the Network, the higher in the building they place your office, he'd joked.

On the third level, Coventry poked her head from the door of the deserted stairwell, only to jerk it back again quickly. Two men approached. She waited, ear pressed to the door as they passed. "Too bad he got away. Now our asses are on the line." The voices faded as they moved on. Had they been talking about Dalton? Was he safe?

Silence. Slowly she opened the door a crack and peered cautiously into the hall. Empty. Stepping out, she located the elevator and began counting doors. Within seconds, she was inserting Dalton's card into the I.D. slot outside his office door and keying in his personal access code. Without hesitation, she stepped into the shadowy chamber beyond and closed the door.

Thank the stars, Dalton had an outside office and a small amount of the city's artificial daylight came through the windows to illuminate the room. She couldn't risk requesting increased lighting because she didn't know what capabilities the maintenance computer possessed. It was possible that, like home computers, it had been programmed to identify the voiceprints of authorized occupants, or in this instance personnel. In which case it might sound an alarm. And that was the last thing she needed.

She studied the office, noting and dismissing the microchip and computer disk cabinets where Dalton no doubt kept backup copies of his data. She wouldn't have time to search through reams of information. No, she needed something simple, to the point. Which is exactly what Dalton would have left if he'd suspected she might come here.

The desk sat before the window, facing the door. It would be her best bet. Quickly moving around it, she sat in the chair and began rifling through the plastic-textured pseudo-paper littering its surface. It looked like somebody else had already searched the papers thoroughly. But they could have overlooked something. There!

She'd come across a handwritten note containing one word, scribbled in obvious haste, *fridge*. Sitting forward, she attempted the letter substitution code she and Dalton had developed as children. Gibberish. It didn't work. Damn!

She began her search again. The door burst open with a bang. Her brain had barely begun to process that information when a male voice shouted, "Freeze, lady."

Coventry froze. Not because of the command to do so, although that had been frightening enough to arrest her heart in mid-beat. No, it was the sight of two ominous black instruments of death pointed directly at her. The wide-nosed muzzle on one proclaimed it a blaster while the other, which flashed a small red light into her face, could only be a laser. If either one of them fired, she'd be dead. She suddenly realized she had an intense desire to live.

"What are you doing here, lady?" The man's growled query distracted her from her contemplation of the terrifying harbingers of death. She looked up. The man on the right was one of the two who'd followed her earlier. The other was an enormous brute whom she didn't recognize, but he looked like he enjoyed terrorizing helpless females. His eyes gleamed avidly from a face containing more mismatched features than Coventry would have thought it possible for one person to lay claim to. "I asked you a question, lady." It was the man in black who spoke.

Coventry's mind raced. She didn't think she had a hope in hell of talking herself out of this, but she had to try. *Act, Cov. Act like you've never acted before.* She took one last nervous look at the artillery pointed at her. "Well you see, sir, my son is sick and he asked me to come by and pick up some papers from his desk." Stars! That was no good. If they thought she was Dalton's mother she'd still be in danger. Besides, a man working within the G.I.N. would probably have his employment terminated for allowing a civilian to gain access to a security building. But there was no way to recall the words now. She'd simply have to go with it and see what happened. "But you see—"

"The mother of the man that had this office died last year." The man interrupted with a snarl. "You wanna try again, lady?"

Had this office! Why the past tense? Dalton, where are you? Coventry swallowed against the knot of dread lodged in her throat. She couldn't allow herself to be distracted now. "I was just going to say, I think I've blundered into the wrong office."

"You don't say," he responded with disbelief. "And how exactly did you manage to get in *here*?"

"The door was open." Coventry's eyes shifted once more to the weapons. "Could you please lower your weapons? You're really in no danger from me."

For an instant her lie seemed to work. She could almost see the functioning of his mind. He would be wondering if somebody else had broken in and then escaped before she came along. He lowered his weapon slightly, although the silent brute beside him kept his pointed dead-center at her forehead.

"What's your son's name?" His tone wouldn't win any awards for congeniality.

Coventry searched her mind with lightning speed. She had to give the name of somebody who actually worked in the building. She'd read the names on the doors she passed. "Floyd . . . Floyd Rolls."

Both men simply stared wordlessly at her for a moment. Then the brute burst into loud, snorting guffaws as he slapped his partner's shoulder. Even the man in black had lost his scowl as his lips twisted in what could almost have been categorized as a smile. *What the hell is so damned funny?* Coventry pinched her lips together before her temper could put her mouth into gear and get her into more trouble.

"Well now, that's something. That's really something. Mom, I know I haven't seen you in a while, but you sure have changed." The man in black, Floyd, chuckled as he raised his gun to center again. "Want to try again, Ma?"

Coventry compressed her lips in silence. She couldn't believe it! She'd given the man his own name! How preposterous! Whatever small chance she'd had to talk her way out of this had just evaporated along with all the moisture in her mouth.

"All right. Move it!" Floyd stood to one side and gestured at the door with his blaster. "There's someone upstairs you've got to meet."

Coventry preceded her two captors down the corridor. Behind her she could hear them as they laughingly replayed her blunder for their own sadistic enjoyment. From the sound of their voices, she thought they must be at least five feet behind her. Not far, but perhaps enough. Her best chance at escape was now. Escape by elevator was entirely unlikely because of the computer override capabilities. Therefore she had to try to flee before she found herself so high up in the building that escaping by using the stairs would become a physical impossibility.

As she came abreast of the stairwell door, she closed her mind to the memory of the blaster and made her move. She shoved the door open. A bellow of wrath spurred her on. She practically flew down the steps. The echo of booted feet pursued her and despite her determination to ignore the presence of the weapons, she found herself waiting for the blast of white-hot heat that would end her life. It didn't come. She made it to the landing.

Turning, she began to descend the next flight. She felt something tug at her head and heard a curse behind her. As blonde tresses fell over her face hindering her vision, she realized that one of the men had grabbed her wig. They were close. Too close! She tried to put on a burst of speed. In the next instant her head was nearly wrenched from her shoulders as one of her pursuers caught a fistful of genuine hair.

She screamed in pain and fury. Pivoting, she attacked like a wild thing. Terror goading her, she clawed at the face of her tormentor. Something struck the side of her head. Tiny pinpoints of light flashed in her mind. She tried to fight the descending darkness. No! she screamed her denial, but she heard no sound. The blackness swallowed her.

"Wake up, bitch," the rough male voice growled at her from a distance. She frowned at the irritation. She felt so tired.

Suddenly, an explosive wave of pain tore through her left wrist. "I said, wake up." The voice accompanied the suffering, was part of it. Coventry whimpered, struggling against the leaden weights on her eyelids. *Don't hurt me any more.* But her tongue refused to form the words. Slowly, she opened her eyes and saw . . . death glaring from stony eyes.

Floyd. That was his name. Floyd, his face scarred with scratches seeping blood, looked at her with murderous intent. "Get up."

Coventry struggled to rise. Blackness hung like a shroud at the periphery of her awareness. "Come on. We haven't got all day." She'd managed to achieve a sitting position when suddenly he grasped her arm and hauled her unceremoniously to her feet. Her rubbery legs refused to support her and she swayed dangerously. A second later, her other arm was seized and she felt herself being dragged up the stairs.

"Why the hell did you hit her so hard? The boss is gonna be madder than a hermit on census day if she can't talk." Coventry didn't recognize the smooth voice and looked blearily up into the face of the speaker. It was the big guy with the homely countenance.

"Look at my face and you tell me," Floyd snarled at his associate.

They half dragged, half prodded Coventry into the elevator and propped her up in the corner. "Thirty-nine," the big man demanded of the elevator computer. Silence descended.

Coventry reached up to massage her aching head but desisted immediately when she discovered that the slight pressure of her fingers against the swelling above her ear induced a surge of pain that had the blackness hovering dangerously close once more. Her fingers brushed against her cheek. Oh no! Her mask had been removed! After running her fingers lightly over her features to verify the perception, she closed her eyes in dismay. They knew who she was then. Floyd Rolls would have recognized her.

Coventry had run out of strategy . . . and courage. She had to forcibly grit her teeth to prevent herself from pleading for mercy. The knowledge that such evidence of fear on her part would merely serve to provide entertainment for her captors had her clenching her jaws together until they ached.

She watched with detached eyes as Floyd rummaged through her shoulder bag, examining its fabric with the same exactitude that the Thadonian had used on the carryall. Floyd must have removed the bag from her person after knocking her unconscious. He opened the case containing her accumulation of contact lenses, looked at her speculatively, and closed the container again without comment. Apparently satisfied that there was nothing of interest to them in the bag, he tossed it to her with an abrupt motion that Coventry barely registered in her foggy mental condition. She missed. Bending to retrieve the satchel from the floor, she almost passed out as blood pounded in her injured head. Gritting her teeth, she stifled the groan hovering on her lips.

Minutes later, having been roughly herded down another unexceptional hallway, Coventry found herself propelled forcibly into an office. It was dim. The overhead lights were not on and, being an inside office, there was no illumination from the street. The ineffectual light of a desk lamp fought to overcome the shadows and failed abysmally in the attempt. The office was enormous.

Coventry noticed a figure seated in the gloom behind the desk—silent, motionless. She studied him as well as she could. He'd formed a steeple with his index fingers upon which he rested his prodigious chin, or rather chins. His body, so rotund that it strained the buttons on his vest to the breaking point, sprawled almost nonchalantly in the chair. Her eyes moved to his face.

She blanched. Small, beady, black eyes inspected her with viperous intentness. His tongue darted from his mouth to moisten his lips and disappeared with equal rapidity. "Lights." His voice sounded like the rasp of a scaly body moving through dry grass. There was nothing about this man that did not remind her with phobic strength of a loathsome reptile. And the increased illumination did nothing to alleviate her impression.

"Coventry Pearce." Even her name sounded repulsive coming from his lips. "I'm pleased that you came to visit us. It should save valuable time.

"Now then, we know that your brother concealed a computer disk in a bag he sent you. Where is that bag?"

Coventry swallowed. "I . . . I left it at Dalton's apartment."

A movement to his left attracted her attention. A man stepped away from the wall where he'd been partially concealed by a cabinet. Coventry's jaw dropped. The Thadonian! She'd known he wasn't a friend, yet she'd assumed his business association with Dalton had been a cordial one. She'd been wrong. He was an enemy. Her fear crawled into a narrow corner of her mind, crowded out by the intensity of the rage that consumed her. Her sagging spine stiffened with the retaliatory desire to tear him limb from limb. She hadn't hit him nearly hard enough. He showed no evidence of being struck at all.

"Pearce." The hiss of her name drew her eyes back to the man behind the desk. His eyes bored into hers unblinkingly. "And where is the disk?"

Surprise . . . confusion choked her. They didn't have the disk? But . . . Her eyes flicked back to the Thadonian. He shook his head almost imperceptibly. He hadn't given it to them! Maybe . . . but she refused to hope for too much.

Coventry feigned ignorance. "I . . . I don't know about any disk. Dalton sent me the carryall and asked me to use it to bring him a costume. He didn't show up and I decided to try to find him. That's why I came here."

He studied her for endless seconds as he weighed her words. Her flesh crawled as his soulless eyes raked her body. "So, you're saying that the disk must still be in the bag?"

"If there was a disk hidden in it, as you say, it must still be there. I certainly didn't remove it."

A downward movement of his head simulated a nod. "Pitt." He looked at the big man still standing on her left. "You and Rolls take her down to detention."

"Yes, sir." He grasped her arm in readiness.

"Trace," Ustin shifted his head to include the Thadonian in his range of vision, "you go to Pearce's apartment. Find the bag and see if she's telling the truth."

"I would prefer to stay in the building. I am expecting a communication." Trace's familiar deep baritone voice sent a tingle of reassurance down Coventry's spine despite the confusion his presence generated in her. His uncivilized manner was infinitely preferable to the brutal behavior of her current captors.

"Fine," Ustin snapped. "Rolls, you go to the apartment. Trace, Pitt, watch the girl." He lowered his eyes to his desk, effectively dismissing them as Trace calmly moved forward to grasp her other arm. "Goddamn Thadonian upstart." Coventry was certain she'd misheard the muttered comment until she felt Trace stiffen beside her.

"This way, lady." Pitt pulled her in the direction of the door.

Coventry didn't know what these people ultimately intended for her. But whatever their plan, she was determined to circumvent it. As they walked down the corridor, she surreptitiously observed Trace. She'd kept his secret. Would he help her in return? From the set of his chin, he looked angry enough to eat a bowl of microchips without so much as flinching. A muscle jumped rhythmically in his jaw. Hell! After the clout she'd given him he was probably furious enough to kill her himself. She couldn't count on him. Besides she didn't know what his tie was with the G.I.N. and right now everyone associated with the Network—with the exception of Dalton—ranked rather low on her list of dependable people.

They rounded a corner and progressed down another hall. If only this blasted headache would go away, maybe she could think. Suddenly she was shoved from behind. Unable to catch herself, she fell to her knees. Her arm twisted painfully as the force of her weight pulled it from Pitt's solid grasp. An almost musical succession of beeps sounded, followed by a grunt and a thud. Dazed, Coventry looked over her shoulder.

Trace bent over Pitt's motionless form as he thrust something into the waistband of his trousers against the small of his back. The stunner! "Run. The elevator." He pointed in the direction from which they'd come. "Go." His expression as he issued the order was unequivocally homicidal. Coventry grasped the strap of her bag and ran. As she passed him she saw him pull the blaster from Pitt's holster. Seconds later she felt him breathing down her neck. He gripped her arm in a painful hold, practically dragging her. "Faster," he urged, "or we will both die."

Chapter Four

As Tiern pressed the button to summon the elevator, he attempted to calculate exactly how far they could descend before the alarm sounded and the lift sealed, becoming a prison. Pitt should be out cold for three minutes, but his enormous body size could shorten that.

Tiern wished he had dared use *Sotah* fighting techniques. He could have incapacitated Pitt for a lot longer, even permanently. But the Thadonian council had not wanted the capabilities of the *Sotah* to become general knowledge to those on Earth. Not yet. The council had decided it was best that Earthers thought of all Thadonian fighting men as no more than the primitive sword-wielding warriors they appeared to be. That image would be maintained until it had been ascertained that those in power on Earth were truly dedicated to harmony between the two worlds and not the domination of the Thadonian people.

So, say two minutes before Pitt raised the alarm. Tiern and Coventry could not escape the building in two minutes but, if he calculated correctly, they could be out of the elevator and much closer to ground level.

A bell sounded and the door opened. Grasping Coventry's arm and signaling her to silence, he motioned her to slide to the right of the door. In that position, she stood directly beneath the surveillance camera, out of its range of view. Then he entered, choosing a position in plain sight. The guards monitoring the camera output should not be alarmed by Tiern's presence; they were used to it. "Level three," he directed the elevator computer.

His stomach lurched as the elevator began its sickeningly swift descent. But, for the first time since he had arrived on Earth, he was glad of its speed. He looked at Coventry. She was hugging the wall beneath the camera, panting slightly as she struggled to secure the strap of her satchel around her waist. The rapidity of the drop didn't seem to bother her, but then she had had a lifetime to get used to it.

The elevator began to slow. Tiern looked at the digital display. Level Eight . . . Six . . . Four. He took a step forward. Level Three. The doors opened. Silently he motioned Coventry to precede him. Emerging into the corridor he immediately located the surveillance camera. It was on! The elevator door closed behind them. A faint buzzer sounded. Looking at the display over the elevator door, Tiern read two words. NO ACCESS.

"We must move quickly. They know where we are."

Coventry had seen the camera, now she followed his gaze. "Right." She headed for the stairwell. She didn't know who Trace really was or why he was helping her. But she didn't think she cared anymore. The situation had gotten out of control. She winced at the pain that stabbed at her bruised head with each step. Painfully out of control! She'd simply accept Trace's aid and try to keep from becoming any more embroiled within this nightmare. "How are we going to get out of here?" She spoke over her shoulder in a whisper as she opened the door. "Won't the front entrance be sealed?"

Trace moved ahead of her and began to descend the stairs at a rapid pace. "We will try the rear freight entrance."

Imitating him, Coventry took the stairs two at a time. "Where . . . is . . . that?"

"Sub-level one."

Coventry froze. *Sub*-level one? Oh hell. She closed her eyes. When she opened them an instant later, Trace had turned a corner in the stairwell and moved from view. Swallowing her irrational fear with an effort, she resumed her pace. Stars! "You can do it, Cov," she muttered under her breath.

Trace's broad back came into view again. He passed the landing in front of the door to the main level and kept going. *Mind over matter, Cov*, she told herself as she followed. *You can do anything you set your mind to. Remember!* She passed the main level exit without allowing herself the slightest pause.

Two giant strides took her down four steps. Three more to the landing. Good, now turn. The air took on the consistency of water, slowing her down. She fixed her eyes on Trace. Follow. Don't think. She began to descend the final flight. The atmosphere thickened. *No!* She fought the pressure. Took another step. Trace pulled open the door to sub-level one and peered out, checking the corridor. He seemed so far away. The distance increased with every passing second. Fog encroached on her peripheral vision. Coventry closed her eyes. Took one small step. Every movement became an effort of will. Another step. Her hand clutched the banister like a lifeline.

"Quickly or they may trap us." Trace's voice came to her from a distance.

She opened her eyes. He was looking up at her impatiently. She looked at the stairs. Just six more steps. "Okay, Cov. This is it," she whispered. She felt sweat beginning to trickle down her face. Her lungs labored. Releasing the handrail, she gathered her resources. *Three giant steps, Cov. That's all.* She leapt forward. *One.* Again! *Two.* So great was her concentration on her descent, that she didn't see the hand Trace extended to her. Again! *Three.* She'd done it! Leaning against the wall next to the door, she saw Trace lower the hand he'd offered. "I'm sorry." She gasped an apology without really knowing what in particular she was sorry about.

He nodded as he studied her. "What is the matter?"

"Why . . . why do you ask that?" Coventry hedged. She despised her weakness.

He gave her a wry look tinged with annoyance. "You are perspiring so heavily that you look like you have just left a shower. You are having difficulty breathing. And, your eyes are . . . strange."

Coventry sighed. He was too observant. She wouldn't be able to pass it off. "I have a fear of subterranean places."

"Why?"

"How the hell should I know? It's a phobia. A groundless fear. Okay? Can we please talk about something else?" Coventry brushed at the tangled mass of perspiration-soaked hair hanging in her face.

Trace nodded and opened the door to peer into the corridor again. "There is a guard—not too alert, but I think he would notice if we passed by."

Suddenly the sound of a male voice reached them. "You go up. I'll check down here," it said. The response was muffled and indistinct, but the sound of booted feet drawing near was unmistakable.

Coventry felt her cold, trembling hand engulfed by Trace's large, warm one as he led her to the back of the stairwell. Pointing, he indicated silently that they should squeeze into the space beneath the final flight of stairs. Coventry stared at the small area. Her throat convulsed with phobic fear. But the echo of boots treading the staircase grew louder. The threat of capture loomed large. It represented the greater danger. Hastily, without allowing herself time to consider the small space, she crawled into it.

Crouched beneath the staircase, Coventry held her breath as the heavy footsteps approached. She looked at Trace. A formidable scowl firmly in place on his rugged countenance, he met her gaze with glittering midnight eyes and ... winked. Winked? Was he actually enjoying this? Placing his finger over his lips in a gesture for silence, he slowly altered his position so that he could peer around the edge of the stairs.

Coventry heard the door to sub-level one open. "Hey, Marv, you see anything?" Muffled response. "Maybe you should check. Make sure." Another inaudible response. The door closed. Footsteps ascended. Minutes passed. Silence.

"Stay here." By the time Trace's whispered comment reached her ears, he was already gone. Silence, growing heavier by the second. Stairs, pressing down on her. She couldn't breathe. *It's all in your mind, Cov. You're fine.* But it didn't help. Her lungs were starving for oxygen that simply wasn't there. Surging blood impelled by the frantic contractions of her pounding heart roared in her ears. Gulping in terror, she crawled to the side. She had to get out!

Writhing out from beneath the stairs, she looked up. The ceiling rippled, swelling downward. Paralyzation gripped her. A scream rose in her throat. *No!* In her mind, an image of Trace motioning her to silence. *Quiet! Must be quiet.* Cowering, she curled herself into a ball, sheltering her head with her arms.

Something touched her shoulder. Suppressing a moan, she pressed herself closer to the floor. The pressure faded. Then, she was being lifted. She opened her eyes. The ceiling still shimmered with instability. She turned her head. Trace!

Reacting instinctively, thoughtlessly, Coventry flung her arms about his neck and burrowed her face into the warm hollow between his shoulder and his jaw.

"It is all right. I am here." His repetitious whispered words of reassurance gradually penetrated the murk of her unreasoning fear. Sluggishly, awareness returned, bringing acute embarrassment in its wake as she realized she was being held and comforted like a child.

Releasing her death-grip on his neck, she avoided his eyes. "I'm fine now." Her whisper emerged shakily, but she continued. "You can put me down."

"You most definitely are *not* fine." As he released her legs and continued to support her against his side, Coventry once more became sharply aware of the magnificent body she was being held against. He gripped her chin with one hand, forcing her to meet his gaze. "But we have to get moving. Just a few more minutes, hmmm?" The smile he bestowed on her was so gentle, so at odds with the expressions she'd seen previously on his face, that Coventry stared in amazement. He released her to grip her hand firmly. "Come." Opening the door, he led her into a gray area of subterranean concrete.

As soon as she was forced to move, she once again lost all perspective of time and space. Trace's hand became an anchor as she walked forever through an endless fog of fear. Tiny sounds echoed. Water dripping. The scrape of something being moved. Footsteps.

"*Zyk!*" The abruptness of the whispered expletive startled Coventry back to awareness for an instant as he halted. "I must leave you again. Just for a moment." He positioned her behind a large crate. "Stay."

Coventry closed her eyes, refusing to look up, refusing to succumb to her phobia a second time. She concentrated on the sounds around her. The footsteps drew nearer. Stopped. A brief shuffling noise. A scrape.

"Come." She opened her eyes. Trace was back, extending his hand to her. Gripping it without hesitation, Coventry followed him as he led her to a door at the rear of the building. Seconds later, Coventry heaved a sigh of relief as he carefully closed the door behind them and they began to ascend a concrete ramp. Raising her eyes heavenward, Coventry took a deep breath. Slowly, rationality returned.

"What did you do to the guard?" Her whisper was barely audible.

Trace cast an impatient glance her way. "Do not distress yourself. He will simply sleep for a time."

Coventry nodded, but it was a wasted motion for he was already looking away. The twenty-four-hour city lighting didn't provide much illumination here at the rear of the building, but as she looked up at the dome overhead, she realized dawn was breaking. In a crouching run, Trace led her from shadow to shadow, insubstantial though they were, until they'd left the G.I.N. building behind.

Stopping in the shadow of another building, Trace waited for her. Reaching him, she sat down on a low concrete divider. "What now?"

"We must get to the Thadonian ambassador and seek aid in finding a ship to take us to Thadonia."

"What?" Coventry stared at him in disbelief. "I am *not* going to Thadonia!"

Trace stalked toward her, halting a scant foot away to look down at her threateningly from his superior height. Coventry refused to back down.

"Don't you dare try any more of your intimidation tactics. I'm not taking another step with you until you tell me what's going on." She was reversing her earlier decision not to become any more involved in this nightmare, but she didn't seem to have a choice. It sounded like Trace planned to keep her involved in it for an indefinite period of time. It would take weeks to get to Thadonia.

Tiern considered his position. Perhaps it was time to tell Coventry Pearce the truth. As a woman of Earth, she remained something of an unknown to him, unpredictable. And if she ran from him again, he might not be able to deliver her from her captors a second time. Yet his promise to Dalton in exchange for the information—which, as Dalton had pledged, Tiern now had in his possession—would compel him to try. "I will tell you." He looked over his shoulder in the direction of the G.I.N. building. "Later. Now we must reach safety."

Coventry stared at him obstinately. "Now! I have to find Dalton, get this mess sorted out, and be at work in two hours."

"You are not going to make it." How could he make this stubborn female face reality?

"What do you mean, I'm not going to make it? I have to make it. I've worked hard to get where I am. I can't just throw it all away."

Tiern gripped her chin, forcing her to meet his gaze as he whispered hoarsely through gritted teeth. "Look, we do not have the time for this. You know you can not return to work. If you did, they would have you back there," he nodded toward the building they'd just escaped, "in an instant."

Coventry swallowed, broke eye contact. Her large, soft, brown eyes shimmered with moisture. Tiern softened. "I know you want to cling to the life that was yours until so short a time ago. But, it is useless."

She swallowed. "But I have to know why," she whispered. "Don't you understand?"

Her eyes pleaded with him and Tiern felt a thawing within him that he did not want to feel. Especially now. "All right." He released her chin and pulled her more deeply into the shadow behind the building.

"A few days ago, your brother contacted me, wanting to arrange a clandestine meeting. At that meeting, Dalton informed me that certain information, which he should never have seen, had been inadvertently directed to him. The nature of the data was such that . . . even had he done nothing, ignored its existence—his life would have been forfeit." Tiern paused. "The mere fact that

71

he'd seen it was a death warrant." Plucking a small landscape stone from the ground, he rolled it between his fingers as he stared overhead.

"Oh, my God!"

He ignored Coventry's hoarse whisper, pinning her with his gaze, trying to impress upon her the importance of what he was telling her. "The information that Dalton possessed concerned Thadonia. It was on the disk he had you bring to the apartment. I haven't had an opportunity to look at much of it, but from what your brother said, thousands of Thadonian lives may depend on this data reaching Thadonia as quickly as possible. I believe he is right."

"But why were those men following me? Why did Dalton want a disguise? And, what were you doing in the office of that horrible man?"

Tiern hesitated. "I do not know about the disguise. Dalton said he had a refuge to which he could go. Perhaps it was part of his plan to use a disguise. As for your involvement: Dalton knew that as soon as the error was discovered, they would suspect that he had told someone. A good friend . . . a wife . . . family members. Somebody. But Dalton is not married. And, he has only one family member . . . you. Therefore, no matter what Dalton had done or not done, you would have been in danger. In searching for a means of saving your life, your brother came up with a plan.

"He would pass this information on to me, in exchange for my . . . promise to provide you with protection and escort to sanctuary. He planned to complete his arrangements and meet me at the apartment where he would give me the data disk and provide me with the directions for taking you to safety."

"But he never showed up," Coventry finished for him. "You think Dalton's dead, don't you?"

Tiern sighed. "I do not know, Coventry. There is, perhaps, still reason to hope. He did say he had a place to go."

"He's alive. I know he is."

"Yes. You are probably right." He looked back toward the G.I.N. building. "I hope it is so. I do not know him, but I think he is a good man. He could have asked for credit—a lot of credit—in exchange for this information. Yet, he did not seem to even consider personal profit. That is a rare quality . . . on any world." He paused. "Now, we *must* go."

Coventry shook her head. "You didn't tell me what you were doing in that man's office."

Tiern sighed impatiently, gazed at the dome overhead. "I was sent to Ustin by the Thadonian council as an employee. My chief function has been to use my talents to locate things and people who have disappeared. To trace them. Thus, the name Trace. But it was obvious, even from the beginning, that Ustin was not happy with this arrangement. I suspect that he was pressured by his superiors into accepting a Thadonian agent as a gesture of goodwill. I also suspect that those *particular* superiors are not aware of Ustin's other strategies involving Thadonian relations." His eyes narrowed with rancor.

"So how do we go about sorting this mess out? Can you find Dalton?"

Tiern shook his head. He wished he could take the time to discover the fate of Dalton Pearce. But he just could not. Too many other lives were at stake. "There is nothing more we can do here . . . on Earth. I must deliver the disk to Thadonia as soon as possible. Once the plot has been revealed, and justice meted out to those involved *here*, then you can return."

Coventry stared at him, stubbornness etched on her beautiful face. "I'm still not going to Thadonia with you, even if you are who you say you are. My life is here! And what about Dalton?" She shook her head.

Trace whipped around to face her. "What life? You no longer have a life." He ground the words out brutally. "Only death awaits you here. Can you not understand? You can do Dalton no good by staying. His own arrangements, had he completed them, would have taken you away from here." His accent intensified as his agitation increased, but he didn't care. How could he make her comprehend? He rose, pacing before her. "These people care not if you actually saw the data. The mere possibility is enough. They cannot take the risk of having their plan exposed. To them you are a liability which *must* be eliminated."

Coventry shook her head in denial. "I can't believe this! Why should I trust you? For all I know, you could have concocted this whole story."

Women! Why must they always confuse a situation with irrational suspicion? "Why would I do that, Coventry? What reason could I possibly have? Abduction? I like my women slimmer," he lied as he cast a meaningful look at her generously endowed chest, "and obedient." That was a definite truth. "*And*, I like my relationships with them short-term.

"Ransom perhaps? Do you know anyone to whom you have value; someone who has enough credit to make such an enterprise worthwhile? I have no more wish to be encumbered with you, than you with me. But, circumstance has removed the element of choice."

Coventry's fury mounted with each word he uttered. No wonder he'd been able to gag her and withdraw into his musings. She wasn't his type. The hints he'd dropped later must have been ploys to play on her fear of the situation. Incensed, she didn't stop to examine the source of her pique, knowing only that she did not want to spend another minute in the company of this . . . this insulting boor.

But they couldn't stay here arguing forever either. And he was right. She couldn't think of a reason why he would have lied. Although she probably could have if she wasn't so tired. Her only options seemed to be months of misery in the company of an insulting Thadonian, or death. Which was really no choice at all. "I get the point." She spat the distasteful words from her mouth. "I'll go with you. For now anyway. So what do we do?"

His lips twisted in a brief triumphant smile as he extended his hand to help her up. "We go to the Thadonian ambassador's."

Pointedly ignoring his offer of aid, Coventry rose. "Before we go anywhere, especially to an ambassador's, I'm going to discard this ridiculous clothing. It's filthy anyway." Suiting action to words, she began undoing the closures of the shirt she'd donned over her own blouse.

"*Magar!*" He scowled menacingly. "Hurry, will you. We have not yet even escaped their territory." He moved a couple of steps into the shadows, looking back the way they had come as though he expected at any moment to see someone in pursuit.

"What are those words you keep saying?"

"What words?" His impatient growl was barely audible.

"*Magar*, and . . . *Zyk*." Coventry hesitated on the pronunciation, but thought she achieved a fair representation.

"Do not say that!"

"Why?"

"They are not nice words."

"I thought you said Thadonians didn't use profanity." Coventry stared at his broad back, waiting for a response. "Well? Didn't you?"

"I said Thadonian *women* do not use profanity."

"Oh, I see." Coventry bristled. "But Thadonian men do, right?"

"Right."

Coventry stuffed the trousers and shirt beneath the edge of a low-growing plant with spreading branches and pulled her bag over her shoulder. "I'm ready." Almost choking on her indignation, she looked into his face as he approached. "So why is it that profanity is permissible for Thadonian *men*?"

"They must have some release for the frustration of dealing with women." Grasping her arm, he turned her in the direction he wanted to go. "Come." He loped off into the shadows.

"Come," Coventry mimicked beneath her breath as she followed. "Next, he'll be telling me that women on Thadonia are kept leashed. If he tries taking me for a collar fitting, he—"

"Quiet!" His order drifted back to her on a hoarse whisper.

He was bent over, peering around the corner of a building. She studied the tight male buttocks outlined before her with a contemplative eye. One well-placed kick. Stars, it would be satisfying to boot that arrogant backside. But, now was not the time. Opportunity would arise again. She was certain of it. "What's the matter?"

"We must cross a main avenue."

Coventry looked over his shoulder at the brightly lit thoroughfare. It was crowded. Morning rush hour had begun as nightshift personnel headed home and dayshift employees headed to work to take their places. She eyed a nearby taxi stand with covetous eyes. "How far is the ambassador's?"

"Seven or eight . . . city squares."

"You mean blocks?"

He nodded curtly, continuing his perusal of the street beyond.

"That's a long walk. Can't we risk taking public transport?"

"No. They would trail us immediately."

"Well, what are we going to do?" Coventry asked in exasperation. "Waiting for the streets to empty might take a few years."

He flashed her an icy look over his shoulder. "Sarcasm does not help. Come." Grasping her hand before she could protest, he moved into the street, pulling her with him. "Keep your head down. We do not want the surveillance cameras to get a clear picture." Strolling casually, he stepped onto the promenade and found a seat. Within minutes, the conveyance rolled across the avenue as traffic dipped beneath them.

Thirty-five minutes later, Trace guided Coventry toward the building housing the ambassador's penthouse. He approached the door, hesitated, looked around, spotted the monitor and, releasing his grip on Coventry's elbow, moved toward it. "How do you use this?"

It was the first real indication that Trace was not as proficient with Earth technology as he liked to let on. Coventry was elated. It went a long way to making her feel more at ease with his version of who he was and what he was doing. "You stand on that plate." She indicated a metal square embedded in the concrete, "face the monitor squarely, and press the buzzer for the apartment."

He nodded, following her instructions. Within a moment, a man's visage appeared on the screen. "*Kwoa?*" Pure Thadonian, Coventry surmised. She wasn't surprised when Trace's response, although more protracted, was equally unintelligible. Trace must have managed to convey his wishes without sounding too much like a lunatic because a moment later the exchange ended and he took her arm as he approached the door once more. A brief buzz sounded and Trace pulled open the portal to guide her within.

The green light on the motion detector didn't even flicker as they bypassed the handprint identifier—which was only practical for building residents and regular or long-term visitors—so the ambassador must already have authorized the computer to receive his guests. They entered the elevator. "Forty-five," Trace directed the waiting computer. The elevator began to move.

Tired after a virtually sleepless night, her head throbbing where she'd been struck, Coventry leaned back against the wall relishing the silence, content to study Trace/Tiern Rainon. She still didn't trust him completely. He *was* after all one of the most arrogant and infuriating members of the male species she ever had the misfortune to come across. But she'd grown more comfortable in his presence.

He, too, showed signs of the chaotic night. His midnight-blue eyes were heavy-lidded, his jaw stubbled with thick black bristles. As she observed him, despite her weariness, she once again felt her body stir to life at his nearness. What was it about this man that excited her? He wasn't even handsome. He was rugged with an air of barely repressed savagery about him that suited his powerful physique. He had a steely aloofness which gave him an air of unapproachability and he was about as domineering as a man could get. All of which suggested that he was not the type of cultivated and sophisticated individual that she'd always dreamed of.

Yet, he'd bent enough to explain their situation to her. Something she sensed was unusual for him. And she'd seen his stony mask crack for an instant when he'd comforted her. She was honest enough to admit to herself that she wanted to see him smile like that again. She wanted to be held against the fiery warmth of his body and burrow her face against his neck. She wanted . . . him. All of which was ridiculous in view of the fact that she didn't like him at all as a person. And he'd told her quite bluntly that she was . . . too full-bodied for his taste. Well, she'd just have to curb her body's lustful inclinations. His disinterest should help in that regard. Mind over matter. She was not about to make a fool of herself over any man.

Suddenly she became aware that he, too, observed her. The expression in his eyes made her feel naked. She swallowed the nervous moisture that flooded her mouth as his perceptive gaze captured and held hers. She felt as if he'd somehow gleaned her thoughts from her facial expression.

Chapter Five

A tone sounded, freeing Coventry from the hypnotic hold of his eyes. The elevator door opened. Trace reached to grasp her elbow once more—the mannerism was taking on the predictability of a habit—and escorted her into an opulent foyer. The man whose visage had shown on the monitor—a stick-thin, dark-haired person in a suit—greeted them. "Be seated . . . please. The ambassador will be with you shortly."

Coventry sat while Trace paced the chamber. The more he paced, the smaller the room seemed, until Coventry was ready to scream at him to sit down. Battling her irritability, knowing it was merely a product of her tiredness, she examined the decor. Its uniqueness proclaimed it Thadonian in origin.

The mosaic flooring consisted of brilliant hues, in every shade imaginable, of yellow, green and blue. The walls, if indeed there were walls, were hidden behind floor-to-ceiling curtains of a beautiful turquoise shade. Ornamentation, rather than decorating the walls as she was accustomed to, took the form of sculptures which resided on their own stands at varying heights around the room.

Coventry's attention was distracted by the approach of a man. Her eyes widened. He was one of the handsomest men she'd ever seen. He wore

some type of belted robe, bright yellow with turquoise patterns. Thick dark auburn hair framed
perfectly proportioned features and a tangle of
lashes many women would have killed for intensified the magnetism of his large expressive eyes.
"Rainon?" His deep bass voice rumbled pleasantly.

"Imnen." Trace bowed slightly from the waist.

The man responded in the Thadonian tongue
and Coventry watched with inquisitive eyes as
the men fell into conversation. Their facial
expressions were strangely subdued; smiles were
insignificant, surprise only faintly indicated by a
slightly upraised brow. Perhaps Trace's predominately stony countenance was a Thadonian trait.

"Coventry." Trace turned to her, extending his
hand in invitation. She rose, taking his hand as
she moved to his side. Although his face revealed
nothing, his eyes shone, and Coventry assumed
that the brief exchange had pleased him. "I'd like
you to meet Ambassador Kalare." He looked at
the ambassador. "Ambassador, Coventry Pearce."

"I am pleased to make your acquaintance."
His accent was more pronounced than Trace's.
Grasping her free hand, he lifted it gracefully to
his lips. Coventry's eyes widened in surprise as
the ambassador brushed her wrist with a light,
tickling caress. "May I call you Coventry?"

"Of course, Ambassador."

Kalare beamed. His hazel eyes twinkled as he
smiled the most open smile Coventry had yet seen
on a Thadonian face. Yet, despite his incredible
handsomeness and his beautiful smile, she noted
that her body did not respond to his nearness in
the slightest. There was definitely something the
matter with her.

"Come with me. I have made arrangements for

refreshments." The ambassador grasped her arm and began leading her into another chamber. Trace fell into step beside her.

They entered an enormous T-shaped room. Each of the T-sections, raised about three steps, opened onto a central sunken square. Within the square, giant cushions surrounded a low wooden table polished to a mirrorlike sheen. At one end of the rectangular table, a woman knelt on a cushion. Thick midnight hair, without a ripple of wave or curl, fell to her waist in a shining cascade. Her eyes, a brilliant emerald green, matched identically the shade of the luminous belted robe she wore. Although she didn't appear petite, her features were so delicate, her figure so slender, that she looked almost fragile. Coventry felt positively gauche. It was a feeling she was unaccustomed to experiencing for, although she was full-figured, she was not overweight and she had always felt that her height lent her poise. Coventry glanced at Trace. He too had noted the woman's beauty. In fact, he seemed positively mesmerized.

"I would like to introduce my consort." Ambassador Kalare's deep voice rumbled next to Coventry's ear. "Lietta." The woman smiled a welcome, her face definitely more expressive than the men's. "Lietta, greet Coventry Pearce and Rainon." He added a few words in Thadonian.

"I am pleased to make your acquaintance." Lietta's voice, as soft and musical as her appearance suggested, sounded exotic. Coventry returned the woman's smile.

"Be seated." The ambassador waved his hand in a gesture that included both Coventry and Trace. "Eat. We will talk." The table was laden with dishes of foods and decanters of beverages.

Coventry's stomach growled noisily. Thankfully, if anyone heard the sound, they ignored it.

Kneeling on a cushion to the right of Lietta, Coventry looked at Trace, who had seated himself across from her. He'd managed to pull his eyes away from the beautiful Lietta and was busily engaged in incomprehensible conversation with the ambassador who'd taken a seat opposite Lietta. She watched Trace for clues concerning what deportment might be expected of her.

"Please help yourself to anything you would like to try," Lietta directed her. "Most of the dishes will probably be unfamiliar to you, but I hope you will enjoy them."

"I'm certain I will." Coventry found that the initial stiffness she'd felt toward Lietta was dissipating in the face of the woman's genuine cordiality. She looked at the strange plate (bowl?) in front of her. It was oblong, about a foot long and six inches wide with raised sides. Within, the container had been divided into three sections. Glancing across at Trace's dish, she noted that he'd filled all three of the sections. Choosing some appetizing looking selections near at hand, Coventry followed his example. Then, picking up the two-pronged fork to her right, she sampled the dishes.

"Do you like it?"

"It is delicious." Coventry's enthusiasm was unfeigned, and Lietta glowed with pleasure.

"When you have finished, I will take you to a chamber so that you can . . . freshen up. Is that the proper term?" She looked at Coventry hesitantly.

Coventry, her mouth full of delectable vegetable-filled pastry, nodded.

Lietta smiled. "Good. If my English is mistaken,

correct me . . . please. I still have much to learn."

"I think you speak the language very well. Certainly much better than I do Thadonian."

"Do you know some Thadonian then?"

Coventry hesitated. Did a profane word or two count? "No, not yet. But I plan to learn."

"Then I will teach you a little while you are here. If—" she hesitated. "You are truthful. You were not just . . . being polite."

Coventry smiled, wanting to reassure the woman who, obviously lonely, so clearly sought female companionship. "I am being truthful."

"I am glad."

Fifteen minutes later, Coventry had finished her meal and learned, or tried to learn, the Thadonian name for everything on the table and in the room. Trace and the ambassador, still deep in conversation, gave no sign that they would be concluding any time soon. Pleasantly replete, Coventry tried, and failed, to suppress a yawn of exhaustion.

"You are very tired," Lietta observed. "Come, and I will show you where you may bathe and rest."

Unable and unwilling to argue, Coventry rose. The prospect of a comfortable rest was just too appealing. Glancing back at Trace from the doorway, she saw him observing her departure with an apprehensive expression. What was the matter with him? It was he who had wanted to come to this presumed haven. Did he think she'd try to escape his protective custody again? Compressing her lips with annoyance, Coventry decided she just didn't have the energy to worry about it.

Lietta escorted Coventry to a room decorated entirely in peach. A luxurious private bath just off the bedchamber had her virtually trembling with anticipation; but, she allowed Lietta to proudly display the suite to her. An enormous king-size bed dominated the room from its central position upon a dais. Behind one of the curtains, which Coventry had thought concealed a wall, another bed—this one much smaller, circular, but just as appealing—rested upon a less grand platform.

Coventry frowned. Why two beds? She turned to question Lietta, but the woman had already moved on to another curtain. This one, when pulled aside, revealed an enormous closet containing a number of the belted robes favored by the ambassador and his wife.

"You are welcome to use whatever appeals to you." Lietta smiled hesitantly, placing one of her delicate hands on Coventry's shoulder as she fingered a magnificent shimmering burgundy garment. "I think this would suit you very well. These garments have been provided for guests. You may keep one, if you like."

"You're too generous," Coventry objected. "I couldn't accept."

Lietta's eyes clouded. "You do not like them?"

"Of course I like them," Coventry hastened to reassure her. "I've rarely seen such beautiful fabrics. But they are too expensive, and I have no way to repay you for your kindness."

Lietta smiled. "You must not worry about such things. Take what you need. You have already repaid me." She paused to take both of Coventry's hands in hers. "I recognize your. . . . No, that is incorrect. I *thank* you." Then, before Coventry could respond, she continued. "And now I must go. When you wish to rest, you may extinguish the lights by saying, *lumo fos.* It is now eight A.M. I will have you awakened just past midday."

"Thank you," Coventry belatedly called after her, uncertain if she had heard or not.

Forty-five minutes later, having availed herself of the supplies in the elegantly appointed bathroom, Coventry, refreshed and pleasantly languid, donned the burgundy robe that Lietta had suggested. Then, turning her attention to her freshly washed hair, she hesitantly touched the sore spot above her ear. The area was still tender, but the swelling had begun to disappear. Then her attention was suddenly caught by her reflection in the full-length mirror.

Lietta had been right. The rich burgundy color looked beautiful on her, lending a rosy flush to her pale complexion. The long flowing lines emphasized her height, while the wide belt complemented her full figure and narrow waist. Perhaps a little too much. She studied her profile critically. What was she worried about? She was not likely to see Trace while dressed like this. She'd purposely washed her clothing and hung it to dry in preparation for their leave-taking. Besides, even if she did, her full bosom was not likely to stir him to lust when that was the particular aspect of her that he'd criticized. The matter decided, she left the bathroom and looked at the enormous bed with anticipatory eyes. Deciding against turning out the lights in a strange place, she crawled onto the soft bed.

Coventry stirred. There was a deliciously warm furnace at her back. She moved, seeking to press herself more firmly against the heat. Her leg brushed something solid. She froze; sleep retreated. A man's muscular arm rested casually across her waist. She rose up on an elbow to look over her shoulder.

"Dammit!" Although hushed due to her aware-ness of where they were, the word was never-theless potent and furious as she landed a solid punch on the shoulder of the sleeping male beside her.

"Kwoa?" He sat bolt upright, his face thunder-ous, his eyes instantly alert.

"What the hell are you doing in my bed? Damn you! Who the hell do you think you are? Get out!" Coventry punctuated her words with force-ful shoves against his massive form. "Get out!"

"Watch your language, woman!" He caught her hands in his enormous fists as he hissed the order at her. "What is the matter with you?"

"You're the matter with me, you—" The dan-gerous glint in his eyes gave her pause. "You jerk," she finished ineffectually. "What are doing in my bed?"

He sighed. "I am not in your bed. You are in mine. The smaller bed was for your use."

"Well, how the hell was I supposed to know that? Nobody told me. Besides, you could have used it when you saw I had this one."

He gave her an incredulous look. "I could not have used that bed. It is a woman's bed. It is too small." His eyes roamed her flushed face and dipped to the broad expanse of snowy white cleavage left exposed by the neckline of her robe. She thought she saw something flicker in his eyes, but it was gone in an instant. "Besides," he continued as she opened her mouth to comment, "this bed has plenty of room for two to sleep."

"I don't care if it has enough room for an army. I am not sleeping with you." Jerking her hands from his grasp, she rose, stalked across the chamber, and pulled the curtain aside to reveal the smaller bed. "And what do you mean this is a woman's bed? Stars above! How many ways have you Thadonians devised to maintain disparity between the sexes?" Heaving an exaggerated sigh, Trace lay down and considered the ceiling. "Well? Answer me!"

"Woman, you are trying my patience." His low growl only served to inflame her volatile temper.

"Woman? . . . Woman? You . . . you ass! We accord our *pets* the affection and respect of a name and you dare to call me *woman*. I have a name and you'd better damn well remember to use it. Do you . . . ? What are you doing?" Coventry eyed him warily as he rose. He wore a black robe with silver embroidery that did nothing to disguise the sheer powerful mass of him. In fact, it seemed to emphasize it. Barefoot, he stalked slowly, purposefully toward her. Refusing to back down, she stood her ground. "Don't you—!" But whatever she'd been about to say flew out of her mind with the speed of light as his dark, menacing face swooped down on hers.

His full-lipped mouth claimed hers; his muscled arms enfolded her, imprisoning her against the hard, heated length of his body. Instinctively she opened her mouth beneath the brutal pressure of his lips. It was a mistake. His hot tongue invaded; Coventry's senses exploded. Every mental faculty she possessed went into full retreat, helpless against the potent male assault. Her arms raised of their own accord to wrap themselves around the thick warm column of his neck as molten heat flooded through her. His hands slid down to cup her rounded bottom. And . . . then it was over.

Coventry almost fell, so abruptly did he release her. She stared at him with dazed eyes. He, too, was breathing irregularly. "Why—" her voice emerged on a hoarse croak. She swallowed, tried again. "Why did you do that? You don't even find me attractive."

"Where the *hell* did you get that idea?" Coventry noted that her syntax was rubbing off on him.

"From you." She was still disoriented by the intensity of the emotions raging through her. "You . . . you said you liked women who are slimmer. You implied I'd be safe with you." She frowned. "Were you lying?"

He turned, raking his fingers through his hair as he walked toward the bed. "No. No, of course not."

"So why did you kiss me?"

He shrugged. "To silence you."

"Silence me?" Her eyes blazed with outrage. "I can't believe, even you, would resort to such vile tactics. I—" A knock sounded.

"Imnen, Imnana, it is past midday." The voice was female, but unfamiliar. An employee?

Coventry opened the door. A young woman stood before her. "It is one-thirty, Imnana."

"Thank you." Coventry closed the door. "I'm getting dressed." She threw the comment over her shoulder as she strode in the direction of the bathroom. Her clothing should be dry. Maybe she'd feel more tolerance after she showered and dressed. She certainly hoped so because right now she was on the verge of becoming homicidal.

She closed the door to the washroom and stopped short. Her clothes were gone! Gritting her teeth, she yanked open the door and forced herself to take a deep calming breath before opening her mouth. "Where are they?" She was pleased at the steady, reasonable tone she managed.

"Where are what?" Trace lay on the bed looking at the ceiling again, his expression decidedly surly and disinterested.

"My clothes. Where are they?"

"They are being packed along with some other things the ambassador has been kind enough to offer."

"I see." Coventry smiled tightly. "And just what am I supposed to wear?"

"We will be traveling as Thadonians returning home." He rose with a sigh and began walking toward the closet. "Therefore, I suggest that you wear Thadonian clothing. Our deception might be rather difficult to maintain if you do not." He extracted an article of clothing. "Something like this should do." He held it out to her.

Her jaws were beginning to ache from gritting her teeth, but Coventry was determined to sustain her composure. Walking forward, she took the outfit from him and studied it. Sapphire blue, it appeared to consist of exceptionally wide-legged trousers with a wraparound belt of the same fabric, and a flowing tunic-style top. "Thank you." Spinning on her heel, she stalked back to the washroom to complete her ablutions.

By mid-afternoon, the arrangements for their journey had been completed. They had eaten a large meal after which Coventry had been coached by Lietta concerning the proper deportment of a Thadonian woman. Clothed as a Thadonian couple, they were able to take their leave of Ambassador Kalare and his wife.

Coventry, wearing the sapphire blue ensemble and a pair of dainty sandals supplied by Lietta, had had her hair braided and twined into a looped style commonly worn by Thadonian women. She'd also dipped into her array of contact lenses and altered the colour of her eyes to a shade of blue that matched the outfit she wore. This, she'd been told by Lietta as she instructed her concerning cosmetic applications, was a very effective part of her disguise because brown eyes were extremely rare on Thadonia.

Now, as she watched Trace bid good-bye to their hostess, she felt tears inexplicably burning her eyes. They'd reached a point in Trace's plan where Coventry once again felt hesitant. Dammit, she *did not* want to go to Thadonia. Unable to leave word with anyone concerning her destination or the reasons that necessitated her departure, she was leaving everything and everyone familiar to her. She couldn't even return to her apartment to retrieve any of her belongings.

At least her lease was paid up for six months. When she did return, everything she owned should still be there waiting for her. And she was leaving almost nobody behind who would miss her unduly. Like Dalton, most of her friends had been people she worked with. They might wonder for a few weeks what had become of Coventry Pearce, but they wouldn't be excessively concerned. Nikki would miss her though; and *she* would miss Nikki. They had been best friends since childhood and had remained so even though Nicole was now married and the mother of two beautiful children. Coventry wished she'd had some way of letting her know she was safe. But there was nothing to be done about any of that now. It was time to go.

Lietta grasped her hands in farewell. "I hope you enjoy the voyage and the hospitality of our people."

"I'm certain I will." Coventry was certain of no such thing. But she couldn't burden this gentle woman with her insecurities and fears for the future. "Thank you for everything." Lietta smiled and nodded, saying nothing more as she released her grip on Coventry's hands and left the foyer.

Coventry donned the cape that had been provided for her and stood back, waiting for Trace to complete his farewell to the ambassador. He looked almost handsome—although somewhat more sinister—in his traditional Thadonian clothing. Where the women's clothing consisted of soft, delicate materials, his clothing had changed only subtly from that he'd worn earlier. His trousers consisted of snug-fitting black leather studded with a strange array of loops for which she could discern no purpose. A matching vest had been layered over a red balloon-sleeved shirt. He wore the same sturdy, black leather boots, knee-high and laced in front, that he'd worn earlier. An ebony cape of some shiny material fastened at his throat and wrists, completing the ensemble. How had he managed to secure it to his wrists?

She studied the inside edge of her own cape, saw the large loops sewn there and slipped them over her hands. There! Looking up she saw that Trace had finished his incomprehensible conversation and was beckoning to her. She picked up the small case containing her new supply of belongings and moved forward. Grasping her elbow, Trace allowed her time for a very short farewell of her own to the ambassador before propelling her toward the waiting elevator.

The doors closed. "Main level." The tightness of Trace's tone drew Coventry's eyes directly to his face for the first time since their argument. There was a peculiar tenseness to his somber features that she hadn't noticed earlier. She almost asked if there was something wrong, but closed her mouth with a snap at the last instant. She wasn't talking to him. She refused to give him an excuse to *silence* her again.

*   *   *

Sitting in the taxi en route to the spaceport, Tiern reviewed his meeting with Kalare. He had told the ambassador virtually everything he knew. Had he told him too much? The ambassador's trustworthiness would depend on where his loyalties lay. And Tiern really had no way of knowing that. Still, he did not see how he could have done differently. Besides, he had provided himself with a safeguard.

He had told the ambassador that he had left the information in safe hands. Those safe hands were, of course, his own. But Kalare would naturally assume there was another party involved. Therefore, if Kalare *was* involved in the plot against Thadonia, neither he nor his superiors would attempt to neutralize Tiern until they discovered where the data was. He hoped.

Both Tiern and Coventry had been supplied with alternate identities, complete with identification and debit cards. But Kalare had been unable to alter any of the data filed directly within Central. He had said that there had been insufficient time for so complex an undertaking. So, although they had new names, they would still have to guard against all security devices linked directly to Central. Which, if they were careful, should not be too much of a problem.

They were going directly to the space port—which had a few cameras to avoid, but nothing more complex that he knew of; from the terminal, they would board the shuttle with standard identification cards; and then, they would make a final transfer, again using standard identification cards, to the *Lunar Princess* ship in space dock. Nothing should go wrong.

Then why was his gut telling him otherwise?

Had he overlooked something? He wished he had been able to maintain possession of the blaster appropriated from Pitt. But carrying such a weapon required special authorization which, under the circumstances, had been impossible to get. Any attempt to smuggle the weapon would be futile. Terminal sensors would detect it immediately.

He looked at Coventry and some of the tension in his gut eased. Woman! He did not know why she disliked the term so. She was the embodiment of the word. So many women he had met had been merely people, totally lacking something—something undefinable even to himself—that made him see them as women; woman to his man. His reaction to Coventry this morning had made him see her more clearly than he wanted to. And he wanted her more than he had wanted a woman in a long time.

But perhaps his attraction to her was simply due to his extended stay on Earth under orders not to succumb to feminine allure. It had been almost three months since he had enjoyed the company of a woman. Besides, the last thing he needed in his life was more complication. And that is precisely what Coventry was—a complication, in a very nice package.

She reminded him too much of Aneire. Aneire who had sacrificed everything, ultimately even her own life, in her efforts to preserve her beauty. Like Aneire, Coventry was exceptionally beautiful although she was, perhaps, less aware of her appearance than Aneire had been. But she was an actress and that, in his opinion, indicated a personality that craved adulation. According to Dalton, Coventry was twenty-eight years old. Yet, she remained unmarried and childless. A situation that—based on the assumption that her appearance alone would have generated at least one proposal—must be her preference. No, she would be much like Aneire. And since Aneire, Tiern had avoided relationships with all women save those he compensated.

Instinctively he knew Coventry was not the type of woman to indulge in a casual relationship. Her naiveté this morning had revealed that, although somewhat familiar with men, she did not understand them well. And even if he had been able to partake of her abundant charm, he would offer her no more than a temporary dalliance. Having a woman as a permanent fixture in his life was not for him. As he had told Coventry, he liked his women short-term. But he could not prevent his eyes from roaming her exquisite profile and his lust grew. Angrily he jerked his gaze away. *Zyk!* He wished fervently that he had never been placed in this position.

The taxi pulled up to the spaceport and stopped, jerking Tiern from his thoughts. He made a careful examination of the area. Seeing nothing suspicious, he turned to Coventry. "Ready?" She nodded, avoiding his eyes as she had all morning. "Come then."

Trace led Coventry into the crowded terminal and began to negotiate their way through the press of bodies. Many people wore the uniforms of space station personnel, presumably returning to their posts. Trace didn't stop at any of the computer outlets and Coventry assumed that their passage price must have been taken care of previously. Reaching a long queue before an exit with the number 513 flashing overhead, he stopped.

"We will be taking a shuttle to Launch Station One, then boarding the *Lunar Princess* for

Thadonia." Coventry nodded in acknowledgment. Although she had been speculating on their itinerary, she wondered what had prompted Trace to explain. Was he learning to read the expressions on her face? Heavens, she hoped not!

Within fifteen minutes, they had cleared the exit and were in line for the authorization booth, the final checkpoint before boarding. The line progressed slowly and Coventry found that her arm was beginning to tire from carrying her case of belongings, despite its smallness. Of course, it *did* contain the additional weight of her shoulder bag. Unable to wear it openly because of her Thadonian identity, she'd nevertheless refused to abandon it. Instead, she'd transferred a few of the items in it to the small drawstring bag worn at her waist, and packed it. The gesture was purely sentimental, but she didn't care.

Trying to ignore her discomfort, she looked around. Of the five shuttles on thrust-pads, only three were boarding passengers. A number of skimmers, private fliers not authorized for commercial flight paths and not designed for space travel, sat preparing for take-off on smaller pads. Coventry swallowed. Seeing the conveyances brought home to her for the first time that she was about to take her first spaceflight.

"Magar!" The timbre of the hissed expletive coming next to her ear set her pulse hammering in her throat apprehensively. They had moved forward a good distance since she'd last checked, but she couldn't see anything to cause alarm.

Sidling closer to him, she broke her vow of silence. "What is it?" she whispered.

He nodded toward the authorization booth. "They are using a portable palm scanner." She had to strain to catch the words. "Come." Gripping her elbow with almost painful firmness, Trace stepped out of the line and began to walk calmly back toward the terminal.

"Stop!"

Tiern ignored the shout and kept walking, scanning the area for a means of escape. Feigning confusion, as though wondering who the shouted command was aimed at, he risked a glance over his shoulder. He did not want to risk drawing attention to them by running if it wasn't necessary.

"Security! Halt, or I'll shoot." The official was definitely looking at him.

There! A skimmer in operation and ready for take-off, its portal open and waiting for a pilot. He jumped to one side, almost losing his grip on Coventry's arm when she, unprepared for his move, didn't move with him. A series of beeps from a stunner announced that the official—if indeed that's what he was—had made good on his threat, but missed. Running, Tiern considered and discarded the idea of extracting his own stunner. Too many officials. Dragging Coventry after him, he raced toward the small ship. Almost there. He risked another glance over his shoulder. A blaster! Heedlessly abandoning his suitcase, he shoved Coventry to the ground and dropped over her.

Chapter Six

A streak of white-hot light flashed overhead. They had mere seconds while the weapon recharged itself. He was up and pulling Coventry with him as he sprinted forward in a crouch. She lost her grip on her case, tripped over it and almost pulled out of his grasp. He lifted her, carrying her the last few steps. Depositing her in the waiting skimmer, he jumped in after her and closed the door.

The small ship shuddered. A hit! Sparks flew. Coventry screamed and cringed. Tiern ducked. Depressing the switch for impulse power, he yanked the thrust lever down. A high-pitched whine filled the cabin. They were airborne. Now, to escape the trap of Providence City.

The craft bucked. Another rain of sparks deluged them. The readings fluctuated wildly. They needed more altitude. Another strike could paralyze the ship. Setting his jaw, Tiern grappled with the bucking, resisting craft and flew straight for the dome overhead.

"What are you doing?" He barely heard Coventry's terrified shriek as he concentrated on the fast approaching dome. He was gambling that what he had been told concerning it was true. If it was not . . . If it was not, both he and Coventry would be dead within the next minute. The dome's surface looked near enough to touch. Instinctively his body braced for impact.

Impact never came. At the last possible second, an opening appeared in the surface of the dome. The tiny skimmer limped through. He heaved a sigh of relief. He had been told the truth. The dome protected itself from possible damage by providing bypass openings for objects on a collision course. He risked taking his eyes from the controls for a second to glance at Coventry. "You can open your eyes now." And then he had no more time to think of her. The reeling craft had given its all. They would not make it to the next city.

"We're going to crash." Coventry's anguished wail sounded above the shriek of the ship.

"Close your eyes. It worked last time." He fought the controls. His attention monopolized by the skimmer, he did not look at her. But she fell silent.

It was raining. They no longer had the advantage of the controlled atmosphere of the dome. Tiern narrowed his eyes, peering through the viewshield. He needed to find a spot to land—quickly. Old buildings, dark and threatening, rose starkly to meet the somber sky. Abruptly he realized where they were.

The Fringe! He had been told little about it beyond the fact that it was a dangerous place. But there was no avoiding it now. Lightning flashed. The skimmer continued its plunge, dipping and swaying as he maneuvered it through the press of ancient buildings.

There! An open space. An old intersection, perhaps. Continuing to battle the obstinate controls, he managed to manipulate the skimmer into rendering a reasonable facsimile of a landing. He was thrown slightly forward as the craft came to a shuddering halt. Shutting it down, he heaved a sigh of relief. Tension began to seep from his taut muscles. He looked at Coventry. She was unhurt. "You can open your eyes," he informed her, noting that she actually had taken his advice. "We are alive."

She peered cautiously through the viewshield as though she didn't quite believe him. "Where are we?"

"I believe it is known as the Fringe. What do you know of it?"

Coventry swallowed. "Almost nothing. Nobody talks much about it."

"So I discovered also. Tell me what you do know."

"Well . . . supposedly the Fringers were the dregs of society at the time that the domes were constructed about a hundred years ago. They were said to have been responsible for ninety percent of the crime that existed at that time. Based on that statistic, most people felt that they could never be part of any productive society, and it was decided that the Fringers would be sealed out of the city." She hesitated, shivering. "They're said to be quite violent."

"Hmmm." Tiern looked around them carefully. "You know nothing more?"

"Nothing," Coventry affirmed. "Except—"

"Except what?"

"Well . . . Dalton doesn't believe what I just told you. He calls it propaganda."

"Propaganda." Tiern looked at her sharply. "I am not familiar with that word. What does it mean?"

Coventry shrugged. "A distortion of the truth— a lie."

"And what does he believe is the truth?"

She frowned. "I don't remember him ever telling me. He used to have lots of theories on what could be done to rectify the situation, but that's all."

Interesting. But nothing Coventry said was any help in formulating a course of action. They still had to depart Earth. They needed transport. And, they could no longer follow normal procedure. What did that leave?

A freighter! Freighters for Thadonia left on a regular basis. He would have to find a captain amenable to bribery, of course. And he and Coventry would have to get back inside Providence City without being disposed of as Fringers. Still, it was the basis of a plan and he began to feel more optimistic about their chances. The freight depot was on the north side of the city, very near the periphery of the dome. They were on the west side of the city. Perhaps . . .

Turning, he began to search the interior of the skimmer for anything useful. There were tools—for performing minor repairs on the craft, no doubt, but not much use to him. A flashlight. He deposited it into a pocket in his cape. Unfastening a square lid on the raised deck, he looked into the compartment beneath. Food stocks? He eyed the oblong brown things in their individual wrappings with distaste. Better take them. Scooping them out of the recess, he deposited them in another of the capacious pockets lining his cloak. Next, he thumbed open a compartment in the side of the craft. Frowning, he removed a weapon. "A laser?"

Coventry looked at it closely. "I'm not certain, but I think so. Perhaps it's an older design."

Tiern nodded. Laser weapons were less certain than blasters, but much more effective than stunners. It appeared to be fully charged and he tucked it securely into one of the loops on his trousers beside his stunner. Taking one last probing glance around the skimmer, he opened the door. "Come." He held out his hand to Coventry.

She shot nervous looks in all directions as she squinted against the rain. Then, as she moved forward to take his hand and the moisture actually struck her face, she started, touching it with curious fingers and a vague expression of distaste. "Where are we going?" Her voice quavered.

He almost smiled. He hoped she was not losing her spirit. "To Thadonia, of course." He began walking north.

"Right." Her exaggerated drawl of resignation as she fell into step beside him was heartening. She was still Coventry. "I don't like it here. It smells strange."

"I agree. However, there is nothing we can do about that now. You did well back there. I am proud of you."

She frowned at him, not understanding. "I just followed your lead. I didn't do anything."

"Exactly."

Her eyes shot sparks at him and he knew she was fine. "What did you expect me to do? Throw some kind of fit like a child? I'm a grown woman."

"Exactly." He placed more emphasis on the word this time.

Narrowing her eyes against the drizzle, Coventry drew the cape around her as she skirted another patch of strange-looking vegetation that had forced its way up through the cracks of the ancient asphalt. She directed a murderous glare at the dark figure strolling along the deserted street before her as though he knew precisely where he was going. She didn't have a clue what the little verbal exchange when they'd first left the skimmer had meant. And it irritated the hell out of her. Trace had looked faintly pleased, as though he'd won some kind of argument, and that compounded her vexation. She'd been so involved in trying to puzzle out the meaning behind the ridiculous exchange that she hadn't noticed the passage of time. But now, her feet like twin blocks of ice in the thin sandals, she realized they'd been walking for some time.

"Quickly, Coventry." Trace's voice was hushed but clear. She looked for him, discovered that she'd fallen more than a few yards behind, and realized that she could barely see his dark form in the lengthening shadows of early evening. The buildings on either side of them had become black monstrosities looming out of the gathering darkness. It was decidedly spooky and she quickened her step, anxious now to catch up with Trace no matter how infuriating he was.

"Where do you suppose they are?" she asked as she matched her stride to his.

"I do not know. If we are lucky, perhaps we will not have to find out. Hmmm?" She found his smooth baritone comforting, and offered no resistance when he grasped her elbow to lead her across another street. "We must find shelter for the night. It would be best, if a confrontation *does* occur, to be able to see our opponents. Yes?"

Coventry nodded. She couldn't agree more. Her spine tingled. She had the sudden impression that she *was* being watched. *Imagination, Cov.* She tried to turn her mind to other things. Her cold feet should do the trick. The sandals she wore

103

were no protection against the cold rain. She shivered, but it wasn't entirely from the temperature. Her skin prickled as gooseflesh formed. She wasn't accustomed to dark streets.

"Here." Stepping in front of her he tried the door of an enormous concrete building. It gave with a ominous shriek of rusty hinges.

Coventry swallowed nervously. "You don't suppose there will be *things* in there, do you?"

Glancing over his shoulder, he frowned at her. His grim countenance was tinged with annoyance, but Coventry found she was becoming used to his scowls. "What kind of *things*?"

"You know. Living things. Creeping, crawling things."

"Surely you are not frightened of a few rodents and insects." He stepped into the gloomy interior.

Warily, Coventry followed. "I don't know. I've only seen insects in pictures or pinned onto boards. And the only rodents I've seen were stuffed. Are they dangerous?"

"Rarely."

He fished for the flashlight he'd appropriated from the skimmer. Coventry wrapped a fist apprehensively in the material of his cloak, moving blindly in his wake through the impenetrable blackness. Then, he triggered the light. Coventry almost moaned. The pale beam did little more than cut a narrow swath through the inky void of the enormous interior. Within the beam she detected filth, broken crates, glinting shards of broken glass. A faint scurrying sound made her jump.

"Do—" Her voice emerged as a hoarse squeak. She swallowed and tried again. "Do we have to stay here?"

He didn't even look at her. "It is dry." He direct-ed the paltry shaft of light in a half circle.

Coventry huddled miserably behind him. Now that they'd stopped moving, the cold began to seep into her limbs. He was right; it was dry. But *dry* was the only positive word she could find to describe it. It was horrible!

"Stay here."

"No." Shivering, Coventry barely had time to coax her numbed fingers into a death-grip on his cloak before he moved off. She riveted her eyes on the inconsequential beacon he trained in front of them. Something crunched beneath her feet. She ignored it, trying to match her gait to Trace's as he moved forward. He stopped. Turn-ing, he grasped her by the upper arms and placed her firmly in a position next to a square wooden pillar.

"Stay here." This time his tone brooked no argument.

Cold, wet and tired, she huddled miserably in the darkness. With detached awareness she noted the dim stream of light cease its movement as Trace placed it on top of something. She shiv-ered. The concrete seemed to have intensified the damp cold. Something scraped the hard flooring. She caught a brief glimpse of Trace's features. Then she heard more scraping and the sound of wood splintering. There was a momentary flare of light, not from the flashlight. A fire! She stared at it, mesmerized.

"Come." Trace was beside her, grasping her arm to pull her forward. "You will feel better when you are warm." The low rumble of his voice was almost solicitous. As she neared the glowing warmth, Coventry could see that Trace had built the fire in an old barrel. Although crates had been placed around it for seating, she rejected them in favor of standing as near the blaze as possible. She watched as Trace removed his cape, which, despite its apparent water-resistant properties, had begun to look somewhat sodden. He hung it from a rafter near the fire to dry. "Give me your cloak."

Coventry stared at his outstretched hand incredulously. "No. I'm freezing." To add emphasis to her statement, her teeth chattered convincingly.

He strode toward her with that familiar look of impatience stamped firmly on his face. "You will not warm yourself," his fingers were at her neck unfastening the clasp, "by wearing wet clothing." Disengaging her wrists from the fabric, he swept the cape from her shoulders as he finished the statement. Coventry made an aborted attempt to maintain possession, but the effort was futile.

Hugging her arms about herself, she tried to control the shivers that racked her. "I h–hate you," she muttered peevishly through vibrating jaws. He ignored her, hanging her cloak next to his. "In c–case you d–didn't notice, the clothes I'm w–wearing are a l–lot thinner than yours." This time he turned to look at her.

Walking back around the fire to her with that effortless stride of his, he grasped her shoulders and turned her backside to the fire. Coventry stared up at him petulantly, waiting almost apprehensively for his response to her grumbling. Then, before she even had time to anticipate his move, he wrapped his arms around her, pulling her close against him. She struggled. "What . . . Let me g–go!"

"Be still. I am warming you." His low baritone emerging on a breath next to her ear sent another shiver down her spine. Stars above! She didn't want to be warmed *this* way. She continued to resist, but her arms were firmly shackled against her sides. Warning bells tolled in her brain. Yet, even through the clammy leather he wore, the delicious furnace-like heat of his body began to seep into her. A minute or two wouldn't hurt.

Tired and chilled, Coventry relented, standing passively within his embrace absorbing his body heat. Slowly, the stiffness began to ease from her muscles. He propped his chin against the top of her head and she realized that unconsciously she'd allowed her head to rest against his broad chest. His hands began to massage her back, dispersing the warmth of the fire. The sensation was heavenly. Enervated, she closed her eyes. Her stomach rumbled with discontent. "I'm hungry," she murmured drowsily.

"Me too." Coventry opened her eyes as she heard the reverberation of his voice deep in his chest. There had been something strange about his tone. Slowly, she raised her head to look into his face. The fire flickered peculiarly across his swarthy features creating shadows and sharp angles, molding his visage into that of a stranger. He bent his head to meet her gaze. His eyes smoldered; lurid portent flickered in their depths. And he . . . just stared. Waiting. Suddenly Coventry was no longer in the least bit cold. Molten heat swirled through her veins. Her lungs constricted.

And then, like shutters on a window, his eyelids closed. When they opened, the expression was gone. Had it been a trick of the erratic firelight?

"I have some provisions." He released her as he spoke and Coventry remembered idly that she was hungry. Walking around the fire, he removed his cloak from the rafter, extracted something from an interior pocket and rehung the garment.

Coventry couldn't tear her eyes away from him. A body like his should be classified and carry a warning label, she thought. *Caution. Inflammatory to the senses.* At least from a feminine viewpoint. Or was it only her viewpoint?

Why did he affect her this way? She didn't like it. Not one bit. She felt ... intoxicated, out of control. She'd always been a person who maintained control in *every* aspect of her life. She even budgeted for impulse spending, for heaven's sake. Since receiving Dalton's note, her entire life had spiraled out of control. And now she'd even lost command of herself.

Trace returned to her side of the fire and took a seat on a crate near where she stood. He looked up suddenly, pinning her with his glittering midnight gaze. "Are you going to eat standing up?"

Coventry closed her mouth with a snap—she hadn't even realized it was open until that second—and sat on the other crate. All right, she admitted it. She had no control where Trace was concerned. He might not be her type of man—violence and danger were too much a part of him—but she craved his body. So now, what should she do about it? Would it hurt to surrender to a sensual craving just once in her life?

Some of the women she knew seemed to change men almost as regularly as they auditioned for new roles, despite the hassle of applying for medical clearance for each new relationship. Of course a few of them merely disregarded the policy. But Coventry had never done that. The penalty for transmitting a sexual disease, whether knowingly or unknowingly, was too frightening. Probation. Just the thought of having a microexplosive implanted in her skull to make certain she never left the designated probationary zone made her break out in a sweat. Besides, she'd always prided herself on being discriminating. Male companionship had simply never been a big part of her life. Sex, when it happened, had always been a pleasant experience, but she'd certainly never found it particularly extraordinary. Which only served to confuse her more. Why did she yearn so intensely to share that pleasant, but singularly unexceptional, experience with a man she barely knew? She'd never craved a *man* before. About the only thing she'd ever craved was chocolate. She swallowed. She knew what happened when she yielded to her craving for chocolate. She couldn't get enough! She gorged herself on it until there was nothing left. That settled it. She couldn't allow herself to give in to this inexplicable yearning. Trace would never be more than a passing influence in her life. She simply did not want her association with him to be unforgettable.

"Here." His gruff voice drew her eyes momentarily to his face. She extended her hand, palm up, and he dropped something into it. Stars, he looked ferocious! He didn't look in the least like he'd have been a willing participant in his seduction, so it was probably a good thing that she'd decided against it.

"Thank you." She looked down. Their meal was to consist of hard biscuits. Biting one of the two he'd given her, she crunched absently, desperately searching her mind for a topic of conversation that would take her thoughts off him. "Tell me about Thadonia."

The look he gave her was enigmatic. "What do you want to know?"

"I don't know. Everything. I'd like to know what to expect."

He nodded. "It is big. About one and a half times the size of your Earth. It has three moons. It is the second planet from our sun, so it is warmer than Earth. We have no polar ice caps." He paused. "What else would you like to know?"

Coventry cast him an exasperated look. "What about the society? The people? Dalton said he'd read some scientific theory that suggested that life on Earth and Thadonia must have shared origins in some dark distant past because it is so similar. Do you see it that way?"

Trace chewed silently for a moment. "Animal life on Thadonia has some similarities to that found on Earth. But, I think there are more differences than likenesses. The people . . . yes, there are a great many similarities. But the society is much less technologically advanced. Probably a few hundred years behind that of Earth. Thadonia is divided into eleven large empires. The smallest empire, Rafat, contains three nations. The largest, Sulaiv, contains nine. This is the empire to which my country, Stanish, belongs."

Coventry nodded. "And where in Stanish do you live?"

"When not in service, I live on my estate in the country. It is near the property where I was raised. My parents still reside there."

Coventry stared. Property in the country? Stars above! She couldn't even imagine such a life. "What is your estate like?"

He shrugged. "By Earth standards, it is large. If you stand in its center, all the land you see in every direction is mine. But it is only an average-sized estate by Thadonian calculation. My home is a single-story dwelling with large, airy rooms

decorated in much the same manner as those you
saw at the ambassador's penthouse."

"It sounds beautiful." Coventry smiled wistfully.
What must it have been like to grow up in such
openness? She studied her companion. "And,
what do *you* do there?"

Trace stared at her uncomprehendingly.

"You know. How do you earn a living? What
kind of job do you have?"

"I am *Sotah*."

"And what exactly is *Sotah*?"

Trace popped the last of his biscuit into his
mouth and rose to replenish the fire. "It is
like a combination of a private investigator
and a bounty hunter. The *Sotah* are under the
principal authority of the emperor. When the
emperor receives word of a crime that cannot
yet be proven, or hears that a criminal has
escaped justice into another nation, the *Sotah*
are sent to investigate. The *Sotah* are the only—"
he hesitated, pursing his lips thoughtfully, "law
enforcers?" He glanced at Coventry as though
seeking assurance that he'd chosen the correct
term. She nodded. "The only law enforcers whose
activities are not curtailed by borders."

"So why were you sent to Earth?"

He stared at her for a moment, his somber
face even more expressionless. "To learn." His
tone was curt.

Must have stumbled on a sore spot, Coventry
mused. Or a forbidden topic. "You speak the language very well. How long have you been here?"

"Three months," he growled and stalked off
into the gloom at the edge of the firelight.

A definite sore spot! Coventry listened to him
banging things around in the darkness. She
looked at the windows high on the concrete

walls of the warehouse. The moon was up, luminous, yet ethereal and indistinct due to the atmospheric haze. Even so, to Coventry's eyes, it appeared more substantial here than it did through the distortion of the city dome. Her eyes had grown accustomed to the murky interior and now, with the added lunar glow, slight as it was, the area seemed less frightening. A faint scurrying sounded in the darkness. She shuddered. Well, marginally anyway.

Trace had returned to the barrel and was throwing more splintered wood into it. "You had best remove the braids from your hair. It is time to sleep."

"Sleep!" Coventry echoed incredulously. "How are we going to sleep in here? The floor is like ice."

"I found two narrow bench-like things that I have placed together to form a bed."

Coventry swallowed nervously. A bed? *One* bed? "I am *not* going to share a bed with you."

"Listen!" he pivoted to face her, his eyes glittering with fury. "I have no more wish to share a bed than you do. But as you so accurately pointed out, it is cold. Body heat is important."

His tone proclaimed in no uncertain terms that he meant what he said. Her feminine vanity punctured, Coventry thought spitefully that he could at least have feigned a slight appreciation for her person. So what, if she'd decided not to succumb to . . . to this annoying craving. *He* couldn't know that. She raised her hands to her head and began to unfasten the braids. A sudden thought occurred to her. Maybe there was a reason . . . "Are you married?" She was sorry the instant the words left her mouth, certain that he would perceive the direction her mind had traveled.

112

He looked at her beneath lowering brows. "No." He removed their cloaks from the beams over the fire, testing them for dryness. "I am not married." He ground the words out between clenched teeth and carried the two capes in the direction of the benches.

Her vanity thoroughly deflated now, Coventry found that pique stiffened her spine. She raked her fingers through her long hair, kinked and thickened by the braids. Then, removing the container of contacts from the drawstring bag at her waist, she replaced the sapphire lenses.

"Come now. We must get some sleep." He'd returned without her hearing him.

"Fine." Rising, she walked a couple of steps into the gloom beyond him. Reaching the so-called bed he'd created, she studied its shape apprehensively. The benches were narrow. They'd been placed together with their backs toward the outside, and the space provided for sleep looked exceedingly small. Especially when she envisioned a certain rather large Thadonian stretched out on them. Oh hell!

"Take off your shoes."

"What?" Coventry swung to face him. Only the glitter of his eyes revealed his position in the darkness.

"I said, take off your shoes. They are wet. I will put them near the heat. Perhaps they will dry before morning."

"Oh. Sure." Coventry sat on one end of the makeshift bed to remove her sandals. After handing them to Trace, she hugged her knees to her chest and wrapped her fingers around her cold toes.

She barely noticed when he returned and

113

crawled past her onto the bed. This was ridiculous! She had nothing to be nervous about. It wasn't as if she had to worry about . . . anything happening.

"Are you going to sit there all night?" She looked back at his dark, nebulous form stretched out on the narrow bench. He lifted the edges of the cloaks in invitation. "Come."

Rising to her knees on the bench, Coventry crawled hesitantly toward him. Reaching him, she lay down stiffly with her back to him. Immediately his arm descended to wrap around her waist.

"Relax." His husky voice emerged on a breath at the nape of her neck, sending a shiver down her spine. He shifted and she realized he'd moved a little closer. She could feel the heat of his body. And yet, he managed to maintain a distance between them. "I said, relax. Sleep." Slowly Coventry allowed the tension to seep from her muscles.

Tiern knew that Coventry slept. Beneath his hand her gently rounded stomach rose and fell with each rhythmic breath. He was not so fortunate. An image had been engraved on the back of his eyelids, and each time he closed his eyes it returned to plague him. An image of Coventry— pure fantasy, pure idiocy. It had burst into his mind, suddenly, explicitly, when he had seen her raking her fingers through her long golden hair in the firelight. And it made absolutely no sense!

In it, Coventry sat on the floor before a roaring fireplace, her legs curled to one side as she ran a comb through luminous hair tinged with flame. Wearing a modest white robe, she stared pensively into the blaze. One delicate hand rested on her swollen belly—a belly swollen with child, his child. Madness! Pure lunacy. He'd long ago resigned himself to the fact that he would father no children. And he had taken care not to, ever since he had made the decision.

He closed his eyes. Saw the picture again. Saw her breasts, bounteous with impending motherhood, pressing against the fabric of her gown. Saw her turn to him with a smile and extend her arms in welcome. He tensed. *Zyk!* What was the matter with him? Frowning, he kept his eyes closed. Perhaps it had been Coventry's question concerning marriage that had provoked the image. Resolutely he banished thought. Sleep. He needed sleep. Slowly, the image faded.

He woke. Looked around. It remained dark within the warehouse, but the sky beyond the high windows had begun to lighten. Coventry still slept. He could discern her features slightly. He frowned. What had awakened him? All was quiet. He laid his head down.

Suddenly Coventry moved. He jerked, suppressing a groan. *That* was what had awakened him. Sometime during the night she had pressed her body more firmly against his for warmth. He gasped as another explosion of heat radiated out from his pelvis. He was swollen and hot. Each move of her backside against his groin aggravated the situation. His hand tightened briefly in reaction, closing over something decidedly soft. He jerked his hand away.

Coventry moaned in her sleep. He rose up on one elbow, lifting the edge of the cloak, to study her more closely. She had her arm curled, cradling her face in her palm; the other arm extended straight down her side, the fingers clutching convulsively at the cloth of her tunic. Her breasts . . . He swallowed the sudden moisture in his mouth. Her breasts swelled against the thin fabric of her tunic and undergarment, the nipples turgid and alert.

Fascinated despite himself, heedless of the consequences, he grasped one of the hard little peaks between thumb and forefinger.

She moaned—he thought she had awakened—and he yanked his hand back guiltily as she moved her hips again in a manner that was unmistakable. He closed his eyes with the effort required to subdue his reaction. *Magar!* She was as hot as he was, hotter.

This was madness! Regulations forbade *Sotah* . . . He leaned forward intending to shake her awake. She made a tiny sound deep in her throat and her chest swelled. Of its own accord, his hand closed over her upthrusting breast. And he held it, torn by the conflict of duty and desire and the consequences of having sex with a woman who, he was certain, would expect more than a casual union.

The regulation had been made for a reason. To keep a man thinking clearly in hostile territory. That regulation had already saved his life once: when an enemy had sent a seductress to murder him. Could he forsake it now? The danger had not yet passed.

Coventry made another small sound in her throat. *Zyk!* She was fiery. Fleetingly, he wondered who she dreamed of, then decided he really did not care. It would be good with her. His thumb boldly stroked the impudent nipple that thrust so eagerly against the fabric of her tunic. Her breath caught in her throat and she shifted her hips against him again as she began to stir to wakefulness. He groaned. Grasping her shoulder, he pulled her onto her back in one swift motion, pinning her legs with his as he bent his head to devour her full pouting lips. She returned his kiss, eagerly, hungrily. And then she stiffened. Her hands began to push ineffectually at his shoulders. He lifted his head, studying her expression, waiting.

"What . . . what are you doing?" The thickness of her voice betrayed her lingering state of arousal.

"What does it look like?" His own voice, too, was deeper, less steady.

"Why?"

Tiern made no response, merely waiting. This was the test. If she still wanted his touch as intensely while awake as she had while asleep he would take her and worry about regrets and guilt later. If not . . . if she resisted he would do nothing to change her opinion. But he found that the thought of *if not* angered him despite his resolve. He was swollen and hot and hard. Uncomfortable. And she had caused his misery. Inadvertently perhaps. But . . . He looked into her soft brown eyes and waited.

Coventry met his glittering gaze. In the gray morning light, he looked . . . appealing. His chin covered by a thick coat of black bristles, his wavy ebony hair tousled, his eyes afire from within, he was male, potent male. And she wanted him. Stars, how she wanted him. But, it wasn't right. She needed more than just an appeasement of desire. She wished . . . She wanted him to . . . Hell! She didn't know precisely what she wanted from him. But . . . "Get off me, please."

"Magar!" Cursing and sullen he rose and stalked away from her. Coventry was surprised. She had felt the hard length of his arousal against her thigh and had expected to have to be quite forceful.

117

He returned, threw her sandals on the bench beside her and grabbed his cloak, throwing it wrathfully over his shoulders. "Get up. We are leaving."

Coventry bristled at his cavalier treatment. "What are you so mad about? You started it."

He pivoted to face her, his face so dark with temper that she thought for a moment he might actually strike her. "I started it? *I* started it!" He threw back his head in a gesture that showed just how furious he really was. "I woke this morning to find you grinding that cute little backside against me like . . . like a *chayah* against a stone."

Mortified, Coventry stared at him openmouthed as he stalked across the building to the door. No wonder he was seething. Her face flaming with the heat of her embarrassment, she pulled on her sandals and threw her cape over her shoulders. How could she have done such a thing? Even in her sleep? But she did not doubt his words. He was too obviously livid to have been lying. She would never be able to look him in the face again. Hastily, keeping her eyes on the floor in front of her, she began to follow him.

"Stay here."

Her eyes flew to the door, but he was already gone. Stars, he wasn't so angry that he'd abandon her in the Fringe, was he? "Trace—?" Ignoring the obstacle course of clutter on the floor, she hurried to the door and looked into the street. There was no sign of him. Panic began to claw at her throat. She didn't want to be alone in the Fringe.

She stepped into the street, looking for him. A voice growled behind her. She squealed, spinning on her heel.

"Be quiet! What is the matter with you,

woman?" He gripped her shoulders hard.

Thank heavens! He hadn't abandoned her. Although at the moment he was staring at her in a distinctly unfriendly manner. "I . . . I didn't know where you were."

He released her with an exasperated shake of his head. "If you need to relieve yourself, you may go around the corner of the building. There." He pointed. "I will wait here."

"Oh." Coventry felt mortification once again creeping into her face as she moved in the direction he'd indicated. *That's* where he'd gone.

Coventry walked into the narrow space between the buildings. It was decidedly filthy, and unpleasant. But, she was enough of a realist to know that she was unlikely to find bathroom facilities any time soon; so, although she'd never had to relieve herself in the open before, she managed to accomplish the business satisfactorily. Adjusting her wrinkled tunic and trousers, she stepped back into the street.

Trace looked at her, his face unreadable. "Come." Coventry followed. He set a distance-eating stride, the thick muscles in his thighs flexing beneath the black leather of his trousers with each step. She couldn't help admiring those muscles as she did her best to match his pace. It was no longer raining and the sky was clear with the exception of a few clouds, but it had an unpleasant brownish cast to it. The odorous air was even more unpleasant without the rain. The buildings on either side of them looked just as somber and repugnant as they had the previous day. Patches of greenish-brown moss clung to many of them. Coventry avoided a puddle of muddy brown water as she followed in Trace's wake. Trying to ignore the prickling of her spine, she turned her thoughts inward.

She felt positively unclean, a sensation totally unfamiliar to her. Her skin felt clogged, suffocated. Her clothes were wrinkled and clung to her unpleasantly. Her hair hung in tangles. Well, at least that was one thing that she could remedy.

Opening the drawstring of the pouch at her waist as she walked, she withdrew the comb and began to work on her hair. A few blocks later, the task completed, she replaced the comb and hurried to catch up to Trace. His profile remained stony. She swallowed nervously. She wanted to know where they were going but she wasn't quite sure how to broach the subject. Dammit, she *would not* allow him to intimidate her. She ignored his stern expression. "How are we going to get to Thadonia?"

He glanced at her, then away, his expression cryptic. "By freighter."

"How—?"

"Quiet!" His low-voiced growl interrupted her. "We are being followed."

Coventry cast a hasty look at the buildings across the street. "Where—?" Her apprehensive whisper was once more interrupted.

"Do not look for them."

As Coventry trod silently at Trace's side she tried to suppress the fingers of apprehension ripping at her stomach. They progressed two more blocks without their observers giving any overt sign of their presence. Suddenly, halfway down the third block, a figure stepped into their path. Coventry froze.

A thousand impressions erupted in her brain within the space of a few seconds. The figure was male. He wore dark greenish-brown clothing studded with weaponry. Thick-soled boots rose to his knees. He carried the largest gun Coventry had ever seen. More than two feet long, it was neither a blaster nor a stunner. Yet, the way he kept it trained on Trace's back as he moved past him left no doubt in Coventry's mind that it was indeed a gun of some type.

Oh hell! Trace hadn't stopped. He'd just kept walking, ignoring the man. And now the man sent Coventry a look that spoke volumes, indicating with a motion of his head that Coventry should make haste in following Trace. She did. Willingly.

As she moved up to fall into step with Trace again, she cast a glance over her shoulder. The man fell in behind them. And now, other people, nasty-looking people with more of the strange guns, began to materialize from between buildings, following. Coventry's heart was in her throat. "Trace," she whispered, "there are—"

"I know."

Chapter Seven

Suddenly a woman, flanked by two armed men, stepped directly into their path. Tiern stopped, felt Coventry halt at his side. The woman said nothing, contemplating them. She projected an image of wildness. Tendrils of long black hair whipped by an errant breeze fluttered around her milk-white face, drawing attention to her black, fearless eyes. Her bold stance drew his gaze to her body. Lithe and slender, narrow-hipped and small-breasted, she wore trousers and a man's jacket with casual elegance. She was an untamed beauty—a savage beauty.

"Give me the stunner." Her voice, deep and husky, focused his attention on the fact that he had instinctively adopted a fighting stance and drawn the weapon closest at hand. He hesitated. He was dreadfully outnumbered, but he hated to be disarmed.

The woman nodded to the man on her right. He shifted the aim of the strange long weapon he carried, directing it to Tiern's left. Instantly, an explosion of sound, an unbelievably fast succession of popping noises, rocked Tiern back on his heels. Automatically he pushed Coventry behind him, shielding her from flying splinters as holes punched through the two-inch thickness of the door. What manner of weapons were these?

The noise stopped. "The stunner." The woman reiterated, extending her hand, waiting. The Fringers did not seem bent on murder, so in the interest of discretion Tiern placed the weapon in her hand. "Search him." She had looked at neither of the men at her side when she spoke. Yet, the man on her left moved forward without hesitation. Lifting the cloak away from Tiern's body, he appropriated the laser from the loop on his trousers, sticking it into his own waistband, before proceeding to search the pockets of the cloak. He removed and examined the contents but, apparently satisfied that nothing could be construed as a weapon, replaced them. Stepping back to his position, he handed the laser to the woman.

"What about her?" The man nodded to Coventry.

For the first time, the woman's gaze shifted from Tiern to Coventry who stood partially behind him. "Are you armed?"

"No." Coventry's voice was quiet, but firm, even though she must have been terrified.

The woman studied her for a moment more, her expression faintly disdainful. Then her eyes shifted back to Tiern. "Follow me." Turning she headed to her right. The small army of Fringers closed in around Tiern and Coventry. No one spoke. Only the slight sound of carefully placed booted feet on cracked, ancient concrete divulged their passing. Within a block, the woman halted and entered a crumbling brick building. Tiern and Coventry were silently herded into the building and up a flight of stairs. Almost immediately, Tiern noted an improvement in the air quality. Perhaps it had something to do with the strange black convex devices he had seen attached to the windows of this building.

123

The stairs opened onto an enormous chamber that must have occupied almost the entire second floor of the building. It was clean but entirely devoid of luxury. "Be seated. There." She indicated a scarred wooden table around which sat eight equally maimed chairs.

Coventry looked at Tiern's face, trying to discern his thoughts. But his dark visage was unreadable. He grasped her elbow, led her to the table and seated her before sitting himself. Coventry looked at the woman, saw her watching them, a faint look of contempt once again etched on her features. Then she turned to the men and women who'd provided armed escort.

"You," she indicated a muscular young man, "and you," she gestured to a woman slightly older than herself, "stay, please. The rest of you may go." Within a moment the room had emptied—silently and efficiently. The two who had stayed took up a position at the opposite end of the room. Coventry still had heard no one, other than the woman, speak.

Now she turned back to face Trace and Coventry. "My name is LaReine. Welcome to the Fringe." Grasping a chair she swung it around so that the back rested against the table and straddled it. "Well now, Coventry Pearce, I had hoped you would not end up here."

Coventry's pulse leapt. "How do you know me? Do I know you?"

In response the woman fished in her jacket pocket, retrieved a small white square, and tossed it on the table before Coventry. Coventry clenched her hands in her lap in an effort to control their trembling before reaching out and sliding the object close enough to see clearly. She gasped. It was a two-dimensional snapshot of herself. The picture had been taken about a year ago. The only people she'd given copies to had been her parents and Dalton. Slowly she slid the picture to Trace. He looked at it, frowned slightly, and looked back at her, saying nothing.

Coventry looked at the woman calling herself LaReine. "Where did you get this? How do you know my name?"

LaReine's lips twisted in a half-smile, a smile of cold amusement. "From Dalton, of course. And if the information he's given us is accurate, then you," she shifted her gaze to Trace, "must be the Thadonian. They call you Trace?"

Trace lowered his head slightly in a nod; remained silent. Coventry's heart was in her throat. "Dalton is here? Is he all right? May I see him?"

LaReine's eyes shifted back to Coventry. "He *is* here. No, he is *not* all right. He was badly beaten and barely made it here. And no, you may *not* see him yet."

"Dalton came *here*?" Coventry asked incredulously.

The expression of scorn returned to LaReine's countenance. "You don't even know your own brother, do you, Ms. Pearce? He is a courageous man. A decent man, who has worked and fought for what he believes in for years now. And you . . . you spend your hours pretending to be someone else in order to provide meaningless entertainment—" She broke off suddenly as though to control her temper. Her tone, which had risen angrily with each word she spoke, returned to normal. "—entertainment to people who close their eyes to murder and oppression while they worry about what to wear to the next *society* function."

Coventry stared at her openmouthed. What was she saying? "Are you saying that Dalton is a . . . Fringer?"

"Up until two days ago: no. He worked for our cause from within. Now: yes. Dalton is a Fringer because he is dead to society. And so are you, Coventry Pearce, or I would not be telling you even this little bit about our activities. Orders have been placed within Central to execute you and your companion," she nodded to Trace, "on sight."

Coventry was stunned. She glanced at Trace. How could he sit there so impassively? Didn't he understand what this meant? If this woman told the truth, she could never go home. Dalton would never again go home. Her whole life, everything familiar had now completely disintegrated . . . not just temporarily, but forever. She would be stuck *here* with this . . . this spiteful woman. And Trace, too, would be unable to leave because it would be impossible to reenter Providence City, even to find a freighter.

As Coventry grappled to understand how such monumental changes could have occurred in just a few short hours, LaReine began to speak again. "I suppose I should pity you. But I don't. If you had once thought to see beyond your own little world—"

Coventry didn't bother listening to the remainder of the harangue. LaReine's continued vilification of her character—which Coventry had been doing her best to ignore due to the nature of the current predicament—only seemed to aggravate the hopelessness of her situation. She was helpless to take control of her own life, and that made her furious. The woman droned on, heaping condemnation upon Coventry's head. All the pent-up anger within Coventry began to take on focus. LaReine. Calling upon her acting talent, she masked the emotion beneath a veneer of calm acceptance. "You don't like me very much, do you?" Now was *not* the time to lose control of her temper. She needed to understand the situation more completely.

"I don't like self-centered people who see nothing beyond their own comforts and aspirations. Why is it, do you think, that *I* know your brother better than you do?"

Coventry swallowed uncomfortably. There was a germ of truth in what she said. And it stung. "I'm sorry. I didn't know. . . . He never said anything."

"You never bothered to find out." LaReine spat the words contemptuously. "How could he tell you anything when you never showed the slightest interest? Was he going to place lives in jeopardy by gambling on your code of ethics?"

Coventry's temper was beginning to boil despite her best efforts to control it. She'd never liked being reprimanded. Who did? But to be castigated here, now, in front of Trace and the two impassive guards, by a woman quite probably younger than herself was just too much.

"Despite everything you say," Coventry ground the words out evenly, between clenched teeth, "I love my brother. I would never do anything to harm him or place him in danger. As for my being self-centered: perhaps I am. But at least I am not a judgmental *bitch* who condemns people before getting to know them."

LaReine stared at her coldly through narrowed obsidian eyes. A pulse leapt in her temple. Then, slowly she nodded. "Point taken," she said expressionlessly. "I'll reserve judgment for now."

"May I see my brother now?"

LaReine shook her head. "Trace first. Dalton thought you might show up in the Fringe and asked us to watch for you. He says he needs to speak with the Thadonian." She nodded in Trace's direction although her attention stayed on Coventry. "When they are through, if Dalton is not too tired, you may see him."

Coventry didn't like the arrangement, but couldn't see any way around it, so she nodded agreement.

"Wait here," LaReine directed. And then to Trace, "Come with me." Coventry tried to smother her resentment as she watched Trace rise, his swarthy features as devoid of emotion as ever. If Dalton needed to see Trace so desperately, then of course she could wait.

Tiern followed the woman across the large upper chamber to a door near where the two guards stood. LaReine opened the door and preceded him into a small room. An old bed placed in the center of the wall opposite the door dominated the chamber. On that bed lay a man whom Tiern assumed must be Dalton Pearce, though he would not have recognized him. The man he had met had been tall and lean, possessing regular features and that particular blond handsomeness many women seemed to find so attractive.

Tiern watched as LaReine sat on a chair near the head of the bed, and gently stroked the man's hair from his brow. "Dalton?" Her low voice was gentle, concerned.

So, thought Tiern, *that* is how it is. No wonder she is so fiercely protective of him. He studied the man on the bed. His face distorted by purplish, swollen bruises, he looked nothing like the handsome young man Tiern had met. Although he could see nothing of Dalton's body beneath the concealing blankets, something about his position revealed tremendous pain. The injuries were not limited to his face.

Dalton opened one moss-green eye—the other was swollen shut—and, with a grimace of pain, looked at LaReine. "I have brought your Thadonian," she said. Glancing at Trace, she waved him forward.

Conscious that every slight movement caused Dalton pain, Trace moved to stand at LaReine's side so that Dalton would not have to move his head to see him. Tiern was uncomfortable. He felt he should do something for Dalton's pain. Could he use *Sotah* in this situation? Without Dalton, there would have been no computer disk to take to Thadonia. Yet, Tiern could do nothing with LaReine present. "Dalton." He nodded his head. Then to LaReine, "Would you consent to leave us for a moment?"

She looked surprised by the request, and wary. But Dalton nodded slightly and she acquiesced, rising and moving to the door. "I'll give you five minutes. No more."

Tiern nodded and took the seat she had vacated. He looked at the battered, virtually unrecognizable man before him. "I know a means of relieving your pain somewhat. If you give your consent, I will use it, asking only that you tell no one of what transpires."

Dalton studied his face hesitantly with his single eye. Then with a slight movement of his head nodded affirmation. Tiern took Dalton's hand in his. He examined it. The knuckles were abraded and stiff. A cut, not deep but inflamed, slashed across the palm. He closed his eyes.

Slowly, he expanded his energy, allowing perceptions to penetrate his mind, to access the power of *Sotah*. And *Sotah* moved through the body he touched, enveloping the two men in its radiant strength, equalizing and balancing the energy within its shimmering field. One of the disciplines of *Sotah* was balance, symmetry in all things.

As Tiern felt the drain of his energy cease, he knew he had done all he could for Dalton Pearce. But he thought it was enough. Dalton would now have the strength to battle his injuries, to survive. Tiern released the hand clasped between his and looked at the man on the bed.

"I feel much better." Dalton stared at him incredulously through his single eye. The swelling of his face was already lessening. Soon he would have both eyes. "What did you do?"

Tiern shrugged. "It is merely a fighting man's technique for transferring energy to an injured comrade."

"I don't understand."

"It is not necessary that you understand." Dalton's persistence made him uncomfortable. He could tell him nothing. "Why did you wish to speak with me?"

Dalton's eyes clouded. "Coventry." He swallowed. "The contact . . . the person to whom I'd thought to send her to begin a new life has been compromised."

Tiern swallowed, uncomfortable with the rush of relief that raced through him. He was glad that his journey to Thadonia would not be postponed. Time was important.

"Yet she can't stay here either," Dalton continued. "She has spirit, but not the strength a person needs to survive *here*. I want you to take her to Thadonia with you. Help her start a life there."

Satisfaction swelled within Tiern, and this time he could not explain away its source. Coventry would not be staying here! The emotion angered him. What was the matter with him? His confusion compelled him to argue against the situation.

"I think you underestimate your sister." Tiern spoke nothing less than the truth. Coventry might not know her brother, but neither did he know her. "In the past hours, she has struck a man unconscious to escape his custody." He did not feel it was necessary to reveal just *who* that man had been. "She has broken into G.I.N. headquarters and your office in her determination to search for you and she has eluded capture by tenaciously battling a crippling phobia without complaint. She has been shot at by men with blasters, walked miles through drenching rain and spent the night in a cold, dirty warehouse. Coventry has faced the reality that her entire life has crumbled, and gone on . . . fought on. If that is not strength, I do not know what is. It certainly requires more than spirit."

Dalton stared at him astounded and Tiern felt rather foolish. Had his speech, perhaps, been a bit too impassioned?

"You're kidding!" Dalton exclaimed, wincing at the pain in his face as he moved the muscles too quickly. "She did all that." He shifted his gaze to the ceiling overhead. "I told her once where to find my duplicate identification card. And I suppose I've told her something about G.I.N. security measures over the years. But she never appeared to take conversation with me seriously. She always had the same expression on her face as

131

she had when we were younger and she suspected me of pulling a practical joke on her. Humph." He snorted in disbelief. "But, I still don't think she'd do well here. I'll acknowledge that there seems to be more to her than I thought. But she's nothing like LaReine. She doesn't have *that* kind of strength."

"No," Tiern acknowledged. "Coventry's courage is different. But it is there. She would adapt to life here. She is a grown woman, and your *sister*, not your wife. I thought the women of Earth valued their independence. Should you not let her make her own decision?" Tiern knew precisely what Coventry would decide. *Magar!* He wanted . . . needed to be rid of her.

Dalton shook his head slightly, wincing as he did so. "No. Not in this. Life here is hard. I want Coventry to have an opportunity to enjoy her life."

"Perhaps you overestimate the ease of life on Thadonia."

"You have fresh water? Plentiful food? Peace?" Dalton asked the series of questions almost belligerently.

Tiern nodded. "We have plenty of fresh water and food. And peace?" He shrugged. "For the most part our life would be more peaceful than that of the Fringers, perhaps."

"Then it's settled. You will take Coventry to Thadonia and help her to begin a new life." Tiern opened his mouth but didn't get the chance to utter a single word. "You have the computer disk?" Dalton reminded him pointedly of their bargain.

Tiern nodded sharply. "Very well. I will escort Coventry to Thadonia. But when you inform her of your plans, you must promise her that, if within one year she has not adapted to life there and is unhappy, you will find a means of returning her to Earth."

The door opened and LaReine stepped into the room. "The five minutes is up."

Tiern looked at Dalton, waiting. "Agreed," he said finally, sighing. "Speak with LaReine concerning your plans for getting to Thadonia. She and her people can help you with arrangements." He did not look at Tiern as he spoke the last sentence, but at LaReine.

Tiern shifted his gaze to her in time to witness her nod brusquely, unsmilingly, in agreement. Ohhh. The transition of power would not go smoothly. The savage beauty, queen of this small band of Fringers, might have fallen in love with Dalton Pearce, yet she would not hand over the reins of her command easily. But that was none of his concern. Rising, he nodded at Dalton, and left the room. Just before he was out of earshot he heard Dalton say, "Send in Coventry now, please." LaReine murmured something in reply.

He looked at Coventry. Sitting alone at the scarred wooden table, she appeared rather forlorn. It was obvious that she was worried about her brother. Her eyes clung anxiously to LaReine, as she waited to be allowed to see Dalton. How would she feel about him after their reunion?

"Coventry—" LaReine called, and Coventry rose instantly to walk swiftly across the ancient tiles toward her. Her gaze met Tiern's searchingly as she passed, but she said nothing.

Tiern took a seat at the table and observed her entry into Dalton's room. LaReine followed her, and the door closed. Tiern waited, half expecting LaReine to leave the room and allow brother and sister a private reunion. Two minutes passed, and still she did not come out. He should have realized she would not. He had seen the situation before. She could not believe that Dalton was actually here, and she feared any influence which could possibly induce him to leave. Insecure in her newfound love, she was possessive of Dalton, not wanting to share his love with anyone, not even his sister.

Tiern heard no sound coming from within the room, yet his mind clung to Coventry, trying to envision her reaction. Finally, he forced his thoughts away from her and began to go over the things he would need to discuss with LaReine.

Five minutes later, Coventry emerged from Dalton's room followed by LaReine who closed the door to the chamber firmly behind her. LaReine looked . . . satisfied. Coventry—her eyes stone-hard; her features rigid—appeared to be holding onto the reins of her temper by the merest thread. Returning to the table, she sat, folded her trembling hands before her and looked at Tiern. "So, how are we going to get to Thadonia?" He was slightly amazed by the evenness of her tone.

"LaReine and her people are going to help us with arrangements."

She switched her gaze to LaReine, who had just reversed a chair and straddled it in what was, apparently, her favorite seating position. "How kind." The sarcasm of the statement was evident, even to LaReine who did not know Coventry well. She returned Coventry's gaze sharply and then ignored her as she began to discuss with Tiern the details of the upcoming venture.

The day had passed. Coventry sat in the center of a narrow cot hugging her knees as she stared sightlessly at the colorless wall opposite. The small room was barren, devoid of ornamentation and lacking amenities except for a small stand in one corner which contained a washbowl and a container of precious water. Yet Coventry barely noticed the austerity, so suffused was her mind with impressions, events and emotions.

She had tried to sleep, but sleep would not come. At first she had thought the fault lay with the strange metal coiled thing in her bed that, no matter what position she adopted, had persistently jabbed her. But she'd folded her cloak and placed it over the thing, successfully suppressing its propensity to torture her, and still found herself awake, her mind cluttered with thoughts.

She was still absolutely furious with Dalton. He had all but told her that she was not welcome here. Had he not been so severely injured—stars, he'd looked terrible—she would have clouted him and told him in no uncertain terms what he could do with his plans. But what really bothered her was that she hadn't done that anyway. Oh, she wouldn't have clouted him. But she could have refused to do as he asked, no matter how much worry it might have caused him. She frowned at the memory of the attempt he'd made at justifying his request; *he wasn't in any shape to expend energy worrying about her.* Hah! It was just an excuse and she knew it. So *why* had she allowed him to manipulate her?

She was angry with LaReine too. The woman had refused to leave her alone with Dalton, hovering over him protectively as though she thought Coventry might hurt him. Coventry narrowed her eyes thoughtfully. She hadn't liked the looks that had passed between the two of them either. It was beyond Coventry to understand where a romance between them could possibly lead. Although her own perceptions of the Fringe were being altered swiftly and radically, there was still a world of difference between inner and outer city cultures. She suspected that a relationship would be anything but smooth. But it wasn't her business. Dalton might be her brother, but he was also a grown man. If he wanted to burden himself with a man-eating virago, that was up to him. In fact, he probably *deserved* LaReine.

Coventry *still* wanted to knock the woman onto her bony backside for the way she'd treated her after Coventry's meeting with Dalton. LaReine had asked Trace to accompany her to the "Operations Center" on the third floor where they would devise a plan for transportation to Thadonia. Coventry, not knowing what else to do since she'd been ordered to let Dalton sleep, had followed. At the door to the "Operations Center," which turned out to be a room full of electronic equipment and computers, LaReine had placed a small white hand on Trace's arm in a proprietary manner and turned to Coventry. She had then suggested, rather condescendingly, that Coventry might be more help in the communal kitchen. "Corie will show you what to do." Coventry's face twisted in angry mockery of LaReine's statement as she replayed the scene in her mind.

Coventry had been so furious she'd thought she was going to explode. And she'd been prepared to argue against her banishment, rather forcefully, when Trace had caught her eye. With a slight negative shake of his head and a nod to the stairs, he'd let her know what he wanted her to do. And he hadn't bothered to object to LaReine's hand on his arm either, Coventry had noticed. Though now, when she thought about it, she couldn't understand why she should care one way or the other anyway. Trace meant nothing to her. LaReine was probably just his type. Slim— everywhere.

Coventry sighed. She was tired, but she knew that her mind was still too active to let her sleep. Leaning her head back against the wall, she studied the small chamber. Heating pipes, carrying hot water, ran along the floor near the walls. Seeing them reminded her of the time she'd spent in the company of Corie, the young woman in the communal kitchen. The time had not been as unpleasant as LaReine had, no doubt, hoped.

Corie had attempted to explain the life of a Fringer to Coventry. "All water has to be distilled to remove chemical poisons before being used, even for washing," Corie had explained. "The domed-cities do so, too." Coventry had been unaware of that. "But water here is more precious because we don't have the massive facilities that the inner-cities do. You must never waste water." She had proceeded to demonstrate just how diligently the precious substance should be conserved.

Coventry shook her head. Why had she never stopped to imagine life in the Fringe? She tossed her head back in self-disgust. As she did so her eyes fell on the bare light bulb overhead. "Electricity within the Fringe is produced by wind-mills," Corie had told her as she demonstrated an unfamiliar food preparation device, electric in nature. "You probably know that the cities use power that comes from solar energy collectors in orbit?" Coventry had nodded knowledgeably while wondering how Corie had become so well-informed.

Coventry found the complexity of the Fringer

society amazing. And so, as they worked companionably together, she'd finally asked Corie the question she wanted most to know the answer to. How had the Fringers *really* come to be?

According to Corie, many of the Fringers *had* once been criminals, but not all. In truth, the Fringers had been the impoverished, the uneducated and unemployed. Faulty economics and war had left governments decimated, and their response to the problem of ever-increasing poverty and crime, a battle they'd fought for centuries with little success, was to simply give up. When the domed-cities were constructed to create a healthy environment for Earth's citizens, the people who'd always been on the fringe of society had been left there to fend for themselves.

Coventry shook her head. There was so much about her world that she had neither known nor understood. The meal Coventry had helped to prepare had been frugal and meatless, the vegetables grown by the Fringers themselves in carefully sterilized soil. Nevertheless, it would have been delicious had she not been obliged to watch LaReine and Trace conversing quietly together at the other end of the table.

She jumped, startled from her thoughts. Male voices, in apparent conversation, passed her door, and she recognized Trace's deep baritone. She could no longer delay dealing with the persistent thoughts of him. Sleep would refuse to come if she merely tried to avoid examining them. But thinking of him invariably induced the return of the embarrassment she'd felt that morning when . . . Hell! How could she have acted that way? Being asleep was no excuse.

And when she'd awakened to find him kissing her . . . Her stomach had plunged down to her toes, and she'd *wanted* him. She'd wanted him more than she'd ever wanted a man in her life. So why had she said no? What was that feeling . . . of wrongness, of something missing? What was lacking that had been there in the previous relationships that she'd had?

Her eyes widened in sudden enlightenment. Love. Though, of course, it wasn't love exactly, because she'd eventually discovered that she didn't love the men with whom she'd had alliances. But it was the conviction of being in love that had been missing; the words of promise for the future. Coventry had always *felt* that she was in love before initiating a sexual relationship. She only wished she knew what the *real* thing would feel like.

When it did happen, she was certain it wouldn't be with Trace. She wouldn't let it be. She wasn't his type anyway. And he definitely wasn't the type of man she'd always wanted. She was more than a little attracted to him physically though, and that bothered her because she suspected that it was muddling her thought processes. At times she just didn't react characteristically. Allowing Dalton to manipulate her into going to Thadonia was a perfect example of atypical behavior. But, it was one that she intended to rectify. She'd simply refuse to go to Thadonia.

She could stay here, become part of the Fringers' cause. What was it Corie had said? The Fringers did not want to seize power because such an attempt only invited opposition and killing. Rather, they worked for lasting change from within, lending support to men and women who understood the Fringers' situation. When these people eventually gained power within the government, the fate of the Fringers would change. It was a good plan, a well-conceived plan. And it was something Coventry could see herself becoming part of. Yes. She would stay!

A knock sounded, startling Coventry from her thoughts. Glancing down, she realized she could not answer the door dressed as she was. She was only wearing the Thadonian tunic and, although longer than a blouse, it revealed a substantial amount of white thigh. She quickly fumbled with the covers, removing a blanket to drape around herself before walking to the door.

Tiern had almost passed Coventry's door, when he noticed a light shining from beneath it. He halted. Before he even realized what he was going to do, he had knocked. He waited indecisively for a moment, uncertain what it was he had wanted to say. There was no immediate response and he had begun to turn away when suddenly he heard the door open. He turned back.

Coventry was peering around the wooden barrier at him. Her eyes were wide and startled.

"Is something the matter?"

"No. Nothing. Was there something you wanted?" She seemed preoccupied, distant.

Her coldness triggered irritation, and he responded brusquely. "I am sorry I bothered you. I wanted to let you know that all arrangements are now complete. We will leave early in the morning."

She shook her head. "I'm not going."

Chapter Eight

"What do you mean you are not going?"
Trace's question sounded distinctly unfriendly
and Coventry swallowed nervously as she raised
her gaze to meet his. Clean-shaven again, he
looked almost handsome. No . . . not handsome,
his features were too rugged to be truly handsome. But, he was definitely dynamic, riveting.
She struggled to focus on his question.

"Just what I said. I'm not going." She tried to
put more strength and conviction in her tone,
although it certainly wasn't easy when you had
to look a large, ill-tempered Thadonian in the eye.
"I refuse to allow Dalton to manipulate me into
doing something I don't want to do."

"I see. You do realize that my providing escort
for you to Thadonia is part of my agreement with
Dalton in exchange for the data disk." Both his
face and his tone were bland, expressionless.

"Yes. So? What about it?"

"So, if I do not conduct you to Thadonia, I am
no longer entitled to possession of the data."

"You're mistaken," Coventry protested. "Dalton
would never blackmail somebody that way."

"You are wrong. He has already reminded me
of our bargain where you are concerned."

"Why that—" She would get Dalton for this if
it was the last thing she ever did.

Trace interrupted her thoughts. "Do you understand what that means?" His tone was still bland, smooth. He was trying to intimidate her again.

"No." She narrowed her eyes. "What?"

"It means that you are going to Thadonia if I have to tie you, gag you and throw you over my shoulder." He ground the words out forcefully between teeth bared in the semblance of a smile.

"You wouldn't!"

"I will if you force the issue." His eyes glinted at her from between narrowed lids. "I think LaReine would enjoy the show. Yes?"

"You bastard!" Coventry stared at him in disbelief.

His counterfeit smile disappeared. "That word has nothing to do with this conversation. And I warn you, profanity is ill-advised at this moment."

"Go to hell!" She slammed the door with all the force she could muster, but the ensuing noise was unsatisfying. The gall of the man! How could she have been worried that she was falling in love with him? The very idea was preposterous.

Fine! She'd go to Thadonia. She didn't seem to have much choice, short of running away, and she had nowhere to go. But she was going to find a way to make Trace/Tiern Rainon wish he'd never met her.

The next morning, she awoke to a quiet knock on the door. "Coventry? It's Corie. Are you awake?"

"Yes." She opened her eyes to darkness. "Yes I'm awake. Come in." She brushed her tangled hair from her face as the door opened and Corie switched on the light.

"Good morning. I brought some clean clothing

for you." Corie stepped into the room and closed the door behind her. "There's a pair of boots too. Definitely not fashionable, but I hope you like them."

Coventry smiled, welcoming the tall, pretty, dark-haired girl who seemed to be the only genuinely friendly person in the Fringe. "I'm certain I will. Thank you." She wrinkled her nose. "I was dreading the thought of wearing this tunic another day." She took the clothes from Corie and examined them. There was an olive green shirt and slacks to match, a black tank top and black boots. As Corie had said, definitely not fashionable but clean, and certainly more practical than the Thadonian outfit.

"We matched the boot size to your sandals, so they should fit. The shirt and pant measurements we had to guess at." Corie shrugged expressively. "Unfortunately, the selection here isn't large."

Coventry frowned. "We?"

"LaReine asked me to help her choose something for you."

"Oh." Coventry didn't know what to say. A kindness from LaReine? Should she accept it at face value or suspect an ulterior motive? Oh well, she didn't suppose it mattered much at this point. "Thank you."

"You're welcome." Corie turned to go. "I'll leave you to get ready. Breakfast is waiting. If I don't see you before you go: Good luck. Maybe we'll meet again some time."

As though suddenly uncomfortable, she opened the door and left before Coventry could do more than call another "Thank you" in her wake. Rising, Coventry washed herself as thoroughly as possible with the small amount of water provided at the washstand, before turning her attention to the clothing.

She held up the slacks to examine them before trying them on. More than a little snug in the hips, they nevertheless had more than an inch to spare at the waist. The fabric did not have the elasticity that her leggings had had, but its ruggedness was a definite improvement over the delicate material of the Thadonian trousers.

Removing the wrinkled Thadonian tunic, she lifted the shirt. It certainly looked large enough! At least she wouldn't have to worry about revealing too much; the voluminous shirt would easily camouflage her full figure. Donning it over the snug elastic tank top, she rolled up the sleeves to a manageable length, tucked the tails into the waist of the trousers, and secured the drawstring purse that had accompanied her Thadonian outfit around her waist.

Moving to the small mirror over the washstand, Coventry removed a comb from the purse and began to work it through her tangled hair. She would have given anything for a decent hairbrush, but knowing that she would have to make do with the comb for some time to come, she decided to braid her long hair into a single long plait. It would tangle less easily that way.

She studied her reflection. The permanent pale peach pigment that she'd had infused into the skin of her cheeks and lips stood her in good stead in a situation like this. Without it she would have been as pale as a ghost. Against her fair skin, her black lashes—even unenhanced as they were— magnified her eyes, making them seem enormous, drawing attention to their unappealing shade. She frowned. Habit prompted her to reach for her contacts, but she hesitated. The present situation certainly didn't call for attractiveness. In fact, it might be better if her eyes remained drab and unremarkable.

Moving away from the small mirror, she pulled on the thick-soled black boots. Despite the fact that they fit, they were still a little uncomfortable. It was the weight of them that Coventry decided she would have to adjust to. They felt heavy on her feet.

Feeling ready to face the world, she folded the Thadonian clothing around the sandals and anchored the bundle beneath one arm before picking up her cloak and leaving the room. She descended three flights of stairs, passing two other rooms designated as dining areas, before she reached the second floor.

When she entered, there was no one in sight. A plate of food, predominately fresh fruit and vegetables, sat at one end of the table. Assuming it was meant for her, she sat down to eat before facing Dalton. Despite her pique with him, it wouldn't be right to leave without saying a farewell. He was the only family she had left.

She had almost finished her meal when the door to Dalton's room opened and LaReine emerged carrying a bowl. She stopped as she caught sight of Coventry. She looked troubled and Coventry hoped Dalton's condition hadn't worsened. "I see the clothes fit reasonably well."

Coventry nodded. "Yes. Thank you."

LaReine shrugged off her appreciation. "Dalton would like to see you when you've finished. I have some things to do, so I'll trust you not to tire him." Coventry nodded but didn't have time to say anything before LaReine continued, speaking quickly. "When you're through, come down to the main level. Trace is waiting for you there. You will have to hurry." She put the bowl she held down on the table and looked at Coventry.

"We have just received word that strangers, possibly dome-guards, are searching the Fringe. Oh, it is nothing to worry about." LaReine waved a hand, dismissing the matter when she saw the expression on Coventry's face. "It is just very unusual. No matter how much superior firepower they have, they are never permitted to leave the Fringe after having seen us. Parliamentary opposition must remain in ignorance concerning us until the appropriate time. So . . . we must assume that they are very desperate and that the reason for their desperation is the Thadonian . . . and you and Dalton." She frowned, seeming to speak almost to herself now. "Few, if any, of them should get this far. Nevertheless, we will have to be careful." She began to leave the room. "Oh, I almost forgot. Corie packed a knapsack of supplies she thought you might need." She gestured to the bag sitting to one side of the door.

"Th–thank you," Coventry stammered after her, receiving no response. She swallowed another mouthful of food, but it had grown tasteless. Would their pursuers never give up? What exactly was so important about that damned data disk?

She eyed the door to Dalton's room apprehensively. What would she say to him? Had LaReine informed him of this new danger? Coventry decided she would say nothing about it unless Dalton brought it up. Knowing that Trace was waiting for her and that speed was important, she rose.

"Dalton?" She opened the door to his room.

"Come in, Coventry."

She stepped into the chamber and approached

the bed. He looked much better today. Some of the bruises had begun to fade from his face. "I'm leaving now. I came to say good-bye."

He extended his hand to her. "Come here, Coventry." She grasped his hand and knelt by his bed. It felt so . . . strange. His long fingers gripped hers with almost painful intensity. She couldn't remember the last time she'd held Dalton's hand. She couldn't remember the last time they'd had *any* physical contact. Oh yes, it had been at their parents' memorial service. "I love you, Coventry. You know that, don't you?"

Her throat was suddenly tight. She nodded, cleared her throat. She acknowledged that he loved her because she loved him. But they no longer knew each other. "What happened to us, Dalton? How did this distance grow between us without our being aware of it? As kids we fought and played and laughed like . . . friends. We used to be friends, Dalton. When did that change?"

"I don't know, Cov. We just grew up in different directions, I guess." He gave her hand a squeeze. "I know you don't want to leave, Cov. But I'm doing what I am because I love you. You have to believe that." He stopped, studying her eyes anxiously.

"I believe you, Dalton." She shrugged. "I just think that you've made the wrong decision. I think I'd be happier here."

"I doubt that, Cov. I based my decision on a lot of factors, and I think I'm right. But, if I'm wrong . . . if after one year you aren't happy on Thadonia, then you need only contact me and I'll make arrangements for you to return. All right?"

Coventry's lips thinned. "I won't pretend I'm happy about it, Dalton, but I'll do as you ask. I

147

really haven't much choice anyway. Since escorting me to Thadonia is payment to you for that damned data disk, Trace assured me that he was taking me to Thadonia—forcefully if need be. And *you* can be assured that you *are* going to pay for this when you're feeling better."

The impish grin that she'd always associated with him appeared on his battered face. "Really? Trace said that?"

Coventry frowned. He wasn't regarding the situation with proper gravity at all. "If I'm not mistaken, his words were something to the effect that he was going to 'tie me, gag me, and throw me over his shoulder.'" Dalton withdrew his hand from hers, throwing his arm back over his face with a groan. His body began to shake alarmingly. "Dalton?" Coventry rose anxiously to her feet. "Dalton? Are you all right?" She grasped his arm, gently pulling it down. "You . . . you dolt." He was laughing, laughing so hard there were tears rolling down his rainbow-hued face. "What the hell is so funny?"

He made an obvious attempt to control his levity. "I . . . I'm sorry, Cov." She frowned at him in annoyance. "Really," he protested with a straight face.

"Like hell you are."

"You're right. I'm not. I can just picture you—" his voice faded beneath a spate of giggles, "picture you thrown over Trace's shoulder." He dissolved into laughter again. He grabbed his ribs. "Oh, damn it hurts to laugh."

Despite herself, Coventry felt an answering smile hovering on her own lips. "Well," she said with an exaggerated sniff, "I can see you're not nearly as ill as I'd thought. I guess I shouldn't have worried. You'll do just fine without me." The statement reminded them both of her imminent departure. All signs of levity faded. "Good-bye, Dalton." She leaned forward to plant a quick affectionate kiss on his poor bruised face.

"Good-bye, Cov. Take care of yourself."

"I will. You too, all right?" He nodded. Turning, she walked out of the room before she embarrassed herself with tears.

Coventry picked up the knapsack and placed it on the table. It was heavier than she expected and she wondered absently what Corie had packed for her. Unzipping the top, she placed the folded Thadonian tunic and trousers inside. Then, throwing her cloak over her shoulders, she hefted the knapsack and began to descend the cracked concrete stairs of the crumbling old building. She had gone down only half of the first flight of stairs when she heard a noise below that attracted her attention and she looked over the railing at the next flight. A man bent over something just at the base of the stairs. She jerked her head back and froze.

It couldn't be! How could Floyd Rolls be here? And where were Trace and everybody else? Her first instinct was to run to one of the upper levels and hide. But she couldn't do that. Dalton lay injured on the next floor, unable to protect himself. Somehow, *she* had to stop this man. But how? She couldn't call for help and hope that someone was within earshot because that would give away her presence. Also, he might have companions just outside.

Biting her lip, she risked another glance down. Rolls was standing, looking around. She searched frantically for something . . . anything to help her. Her eyes lit on a large red cylinder hanging on the wall by its handle. Carefully, she eased out of her

149

Christine Michels

cloak and moved across the stair to the object. It was quite heavy and constructed of good solid metal. Uncertain yet as to exactly what she would do, she carried the heavy knapsack and the red cylinder as she slipped down the stairs. Her heart hammered in her chest.

Hugging the wall, she reached the landing and slowly peered around the railing at the next flight. Rolls was not in sight. Where had he gone? Continuing to cling to the wall, she moved forward, her eyes searching every corner fearfully. As she neared the head of the final flight of stairs, she saw what Rolls had been bending over. A body! Coventry swallowed. The body had been pulled partially out of view, but she could see a pair of legs wearing the thick-soled boots that the Fringers favored.

A door was open on the left, in the same wall against which she was pressed. Slowly she proceeded down the stairs, the fabric of her clothing scraping against the wall as she slid along it. The rasp it made seemed unnaturally loud and she tried to ease herself a little away from the rough concrete surface.

She reached the bottom step. Resolutely, she avoided looking at the body of the man at her feet. Holding her breath, she slowly moved her head toward the frame of the open door until she could see around it with one eye. Rolls! He was in there sneaking around. She pulled her head back out of view.

Breathing shallowly, feeling a pulse pounding in her throat, Coventry tuned her ears to the slight sounds of his movement within the room. If she was lucky, maybe somebody with a *real* weapon would come and handle the situation. But she knew she couldn't count on it.

Was he coming closer? He was! Oh, hell! She took a firmer grasp on the heavy knapsack. He was almost at the door. All her muscles tensed. A hand appeared in the doorway. She didn't wait to see more. Swinging the knapsack with all her strength at where his midsection should be, she was rewarded by a loud "Oof," as he bent forward and his head came into view. Without pause, Coventry grasped the red cylinder firmly and brought it down on the back of his head. He fell and lay moaning. Why wasn't he unconscious?

Terrified, knowing she had no other means of disabling him, Coventry struck him with the cylinder a second time. He lay still. Breathing heavily, Coventry examined him, trying to decide what to do. It wasn't Rolls, she realized with a shock. It was the other man in black who'd first followed her on the promenade. Was he alive? She didn't want to touch him, but she had to find out. Her stomach knotted as she reached out a trembling hand to check for a pulse in his neck. She sighed with relief. He was alive. Good. If his destiny was to die in the Fringe, she'd prefer that the onus lay with the Fringers. She didn't want to be a murderess.

Would he be out long enough for her to find the others? She wished she had some rope. Her eyes traveled the small foyer, lit on the main door to the building. She couldn't leave him lying *here*. If any of his compatriots came to the front door of the building, he'd be in plain view. Grasping his legs, grimacing at his weight, she pulled him back into the room from which he'd emerged.

Straightening up, Coventry studied the room. It had no other doors. She looked across the foyer to the closed door on the other side. Maybe everyone was in there. She had just taken a step in that direction when she heard a strange noise to her left. She looked back. Her mouth dropped open. One entire wall of the room was rising, disappearing into the ceiling. She watched as scores of booted feet came into view. So that's where they were! A concealed room.

"What is going on?" LaReine's imperious voice pierced Coventry's daze.

Coventry looked at the woman striding toward her with Trace at her side, then nodded to the body at her feet. "G.I.N.," she said.

Immediately LaReine snapped her fingers and made a sweeping motion with her hand. A score of armed young Fringers trotted from the room. "Where is the guard that did this? He should know better than to leave a prisoner without ensuring confinement."

"This man disabled your guard." Coventry nodded at the body still lying in the foyer. "And I wasn't going to leave him without *ensuring confinement,* but I couldn't find any rope."

LaReine waved a hand and another Fringer moved to check the body of the guard. "Where are the other guards? There are always four on duty on the main level."

"I didn't see any others." She looked at Trace, who'd moved to stand at her side. He stood frowning down at the body of the man on the floor in silence, his dark face unreadable.

Then, LaReine nudged the G.I.N. agent's body with her foot. "*You* did this? How?"

Coventry grimaced. Why did this woman insist on assuming she was helpless? "I hit him with that red thing when he came into the foyer."

"A fire extinguisher!" She almost smiled. "Well, your methods may be unique, but they are effective."

"Telli's dead. A laser strike." The voice was that of the young woman sent to check the body of the guard in the foyer.

LaReine nodded. "See if you can find out what happened to the others. And let me know as soon as the team returns." She turned to Trace and Coventry. "As soon as we know it's safe, you may leave. I'll provide you with armed escort to the dome entrance. From there you're on your own until you contact Captain Remes."

Coventry chewed her bottom lip apprehensively as she watched Trace and a Fringer by the name of Stevens attach a device to the dome's surface with suction cups. Whatever they were doing she hoped it worked. The dome was opaque at ground level, but Coventry thought she could just make out the shadows of buildings on the other side. She swung her eyes back to the apparatus stuck to the dome surface as it began to make a series of musical beeping noises. Trace and Stevens stood back, watching.

"What are you doing?" Coventry whispered to Trace.

"Convincing the dome that there is a threat to it, so that it will open a section. And, short-circuiting the alarm system."

"Oh." There didn't seem to be much else to say, so Coventry merely stood beside him watching the device curiously for any sign of progress. Nothing. She looked over her shoulder at the Fringe. The armed escort was still there, she knew, hidden by the ruins of ancient buildings. But if anything went wrong now, there was little help the Fringers could offer.

"Come." Trace grasped her elbow and Coventry looked forward. Her eyes widened in amazement.

A complete section of the dome—large enough to accommodate a bus—was opening in absolute silence. "Thank you," Trace said to Stevens as he gripped his shoulder in a brief squeeze before beginning to back through the opening, pulling Coventry with him.

"Good luck." Stevens raised the hand in which he held the strange suction-cup apparatus in farewell as he began moving away. Then, he turned and loped off. Within seconds he was swallowed by the shadows of the Fringe.

"Quickly." Trace moved to one side, pulling Coventry into the dimness of a large low building.

"Where do we go from here?"

"We find the warehouse belonging to Nova Enterprises and contact Captain Remes." Trace withdrew a palm-sized computer from a pocket in his cloak and began to study its data.

"Where did you get that?"

"A man named Kal. He also provided us with disks that will allow you to learn a good deal of the Thadonian language. Although how he got them is anybody's guess." He paused, looking around. "The Fringers did a pretty good job of estimating the best place to enter. This warehouse belongs to Collins Research." He nodded to a small sign near a designated parking stall. "So, Nova Enterprises should be just two buildings that way." Moving to the corner of the building, he peered around it.

Coventry sidled up beside him. Pulling his head back quickly, he pressed her back against the building with one hand. They waited. Finally Trace looked around the corner again. "Come." He grasped her hand and they sprinted to the rear of the next building. After carefully crossing the next property, they reached the rear of Nova

Enterprises without incident.

Trace checked his wrist chronometer, another acquisition that Coventry hadn't seen before. "We are five minutes early. We will have to wait." Crouching down, he leaned his back against the rear of the building and closed his eyes. Coventry removed the knapsack from her back and followed suit, although she didn't feel quite safe enough to close her eyes. After several deep cleansing breaths, she found tension she hadn't been aware of seeping from her muscles.

"It is time." Trace rose in a sudden fluid motion and Coventry wondered how he knew the amount of time that had passed. He hadn't even glanced at his wrist. She stood, grasping the straps of her knapsack in one hand, and followed him as he moved to the rear door and placed his ear against it. Apparently satisfied, he knocked precisely three times, paused, and rapped twice more. The door opened almost instantly.

Trace grasped her elbow, guiding her into the building. In the sudden gloom of the interior, Coventry caught no more than a glimpse of the man preceding them. She received an impression of a vast open space filled with crates of all sizes and descriptions. After skirting many of these, the man they followed stopped and turned to face them. The corner he'd chosen was secluded, walled off from the rest of the building by crates stacked from the floor to the high ceiling overhead.

He flicked the switch on a portable lamp he carried, illuminating the area with cold blue light. Coventry felt suddenly wary. Too much had happened to her recently for her to trust this man easily. He turned to Trace. "You're the Thadonian, Rainon." His voice was brusque, but not unpleasant.

"I am. On Earth I am called Trace." He handed the man a package which swiftly disappeared, without examination, into a pocket.

"Captain Remes." The man extended his hand to Trace in self-introduction. "And your companion?" He turned to look at Coventry.

"Coventry Pearce," Trace responded as Captain Remes extended his welcome to Coventry.

"Pleased to meet you, captain." Coventry found his grip pleasant, firm and warm. His eyes were pale blue, a color that she'd always found difficult to read. She studied his face—that is, what she could see of it. The captain wore a very full beard, something that was seldom done these days, and Coventry found herself staring, trying to pierce the thick, reddish hair-covering with her eyes to discern the expressions it concealed. It was useless. He released her hand and turned back to Trace.

"Earth security for freighters is quite lax, but customs is another matter. I have arranged to take you on as temporary staff until we're past the excise officials on space dock." He reached into a pocket to withdraw a clump of shimmering silver material. "These are the uniforms used by personnel of the freighter *Payload*. The insignia is on the chest. The uniforms are designed to fit virtually any body size ranging from seventy-five pounds to two-hundred and seventy-five." He looked critically at Trace as he gave him one of the uniforms. "No problem, is there?"

Trace shook his head.

"Good. It is recommended that you do not wear underclothing when wearing the uniforms.

It can hamper their efficiency. They are specifically designed to automatically regulate body heat during space travel. They breathe, and they absorb perspiration. So, you should feel comfortable." He turned to Coventry, handing her the other uniform. "I wasn't certain of your foot size, so I was unable to obtain gravity boots. Here." He extracted a duffel bag from between two crates and opened it to withdraw something metal. "These magnets will attach firmly to your existing footwear and serve the same purpose."

Captain Remes glanced at his wrist. "We haven't much time. The shuttle will be finished loading within minutes and we'll be leaving for space dock. Any questions so far?"

"No," Trace responded.

"Fine. I'll leave you to change then. Just choose any crate as a dressing room. You can use this duffel bag for your own clothing." He handed the now empty bag to Trace. "When I return, I'll finish briefing you." In two steps he had disappeared from sight between the myriad containers.

Coventry, suddenly feeling extremely uncomfortable, held up the uniform she'd been given, pretending to examine it. For some reason the thought of undressing anywhere near Trace bothered her. But it had to be done. Out of the corner of her eye she saw him walk around the edge of a large container. Walking toward some crates in the opposite direction, she began to study them.

Actually using one of the containers as a dressing room was not as bad as she thought. The crates had all been placed on their sides, so they were completely enclosed on the top, sides, and bottom. By choosing one with the rear of another container in front of it, she managed to feel relatively shielded. She hated to abandon her comfortable, oversize shirt in favor of the uniform though. The supple, shimmering, silver cloth fit like a second skin and Coventry felt naked. If she'd had a wart on her bottom, she was certain it would have been discernible. After stuffing her discarded clothing into the already bulging knapsack, she smoothed the fabric of the uniform self-consciously and stepped from the makeshift changing room.

Finding her way back to the clearing among the containers, she saw that Trace stood waiting. She swallowed self-consciously as she walked toward him. Despite herself, her eyes were drawn to his body. If she'd thought he looked magnificent in the snug suppleness of leather, words completely failed her now. As her eyes traveled slowly over his physique, her gaze contacted his and she flushed. The knowing expression in their depths was enough to make her want to smack him.

"Ready, I see. Good." It was Captain Remes returning. "Now then, these are your new identities, at least until we clear customs." He handed a package to each of them. "You," he said to Trace, "are now Officer Kurt Fielding. And you"—he turned to Coventry—"are Officer Gina Bell. Read the material in the packages to learn the details of your lives that might be asked by customs personnel: where you were born, et cetera." He stopped and looked at Trace thoughtfully. "I've noticed you Thadonians, no matter how well you learn our language, seldom use contractions in your speech. Do you think you might be able to throw a few in until we're safely away from space dock?"

Trace nodded. "I will . . . I'll do so."

Remes smiled and nodded. "You'll have no duties on the shuttle so, after you check your documents over, you can just strap yourselves in and enjoy the flight. Once we achieve space dock, you will be required to help with the cargo transfer from the shuttle to *Payload*. Just follow the directions of the Officer in charge and there should be no problem. All right?"

"Understood," Trace replied. Remes looked at Coventry expectantly. She nodded.

"Fine. Let's go then. The shuttle is on the pad.

"Oh. You are aware that accommodations aboard a freighter will not have the conveniences of a passenger ship. If I am bombarded with complaints, I may be tempted to jettison the cause of my headache. Do I make myself clear?"

Coventry frowned slightly. Just what kind of accommodations did freighters have? But Remes appeared to be waiting for her response, and now was not the time to quibble. "You make yourself clear."

He nodded and began to leave with Trace, carrying the duffel bag, in his wake. Quickly Coventry pulled the knapsack onto her back and began to follow.

Tiern watched Coventry expectantly as the shuttle cleared Earth's atmosphere and entered space. As they had taken their seats on the shuttle along with the other employees of *Payload*, she had confided in a whisper that this was to be her first time off planet. Relatively new to space travel himself, Tiern anticipated her reaction. He was not disappointed.

As the force pressing them back into their seats diminished, she turned her head to look out the port. "What are all those lights?" Astonishment colored her voice and he realized that this experience would be even more wondrous for her than it had been for him. She had never seen stars. The atmospheric haze that obscured the moon had virtually obliterated the stars. He waited, not answering immediately because he wanted to see her expression.

Turning to face him, she repeated her query. "All those lights—" She gestured over her shoulder at the port with one finger, "What are they?"

"Stars." He watched her closely, saw the widening of her eyes as comprehension dawned.

"Stars," she repeated quietly. "Of course. I should have known. I've seen them in pictures." She turned back to gaze out of the port. "It's just that they seem so much more . . . real, somehow. And there are so many of them."

He studied her profile as she continued to gaze in wide-eyed fascination at the expansive universe beyond. *Magar!* She was beautiful. The lighting within the shuttle cabin, dimmed to a faint blue illumination, lent a special luminescence to her fair complexion as though she herself radiated starlight. Her golden-blonde hair had taken on a silvery radiance that softened the contours of her face, enlarging her expressive, velvet-brown eyes. She continued to observe the unchanging panorama beyond the shuttle and he decided to make the most of this opportunity to drink in the sight of her.

As his eyes followed the delicate line of her slender white throat past the high neckline of the uniform, his senses absorbed the warmth and fragrance of her. The shimmering suit, bonded to her form like another skin, heightened rather than curtailed awareness of her generous proportions. Her rounded breasts rose and fell with each gentle breath; the nipples, delicately outlined by the thin fabric of the suit, were indistinct. An urge to change that, to hold those exquisite breasts in his hands until the nipples hardened and pressed demandingly against his palms, exploded within him.

With sudden intuition he perceived the reason—hidden even from himself until this moment—that he had wanted to take Coventry Pearce to Thadonia. He studied her fine-boned, partially averted face. On Thadonia the regulation prohibiting involvement with women would be void; he'd be in his own territory. On Thadonia he could take what she, in her sleep, had offered the previous morning. On Thadonia, he could . . .

"What? What is it?" Her words wrenched him from his reverie.

He looked at her, puzzled. "What do you mean?"

"What is it? Why are you staring at me like that?"

He shrugged, uncomfortable at being caught in the depths of a fantasy in which Coventry was the star. "It is nothing. I was just thinking. I apologize for staring." Resolutely, he forced his mind to focus on other things.

Chapter Nine

Trace had been silent a long time, and Coventry hadn't wanted to disturb his thoughts. Astonishment prompted her to forget that resolve. "What is that? It looks like a giant Sea Urchin." She stared wide-eyed at the strange object.

"That is the space dock. Each of those long spines you see is a docking bay. The shuttle will enter the center sphere through an opening in the bottom."

Coventry nodded in mute fascination as the shuttle drew ever nearer. The spaceport was enormous. Each of the spines appeared to be a hundred times the length of a shuttle. Small round circles of light, which she took to be windows, shone intermittently along their length. The colossal center globe—as large as a city!—was ringed with glowing circles at every level.

Within minutes the shuttle had maneuvered between the spines and approached the monolithic formation from beneath. Coventry craned her neck, attempting to look directly up through the limiting viewport. She saw the base of the spaceport open, cavernous and somehow frightening. But the sensation passed and she watched with interest as the shuttle rose into the belly of the enormous globe.

A large glass-like dome enclosed the area of

entry, isolating the shuttle. Beyond the dome enclosure, scores of people and machines moved in an area so vast that she could not perceive its boundaries. The lighting, brilliant in comparison to the muted illumination within the shuttle, almost blinded her. The shuttle moved to one side and settled upon a pad. The huge opening through which they'd entered had already closed.

"Attention please. This is Captain Remes. Prepare to disembark, people." The announcement began as Coventry, enthralled, continued to observe the activity outside the shuttle. She watched the dome, which had sealed the area of entry from the remainder of the base, begin to lift up in sections and white-suited workers begin to move into the area. "After cargo has been transferred, all nonessential personnel will have approximately one hour to take advantage of on-site amenities. *Payload* will be initiating take-off procedures at fourteen-hundred hours."

Even before the announcement had been completed, people rose from their seats to retrieve their belongings from overhead compartments. Trace, too, had risen and was pulling the knapsack from the niche above. Coventry unstrapped herself from her seat and took it from him as he removed the duffel bag.

Minutes later, they stepped from the shuttle to find themselves in a queue filing past a white-uniformed man standing behind a pedestal containing electronic equipment of some type. "Customs Officer," Trace whispered in her ear. She swallowed nervously. They weren't safe yet. But she'd memorized the material in the packet Captain Remes had given her as thoroughly as a script. There wasn't much more she could do to prepare.

Finally it was her turn. She approached the official with what she hoped was a confident step. "Name?" he demanded in a bored tone.

"Officer Gina Bell."

"Date of birth?"

"Fifteen—ten—forty."

"Age?"

"Twenty-eight."

"Place of birth?"

"Oscala City."

He looked at her sharply. "It says here you were born in Bay City."

"No, Sir. I was born in Oscala City. I was *educated* in Bay City." Coventry met his hard gaze. She'd studied the material. She *knew* what it said. So, unless there was an error in the documents Remes had provided, this official was merely attempting to trip her up, as he seemed to have done with a number of people at random along the line. So far, no one had been detained.

Eventually the man gave a sharp nod. "Your identification card, please." Coventry handed it to him and he ran it through a slot on the pedestal. After studying the readout briefly, he returned the card and smiled. "Have a good journey, Officer Bell."

"Thank you, sir." Coventry followed the line slowly forward as she tuned her ears to the exchange taking place behind her as Trace responded to the Customs Officer's queries. It seemed to be going smoothly.

Having helped with the transfer of cargo to *Payload*—which had been a surprisingly easy, if somewhat unique, experience in the gravity-free environment of the loading dock area—Trace and

Coventry were being escorted through a series of corridors and ladder-equipped shafts in search of their cabin. The young man who'd introduced himself as Officer Reece finally drew to a halt before a plain metal door. He waited until Trace and Coventry drew abreast of him before placing his hand on the sensor panel.

The door swished to the side. "These are your quarters. The cabins are not particularly roomy, but they are comfortable."

Coventry eyed the small chamber in dismay. There was only *one* berth. Something was wrong here. Where were her quarters? She turned to broach the subject to Reece, but he continued speaking as though in a hurry to be off. "The galley is down this corridor to the left, and up one level." He began backing away as he spoke. "See you."

"Just a minute—" Coventry ignored Trace as he suddenly grasped her arm. "My quarters?"

"Are fine," Trace finished her statement. She turned to stare at him incredulously as Officer Reece made good his escape.

"What do you mean they're fine? Where are my quarters?"

"You are looking at them." Trace tugged her through the open door and closed it behind them, dropping his duffel bag on the floor.

Coventry eyed him suspiciously. "Then where are your quarters?"

He waved his arm expansively to represent the small area which contained two chairs, a small table and one solitary bunk.

"Like hell!" She glared at him as he turned to face her with an enigmatic expression. "If you think I'm sharing this . . . this closet with *you* for a month you're crazy. I'm going to straighten this out right now." As she reached for the sensor plate by the door, her hand was caught and imprisoned in an iron grip.

"Have you forgotten what the good captain said in reference to complaining passengers?" As he spoke quietly, the warmth of his breath caressed her neck. He stood very near. She could feel the emission of his body heat against her back. Almost instantly she felt the now familiar tightening sensation in her stomach that was the first sign of her body's response to his nearness.

She tried to twist her hand from his grasp. "I don't care what the captain said. We need separate quarters."

Effortlessly, he turned her to face him, capturing her other hand in his as he imprisoned her against the wall of the cabin, his towering form a scant six inches from hers. "Why?"

Shocked speechless by the absurdity of the question, she tilted her head back to look into his face. It was as unreadable as always. She looked into his eyes. There was a disturbing twinkle in their depths. Was he teasing her? Or . . . ? She didn't want to consider *or.*

The situation was spiraling out of control. She felt a pulse beating in her neck. There was a peculiar tightness in her chest. Her instincts told her that it was important that he not become aware of how devastating his proximity was to her senses. But in order to control her body's reactions, she had to put some distance between them.

Becoming more impatient by the second, she struggled to speak in a normal tone of voice. "Don't ask stupid questions. You know *why.* Now let me go." She emphasized the order by attempting to pull her wrists free of his unyielding grip, without success. "Dammit!" Her voice rose slightly despite her best efforts. "I said—" Her sentence was cut off by the placement of a hand over her mouth. How the hell had he managed that? She tugged experimentally at her fists, but her wrists were firmly secured, together now, in just one of his large hands.

"You talk too much, Coventry Pearce. I was going to tell you that—" His words, spoken so quietly that Coventry had to strain to hear them over the pounding in her ears, trailed off. Her eyes flew to his face.

Oh, no! She struggled to speak against his hard palm as she recognized the expression in his eyes. Desire. Despite everything he'd said, he desired her. His gaze began to drop from her face. The sudden knowledge that her body's responses were reciprocated imperiled her resistance. Searing heat swept through her limbs, threatening to rob them of their strength. Desperate now, she twisted her head in his grasp. He ignored her, his gaze riveted on her chest. She saw something flicker in the depths of his eyes as he just stared for endless seconds that seemed like an eternity.

Confusing feelings warred within her. She was furious with him for making her feel so helpless. The sheer size of him as he towered before her, holding her captive with ease, made her feel powerless. And yet, she still wanted him. She didn't recognize herself anymore.

Having met few women with Coventry's unpretentious personality, Tiern had been merely teasing her, anticipating a stimulating encounter with her tempestuous temperament, when suddenly, he had sensed a change, a subtle alteration in the warm female fragrance of her. As *Sotah* he had been trained to isolate and identify scents. The process took place automatically, without conscious thought. Hers was not the smell of fear, it was the scent of anticipation, the beginnings of arousal. A bolt of pure lust flashed through him as he perceived her reaction to him.

Realization induced the return of his earlier fantasy and his longing for them to reach Thadonia. But, even knowing that the charged atmosphere between them was dangerous, he was helpless to check his fascination. He wanted to watch the transformation of her body as her arousal deepened. The clinging silvery suit did nothing to conceal it.

Beneath his avid gaze, her breathing quickened; the soft flesh of her breasts quivered. He let the image of the fantasy return and, as though her body responded to his slightest thought, her nipples began to pucker, tightening and stiffening beneath his eyes. *Magar!* He wanted her.

He closed his eyes, blocking out the sight of her. Beginning a relationship with a woman like her *anytime* was risky. But starting anything with her *now* was out of the question. Although he was certain he could convince her, eventually, that a short-term alliance could be rewarding for them both, he could not allow a physical attraction to hamper his senses until the danger was past.

With an effort he lifted his eyes to her face. This was going to be the longest journey of his life. Realizing that he was still confining her, he released his grip. Her full lips trembled invitingly as she stared at him with those immense, velvet-soft eyes. *Zyk!* He had not intended this to happen. Not now. Not yet. But even as he racked his brain for the thread of the previous teasing interchange, his hands disobeyed him. With a groan of frustration, he pulled her into his arms, more roughly than he had intended. Covering her slightly parted lips with his own, he plunged his tongue into the inviting recess of her mouth as he crushed her against the swollen heat at his groin.

If she'd been an android, Coventry would have sworn there was a wire shorting out somewhere in her abdomen. Her senses swam as the devouring heat of his mouth set sparks off all the way down to her toes. Her stomach churned; her lungs constricted; her knees buckled. Her arms wrapped around his neck and she clung to him as the only solid thing in a vortex of sensation. His hands moved down her back, pressing and kneading, until he cupped the rounded cheeks of her behind. He pulled her tightly against him and she felt the size and hardness of him. Her loins tightened as molten heat flooded through her.

She wanted this. More than anything she wanted his kiss, his caressing hands on her body. In some distant part of her mind she remembered her determination to resist this attraction. But she didn't want to, not this time.

Suddenly his lips left hers to trail over her face. He kissed her eyelids, her cheek, her ear. And then, giving her bottom a final squeeze that threw her senses into total chaos, his caressing hands moved slowly up her back once more. "I am sorry." The whispered words barely penetrated the fog enveloping her mind.

"Mmm." She wanted to tell him everything was all right, but she couldn't seem to get the words out. Then his hands were on her shoulders and she felt him drawing away from her.

Coventry stared at him through passion-dazed eyes as he gently put her from him. What was the matter with him? His hands trembled as he raked his fingers through his hair. "I am sorry, Coventry. We cannot . . . I cannot—"

She continued to stare at him with bemused eyes as he walked a few steps to one of two small doors set into the wall. Stars! *Was* she falling in love with him? Perhaps, if she was . . . and he didn't feel the same way . . . that would explain how he could simply set aside his . . . his physical appetite so easily. Destined to spend weeks, perhaps months, in his company, she would probably fall more deeply in love every day while he . . . he simply looked on her as an inconvenience—the price to be paid for his precious data disk. She swallowed, horrified by the implications.

He walked across the small chamber and slid open a door. "Your compartment is in here," he said as he indicated the room beyond. "Captain Remes explained the arrangement to me earlier, when we contacted him from the Fringe. It was the best he could provide. The chamber is small, but it is private. This door," he indicated the next one, "will be the lavatory." He turned to face her. "*Magar!* Will you stop looking at me as though I am a creature from a nightmare. I have apologized. I was merely teasing you and—" He trailed off with a shrug.

Ignoring her, he retrieved the duffel bag from the floor and thrust it into a compartment over his berth with abrupt, angry motions. Then, lowering himself onto the bed, he stretched out, arms behind his head, and contemplated the ceiling with single-minded concentration.

He had been *teasing* her and *what*? Fury mounted within her until she thought she was going to explode. Gritting her teeth, Coventry silently picked up her knapsack, and began to walk toward the door of the compartment he'd said was hers. Tears stung her eyes at the effort it took to control her anger. It was no good. She *had* to say something or she'd end up crying, and she hated tears. She pivoted to face him. "You—" She paused, steadying her voice. "You are never to touch me again. Do you understand?"

He did not look at her, but merely nodded as he continued to stare at the ceiling. "I will not touch you unless you ask me to."

"Unless I ask you to," Coventry echoed incredulously. "The entire galaxy will explode before I ever ask you to so much as lend me a hand. You . . . You are despicable." Turning, she entered her chamber and slid the door closed with as much force as possible.

An entire week had passed. *Payload* was well on its way to Thadonia. And Coventry was slowly, surely going crazy. She'd settled into her small apartment, trying to make it home by unpacking the knapsack. It had contained an extra set of clothing for herself, some undergarments and toiletries—including a very welcome hairbrush—men's trousers and a shirt in Trace's size, which she'd placed on Trace's bunk, and a blaster wrapped in some type of shielding material and concealed in the lining. Now, she found herself with nothing left to do.

She and Trace had not spoken two words to each other the entire week. In fact, much of the time he seemed to have found something to occupy him away from the cabin. When he was there, Coventry had found that she could not control the inclination to observe him constantly.

Despite her pique and the fact that, as facial features went, his too-aggressive countenance was not a particularly handsome one, despite everything, she found that he appeared more and more attractive to her. She'd caught herself studying the deep blue color of his eyes and the way his hair drooped over his forehead as he read data on the palm-sized computer. She had found herself remembering how it had felt to be crushed against that wide, rock-hard chest; to have those long-fingered hands caressing her behind. In desperation she had finally taken to locking herself in her own tiny chamber, which was large enough for a bunk and nothing more, whenever he was in.

But she couldn't take much more of this. She was not a gregarious person by nature, yet neither was she a solitary one. She needed conversation and companionship. Having tried more than once to strike up a conversation with the ship personnel she'd met in the companionway, she'd eventually given up. The results had always proven disappointing; they were always in a rush, or had duties to attend to, or had a rendezvous to keep. And there was only one female employee, an oriental woman who *was* a solitary person. When Coventry'd asked why there were no other women aboard, she'd been told that most of them preferred the predictability of working aboard the space stations or passenger ships.

Coventry looked at the chronometer on the wall. It was late. Where was Trace? Even as the thought took form, she heard the outer door open and knew that he had returned to the cabin. Perhaps it was time to break her self-imposed isolation. She was still angry with him, but that didn't mean they couldn't *talk*.

Resolutely, she opened her door and stepped into the larger room. He'd begun alternating his

Thadonian clothing with the Fringer ensemble Coventry had found in the knapsack. Tonight he wore the Thadonian garb. In the process of removing his shirt, he stopped in mid-motion and looked at her quizzically.

The words Coventry had been prepared to utter scattered in her mind like so much fluff in a breeze. She'd never seen him without a shirt before. Stars, he was magnificent! The bronze flesh of his shoulders and biceps rippled smoothly as he pulled his shirt back on. Thick black silky-looking hair covered his chest and trailed over his hard, flat belly in a single narrow line before disappearing into the waistband of his trousers.

"Did you want something?" Coventry's eyes flew to meet his. The wicked glint in their depths left no doubt in her mind that the suggestive tone of his voice had been intentional. Her face flamed with mortification. He was embarrassing her on purpose. Why? It was obvious that, although she had felt his body respond to her, he did not want her. Was he trying to anger her to maintain a distance between them? She refused to retreat now.

"Yes. Conversation. I'm bored." She avoided looking at him as she moved to one of the chairs and sat down. When she did look up again, she had managed to control her embarrassment. Trace sat down on his bunk, resting his back against the wall. She wished he would fasten his shirt, but she refused to reveal just how much his naked chest unsettled her by asking.

"What did you want to talk about?"

She shrugged. "I don't know. Tell me about your family. What are Mr. and Mrs. Rainon like?"

"Who?" He looked at her blankly.

173

"Your parents. You know, Mr. and Mrs. Rainon."

"Oh." He smiled slightly. "You are suffering from a misconception. It is my fault, I should have explained."

"Explained what?"

"On Thadonia, we do not use surnames as you do. When a child is born, they are given a name . . . one name. This is the name by which they are known to their loved ones. When the child is older and begins associating with people outside the circle of the family, he or she chooses another name. This is the name by which he is known to all others."

Coventry frowned slightly. "So, then Rainon is the name you chose for yourself, and Tiern is the name you were given when you were born?"

"Correct."

"And nobody calls you Tiern except your family?"

He nodded.

"So what would your family call you if they were speaking of you to a stranger?"

"Rainon. The name Tiern is for private moments when surrounded by loved ones."

"Why?" Coventry was thoroughly confused. "What is so private about a name?"

He studied her intently as though debating his response. "In the Thadonian language there are no words for . . . affectionate names." He hesitated. "No endearments. The name bestowed at birth is known as the heart-name. It is private, the endearment by which that person is known to his loved ones for the rest of his life."

"So why did you tell people your given name on Earth? Shouldn't it have been kept a secret?"

Trace looked to the side and, if she hadn't

known better, she would have sworn that he appeared to flush slightly. He cleared his throat. "You are the only person on Earth to whom I revealed my name. I don't know why I did. Perhaps it was the fact that you introduced yourself with two names." He shrugged. "It does not matter. I ask only that you do not reveal it to others."

Coventry's eyes widened in surprise and she felt an inexplicable glow of pleasure. "All right, I'll keep your personal name a secret. Tell me about your parents. What are their names?"

"My mother is known as Aislyn. She is my father's first chosen consort. My father's name is Rytr."

"Oh, so your parents are separated?"

"No." He frowned at her. "Why would you say that? They have always been very happy together."

"But you said that Aislyn was your father's *first* chosen consort. I just assumed that they had separated and that your father had remarried."

Trace grinned as his eyes glittered with mischief. He shook his head. "You assume so much Coventry. Thadonia is not a monogamous society, although couples can choose to be if they so wish. It is perfectly acceptable for a man to have more than one wife provided his first consort is agreeable."

"You're joking!" He shook his head. No wonder he had a tendency to be domineering with women, coming from such a society. "And is it acceptable for a woman to have more than one husband?" She asked the question jeeringly, feeling certain she already knew the answer.

"Of course. Provided her first husband is in agreement."

Coventry's jaw dropped. "Really?"

He grinned again, obviously enjoying shocking her with this little interchange. "Really."

Coventry's mind whirled. "Couldn't that get awfully complicated? I mean, what would happen if your father's second wife decided she wanted another husband or two? And then each of them decided they wanted another wife?"

"Each marriage alliance is limited to six members. Usually only the first couple has the right to choose another member to join the union. The second, by virtue of his or her lower status in the household, gives up that right."

"Oh." Coventry tried to picture the nature of such a family. "Six members to a marriage. Three men and three women?"

He shook his head. "Not necessarily. The numbers can be five to one of either sex, but such a combination is rare."

How did they get onto this topic? Oh well, she couldn't stop now. She was simply too curious. "I don't suppose infidelity would be as much of a problem in such a society," she mused. "Do people get divorced?"

"Divorce does occur, rarely, and only for a reason that is deemed justifiable by the judiciary. Infidelity is unlawful, but rarely a reason for divorce."

Coventry shook her head in bafflement. "What would be considered a justifiable reason for divorce? And why is infidelity rarely a factor?"

He looked at her quizzically. "Why do you want to know all this? There are many more interesting topics we could speak of."

"But this *is* interesting. And I'm curious. Besides, we have lots of time to cover all the other topics. So talk."

He sighed. "Very well. A justifiable reason for divorce would be . . . violence or . . . complete incompatibility with the other partners of the marriage. It has happened that two people will divorce the other members of a union in order to become monogamous. Infidelity is rarely a factor in divorce. Usually the offender is merely punished by the marriage partner or partners through confinement and ostracism."

"What happens to repeat offenders?"

Trace grimaced and shifted uncomfortably. "I do not think you want to know this." Coventry opened her mouth to protest and he held up a hand to forestall her. "All right. In *extreme* cases, based upon the intervention of a judiciary, a woman may be permanently disfigured or, if the offender is a man, he may be . . . emasculated."

Coventry's eyes widened in shock. If she'd needed proof that she was traveling to a primitive society, she definitely had it now. "Isn't that rather severe?"

"Perhaps, for a monogamous people, yes." He shrugged expressively. "But in a society where it is possible for a man or woman to have up to five partners of the opposite sex, adultery is considered unnecessary and dangerous in terms of disease transmission."

Coventry nodded. "You said of the *opposite* sex. There are no marriages that consist entirely of one sex?"

He frowned at her. "What would be the purpose in that? There could be no children. The family would be extinct within one generation."

"Well, children aren't the only reason to get married. Some people marry for love and remain childless. And some love marriages *are* homosexual."

He shook his head. "There are no homosexuals in Thadonian society."

"None?" Coventry asked incredulously.

"None." His response was firm and absolute. "Have you learned enough for one evening?" He looked at the digital chronometer on the wall. "It is late."

Coventry actually had one more question to ask, but she didn't know how to go about it. How did one go about asking a man from another world, a foreign civilization, if he was permitted to have sex before marriage? The thought had occurred to her during their conversation that perhaps, if sex prior to marriage wasn't approved of, it would explain why he had acted as he had the day of their arrival.

"I can see you have another question," he said. "Ask it. We will make it your last question for the night. Tomorrow you can begin studying the disks that will teach you the Thadonian language. Perhaps the language itself will give you some insights into what to expect on my world."

"You're certain you don't need the computer anymore?" Coventry was stalling for time. She couldn't ask the question. She'd embarrass herself. But her mind refused to come up with any other inquiry.

"I have finished with it. What is your question?"

She looked around the room. Hell! She needed to know. "On Thadonia, are you . . . are people allowed to . . . have relations before marriage?" She risked a look in his direction.

His face had gone still, completely expressionless, his eyes intense as his gaze captured and held hers. "What kind of relations, Coventry?" The question was low, intimate. She tugged nervously at the fabric of her pants without realizing

178

she was doing it until his gaze dropped to her hands.

Clasping her hands together, she met his gaze and said firmly, "Sexual relations."

"Why do you want to know that, Coventry?" Her stomach shuddered in response to his suggestive tone. Stars, how could just his voice affect her that way?

She shrugged in an attempt to portray a nonchalance she did not feel. "I was just wondering if there were rules governing the behavior of unmarried people. That's all." She looked him in the eye unflinchingly.

He put his head back against the wall, facing the ceiling so that she could not see his expression. "No. There are no rules, other than those dictated by a moral upbringing, imposed on unattached people. Rampant promiscuity is not acceptable to most people, but neither is it unlawful." He lowered his head to look at her. His eyes glittering peculiarly, he smiled. "In that respect, Thadonia is very much like Earth. And now, it is time you went to sleep."

"But what about—?"

"Now, Coventry!" Startled by his abruptness, she stared at him openmouthed. What on earth was the matter with him? "Good-night, Coventry," he said silkily.

Puzzled, Coventry rose and walked toward the door of her chamber. As she opened it, she turned to ask him what she'd said to anger him, but she never got the chance. "Out, Coventry. Now!"

She didn't like his tone. She didn't like it at all. But she'd had enough experience with him to know that she rarely, if ever, got the upper hand in an argument. So, squelching her retort, she entered her room and shut the door. Sheesh!

He was as surly as a Central technician who'd been forced to miss a coffee break. Stripping out of her clothes in angry, jerky motions, she donned the Thadonian tunic that she'd taken to using as a nightgown and lay down.

As the door closed behind her, Tiern doubled up his fist, striking the wall next to him in frustration. He knew why she'd asked, he'd known the instant the words left her mouth. She was still angry with him for . . . for not following through on what he had started and sought a reason that would explain his behavior. He supposed he could have explained the regulations of *Sotah* to her, but her anger served well as a buffer between them. And, no matter how much he hated to admit it, he desperately needed that buffer because every other reason against becoming involved with her was quickly diminishing in importance. So, he would continue to maintain a distance between them until they were beyond Earth's territory.

He frowned in sudden thought. Technically speaking, was he not already outside Earth's territory? He was in space, no-man's domain. No! Growling in frustration he rose to remove his shirt and prepare for bed. The *Payload* was an Earth ship. Aboard her, he was surrounded by Earthers. He was merely trying to negate the most important reason for continuing to avoid Coventry, the *Sotah* regulations by which he lived his life. And even if those regulations, technically, no longer bound him, the purpose of them did.

Removing his boots, he ensured that they were firmly magnetized to the floor near the head of the bunk. Although the *Payload* was a large enough ship that it had artificial gravity, the force was perhaps only three-quarters that of

Earth and objects tended to slide around much more easily than he was used to. Looking at the boots reminded him of the disk concealed in a shielded packet in the heel of his right boot. He felt the urge to remove it and study it once more. But it was no longer necessary; he knew what the disk contained: detailed plans for an upcoming attempt to seize control of Thadonia, a coup.

He lay down on his bunk, hands beneath his head, as he once again considered the information. Many of the names of the participants, including those of the leaders of both the Earth and Thadonian contingents, had been coded. But the details were appalling. It was a plan devoted to the personal profit of the people involved and the subjugation of an entire populace as their home world was raped of everything of value. But even the Thadonian men involved could not know the *full* capabilities of the *Sotah*. And Tiern knew that Thadonia would be forever eradicated from the map of the universe before it would be allowed to fall into such hands.

He frowned thoughtfully. Coventry's safety on Thadonia was no more assured than it had been on Earth; but there was little he could do about it. At least the danger was not immediate. The best he could do was prepare her as well as possible for life on his world.

Sitting up he reached into the compartment over his bunk, searching for the educational disks and compact computer. Finding them, he rose to place them firmly on the small table where Coventry would find them easily in the morning. He had no intention of being in his room when she arose. That done, he entered the lavatory to wash and prepare for another restless night.

* * *

When Coventry arose the next morning, Trace was, as usual, already gone. She saw the disks he'd left on the table, but ignored them for the moment as she attended to her morning ablutions and left the cabin in search of the galley. After a solitary breakfast provided by the dispenser, she returned to the cabin to spend the day learning the Thadonian language.

Once she became involved in the process, lying on her bunk with computer headphones attached to her ears as she simultaneously studied the display on the small screen, the day passed quickly. She skipped lunch, returning to the galley for the evening meal. Trace had either eaten previously, or would eat later, for he was not in evidence. Although curious as to where he spent so much of his time, she did not feel comfortable with the inclination to inquire concerning his whereabouts and she remained silent, studying the few other personnel who had chosen to dine at the same time.

She tried to involve the man next to her in conversation, but the attempt proved fruitless. He responded to any question put to him in monosyllables. Finally, frustrated, Coventry put down her fork and grasped his arm, compelling him to look at her. "Is there some reason why I cannot cultivate a decent conversation with a single person aboard this ship?"

The man, Officer Vance she saw on his nametag, turned to her. He looked around the table at the other personnel present. All conversation had stopped; everyone stared at her. Coventry felt the sudden tension in the room. A couple of the men present looked at Officer Vance and nodded. Finally Vance swallowed whatever he'd been chewing and replied. "You are the only attractive female aboard. That position can be . . . dangerous. The captain made it clear that any attempt at . . . fraternization would be punishable."

Coventry's mouth opened in surprise. She could think of nothing to say. Within a minute, those assembled returned to their conversations with each other, ignoring her presence. The situation was ridiculous. Wasn't it? All she wanted was conversation. But she'd never been alone among this many men before for any protracted period of time. Perhaps it was best to assume that the captain knew the nature of his men better than she did.

After finishing her meal, rather than returning to her lonely and confining cabin, Coventry decided to go to the observatory. Although the three-hundred-and-sixty-degree view of the universe had a tendency to increase her melancholy, this was the third time she'd found herself drawn to view the panorama of the stars. As she ascended the companionway ladder into the small unoccupied observatory, her eyes were immediately attracted to the measureless expanse of the star-studded heavens. Always the same, yet ever-changing, she thought she'd never seen anything more beautiful. Unconsciously, without taking her eyes from the spectacle, she moved across the dimly lit room to one of the two padded chairs and seated herself.

Tonight there was one exceptionally bright star just to her right. Studying it, she thought she perceived a planet, large and reddish, suspended in imperceptible orbit. Seeing it, her thoughts strayed to Thadonia, the planet that would be her new home for at least a year. What would it be like? And the question that had been bothering her ever since she'd had the time to really stop and think popped into her mind. What would she do to earn a living there? Did they have theatres? Actors and actresses?

She allowed her mind to drift. Thoughts and questions coming and going without direction. And once again her thoughts turned to Trace. What was she going to do about him? It was hard enough to imagine what life on Thadonia might be like for her. But to imagine her life there without Trace in it was all but impossible. Why? She'd never before attempted to define her life, or the quality of it, based on the presence of another person in it. Was it because her life had changed so drastically? Or was it because she was falling in love with a man totally unsuited to her? She just didn't know. Realizing it had grown late, she rose to return to her cabin.

Coventry was amazed to find the cabin in total blackness. She always left the lights on when she went out because the computer did not respond to either her or Trace's voice commands and she knew she would have difficulty finding the manual switch in the dark. "Trace?" She paused hoping for a response. "Trace, are you there?" Nothing. There was no alternative then. She had to enter and try to find the light switch.

Swallowing nervously, Coventry stepped into the chamber, sliding her hands over the wall. Her breath froze in her throat. She'd come up against something definitely not part of the wall. It was fabric. And beneath it was a very solid shoulder, an unfamiliar shoulder. She opened her mouth to scream. The sound never left her throat. Something struck her face. There was an instant of mind-numbing pain as tiny pinpoints of light flashed in her brain. Her legs began to lose their strength. She struggled desperately to move toward the door. It was no use. Blackness, deeper even than the darkness of the room, imprisoned her mind and deadened her senses.

Chapter Ten

Tiern glanced uneasily at the chronometer. He was in the engineering department where he had struck up a friendship of sorts with a man named Warshaw. His gut was telling him something, but he did not know what. He swept the engineering room with appraising eyes. Warshaw was clanging tools around as he worked; his assistant studied a computer readout. No one else was present. He glanced at the chronometer again. It was too early to return to his chambers. Coventry would still be awake. Coventry! Warning bells tolled in his brain. Without a word, he moved swiftly toward the exit, blindly skirting the machinery in his path.

Barely three minutes later, panting more with alarm than with exertion, he approached the closed door of his compartment. Stopping, he brought his breathing under control. If Coventry was in danger, he would not help her by bursting in unprepared. After checking the corridor to make certain he was alone and unobserved, he closed his eyes and centered, calling upon the energy of the *Sotah*. He felt the power that was part of him become tangible. Slowly, he extended his senses beyond the door.

He found Coventry's presence immediately, determined her exact location, and then swept the chamber for a presence that did not belong. It was there. A male presence directly behind hers. Whoever was in the room was waiting for his arrival, using Coventry as a shield. Tiern withdrew. Pulling the stunner from the loop on his trousers, he palmed it although he doubted that it would do him much good. If the man was competent, he could use Coventry very adeptly as a screen. Triggering the sensor plate for the door, he flattened himself against the wall as light spilled from the chamber into the corridor.

"Come in, Thadonian. Carefully. You wouldn't want me to have to hurt your friend here any more, would you?" Tiern could not identify the voice. Smooth and almost excessively pleasant, he was certain he would have remembered it had he ever spoken to the man. Senses alert to the slightest hint of change in the situation, Tiern turned and stepped into the chamber.

His eyes found and probed his opponent. Attractive, with tawny hair and pale green eyes, he was almost the equal of Tiern in height for his chin barely grazed the top of Coventry's head. He had one arm around Coventry, holding her against him. In the other hand he held a laser, its muzzle pressed firmly against her temple.

Tiern looked at Coventry. Rage, potent and virulent, swelled in him and he fought to control and conceal it. She was barely conscious, her eyes dazed and uncomprehending. Blood trickled from a cut beneath her left eye, forging a crimson trail down her swollen, discolored cheek.

"So I finally get to meet the Thadonian." He spoke the last word with derision, pulling Tiern's gaze back to him.

"Who are you?"

The man shrugged. "They call me Kys." He

grinned, his eyes alert, eager and glowing with madness. "You have one minute to hand over the disk or your friend dies." His calm statement left no doubt in Tiern's mind that he would do as he said. His pale, soulless eyes were those of a man who suffered no remorse—the eyes of a killer.

Tiern nodded, lowering his head slightly as though resigned to the situation, as he drew again upon the power deep within him. He gathered it, focusing it without allowing its radiance to escape the shield of his body. Then, suddenly, just as the man began to get impatient, Tiern attacked. Without raising his head, he suddenly pinned the man with the dark force of his merciless gaze. Kys's eyes opened wide in disbelief and terror as his will was torn from his mental grasp. A brilliant blue-white light, visible only to Tiern's enlightened eyes, charged across the short space between them, disappearing into the man's skull. Without uttering a sound, Kys began to fall. The reflexes of a *Sotah* took over and Tiern leapt to catch Coventry's wavering form and snatch the laser from the man's hand before, in the convulsive reaction of death, it could be fired.

"Trace?" Coventry's voice was weak, confused and panicky.

"Hush. Everything is all right now." Holding her trembling body against him, he looked down at the corpse of the man who had planned to kill them both. Tiern had only recently learned of such men. In Earth terminology, he was termed a plant. A man who, while employed by one company, was on retainer to another organization, inactivated until his services were required. The practice was a common one on Earth, employed even between rival companies. Given the perilous nature of the data he carried and the extensive control manifested by an organization capable of the plot he sought to disclose, he had almost expected to encounter such a person. But when the first week had passed uneventfully, he had relaxed his guard. A mistake—and a lesson he would not forget.

Lifting Coventry in his arms, he carried her to his bunk and gently laid her down. Her eyes were closed, their dark lashes a stark contrast to her pale face. He moved toward the lavatory to get a cold cloth, but halted in mid-stride. Turning, he looked at the man once more. It was unlikely that he had a partner on board, but if he did and Tiern did not act swiftly, he could be charged with the murder of a crew member. If he attempted to conceal the incident or was apprehended with the body in his quarters before he himself reported it, he would look guilty. It would be best if he reported it . . . immediately. Flipping the switch on the intercom, he put in a priority call to Captain Remes, requesting the presence of the captain and a medic, before proceeding to the lavatory.

Returning to Coventry, he began to gently sponge the congealing blood from her swollen cheek. She opened her eyes; they were clearer, more focused. "What did you do to him?"

"Hush. He is dead. He will not hurt you again."

"But—" Her brow furrowed slightly. "How? I didn't see you—" Her voice trailed off, made uncertain by her confusion.

"You must not concern yourself. I merely used a technique similar to the martial arts practiced on Earth." The response seemed to satisfy her, for she nodded and closed her eyes. "Are you hurt anywhere other than here?" He placed the cool cloth over her cheek as much for her comfort as to conceal the damage to her features.

Coventry shook her head slightly. "No. He only hit me once. How does it look?"

Tiern studied her. How would she react when he told her that her face might be scarred for a time? She was a beautiful woman, and an actress, surely her appearance would be as important to her as Aneire's had been to her.

She opened her eyes, awaiting his response. He cleared his throat. "The swelling and bruising will fade, but I am afraid the cut may leave a scar." He watched her intently, waiting for her to dissolve into hysterics, wondering what he could do to ease her pain.

"Is it big?"

"No. About this long." He held up his fingers showing a gap of about an inch.

Coventry smiled. "Now maybe I'll finally be able to get the part of the *warrior queen*. They always told me I looked too soft for the role."

Tiern stared at her in amazement. "You are not concerned?"

"About a tiny scar?" She looked at him in genuine puzzlement as she struggled to sit up. He helped her, placing a cushion between her and the wall at her back. "Why should I be? If the medic here is any good, it will probably be virtually invisible, and I can always cover it with cosmetics. Actually," she grinned lopsidedly, wincing slightly as the movement irritated her swollen face, "I might just emphasize it on occasion. Do you think I might be able to make myself look . . . forbidding?"

"I do not know," Tiern responded absently. Why had he assumed that Coventry would be like Aneire? Because she was an actress and he had always assumed that actresses lived for adoration? Had he judged her unfairly? There were many beautiful women, on Thadonia and on Earth, who had husbands *and* children. He had assumed that because Coventry was a mature woman, unmarried and without children, that that was the way she wanted it. Even now he found it difficult to abandon his assumptions. "Are you not concerned with . . . the flaw to your appearance?" He felt ridiculous even as he asked the question. Why was he pursuing the issue?

Coventry gave him a hard look. "I don't know what your problem is, Trace. But if you think that . . . that a tiny scar is going to make me ugly or something . . . well, then you can just keep your eyes off of me." Her voice warmed to her anger. "Nobody, no matter how good the medical technology available, keeps their looks forever. And—" There was a knock at the door.

"That will be the captain." Tiern rose and looked down at Coventry. "I do not think you are ugly, Coventry." He walked to the door, skirting the body of the man who had called himself Kys, and bade the captain and the medic enter. After directing the medic to care for Coventry, who continued to stare at him with a combination of anger and confusion reflected in her large dark eyes, Tiern directed his attention to the captain.

"What happened here, Rainon?" The captain's voice was brusque, harried, but neutral.

Tiern shrugged. "I returned to the cabin to find Coventry being attacked by that man." He gestured to the spot where the body sprawled on the floor. "I . . . remedied the situation."

Remes stared silently into his face for a moment, as though seeking verification. Then, nodding, he directed the medic to put in a call for a gurney and examine the body. Then, he returned his attention to Tiern. "Kys was a relatively new man. He's been with us about six months. A loner. He never seemed to make any friends among the crew, so I doubt if there will be any further trouble." He looked at the medic as he began to pack away his instruments. "Well?"

"Looks like a stroke, sir."

"A stroke?" the captain echoed in disbelief. He turned to Tiern. "Would you care to comment on how a physical confrontation would result in a stroke?"

"My fighting technique is similar to a martial art. Perhaps my attack merely accelerated a situation that was inevitable."

Captain Remes considered the idea. "Perhaps," he agreed finally. He looked at the medic. "How is Ms. Pearce?"

"I gave her a shot to reduce the pain and swelling. She should be fine in a few hours. I closed the cut and put some surgical tape over it to minimize infection and scarring. It may still leave a slight blemish, but," he shrugged, "it's the best I can do with the facilities we have. She can always have it surgically repaired back on Earth."

The captain nodded and stepped aside as an anti-grav gurney arrived. After hastily strapping the body to the stretcher, the attendants turned and left the chamber. Captain Remes faced Tiern. "I am trusting your word on the nature of this encounter. And I apologize for the fact that it happened on my ship. However, I feel compelled to warn you that, should another incident of this type occur, I will not be as inclined to accept the situation. Do I make myself clear?"

Tiern nodded. "You do."

"Good." The captain left without another word. Tiern turned back to Coventry. She was curled into the fetal position on his bed, her head cradled on one bent arm with tears streaming down her face. Quickly he knelt at her side. "What is it, Coventry?"

She sniffed. "I don't know. For some reason I can't stop crying. I hate crying." The last sentence emerged on a near wail of despair.

He smiled as he brushed a soggy strand of hair from her cheek. "You can cry."

She sniffed again, looking at him as though he were not all that intelligent. "I know I *can* cry. I just don't want to."

"It must be a reaction to the drug the medic gave you. It will pass."

She began plucking at the fabric of her trousers intently. "Are we going to die, Trace?" The question was no more than a murmur and it took an instant for him to make sense of the words.

"No. Of course not." Poor Coventry. Tenderly he stroked her hair. He had never met a more adaptable woman. He wondered how he would have dealt with such complete transformations to his life. Somehow, he did not think he would have handled it as adeptly. She had accepted so much change, so much danger. Only now, under the influence of the drug, was she incapable of hiding the insecurity generated by her circumstances. He wanted to lie with her, gather her into his arms and comfort her. Yet he was mindful of the promise he had made.

"Will we ever escape them?" Tears continued to stream from her eyes and he gently wiped them away with the cloth.

"Yes. You must trust me to protect you." He stroked her silken hair as he spoke, amazed at how beautiful she appeared to him, even with her features bruised and streaked with tears.

"Hold me, Trace." His hand froze in mid-caress upon her hair. She turned her large, soft, brown eyes on him and he saw the pain and fear in their depths. "Please?" She moved over to make room for him on the narrow bunk.

He was lost. Rising from his kneeling position, he stretched out on the bunk beside her and wrapped his arms around her slender form as she burrowed against him. *Magar!* She felt good in his arms, and he felt like a scoundrel for savoring the sensation of holding her when what she needed was comfort. Closing his eyes, he rested his chin upon her head as she pressed her tear-dampened face against the warmth of his neck.

"Can we talk?" Her warm breath caressed his neck.

"About what?"

"I don't know. Anything."

He thought about how she had begun to so thoroughly obliterate his assumption that she would be another Aneire. Although he refused to ascribe any more to his desire to know than simple interest, he felt compelled to satisfy his curiosity. "May I ask you something?"

He felt her nod. "All right."

He hesitated. "If you feel it is none of my business, you do not have to answer. I am simply curious." He cleared his throat. "Why have you never married?"

She sniffed. "No one ever asked me." He raised his brows at her murmured response.

He could not believe that no man had ever asked her. "I do not understand. Have you never loved someone enough to want to marry?"

She shrugged and he felt the warm breath of a sigh caress his neck. "I thought I did. A couple of times. But the relationships ended before marriage was ever discussed."

"Oh." Another question burned in his mind. "Do you not desire children?"

She moved her head back and looked up into his face. She was no longer crying. "I always wanted *two* children," her expression was wistful, "a boy and a girl. But that won't be possible now."

"Why?"

She sighed and rested her head on his shoulder. "Because I am almost thirty. At the age of thirty sterilization procedures are mandatory in order to control population growth. Even were I to marry this year, there would not be time enough to have more than one child."

A tautness that had gripped him without his knowledge eased. "It is not so on Thadonia."

Coventry looked up at him, her eyes wide with sudden comprehension. "No. It wouldn't be, would it? I hadn't thought about it." She brushed a hair back from her face and winced as she inadvertently grazed her bruised cheek. "What about you? Why aren't you married?"

Tiern froze. Why had he not realized where his questions would lead? Uncomfortable with his memories, he responded more brusquely than he had intended. "I was."

"Oh." Coventry's eyes were wide with astonishment. "I just assumed . . . when you said you weren't married—" Her voice trailed off. "What happened?"

"Aneire died about two years after we married."

"I'm sorry." Closing her eyes, Coventry rested her head on his shoulder and grew silent.

Tiern watched her as she drifted into slumber. Already the swelling in her face was going down, the bruising less noticeable. The cut beneath her eye, visible through the translucent surgical tape, was no more than a small red line. Seeing that she rested comfortably, he closed his eyes and sought his own respite.

Coventry stirred. Although she could feel the cover of the ship's silvery, thermal blanket over her body, she was cold. Reluctantly opening her eyes, it took her a moment to remember what she was doing in Trace's bunk. Where was Trace? She looked at the chronometer above the door. It was only five hundred hours. Surely he didn't usually leave this early. Sitting up, she gingerly tested her cheek and found that, except for a slight tenderness, it felt much better. Whatever the medic had given her seemed to have worked well.

She thought of the man who'd accosted her. Trace had killed a man last night, yet she could find nothing in her heart but relief. That bothered her a little. The man had, undoubtedly, been a horrible person but shouldn't she have abhorred the act of slaying another human being? Yet, she found that she didn't. Not in this instance. She remembered the impotent rage she had felt when she'd first seen how badly Dalton had been beaten. When she thought about it, she felt that, in certain circumstances, she herself might have the capacity to kill. Perhaps, deep down, she had much more tolerance for violence than she had been aware of. Maybe no one was ever really aware of what they were capable of until their lives, or the life of someone they loved, were threatened.

She sighed and looked at her clothing. After having been slept in, it looked none too appealing. Entering her own small chamber, she stripped and put on the Thadonian tunic before reentering

196

the main room to hang her clothes in the laundering compartment. As she closed the door, a slight noise behind her made her whirl in surprise.

Trace emerged, barefoot and shirtless, from the lavatory. As he looked at his empty bunk, he stopped and then slowly turned to face her. He had obviously bathed. The bare flesh of his upper body glistened with the cleansing effect of the radiant-shower. Her eyes clung to him, mesmerized by the sheer male beauty of his form. She saw the leashed power in the muscles beneath the bronzed flesh of his arms and recalled how she had fallen asleep within his embrace. Her gaze roamed the hair-covered expanse of his broad chest, and she remembered the sound of his heart beneath her ear. The sight of the powerful, tawny-fleshed column of his neck evoked the memory of how it had felt to press her cheek against its warmth. His eyes . . . Oh stars! His eyes made her realize with sudden clarity that she was wearing nothing more than the short, delicate Thadonian tunic.

The tension in the small chamber magnified. She had to do something, say something to break it. "I . . . I thought you had left." He didn't respond with so much as the flicker of an eye and Coventry became acutely conscious of her long bare legs. Moisture flooded her mouth and she swallowed. "I was just going to go to my room—" Nervously she took a sidestep in that direction. With a tremendous effort of will, she broke the magnetic pull of his burning, midnight gaze and looked at the door to her room. "Good-night."

He made a strange growling noise deep in his throat. "Coventry—" The husky tone of his voice stopped her, but she refused to look at him.

"Yes?"

"Come here." Her stomach fluttered at the soft-voiced command, but she fought it. She just couldn't deal with any more of his mercurial reactions to her.

"No." Taking two quick steps, she reached the door to her chamber but before she could enter she felt his hand close on the soft flesh of her upper arm.

"Look at me, Coventry."

"No. Let me go." Her response sounded petulant, even to her own ears, but she couldn't help it. She knew the effect he had on her.

Grasping her shoulders, he slowly turned her to face him. Resolutely, she closed her eyes to the sight of his naked chest. Raising her chin with one finger, he repeated his demand in a whisper. "Look at me." He clasped the back of her neck with one hand, caressing the sensitive spot beneath her ear with his thumb. Gasping, she opened her eyes and raised her hands to counter the movements of his. But he did nothing more than look into her eyes, paralyzing her with the sheer heat of his gaze. And then, with a muffled growl, his lips swooped down on hers as he pulled her into his arms, trapping her hands between their bodies.

His kiss was gentle, consuming, and just as devastating as Coventry remembered it. He stroked his tongue across her lips and she parted them, powerless to resist the impulse. Her senses exploded and her fingers curled helplessly in the silky hair of his chest. Then, too soon, his lips left hers, trailing tender kisses across her bruised cheek until he reached her ear. "Do you still want me to let you go?" His tone was no more than a ragged whisper.

Coventry shuddered. No! She wanted him. But could she risk telling him that? Yet even as the hesitant thought entered the rational part of her brain, another part took control of her tongue and she answered him. "No." The word was little more than a slight exhalation of breath, but he must have heard it for his arms tightened around her convulsively.

He looked into her face and smiled. Her knees turned to water in reaction to that tender, triumphant, yet wary smile and she clung to him as his head lowered once more. Threading one hand into her hair, he immobilized her head as he plundered her mouth with his tongue. Her equilibrium dissolved as he arched her body over the fulcrum of his arm at her waist, and she twisted in his hold, pushing her arms up through his crushing embrace to grasp his neck.

His arm slipped lower. She felt his hand caressing, kneading, the twin rounded cheeks of her bottom, the thin fabric of her short gown riding up beneath his touch until his hand fondled bare flesh. Nudging her legs apart with his knee, he pressed his leather-clad thigh firmly against that part of her that suddenly burned with desire. He continued to manipulate the soft flesh of her behind, stimulating her body with his hard thigh and she trembled, moaning softly. He answered, groaning deep within his throat, and his mouth left hers. He looked down at her, a savage glitter lighting his eyes.

His gleaming scrutiny clung to her face, holding her eyes captive as he released his grip on her head. Slowly his hand wandered down her body until it closed over her breast. The warmth and strength of his hold burned through the fabric of her thin gown, shooting a jolt of electricity through her. Coventry closed her eyes, biting her lip to stifle a whimper as her nipple tightened almost painfully against his cupped palm. When he found it with his fingers, her entire body quaked. Sensation deserted her limbs, catapulting into the area he caressed. Had she not had her arms locked so firmly around his neck, she would have fallen.

Abruptly, he loosened his embrace. For one mind-numbing instant she thought he was once again going to abandon her. But then he lifted her, carrying her toward his bed. His face above hers was taut, the planes hard and resolute as his eyes glittered down at her with feverish intensity. Her own eyes felt dazed, the lids heavy with passion. Reaching the bed, he sat her on its edge and with a single, expert movement pulled the tunic over her head, discarding it carelessly on the floor. His eyes devoured her and, self-consciously, Coventry covered herself.

"No." The word was a harsh whisper as he crouched before her, nudging her hands aside. "Let me look at you." Her flesh tingled, the nipples of her swollen breasts contracting even more, as his gaze raked her body from head to toe and back again, hesitating briefly at the soft triangle of burnished golden curls nestled at the junction of her thighs. "You are very beautiful." Bracing his hands on either side of her, he leaned forward capturing her lips, ravaging her mouth and overpowering her senses. Vaguely she felt him lift her legs to lay her fully upon the narrow bed, and then he was beside her.

A large warm hand closed over her breast, weighing its softness as his thumb rubbed the taut nipple. Sensation shot through her and she arched her body off the bed, her hands blindly clutching at his shoulders. She wanted to feel his body next to hers. But he resisted her attempt to pull him closer as he murmured something she didn't understand. His mouth replaced his hand at her breast, closing over the turgid tip, tugging at the tiny crest as he raked the sensitive nub with his tongue. His hand trailed slowly down her body, stopping briefly to torment her navel before stroking the insides of her thighs, stoking the hot coals of desire, igniting a raging blaze. She cried out, lifting her hips, pressing against his palm in supplication.

Lifting his head from her breast to look into her passion-dazed face with smoldering eyes, he smiled, a lingering, satisfied smile that sent the blood racing through her veins. "Soon," he promised and lowered his mouth to tease her other breast, in the same instant pressing one finger slightly into the moist crevice between her thighs.

"Trace!" Coventry was unable to suppress her cry of desperation and longing. She wanted him. She *needed* him. Now! Her hands trailed down the silken hair of his warm chest to the waist of his trousers. Perhaps he needed more encouragement. Her shaking fingers fumbled with the unfamiliar buckle clasp. And then his hand was there, stopping her. She moaned in frustration. But in the next instant he rose, his hands going to the waistband of his pants as he undid the clasps and slid them from his narrow hips.

She saw his manhood jutting, enormous and pulsing, from a thick thatch of black hair at his groin. And then, before she had time to blink, he was back on the bed nudging her knees apart to kneel between them. Unconsciously, she lifted her hips in anticipation and invitation. But he merely leaned forward, his sex pressing unsatisfyingly against her, his chest hair tormenting the sensitized tips of her breasts, as he kissed her. Then, slowly, with torturous precision he trailed a path of fire down her body with his lips and tongue, pausing to wrest exquisite penance from each of her throbbing breasts before kissing her navel. Coventry writhed beneath him, flustered by the soft mewling sounds that escaped her throat each time she struggled to control her frantic breathing.

With sudden shock, she felt his warm breath tracking lower. She stiffened. Her thighs tensed as she made a futile attempt to close them. Nobody had ever kissed her there! And then she forgot modesty as his moist, scalding tongue worked a slow, insidious assault on her reason. Her body arched off the bed as she clutched frantically at his shoulders. "Please Trace, *now!*"

He lifted his head. His lips curved in that infuriatingly sexy smile that sustained the elevated temperature of her blood, and he began to trace kisses back up her convulsing body. He paused at her breasts, tugging the crests, each in turn, into his hot, tormenting mouth until she almost sobbed with the frenzy of her need.

Then he entered her. Huge and hard and scorching hot, he filled her. She cried out, her hands clutching at the smooth, hot flesh of his back as a starburst of impressions burst behind her eyelids. Waves of sensation impacted, carrying her away on their surging crests, each higher than the last until she felt she could reach out and touch the stars. She tasted the tangy salt of her body on his lips as he kissed her, absorbing her cries with his mouth until she came floating back from her ascent to the stars. This! This was what other women had felt that drew them irresistibly to men. This was what Coventry had missed over the years. This was the experience that made sex more than a "somewhat pleasurable experience."

Panting with exhaustion, she opened her eyes to look at the man who had so thoroughly thrown her senses into chaos. She thought that her surprise and wonder must have shown in her eyes, for he smiled slightly with satisfaction. Then, with a groan, he pressed into her and she realized that he was still solid and swollen within her. Despite her enervation, she felt a flutter of response.

He raised himself off of her, supporting his weight on his forearms as he withdrew from her body and lowered his head to excite her breasts with lips and teeth and tongue. And then, he pressed forward, slowly, so slowly, squeezing back inside. Stars, he felt good!

He continued the lingering, tender torment until Coventry raised her hips in spontaneous anticipation of each erotic thrust of his pelvis. His cadential movements stoked the fever in her blood until she clutched at him, pulling him down to her as she sought anchorage in the storm of passion that raged through her. And this time when she cried out as the surging waves swept her away, he was there with her, his hoarse shout echoing hers as they rode the breakers together. Their hearts hammered in unison and it was a long time before he rolled to one side, cradling her against him with one arm.

Coventry curled her fingers into the silken hair on his chest and closed her eyes. Never had she felt so complete, so content. And in that moment she knew she never wanted to let Trace out of her life. "I think I'm falling in love with you," she murmured, planting a tender kiss on the soft hair that tickled her lips.

She felt him tense. "Do not say that."

She raised her head, looking into his face. All trace of tenderness was gone, the muscles rigid. "Why? What's the matter?"

With an abrupt motion, he sat up, retrieved his trousers and pulled them on. "I do not want your love." His tone was hard, almost angry. "I do not want *any* woman's love."

Coventry stared at his uncompromising back in astonishment. "What . . . what about what we just shared? Didn't that mean anything to you?"

He turned to stare at her with hard, unyielding eyes. "What we shared was *askauv*."

"What?"

"Good sex," he elucidated. "We shared good sex, but nothing more. Do not start imagining yourself in love over it."

"Good sex!" Coventry echoed incredulously. "It was more than good. It was fantastic!"

He quirked an eyebrow at her in a manner that made her feel distinctly foolish for her enthusiastic endorsement. "Good or fantastic." He shrugged. "It was still just sex. You must accept the fact that there can never be anything more between us."

Her anger making her heedless of her nakedness, Coventry rose to her knees on the bed, leaning forward on her arms. "You . . . you arrogant bastard. Did I ask you for anything more? Do you think I'd ever have considered anything more? In case you've forgotten I'm returning to Earth as soon as possible. All I was doing was stating a simple emotion. But since that frightens you so much, you can just accept the fact that there will never be *anything* between us. Not even *good sex*."

Stepping off the bunk, she retrieved the tunic from the floor and, without bothering to put it on, stalked into her own chamber and closed the door.

Leaning against it, she closed her eyes as the bolstering anger dissipated. She'd lied, of course. She had hoped for more, dreamed of more. But if she admitted that to him, she'd only be leaving herself vulnerable to more pain. She simply could not enjoy sex for its own sake. Her emotions were too strongly intertwined with the act of making love. Her only hope of salvaging her pride lay in having nothing more to do with Trace.

Chapter Eleven

Coventry awoke and stared at the ceiling disconsolately. More than three weeks had passed since she and Trace had last spoken. Yet no matter how angry and hurt she was, no matter how much she avoided him, her mind persistently provided her with the most explicit memories of their time together and her body continued to hunger for his touch. Ruthlessly suppressing the impossible craving—knowing that if she succumbed she would only further endanger her heart—and determined that she would not be dependent upon him when they reached Thadonia, she had managed to avoid him while immersing herself in the Thadonian language disks. In the process, she'd become fairly proficient in Thadonian, and that gave her confidence. But now, they were due to arrive on Thadonia within the next forty-eight hours, and she was scared. In fact she'd wavered between elation and despondency for the past eight days.

Eight days ago she had realized that the time for her monthly flow had come and gone. At first, despite the fact that she'd always been extremely regular, she had managed to ascribe the lack to shock and excitement. But that was getting more difficult to do with each passing day. She chewed her lip. Why had she not renewed her inhibitor?

But she knew the answer. Ever-conscious of her desire to have a child before her time ran out and finding herself uninvolved with anyone at the time that she was due to renew, she had simply not gone.

She wanted a child, desperately. But, why now? She was on her way to another world. She didn't even know how she would support herself. How would she care for a child? But returning to Earth was out of the question. She could not return to her old life until it was safe—if that time ever came—and she found the thought of raising a child in the dismal lifestyle of the Fringe repulsive. In fact, she had not even seen any children during her time there. For all she knew they raised their children separately, and that was something she simply would not do. So, there was nothing she could do but to take one day at a time, and hope that things worked out.

For the millionth time, she considered informing Trace of her possible predicament. But again, she decided against it. If he didn't want to be encumbered by the love of a woman, he'd probably despise the thought of a child. And even if he didn't, if he wanted the child as much as she did, she didn't want him accepting her because of the child. Although she had always imagined herself with a family that included a husband, if that was not to be, she would accept it. Somehow, she would manage.

Rising, she decided to avail herself of the radiant-shower before dressing. Perhaps it would improve her mood. Half an hour later, she had just finished dressing and braiding her long hair when someone knocked. Opening the stateroom door, she found herself facing a tall dark-haired man whom she'd seen once or twice before but to whom she'd never spoken. "Yes?"

The officer's brown eyes appraised her with frank appreciation and Coventry, prey to her present insecurities, felt absurdly pleased by his admiration. "I'm Commander Demeter, Ms. Pearce. Captain Remes asked me to inform you that there will be a farewell dinner this evening at nineteen hundred for you and Rainon. He apologizes for being unable to invite you personally but—" Commander Demeter shrugged. "He hopes that you will be able to attend."

"Oh." She was surprised and pleased by the invitation. It would be good to have an excuse to escape her cabin. "Please tell the captain, thank you. We would be happy to attend." How would she inform Trace? She didn't particularly *want* to speak to him and she didn't have the slightest idea where he spent his time. "But—"

"Is there a problem?"

"Would it be possible for you to find and inform Rainon of the invitation? I'm afraid we don't see each other much."

"Oh." It was a simple word, but his inflection made it seem as though he'd just received a revelation. "Certainly, Ms. Pearce." He smiled. "I'll see you this evening."

Closing the door, Coventry immediately began to wonder what she would wear. The silvery jumpsuit that she'd worn to come aboard had been returned to the captain. Besides, it would have been too revealing. She had nothing other than the clothing she'd been given in the Fringe and the Thadonian tunic and trousers. The rugged Fringer clothing simply was not suitable, which left the Thadonian outfit. But the fragile tunic had begun to look a little the worse for wear after having been worn quite regularly for the past month. Perhaps if she hung the entire outfit in the fine mist of the radiant-shower—would the disinfectants harm the fabric?—and then put it into the cleaning compartment for the remainder of the day, some of the creases—which had begun to look almost permanent—would come out. She would do that before she went for breakfast.

Tiern, not in the best of moods, returned to the cabin at eighteen hundred hours to prepare for the dinner that Coventry had accepted on their behalf. The last thing he needed or wanted was to spend an entire evening in her company. The past three weeks had been pure torment. Rather than waning after having had her, he had found that his desire for Coventry intensified daily. And he blamed her for the situation. Had she not withdrawn from him, her appeal would have eventually palled, as the allure of women always had in the past, and the problem would not exist.

Instead, he found himself thinking of her, picturing her as she had been that night when, magnificent in her anger and heedless of her nakedness, she had risen to her knees on his bunk. The scene refused to fade, every detail replayed in his mind in perfect detail. The way her tousled mane of golden hair had framed her proud, enchanting features as she spoke. The way her enormous, brown eyes had pierced him with daggers of disdain. But most of all, the way she had looked as she had walked past him to her room, composed and haughty despite her nudity.

Scowling blackly, Tiern stalked by Coventry's closed door and entered the lavatory to refresh himself and change his clothing. He would certainly be glad to reach Thadonia *and* his wardrobe. When he emerged, bathed, clean-shaven and carrying the boots that he never let out of his sight, Coventry was just coming out of her room. Unable to help himself, he stopped and stared.

Her hair had been braided in an approximation of the Thadonian style, and she wore the tunic and trousers given to her by the ambassador's wife. At least he thought it was the same outfit because he could not imagine where she might have obtained another one. The delicate fabric, still sapphire but now streaked with ribbons of luminous emerald, clung to her upper body, hinting at the treasures beneath. As the image of those treasures returned to his memory with torturous accuracy, he felt a tightening in his loins.

"Are you ready?"

He nodded, ignoring her cold tone. "One minute." Sitting on the edge of his bunk, he pulled on his boots. *Zyk!* This was going to be a long evening.

The galley had been enlarged, converted to serve as a dining hall for virtually the entire staff of the ship. Captain Remes, at the head of one long table, stood and beckoned to Tiern as he entered escorting Coventry and they moved to the seats indicated: Tiern to Captain Remes' right, and Coventry to Tiern's right. "Welcome, from all of us." The captain smiled, lifting his glass in salute. The assembled officers followed suit and Tiern scanned their faces, remembering most of them from casual associations throughout the journey. He nodded to Warshaw and, finding that the courtesy was beginning to come more easily to his lips, turned to express his thanks to Captain Remes with Coventry echoing his appreciation.

"You're quite welcome, Rainon." He reached for a steaming bowl in front of him and served himself before passing it to Tiern. "Actually, I felt it was the least I could do to express my appreciation for the opportunity to make such a profitable run to Thadonia."

Tiern nodded uncomfortably. The manner in which he had provided payment to the somewhat unscrupulous freighter captain did not sit well with him. He had never before been reduced to trading in black-market goods. But, this time, he had found it the only means of securing passage. Captain Remes had requested payment in the form of Thadonian intoxicants, in particular the wine dubbed *blue passion* by those who plied its trade. Tiern had furnished the good captain with authorization to purchase ten cases upon arrival on Thadonia, and, with the help of the Fringers, he had managed to provide Remes with one case as advance payment. To Tiern's relief, the captain made no further mention of the transaction, turning the conversation to other things.

Tiern, his senses ever tuned to Coventry, heard her converse with the man on her right even as others around the table spoke with each other, contributing to the drone of sound. Although he could not discern their words, something about the man's tone bothered him. It was . . . husky, laden with nuances that should not have been there. The knowledge that the man was attempting to charm Coventry with Tiern sitting beside her infuriated him. As soon as a lull in the conversation with Remes permitted, he leaned forward to determine the man's identity and pointedly made his own presence known.

"Commander Demeter." Tiern nodded his head in greeting even as his senses were flooded with

Coventry's warm, attractive scent. "We met this morning."

"Good to see you, Rainon." Demeter nodded and smiled. "We are not standing on ceremony this evening. Please call me John." He shifted his gaze to Coventry and favored her with, what seemed to Tiern, an exceedingly warm and secretive smile. Tiern opened his mouth to engage the man in further conversation only to have his effort circumvented by Captain Remes.

The meal, although certainly good, became interminable. He could not seem to discourage the captain from his propensity for loquaciousness and the tone of the conversation Coventry shared with John Demeter became increasingly disturbing. What were they talking about?

Finally, the meal began to draw to a close. A few of the men present, no doubt those with duties to attend to, left the room. Tiern glanced at Coventry's dish to see how close she was to being finished. With a sense of shock, he saw a glass containing an azure beverage sitting before her. The *blue passion!* Why would anybody have served it here? He scanned the table. Only two other people appeared to be drinking the beverage—both men. It did not make sense. Tiern frowned as he observed them, saw one stroke the other's arm with a furtive movement. His stomach churned with distaste. That explained why they were drinking the beverage together. But why had it been served to Coventry? Commander John Demeter's doing? It had to be. Tiern's gut twisted with fury. He felt an intense desire to strangle the other man.

Coventry began to reach for the glass. He caught her arm, preventing her from completing the motion. Surprised, she turned to look at him.

"You will not drink that." Although he kept his voice low, he knew his anger made the statement more commanding than he had intended.

Her eyes flashed sparks as she jerked her arm from his grasp. "Do not tell me what to do, Trace." He was momentarily staggered by astonishment as she spoke in fluent Thadonian; only her accent had been slightly off. She picked up the glass.

"Coventry, I warn you. You will not like—"

"Do not presume to dictate what I will or will not like. I am perfectly capable of arriving at my own conclusions." She took a large swallow of the beverage and, short of making a scene, there was nothing Tiern could do to prevent it. Then, turning her shoulder to Tiern, she once again engaged in conversation with Demeter.

Tiern looked at Demeter and fought the desire to drive his fist into the man's face. Coventry took another hearty gulp of the beverage and Tiern saw Demeter assimilate the occurrence with obvious satisfaction. The man's eyes fairly shone as his gaze roamed Coventry with unbridled anticipation. Tiern did not know what erroneous assumptions Demeter had made, but he determined that the man's designs on Coventry would come to naught.

Turning to the captain, Tiern thanked him once again for the meal—he hoped his tone was reasonably cordial although in his present mood he could not be certain of that—and made an excuse for his early departure. The captain nodded, falling into conversation with the man on his left, and Tiern leaned toward Coventry. "It is time to go. Bid good-bye to your friend." He spoke in Thadonian but, even in his own language, he knew that he had been unable to disguise the acrimony in his voice.

Coventry turned to stare at him incredulously, responding in Thadonian. "No. I am enjoying the evening."

"Obviously. However, I warn you that if you do not come with me now, I will pick you up and carry you bodily from this room."

"You would not!" She gave him a shrewd look which displeased him immensely. "Perhaps Commander Demeter would not allow your cavalier treatment."

Tiern stared at her in disbelief. "Then you, not I, will be answerable for any injuries Commander Demeter may sustain." He paused, allowing her to assimilate his statement. "Now you *will* come with me. Yes?"

She stared at him obstinately for a moment, then reached for her glass of Thadonian wine. Tiern caught her arm. "You need not finish your drink. Say good-bye to your friend."

"Let go of me, Trace. Now!" Not wanting to provoke her to the point where she would refuse to leave with him—despite what he had said he preferred to avoid a scene—he released his grasp on her arm and she poured the remainder of the beverage down her throat. Then she turned to Demeter. Tiern rose, waiting as they spoke. Demeter flashed him a distinctly unpleasant look and spoke in a hushed tone to Coventry, apparently arguing the situation. Coventry merely shook her head and rose, allowing Tiern to escort her from the room.

As the door closed behind them, Coventry kicked him in the shin, jerked her arm from his grasp, and stalked off without a word in the direction of their cabin. The corridor was, thankfully, empty. Ignoring the slight discomfort in his bruised shin, he grinned and followed her. She was the first woman he had met with a disposition to match his own. The man who married her would certainly never find life boring—provided he refrained from strangling her, of course.

As Tiern entered the cabin, the door to Coventry's chamber was just closing. Seating himself in one of the two chairs supplied, he propped his feet on the other and waited to see what would happen. He had never seen the effects of *blue passion* firsthand, only read the reports stating the reason for prohibiting its export to Earth. Apparently the beverage, which was merely a mild intoxicant on Thadonia, exhibited potent aphrodisiac properties in a large percentage of Earthers. According to the report, seventy-five percent of Earth women and approximately twenty percent of Earth men were thus affected.

Tiern looked at the chronometer. Ten minutes had passed. He looked at Coventry's closed door with a mixture of curiosity and, despite himself, anticipation. Which percentage would she be part of: the twenty-five percent on whom the beverage had no effect, or the seventy-five percent? He knew the one to which he wanted her to belong. He could not help it. For three excruciatingly long weeks he had wanted her. While she, unable to separate love and sex in her mind, had kept herself away from him. Perhaps tonight . . .

A feminine cry of rage issued from her chamber and the door opened. She still wore the tunic and trousers, but she was barefoot and had unbound her hair. The long golden waves flowed around her upper body like an imperfect halo. With a single furious glance at him, she marched toward the door to the corridor. Alarm swept through him and, jumping to his feet, he pursued her, catching her arm just as she was about to trigger the sensor.

"Where are you going?" He studied her flushed face.

"Visiting. Let me go this instant."

Tiern ignored her demand. "Visiting whom?"

She smiled, her eyes flashing slivers of ice. "Why . . . Commander Demeter. Who else?"

He stared at her incredulously. His gut twisted with rage at the thought that she would turn to Demeter rather than to him. "You are going nowhere."

Suddenly, without warning, she went wild. Kicking him, pounding his chest with her fists, she screamed invectives at him. Avoiding her flailing fists, he caught her to him, crushing her against him as he tried to calm her. She fought his hold so violently that it was all he could do to restrain her without hurting her. This is not how he had thought . . . had hoped, it would be. "Shhh." He stroked her back until eventually she began to quiet down. "Coventry, what is wrong? Tell me." Finally, she shuddered, subsiding, and he enjoyed the sensation of holding her in his arms. Hot tears wet his shirt as her arms crept up around his neck. "Tell me."

She sniffed. "I swear I'm going to kill him."

Tiern frowned in confusion. "Who?"

"John."

"John? Oh, Officer Demeter." Tiern felt a surge of elation. She had not been going to Demeter to offer him her body; she had intended to castigate the man.

She lifted her head from his chest, looking up into his face. "Why didn't you do something?"

"I did try to warn you. You would not listen." Her fingers began to stroke his neck, threading into his hair. He wondered if she was aware of her action.

"I know." She pressed her breasts more firmly against him as her gaze dropped from his eyes to his mouth. "I'm sorry," she whispered, licking her lips.

I'm not, he thought as he caught the faint scent of her sexual excitement. She licked her lips again and he knew she wanted him to kiss her. Yet, now that he understood she would not turn to another man, he found himself holding back. He sensed that Coventry was not used to being the aggressor in a sexual relationship and he wondered what she would do.

"Trace?" Her voice was a hesitant whisper.

"Hmmm?" He stroked her back as he looked down into her large, expressive eyes.

"Will—" She swallowed nervously. "Kiss me, please?"

He wanted her so badly that he almost complied, but inquisitiveness . . . anticipation held him back. "You will have to take what you want, Coventry."

She stared at him, her eyes, already heavy-lidded with passion, uncomprehending. And then, slowly, he saw understanding dawn. "I hate you," she said, but the words had no bite. With a muffled groan she stood on her toes and pressed her mouth to his.

He waited, not making it easy for her. Finally, hesitantly, she gently stroked his lips with her tongue and he opened his mouth. As her small, hot tongue invaded his mouth and he set his own in motion to do erotic battle, her fingers began to fumble with the fastenings on his shirt.

Her mouth left his to trail over his neck and chest. Her hands massaged his back as she found his flat nipples with her mouth and began to excite them with lips, teeth and tongue. Closing his eyes he leaned his head back against the wall. *This* is what he had wanted. He reveled in the tiny, frantic, whimpering noises that escaped her as she strove to seduce him. He reveled in the sensation of her rubbing herself against his thigh. He reveled in the knowledge that she wanted him as much as he wanted her.

Heat flooded his groin as she began to fumble inexpertly with the unfamiliar fastenings on his trousers, and he opened his eyes. They still stood next to the door. Gathering her into his arms, he carried her the few steps to the bunk and stood her beside it. He looked at her flushed face, saw her full-lipped pouting mouth and dazed eyes, and began to tremble with the intensity of his own desire. But, gritting his teeth, he checked it. Swiftly bending to untie the laces of his boots, he kicked them off. Yet even in the heat of arousal he made certain they sat near the head of the bed.

Then, with swift, practiced fingers, he loosened Coventry's belt, removing her tunic and sheer undergarment before unfastening the string of her trousers and allowing them to fall to the floor. He drank in the sight of her as she stood before him clad only in a pair of thin panties. The pink-brown nipples of her full, proud breasts puckered more tightly even as he watched. He wanted to reach out and touch them, but again he restrained himself.

"Your turn." He hardly recognized his own voice.

"Trace, I—" He raised a questioning eyebrow and she broke off. Clamping her lips firmly shut, she began to fumble and then, muttering a curse, to fight with the obstinate buckles on his pants.

Finally, they gave and she knelt, working the soft leather down his legs. "Step out." Absurdly pleased by the husky timbre of her voice, he complied. Then he watched her as she carelessly threw the trousers aside and looked up the length of his body from her kneeling position.

As she slowly rose, she began to trail hesitant, unpracticed kisses up his hair-roughened legs. Twining his fingers into the soft mane of her hair, he marveled at the erotic contrast of her golden fairness to his swarthiness. She reached his hips, and the nuzzling caress of her lips faltered as she looked at his sex with heavy-lidded eyes. He sensed her uncertainty. Then, suddenly, as though prompted by some primal instinct, she took him in her mouth. Slowly, agonizingly, she began to heap attention upon his turgid shaft, nipping with teeth, soothing with tongue, and stimulating the sensitive tip with her moist mouth. He was rocked to the depths of his soul by a surge of lust so intense that he was unable to contain a groan.

Grasping her arms, he pulled her to her feet, crushed her to him, and bent his head to her enticing lips. His hands worked at the waistband of her panties, shoving them down, out of the way as he cupped the cheeks of her bottom, pressing her to him, trapping his swollen shaft against her abdomen. *Magar!* He wanted her. He wanted to drive himself into her until she cried out in ecstasy. He wanted to feel the quaking of her body as he brought her fulfillment. He wanted the intense pleasure of spilling his seed deep within her body.

He tensed, controlling his lust. Not yet. He caressed the warm crevasse of her bottom, slowly working his fingers down between her thighs until they found what he sought. She moaned, sagging against him. She was hot, and succulent, and slick, more than ready. Liberating her mouth, he slowly disengaged her from his embrace and lay down on the narrow bed. Still standing, she stared at him and he savored the expression on her face as her eyes swept the length of his body. She looked . . . hungry, as though she would devour him whole if she could.

"Take what you want, Coventry."

Her eyes flew to his face; she reddened. She looked at his erection and licked her lips in an unconsciously erotic gesture. "Damn you." Her petulant mutter coaxed a smile to his lips despite his tension.

Then, her eyes clinging to his face, she knelt on the edge of the bed and hesitantly moved to straddle his body. Bracing her hands on his abdomen, she positioned herself and slowly slid her hot, moist sheath down over him. The abundant moisture welcomed him as her body clung to his, smooth, tight, and exquisite. She closed her eyes and began to move on him, uncertainly at first until she found her pace, and then more and more fervidly, gradually becoming a feral, sybaritic creature. He smiled as he watched her, magnificent in her abandon. Eyes closed, her head flung back until her long hair tickled his thighs, her full breasts heaving with her flexion, she was beautiful and as sultry as any woman he had ever had. He reached out, cupping her breasts, gently stimulating her taut, flushed nipples with his thumbs. She cried out, reaching her peak. Her hips twisted frantically against him as she clutched at him for stability. The voluptuous palpitations of her body gripped him, pulling him relentlessly over the edge with her. Unbearable pleasure washed through him and with a hoarse, wordless shout he steadied her hips, driving himself deep. She wilted onto his chest and he held her, trembling and winded, as they both panted to regain their breath.

Coventry kept her eyes closed, listening to his racing heart beneath her ear. She could not believe what she had done. She had, quite literally, seduced a man. The fact that she loved him, and that he was the father of the child which she, in all probability, now carried should have made no difference. Knowing he did not love her, she should have felt embarrassed beyond belief. But at this moment, all she felt was contentment—and a faint stirring of renewed desire deep within her. More of the effect of that damned drink no doubt.

It hadn't taken her long to realize something was happening to her body when she returned to her cabin. The intense tingling in her nipples and between her thighs had made the nature of that occurrence all too obvious. From there it had taken only a short leap of logic to ascertain the cause—and the reason Trace had attempted to discourage her from drinking the foreign beverage that Commander Demeter had so persuasively suggested she might enjoy.

She sighed, complacently. She no longer wanted to kill Demeter, but she would dearly love to repay him in some way for his unscrupulous conniving. Unfortunately, there would be little time to devise a plan now. They would be arriving on Thadonia within hours. She would have to rely on the vagaries of fate to repay him.

Trace gently stroked her back and the stirring within her grew in intensity. She raised herself up to look into his face and moved her hips in a manner that she hoped would make him aware of her craving. It did.

He opened his midnight eyes, arched his brows at her incredulously, and said, "Again?"

She smiled at his reaction and ran an affectionate finger over the scar that curved over his left eyebrow. "Yes, please."

His lips bowed in that enticing manner that set her blood boiling. Wrapping his arms around her, he reversed their positions and set about responding to her supplication most competently.

Chapter Twelve

Tiern awoke slowly to the pleasant sensation of Coventry's body pressed against his on the narrow bed. Her back was to him, and he lifted his head to observe her as she slept. They were good together. He could see no reason why they should not share many more nights as wonderful and fulfilling as the hours they had just shared. An entire year of such nights—if their desire remained constant—awaited them until the time came when she would be able to return to Earth as she wished. He hoped she would see the sense of the situation. But, even if she did not, he simply would not allow her to withdraw herself from him again; no matter how she felt about what had occurred between them when she awoke. If he had to seduce her each and every time he wanted her, he *would* have her. Just thinking of her, looking at her, he wanted her again. And he decided he knew the perfect way to arouse her from her sleep.

It was fourteen hundred hours. The *Payload* had settled into orbit around Thadonia. Coventry, the knapsack containing her few belongings once again in hand, followed Trace through the corridors to the shuttle bay. She observed his tall, wide-shouldered, narrow-hipped form with affectionate eyes. All the leashed power and violence

223

she sensed in him had never been directed at her. In fact, it was probably that precise aspect of him that made her feel so . . . secure when she was with him. She still wasn't absolutely certain that she loved him with the enduring type of love that her parents had shared, but she did know that her heart was significantly involved. And whether or not she avoided contact with him, that wouldn't change. He made her feel alive. Even when she was furious with him, his very presence made her feel vital and alive. And, when she wasn't angry with him, she enjoyed being with him despite his intractability and domineering conduct, despite all the . . . character flaws she had catalogued against him. And she certainly enjoyed being with him in bed.

Yet, Trace felt nothing for her beyond an apparently increasing appreciation for her body. She flushed at the memory of just how thoroughly he'd illustrated his esteem that morning. But it was the fact that his appreciation for her was growing that gave her hope. Since her heart was already irretrievably involved, she had decided to allow their relationship to continue for a time and hope that his appreciation would gradually transform itself into something more.

They entered the shuttle bay and Coventry's thoughts focused on the present. The shuttle, a squat, blunt-nosed, semi-rectangular craft, sat waiting, its winged-door open. Coventry wiped her palms nervously on her slacks. This was it. She was almost at the end of her journey. When she entered the shuttle, she would be taking the next step toward a new life and an unknown, unplanned future. She was terrified.

Trace reached the entry and spoke to the pilot and some officers. Then, turning to face her, he

smiled and extended a hand to her. "Come."
Coventry stepped forward, allowing him to grasp
her arm and aid her ascent into the shuttle. A
sense of unreality gripped her and she moved
like an automaton, shoving the knapsack into
the compartment above, and taking a seat next
to one of the viewports. She was only vaguely
aware of Trace settling himself next to her as
some of the officers Trace had spoken to entered
the shuttle and chose seats. Yet, she couldn't even
put the sudden nameless terror that gripped her
into words. She was simply afraid. Conversation
droned around her, but she made no effort to
focus on it.

Trace said something to her and she took a
deep breath as she attempted to cast off the sense
of unreality. "Pardon me?"

"Strap yourself in."

"Oh, yes." She fumbled with the seat belts,
finally managing to secure them properly. Two
minutes later, the shuttle dropped like a stone
from *Payload*'s belly. Coventry closed her eyes
until her stomach settled back in place and then
looked out the viewport. Silhouetted against a
midnight backdrop, an enormous, blue-green
world confronted them. Coventry stared, her
fear diminishing as astonishment crowded it
from her mind.

"Thadonia," Trace breathed unnecessarily at
her side, and she heard the reverence in his
voice.

"It's beautiful, Trace." She was mesmerized by
the incredible colors—blue and green and violet and ochre, streaked with nebulous ribbons
of white.

"Yes." They fell silent for a time, each absorbed
by the indescribable spectacle of a world seen

225

from space. "Coventry—" She looked at him. He stared straight ahead, his face devoid of expression. "I think perhaps you should begin calling me Rainon. Trace is not—" he hesitated as though searching for words, and shrugged. "It is a name that belongs to another world."

Coventry, amazed by the degree of sensitivity his simple statement revealed, nodded mutely as she tried to find her tongue. "Of . . . of course. If that's what you want. But I may slip up occasionally." He nodded and Coventry turned to look again at her new home. It completely dominated the view now. "Where will we be landing?"

"The city is called ReiDalgo. It is in my country, Stanish, and is the only place on Thadonia where a spaceport has been constructed."

She looked at him. "Is it big?"

"ReiDalgo?" Coventry nodded. He shook his head. "Not nearly as large as most of your Earth cities, but it is large for Thadonia. The population is, perhaps, a few hundred thousand."

"What's it like?"

He smiled. "You will soon see for yourself. But, I will tell you a little of what to expect.

"The spaceport will seem much like any such place on Earth. It was constructed according to Earth specifications after contact with Earth. When you leave the port . . . then, you will begin to see the real Thadonia. There is no Central and no government office; only the emperor and his envoys rule here. There are no computerized vehicles; just hundreds of dyre, some ridden, some pulling wheeled conveyances."

Coventry stared, just beginning to comprehend exactly how unsophisticated Thadonia was. "What are dyre?"

"They are animals somewhat like . . . a goat, perhaps. But, much larger. They are very swift, and sure of foot. The best and strongest are bred in Vaileu, a country in the Rafat Empire. My own dyre was imported from Vaileu."

"Oh." Heavens above! She was going to have to ride an *animal* to get around. The only large animals she'd ever seen had been in zoos. She tried to picture a goat large enough to ride. They had horns, didn't they? She swallowed, wiping the image from her mind, resolved to face it only when it became necessary. "So where are we going first?"

"We will find an inn and prepare to see Emperor Riyan."

"See the emperor!" Coventry eyed him in shock. "But—" she looked at the Fringer clothing she wore. "I can't . . . I mean, it's—"

He followed her gaze. "Do not worry. We will arrange for appropriate clothing. In any case, it would be considered extremely rude to request an audience with the emperor without suitable preparation. Only in the most desperate of situations would the audience even be granted." He shrugged. "Protocol is difficult to circumvent here as well. Watch." He pointed at the view of Thadonia. The shuttle traveled from night into day in the blink of an eye. She began to discern landmarks: mountains and lakes and vast areas of greenery which she took to be forests. Things she had only seen in representations.

An hour later—after Trace had spent an unconscionable amount of time withdrawing and replacing items from a spaceport locker and speaking with Thadonian officials—they emerged from the enormous white dome of the spaceport.

Coventry's mouth opened in unabashed wonder. The golden light of a newborn day bathed the land. Stone pathways, softly tinted by the dawn light, threaded through an area the size of four city blocks. Groves of towering trees and smaller beds containing bushes grew in asymmetrically arranged tracts throughout; while, bordering the walkways, flowers grew in a profusion of colors more vast than she had ever imagined. Above them, the clear sky was an incredible shade of violet blue. She noted that Trace, or rather Rainon, was headed in the direction of an extremely long, low building. He had removed his cape and carried it draped over one arm. From his locker, he had obtained and donned a long, narrow sheath which he now wore strapped to his back. A sword? she wondered. She had heard that they were the preferred weapons on Thadonia, but she had never seen one. Suddenly noting that Trace was drawing ahead of her, she hurried to catch up with him.

As they neared the building, she perceived a peculiarly pungent, though not entirely unpleasant odor. "What is this place?"

"The stables," he replied in Thadonian. "I must retrieve my dyre. Once in ReiDalgo I will make arrangements for a mount for you."

"Wonderful." Her dry tone drew a quizzical glance from him, but he made no comment as a voice greeted them from the cool gloom of the building's interior. A little intimidated by the strangeness of the place, Coventry remained in the bright sunlight near the entrance as Trace entered and spoke with the man. A short time later he emerged leading one of the most peculiar animals Coventry had ever seen.

It was glistening black; its coat long and

silky. Two gnarled, charcoal-gray horns rose like enormous spikes from between its ears. Its head, perched atop a long, shaggy, graceful neck at least four feet long, appeared almost elegant despite the beast's size. A contraption of some type was strapped to its back, which was about even in height with the top of Trace's head. Suddenly she realized that it had turned to look down at her from its vast elevation with three glowing, golden eyes. "It has three eyes!"

Trace nodded. "That is part of the reason dyre make such excellent mounts. There is little that they do not see. The eyes on either side of their heads give them remarkable peripheral vision, while the center one is for forward viewing. Come." He beckoned to Coventry. Nervously, she moved to his side. "I want you to meet Faolan. Place your hand before him like this, so he will remember your scent." Trace held his hand, back up, before the creature's nose.

"He . . . he will not bite, will he?" Taking a cue from Trace, who had spoken nothing but Thadonian since exiting the spaceport, Coventry asked the question in Thadonian as she duplicated Trace's gesture rather nervously.

"No. The dyre are gentle beasts, for the most part." The dyre lowered his big, mottled-pink nose to her hand and she felt its warm breath against her skin. When the beast lifted his head, Coventry withdrew her hand. "Good," Trace said. "Come." Grasping her arm he directed her around to the animal's side. "Faolan, kneel." To Coventry's astonishment, the animal immediately lowered himself to his front knees and then dropped his hindquarters in a corresponding manner until his back was once again level, but only half as high. Trace removed the knapsack from her back and secured it, along with the duffel bag he had carried, to ties attached to the apparatus on the dyre's back.

"What is that?" She stared at the contraption. It was black with silver ornamentation. A large depression in its center was flanked, front and back, by a rigid edging.

"It is a saddle." Grasping her by the waist, he plunked her down on it before she had a chance to ask anything further. She sat, both legs hanging down the left side of the enormous and, thankfully, motionless beast. "Face forward. Put your right leg over him to the other side." Coventry squirmed, and managed to follow his directions without making a complete fool of herself—she hoped. As soon as she was settled, Trace grasped the rigid front edge of the thing and slid into the seat behind her. He lifted her slightly until his muscular thighs were situated comfortably, a maneuver which placed Coventry more in his lap than in the saddle. But at the moment, she was so concerned with the alienness of her situation she barely noticed.

"Faolan rise." The instant the words left Trace's mouth, the beast lunged forward as its hind legs straightened—only Trace's arm about her waist prevented her from flying over the creature's head—and leapt to its front feet like a coiled spring. Then, it stood as still as a statue, its ears turned back toward them. Despite her earlier trepidation, Coventry found that she was eager, even impatient, to begin this new experience.

Turning slightly, she looked at Trace over her shoulder. "How do you make it move?" To her consternation, he tossed back his head and laughed; full-bodied, throaty laughter erupted from his throat. It was the first time she had ever heard him laugh. "What is so funny?" she demanded.

He looked at her, still smiling widely, revealing strong, even white teeth. "Not funny," he responded. "Enjoyable. Through your eyes, a simple, ordinary experience becomes new and exciting."

"Oh." That was all right then. He wasn't laughing *at* her. She returned his smile. "So . . . how do you make him move?"

"I often guide him simply with knee signals, and the use of my hands on his neck. However, he also responds to voice commands." He directed his gaze to the beast's head. "Faolan, forward." The animal responded instantly, walking forward with a peculiar swaying gait.

Minutes later, they left the carefully tended grounds surrounding the spaceport and began traversing a rutted road or, rather, trail. Rolling fields of blue-green grass, dotted here and there with clumps of enormous trees, stretched to the horizon. Coventry had never seen so much uncluttered territory. But where were the people, the buildings? She frowned, inspecting the area thoroughly to ensure she had missed nothing. Finally, she asked, "Where is the city?"

"ReiDalgo is about five miles distant. We will reach it soon."

"Why did they build the spaceport so far from it?"

"Two reasons. The first is that, should the city continue to grow, it is preferred that the port remain on the periphery of it. And second, we want to carefully regulate the induction of technology into our world. We are a proud people and the council felt that, if change occurred too swiftly, the Thadonian identity and culture might be lost. We trade only for things that can aid our people without causing disruption, such as medical equipment, medicines, and educational tools. Earth weapons, for example, are illegal here."

"Oh." Coventry remembered the carefully wrapped blaster hidden in her knapsack. She had never mentioned it to Trace. Somehow the subject had never arisen. Should she tell him now? Where were the stunner and laser that he had carried? She looked down trying to see if they were still attached to the loops of his trousers. "What did you do with the weapons you were carrying?"

"I signed them over for storage at the port. If I had attempted to leave the port without doing so, they would have been detected by sensors and I would have been apprehended."

Coventry frowned. So why hadn't the one in her pack been detected then? Did the peculiar covering somehow shield it from sensors? It was the only answer she could come up with and she was suddenly glad that she'd carefully rewrapped it after examining it aboard ship. She decided she wouldn't inform Trace about it. Not yet, at any rate, because she received the distinct impression that he'd confiscate it. And a lady never knew when a weapon might come in handy on an alien world.

"There." He pointed before them. "You can begin to see ReiDalgo now."

Coventry peered intently ahead and could just make out some squarish silhouettes on the horizon. As they drew nearer, the shapes began to become more definite and she perceived them as squat buildings. There didn't appear to be a tall structure in sight. No apartment complexes! Where did people live? But before she could ask about it, her mind seized on another anomaly. The air. Although still pure, it had taken on a distinctive piquant flavour. "What is that scent?"

"You smell the sea," Trace responded. "Rei-Dalgo is a seaport."

Coventry took a deep breath. It smelled . . . vibrant. "Will we see it?"

"Not today, I think. But soon, yes."

A few minutes later, they passed through the city gates. If Coventry thought she'd been amazed before, the confusing inundation of the exotic society inside the gates positively overwhelmed her. The marketplace, Trace called it. Everywhere she looked, she wanted him to acquaint her with what she was perceiving. The noise struck her first, and then the color, and then the constantly changing array of odors.

Every color in every shade imaginable was represented somewhere. Hundreds of people in innumerable apparel styles congested the cobbled streets. Some sat astride dyre; others rode in strange two-wheeled vehicles drawn by dyre; some walked; some stood behind awning-covered booths. And everyone seemed to be shouting. The vendors hawked wares ranging from fruit, vegetables and meats to clothing, animals, and furniture. Behind all the people, low, pink, stone buildings, no taller than three to four stories, lined the busy streets. From each of these hung potted plants, many of them flaunting colorful blossoms.

Eventually, Trace turned Faolan down a side street and the chaos began to diminish. Fewer people moved through the streets, and those who did were less hurried. She saw many incongruities. Clothing hung on cords strung between buildings. Unintelligible signs—which gave the impression that these same buildings contained businesses—fascinated her with their strange drawings. Children played *everywhere*, even in the middle of the cobbled street. It was so vastly different from Earth—where a child under twelve was never seen in public without an adult—that Coventry could do nothing but stare.

Trace halted Faolan before a two-story building. A balcony stretched the entire expanse of the upper floor, and above it hung a sign of equal width. "What is this place?"

"The inn. I've stayed here before. It is clean, and it has bathing facilities. I will arrange for a room and then leave you while I purchase clothing."

As Coventry settled into their room and prepared to bathe, Tiern once again mounted Faolan. His eyes swept the street. He could discern no hint of a threat, yet his gut told him one existed. Not wanting to leave Coventry alone, he had almost stopped to make the purchases they needed before going to the inn, but the crowded streets had decided him against it. Protecting himself from a threat in such streets was one matter. But protecting somebody else would be next to impossible. It would be too difficult to discern the direction from which a threat might come. Coventry was safer at the slightly out-of-the-way inn.

He had concealed his anxiety from Coventry; she believed they were safe now that they had reached Thadonia and he did not want to distress her. But he knew they would not be safe until the disk had been delivered to the emperor and the plot exposed. Even then, repercussions could follow. He moved quickly through the streets, in a hurry to reach his friend's lodgings where he had left his formal *Sotah* attire before embarking for Earth. Leof, friend and brother *Sotah*, maintained permanent lodgings in an old boardinghouse two squares to the north of the inn Tiern had chosen. The streets had a slightly more impoverished quality in this area yet, conforming to Thadonian custom, they were clean.

As he approached the lodge, Leof was just leaving. He wore a trader's burnous. Their eyes met in recognition for a split second before Leof turned and departed. He was incognito and could not jeopardize his work.

Tiern dismounted and entered the boarding-house. After quietly ascending the stairs, he moved down the corridor and approached the door to Leof's suite. Other doors along the corridor remained tightly closed; he was alone, unobserved. Raising the latch, he opened the door and slipped into the room. It was dim, only minimal light entered from the window. He took a minute to get his bearings. He noted wryly that Leof had not become any tidier in his absence. The apartment itself was clean if somewhat disorderly. But Leof had still not retained the regular services of a laundress. The smell of unwashed clothing, piled near the window, assailed him and he wrinkled his nose.

He approached the wardrobe, carelessly kicking aside a quilt left trailing from the bed, and opened it. There, hanging just where he had left them, were his *Sotah* garments. Below, squashed beneath a scuffed pair of boots was his bag. Removing the bag and the clothing, he quickly packed and, after checking the corridor to ensure he remained unobserved, left Leof's room.

Fifteen minutes later, he approached a vendor who specialized in women's clothing. He knew that Coventry preferred the serviceability of the Fringer clothing to the delicacy of the Thadonian ensemble. With that in mind, he attempted to choose garb that, although feminine, was practical. Ultimately, he found what he sought. He purchased three calf-length, leather split-skirts and coordinating blouses in what he hoped was the correct size. Telling the shopkeeper to provide appropriate undergarments, he browsed for an ensemble suitable for their upcoming engagement with the emperor. Choosing one in a rich burgundy similar to, although of a somewhat more substantial fabric than, the Thadonian tunic and trousers she already had, he was about to leave when something caught his eye. It was the traditional outfit of a Vaileun dancer. Consisting of a brilliant red layered skirt, it was designed with particular fullness to flare up from the legs of the dancer. He had always been fascinated by the exotic dances of the Vaileun women and, on impulse, he purchased the skirt and an embroidered, white, scoop-necked blouse to coordinate. After paying the merchant with coin retrieved from his locker at the spaceport, he secured the bundle of clothing on Faolan and directed him back through the crowded streets.

After settling Faolan in the small stable at the rear of the inn, Tiern carried his packages into the building. Their room was situated on the main floor in order to take advantage of the natural, hot-spring bathing facilities. Although the upper floor, too, boasted bathing facilities, these were merely hip-baths filled by inn employees with natural mineral water from the spring. He moved down the deserted corridor. It was dim after the brightness of the day without; its coolness welcome. He had just opened the door to his chamber and moved into the threshold when a sharp, piercing sound set his heart hammering until he pinpointed its source.

A young woman ran down the corridor toward him. "Rainon." The squeal came again. "Is it really you? You are back?"

He placed his case and the package of clothing for Coventry on the floor. "Melise. How are you?" He observed her tall, voluptuous form as she ran toward him. Her thick, sable curls cascaded in abandon down her body to caress her hips. Her dark, sultry eyes glistened with excitement from her oval features. She was as beautiful as he remembered her, yet he did not feel the same stirring within him that the sight of her had always induced in the past.

She launched herself at him, wrapping her arms about his neck as she pressed her lips to his in a fervent welcoming kiss. Instinctively, his arms closed around her as, with a sense of curiosity, he returned her kiss. Pleasant, but no kindling of the senses. Melise no longer excited him. It was the same whenever he found a new woman; interest in all others waned for a time. It seemed that, unlike so many of his countrymen, he liked his women one at a time. And since he had found Coventry . . .

Coventry! He could sense her standing nearby. Carefully disentangling Melise's arms from about his neck, he broke off the kiss. "It is good to see you again, Melise." He turned in the direction he knew Coventry stood. Fresh from her bath, she stood wrapped in an enormous towel. "I would like you to meet Coventry. Coventry, Melise is one of my countrywomen."

The two women stared at each other cautiously. Coventry spoke first. "Pleased to meet you." Then, nodding shortly in response to Melise's mumbled echo of her words, she turned on her heel and walked into the bathing chamber.

What was the matter with her? Melise had more reason to be angry than Coventry did. The thought prompted him to look down at the woman before him. She was staring at him with apprehensive, soulful eyes. She obviously recalled his warning that he had never maintained more than one *kvina* at a time. *Magar!* He had not wanted to deal with this yet. In truth, he had forgotten all about his contract with her. "Melise, I must release you from our contract." Digging into his pouch he extracted the coin necessary to pay out the contract and then added a few *pengi* for compensation until she found a new provider. He pressed the funds into her hands and smiled gently. "You are a beautiful woman. You will not be long without a man." He recalled that he had given her a temporary release from their contract before he had left for Earth. "Perhaps you have already found another?"

Melise shrugged. "There are some prospects." She avoided his eyes as she spoke. "Will I see you again, Rainon?"

"Perhaps." He gently turned her to face the corridor. "Farewell, Melise." He closed the door, retrieved the packages from the floor and moved to place them on the large bed in the center of the chamber.

"Who was that woman?" Coventry's voice was

strident and unfriendly. She had abandoned the Thadonian tongue.

He looked at her questioningly. "I told you. Her name is Melise."

"I mean who is she to you?"

Tiern frowned. He did not like the tone of her voice. He did not understand her anger. "She *was* my *kvina.*"

"I do not know that word. What is a *kvina?*" She spoke in Thadonian.

"A *kvina* is a . . . courtesan, a professional mistress."

"You said, she *was* your kvina. What is she now?"

"A friend."

Her face twisted with sarcasm. "Obviously."

Tiern eyed her with amazement as he suddenly realized what her problem was. She was jealous! Although jealousy persisted on Thadonia as on Earth, it was less prevalent in a society where monogamy was not the norm and Tiern had had little personal experience with it. Yet, the realization that Coventry was selfish where he was concerned delighted him. He grinned. "Curb your jealous tongue and come and see what I have purchased for you."

She came forward to study the clothing displayed on the bed. "I am *not* jealous."

"Hmmm." He picked up the outfit he had procured with the visit to the Emperor in mind. "This is for you to wear today. These," he indicated the leather split-skirts, "are everyday garments, excellent for use while riding."

"And what is that?" Coventry gestured to the brilliant red dancer's skirt.

"It is the traditional skirt worn by the Vaileun dancers." He shrugged. "I do not know when you will wear it, but I thought you might like it."

Coventry fingered the light, silky material. "It is beautiful. Thank you."

He nodded shortly in acknowledgment, studying her as she rearranged the clothing, examining the unfamiliar fastenings. The clean, fresh scent of her titillated his nostrils. Her golden hair cascaded in damp ringlets to her hips. The towel wrap, knotted between her breasts, hung straight, disguising the shape of her body. Yet Tiern, possessing intimate knowledge of its contours, found he was stimulated by the knowledge that only the simple barrier of the wrap kept him from viewing the naked treasures of her body. He reined in his emotions. There was not time now.

"I will prepare myself," he said, picking up the case containing his customary attire, "and then we will dine before we leave."

She glanced at him. "All right."

After Trace had secluded himself within the confines of the natural hot-spring bathing chamber, Coventry set about examining the Thadonian underclothing. Most of it appeared self-explanatory and fairly standard. There were a variety of loose satiny underpants trimmed with lace and matching camisoles. But there was one item she puzzled over momentarily. The fabric, laced up one side to form a ring, had been reinforced with a series of hard strips running vertically the entire one-foot depth of the garment. She held it this way and that, flipping it a few times in an attempt to determine what it was for. Then, as she held it with the laced area between her two hands, she perceived its purpose. It was a brassiere—of a sort anyway. Certain that it would be extremely uncomfortable, she discarded it onto the smaller "woman's" bed in favor of her own supple anti-grav cups. She paused, studying the smaller bed. The beds, Trace had said, were simply the remnant of a tradition carried over from ancient times when it was customary for men and women to sleep separately. The beds had been kept primarily because they did serve a practical purpose: providing separate sleeping accommodations, when desired, as had been intended at the ambassador's residence.

After donning the rich burgundy ensemble and a pair of delicate leather sandals, she sat at a small dressing table and began braiding her hair. She had almost finished the task when Trace emerged from the bath chamber. Her jaw dropped. He looked . . . different. Although still dressed almost entirely in black, he now wore loose-fitting trousers. Only the inside of the legs were leather, while the outside was of fabric that reminded Coventry of expensive cotton or linen. They disappeared into the tops of his laced boots at knee level. His shirt, also black, was of the same fabric with leather ornamentation across the chest. Embroidered onto this strip of leather was a strange red design. He had tied a band of red fabric, sporting a black motif, around his forehead and another corresponding red band encircled his upper right arm. A sword hung from his waist, the bottom of the scabbard secured at his knee.

Coventry frowned. She had not seen anyone dressed in quite this way on their passage through the streets. "What are you wearing? It is not street clothing, is it?"

"This is the standard dress of a *Sotah* warrior when not engaged in covert investigation."

"Oh." She turned back to the mirror to complete her hair. "Like a uniform."

241

"Correct." He pulled a bell-cord hanging near the door as he met her eyes in the glass.

Coventry frowned. "What does that do?" She nodded to the bell-cord.

"A number of things, depending on how many times you pull it. I have just ordered a meal. It should be delivered shortly."

"How do you know what kind of meal you have ordered?"

Trace shrugged. "You do not know. The inns traditionally provide only one choice per day. The menu is altered on a daily basis." He strode toward the door. "I have not yet arranged for a dyre for you, and it would be unseemly to ride together on a visit to the palace, so I am going to arrange to rent the inn's hackney. I will return momentarily."

"All right." Coventry stared at the closed door. Did he seem tense? Or, was it her imagination? A slight frown of anxiety formed between her brows as she finished her hair.

After some initial trepidation, Coventry found the midday ride through the streets aboard the strange hackney conveyance relaxing. She settled back to observe the city and its inhabitants. After a time she became aware of a uniqueness about a few of the people she saw. They were extremely tall; some, she was certain, over seven feet, and remarkably slender. Almost uniformly, they had snow-white hair; yet many of them seemed young. Their skin was so pale that it actually had a bluish cast. And, without fail, they moved with a peculiar unhurried grace lacking in many of the other people traversing the streets.

As they came abreast of another of these people, Coventry could contain her curiosity no longer. "Those people," she indicated the tall white-haired man with a motion of her chin. "Are they Thadonian?"

Trace followed her gaze. "Yes, they are Thadonian. They are merely of a different race. We have many races here, just as you do on Earth."

"But . . . they look so . . . foreign. They are so different from everyone else."

He nodded. "The Fehera are unique, and that distinctiveness almost resulted in their extinction."

"How so?"

"The Fehera are, without exception, telepaths and extreme pacifists. Whether this is a result of their religion or simply a genetic factor, no one knows for certain. Not even the Fehera themselves. But no Feheran has *ever* committed an act of violence or aggression."

Coventry frowned. "So . . . what are you saying? That they are a saintly race?"

Trace shook his head. "They are not completely virtuous by any means. Although most are good people, Feherans have been known to commit crimes. But they are always nonviolent crimes."

"Why did their character almost result in their extinction?"

"Because, like you, others notice their strangeness. In times past, maniacal leaders attempted to exterminate the race. Many of the Fehera were killed because, as pacifists, they never defend themselves. Now, they are a protected species. The Feherans are safeguarded even in times of war."

He grinned. "There was an incident that occurred, perhaps thirty years ago, where two neighboring estates warred with each other over water rights. It is said that a Feheran walked into the midst of the battle, filled his waterskin at the disputed river and set up camp. Effectively, he halted the battle for hours until he moved on because none would take the risk of killing him."

Coventry smiled. "It sounds like there should be a Feheran present at every dispute."

"Perhaps," Trace conceded as he occupied himself with maneuvering the pair of dyre pulling the hackney through a congested area of the street. Coventry turned back to viewing the shifting scenes of the city.

A few minutes later, they entered an area that appeared to be exclusively residential. There were still no apartment blocks—something, she had learned from Trace, which did not exist on Thadonia—but the buildings no longer displayed signs of any kind. As they progressed, the houses gradually became larger and farther from the street. Almost all of them still sported facades of pinkish plaster, but some were ornamented with a black slatelike stone. Eventually, stone walls enclosed the properties, blocking her view of the grounds and houses beyond.

"There." Trace's voice drew her gaze to his pointing finger. "The palatial grounds are ahead."

Coventry saw nothing but a massive stone wall topped with menacing black spikes. In the center of the wall, an enormous wooden gate maintained the privacy of the grounds from prying eyes. It looked impenetrable. "How are we going to get in?"

"There is a gatekeeper." Trace stopped the rig before the gate and disembarked. He pulled a rope dangling to one side of the gate and waited. Within a moment, a small square opened in the wooden portal to frame the face of a man. Trace and the man conversed for a moment, and then Trace returned to the hackney and the gates began to swing open.

As Trace maneuvered the conveyance through the massive gates, Coventry sat stunned by the beauty hidden behind the stone walls. The grounds were those of a massive, and meticulously maintained, park. Asymmetrical, as the grounds surrounding the spaceport had been, they still possessed an ambience that was unique to themselves. Colorful clumps of brush, flowering shrubs, and statuesque trees abounded. Short blue-green grass, like a sumptuous carpet, blanketed the space between them. A profusion of flowers bordered graveled paths, each of a particular shade of crushed stone, as they wound through the grounds, drawing the eye to scattered fountains throughout. The mingled scents of myriad flowers perfumed the surroundings. Birds, the first Coventry had seen, darted between flowered clumps, permeating the air with their musical cries. And dominating the scene was the palace itself.

The entire enormous building was constructed of the blue-black stone Coventry had just begun to see on some of the homes beyond the palace grounds. The pinkish plaster, so pale that it was almost white, provided accents and decorative relief to the starkness of the black stone. A huge portico, supported by six plastered pillars, led to a pair of massive, carved, wooden doors. As they drew the carriage abreast of the stairs, the doors opened and two young men wearing red and white uniforms descended to greet them.

"Would you like me to return your hackney for you, Imnen?" one of them asked Trace.

He shook his head. "I will return it myself. If

you will just park it for a time?" He lifted a hand to Coventry to aid her descent.

"Certainly, Imnen." The young man bowed his head in a sharp nod, then, directing his gaze to Coventry, he repeated the gesture. "Imnana."

As he jumped into the carriage to take Trace's place, his uniformed partner preceded them up the stairs to hold open the doors. They entered an enormous foyer, so long it appeared almost like a corridor. While Coventry stared at the opulent surroundings, Trace took her arm and began to lead her through the foyer toward a man seated at a desk.

Dozens of wax figures, garbed in golden uniforms, lined both sides of the long entryway. The floor, constructed of smooth black stone, was so polished she could see their reflections in it as they walked. Embedded periodically within the white plaster of the walls were mosaic depictions of Thadonian scenes. Overhead, an enormous chandelier, constructed of millions of pieces of glittering glass, contained tiny, glowing cylinders which cast a strange blue-gold light. Coventry looked more closely at one of the wax figures, wondering whom he had been made to represent. Suddenly, the figure blinked and she realized he was not wax at all, but a man standing perfectly stiff and motionless. Stars! What a boring job.

Trace halted and she looked forward. The man seated behind the desk wore clothing of a deep blue color. He was slightly past middle age and had a stern uncompromising face. Yet, Coventry noted that his medium-blue eyes looked kind.

"Sotah Rainon to see Emperor Rion," Trace said with brusque efficiency.

The man nodded, beckoned to a young man wearing a red uniform similar to those of the doormen, and sent him off with the message. Then he looked back at Trace. "I will inform you when I receive a response. You may wait in the salon, Rainon. You know where it is."

Trace affirmed his statement and led Coventry to the right, through a small door and into the waiting room. Thickly padded cushions of forest green rested on the gleaming tiling in various positions around the room. Bowls of fresh-cut, yellow flowers perfumed the air. "Sit," Trace directed her absently as he indicated one of the cushions. He did not seat himself, but paced the room like a caged beast. And once again, Coventry sensed tension in him. What was wrong? What had he not told her?

The silence in the room stretched, broken only by the almost imperceptible sound of Trace's pacing. Perhaps twenty minutes had passed when the deskman finally entered. "I am sorry, Rainon, but the emperor left this morning for his summer estate informing only his secretary. It is said he will return within fifteen days."

Coventry looked at Trace. Although his expression was grim, he said nothing, merely nodding brusque acknowledgment as he helped Coventry to her feet.

Barely two minutes later, they emerged from the palace and Trace ordered the hackney to be brought around. They waited in silence. Suddenly, the young man sent to retrieve the rig came running around a corner, winded and excited. "Imnen, it is gone."

"What is gone?" Trace demanded. "The hackney?"

The boy nodded. "I do not know how or why, Imnen. I followed your instructions to hold the rig."

Trace frowned forbiddingly. "Arrange for a driver to return us to our lodgings."

The young man shuffled his feet nervously. "I cannot, Imnen. There are no dyre in the stables. No drivers. No stablehands. I—" He shrugged his shoulders helplessly. "It is most peculiar."

If Coventry thought Trace had looked grim before, he appeared absolutely thunderous now. "So, we must walk." He ground the words out between clenched teeth. Grasping Coventry's arm, he led her down the steps and onto the graveled drive. More than a little intimidated by the ruthlessness of his countenance, Coventry remained silent.

Having negotiated the palace grounds and streets bordering the larger estates, they entered a less affluent area. The buildings, although still relatively large, were much closer together and only steps from the street. Trace remained broodingly silent as they maneuvered their way through increasing numbers of pedestrians. Coventry wished he would tell her what the problem was. Sure he had been unable to hand the data disk over to the emperor. But he could go to the emperor's summer residence to give it to him, couldn't he? How far away could it be? Another short delay, nothing more. So why was Trace so . . . uneasy?

They drew abreast of a gap between two buildings. Suddenly, a man leapt from the space, sword in hand, yelling something unintelligible to Trace. Coventry did not see Trace draw his own weapon, but it was in his hand as he pivoted to meet the attack, parrying a thrust that would have ended his life had he been a fraction slower. She felt herself grabbed from behind. An arm encircled her throat. She struggled. A knife sailed from her captor's free hand, directed at Trace's back. She screamed. The weapon struck Trace. A light flared. And then the knife fell harmlessly to the ground. Trace did not even seem aware that he'd been struck as he continued to battle. Her captor began to drag her back, away from Trace. She opened her mouth to scream again but the sound was trapped in her throat as a strange-smelling cloth was pressed to her face. Her vision blurred, the strength began to fade from her limbs. She saw Trace knock the sword from his opponent's grasp. And then, awareness fled.

Chapter Thirteen

Tiern heard Coventry scream. A second assailant! Dispatching his opponent as rapidly as possible, he turned to aid her. She was gone! He raced back a short distance along the street, peering into the gaps between buildings. Nothing! He studied the faces of the bystanders who had stopped, interested in the proceedings.

"The woman. Where was she taken?" His heart pounded with the need for action, but his penetrating gaze was met by blank stare after blank stare. No one responded. His keen eyes searched the street. There were no rigs leaving the area, no dyre carrying a suspicious bundle.

Determined to search every building in the area if need be, he turned away from the crowd. Stalking swiftly to the body of the man he had killed, he dropped a small red square of cloth onto his chest. The cloth, embroidered with the symbol of the *Sotah*, would inform the city guards that the kill had been a lawful one. Then pivoting, he scanned the structures bordering the street. He was certain Coventry had been taken into one of them. But which one? They were so close, and so narrow, that only a few steps separated one doorway from the next. He had taken only a single step toward the nearest door when a small high-pitched voice halted him.

"Imnen, for a price I will tell you through which door she was taken."

Tiern spun in the direction from which the call had come. A boy, perhaps twelve years of age, forced his way through the muttering bystanders. He wore the gray garments of a city orphan, an information broker. The orphans sold information to *anybody* without prejudice or loyalty. It was how they maintained their orphanage and contracted the services of instructors. Without hesitation, Tiern dug into his pouch for a handful of coins. "Where?" he demanded, opening his fist to deposit the cash into the boy's grimy hand.

"There." The boy pointed to the door next to the one Tiern had been about to enter.

"Do you know anything about him?" Tiern indicated the body he had left lying on the walkway.

The boy shrugged and his face twisted in a grimace of distaste. "He is a hunter for hire, a bonus tracker. That is all I know."

Tiern nodded and moved to the door the boy had indicated. He did not doubt the truth of the boy's information. The orphans prided themselves on providing accurate details. Standing to one side of the entry, he lifted the latch on the door and nudged it open. It creaked on ill-used hinges. The room beyond was small and dim, obviously abandoned. Piles of broken furniture and pottery littered the floor. The smell of dust and mold met his nostrils. Stepping inside, he searched the shadows with his eyes. No movement.

An arched entry at the rear of the room beckoned. He walked silently toward it. The next chamber was empty, devoid of even the clutter in the front room. A flight of stairs to his left led to the second level. At the back, a door stood open invitingly, leading to the compound beyond. A ruse? He moved toward it, checking the floorboards for trapdoors as he went. As he stepped from the building, he raked the compound with his eyes. Empty. A gate in the rear fence stood open. He moved swiftly toward it, his probing eyes sweeping the dusty soil. The signs of two dyre, one larger than the other, marked the compound along with the booted prints of two men, but there was nothing to indicate Coventry had passed this way. Had she been carried? Wait! There! The smaller print of a woman's foot. Coventry!

He rushed into the alley. *Zyk!* There was no sign of them. Though, even had they been in sight, he did not know what he would have done to pursue them without his dyre. He studied the soil once more in the hope of at least learning what direction the man had taken. It was no good. The hard-packed, alley surface yielded no secrets. He would have to search by other means.

Tiern had the entire network of orphans seeking information throughout the city. There was little more he could do without planning. An hour had passed since the attack. His guts churned with conflicting desires: his need to find and free Coventry, and the need to leave the city, locate his emperor and pass on the critical data. But he could not leave without Coventry, so he had returned to the inn. The chamber he had rented seemed empty, lifeless, without Coventry. Everywhere he looked, he pictured her. Before the dressing table, braiding her hair. At the bed, searching through the clothing he had purchased. Emerging from the bath wrapped in a towel, the golden hue of her long hair tarnished by moisture as it dried.

Abruptly, he shoved aside his emotion. He had

to deliberate, to focus on the power of *Sotah* and determine the purpose of his enemies. Kneeling in the middle of the room, he centered. The leashed force within him expanded, submerging emotion, augmenting lucidity. He recalled the details of the incident.

It had been obvious that his enemies no longer considered the acquisition of the data disk of primary importance. If they had, the man who had attacked him would have attempted to disable rather than to kill him. But the man had definitely sought his death. So, his enemies must assume that the danger the disk represented to them would perish with him. And they would be correct. Distrusting everyone, he had kept the data secret. But the *Sotah* could be trusted, and many of his brothers were near. He *must* share the responsibility he carried, or the enemy would have too great a possibility of prevailing.

But why had they taken Coventry? If they had not attempted to kill him, he would have assumed that they sought to ransom her for the disk. Since they obviously *did* seek his demise, what reason could they have for abducting her? No answer was forthcoming. He relaxed, waiting. Slowly he expanded the scope of his senses, probing the patterns of thought, twining and retwining, creating new configurations. The men were bonus trackers—killers and abductors for hire. Therefore, somebody wanted Coventry enough to pay for her capture. Who? For what reason?

He waited patiently. The answers gleaned from *Sotah* were always accurate, always reliable when they surfaced, but they could never be forced. And sometimes they simply did not come. Abruptly, he received a partial revelation. They planned to use Coventry against her brother. They knew Dalton

Pearce lived and still considered him a threat to their plans. But who, here on Thadonia, acted in the interests of the men on Earth? Who held Coventry? Once more he waited. This time no answer was forthcoming.

Sighing, he gathered the power of *Sotah*, drawing it back, shielding and confining it as he had been taught. Now, he must contact his brothers. Once more he released the force, but differently this time. A shimmering incandescent aura rose from his kneeling form as he bowed his head. Scintillating sparks of energy danced over his body as the call went out. The *Sotah* were not telepathic in the true sense of the word. But, they were linked, brothers of one spirit for all time. They would perceive his summons, not in words or images, but as compulsion. And they would know that one of their number required aid. No matter which emperor they represented—if they were not involved in an investigation and it was possible for them to come—they would arrive to assist a brother.

Gradually the glistening outline faded from Tiern's form and he rose to face the silent, barren chamber. Coventry! his mind shouted as the discipline of his organization failed him for an instant. He ached to do something . . . anything. With sudden insight, he realized that he felt more for Coventry than he had for a woman in a long time. Love? No. His conscious mind immediately denied the thought. What he felt for Coventry was nothing like the emotion he had felt for his wife. And he had loved Aneire. Yet, why did his chest ache as he contemplated the fear she must be suffering? His hands clenched into fists as question after question resounded in his brain. Where is she? Is she all right? What have they done to her? He pictured her in so many ways. Coventry. Delicate and beautiful; courageous and spirited. She would fight her fear and her jailers. And he must help her.

Coventry began to stir. Her head throbbed; her stomach rolled uneasily. Even before she opened her eyes, her subliminal senses told her something was wrong, horrifyingly wrong. But the message was suppressed by her conscious mind. The air smelled dank, unused. There was no sound; absolute silence reigned. She could hear her own pulse pounding in her ears. The chamber was so stuffy and thick with humidity that she could barely breathe. Moaning, swallowing in an attempt to alleviate the dryness of her throat, she opened her eyes.

The room was small, bleak and colorless. Directly across from her a thick wooden door had been set into a gray wall. Slowly she lifted her head, wincing at the roaring headache the insignificant movement caused. All the walls were gray. The floor was gray. Not even a sliver of natural light penetrated the murky chamber to dispel the gloom. The only illumination came from a clear, crystalline container filled with a luminous green substance. From atop a scarred wooden table, it glowed with a sickly, unpleasant light. Coventry opened her mouth. Why was she finding it so difficult to breathe? Where was she?

Moving carefully, she sat up. The room spun disagreeably for a moment, but gradually righted itself. She was sitting on a narrow cot covered with what appeared to be soiled, matted furs. She frowned in an effort to remember how she had gotten here. She was on Thadonia. She and Trace had taken a room at an inn and then . . .

She rubbed her aching forehead. Oh yes, they had gone to see the emperor. Memory burst in on her with the impact of an explosion. They'd been attacked! She remembered being dragged away. Yet, she was certain Trace had survived. Just before she blacked out, she had seen him disarm his adversary. But who had kidnapped her? Why? And where had they taken her? She panted for breath, brushing at the perspiration pouring down her face. What was the matter with her? Why couldn't she think?

Shakily, she rose and walked the few steps to the door. There was no lever, no apparent means of opening it. She knocked. "Is anybody there?" Realizing she had not spoken in Thadonian, she repeated the statement. But there was no response. She placed her ear to the wood. Silence. Fear began to clamor in her brain and she forced back encroaching panic as she studied her prison again.

A large pot sat on the floor in one corner. She had no idea what its intended purpose might be. On the table, beside the glowing container, sat a pitcher. She moved to examine it. Water! Well, at least they weren't going to let her die of thirst. Seeing no glass, she lifted the pitcher to her mouth and hastily swallowed between the panting breaths that she seemed unable to control. Her throat immediately felt better.

She returned to the door. Perhaps, she'd be able to find a way to remove the hinges. She knelt to examine the lower one. Her vision blurred and she gasped, trying to supply more of the moist, oppressive air to her starving lungs. Her fingers, fumbling with the unfamiliar hinge, brushed the wall. It felt strange, rough and damp. She ran her hand over it, trying to see it more clearly in the dimness. Oh, God! It was soil. She was belowground! She closed her eyes, willing herself to stay calm. *C'mon, Cov.* With determination born of willpower and little else, she turned her attention back to the hinge. Perspiration soaked her body, but she couldn't budge the stubborn apparatus.

Dammit! She had to get out! She could feel the panic clawing at the feeble bonds of her restraint. Her eyes raked the small chamber, seeking a tool . . . anything to aid her. There was nothing. Hysteria mounted. A whimper of anguish escaped her tense lips. She pounded on the thick door and clawed at the stubborn hinges. A voice wailed in terror. The sound intensified, becoming a frenzied succession of breathless screams. She was vaguely aware that the frantic sounds filling the room came from her own lips, but fear consumed her, suppressing her will beneath its superior strength. The walls pressed in on her. The atmosphere thickened. She couldn't breathe; the room darkened.

Consciousness returned suddenly; awareness crashed in on her. She stared dispassionately at her hands as she swallowed the hysteria rising inexorably in her throat. They didn't look like her hands. The nails were torn, shredded and bloody. Oozing scratches marred the normal whiteness of her flesh. But she felt no pain.

She gasped. There was no air. She closed her eyes, seeking oblivion. Perhaps she would suffocate and die. The thought was unemotional, detached. But she was cold . . . so cold. Gradually she realized that she lay in perspiration-soaked clothing on the chilly floor. She opened her eyes, staring at the insubstantial and uninviting cot across the room. It would be warm.

Slowly, she shifted her position, trying to rise. The floor rippled, the walls tilted toward her, and she closed her eyes with a moan of despair, defeated. *Move, Cov.* The words became an urgent litany, sounding again and again in time with her racing pulse. Resenting the imperious voice within her that compelled her to fight her crippling fear, Coventry rose to her knees. Keeping her eyes tightly shut, she crawled across the suddenly enormous space. Tiny, desperate whimpering noises escaped her throat and part of her despised her weakness. Finally, she reached the cot and squirmed onto it, pulling one of the unpleasant furs over her with trembling hands.

She could barely breathe. She knew without opening her eyes that the ceiling hung mere inches from her face. Rippling. Bulging. The walls pressed inward seeking to crush her. She knew she teetered on the edge of madness. What would happen to the child she carried if she plunged into dementia? Would she survive long enough to give it life? Would she ever hold it in her arms? She had to defeat the phobia that sought so aggressively to destroy her. But how?

Jyllian, an actress that Coventry had worked with, had practiced meditation. She had once said that she could tune out the entire world by focusing on something and directing herself inward. Perhaps Coventry could do that. But what could she focus on? Her child! Could she block out the fear by focusing on her unborn child? Of its own accord, her hand drifted down to rest protectively over her abdomen.

Tiern half expected his enemies to seek him out at the inn. It would not have taken much investigation for them to discover where he stayed. Yet, when contact did come, it did not take the violent turn he had expected. He answered the knock on the door warily. A child, of perhaps eight or nine years, stood there. Before Tiern could open his mouth, the boy thrust a slip of paper at him and fled down the corridor.

Closing the door, Tiern unfolded the message. *We have the girl. Bring the information to the alley behind the Warrior's Inn at mid-eve. Come alone.* He frowned. He had not expected to receive a ransom demand. What were they planning? He had already determined that they wanted him dead, and that they conspired to use Coventry against her brother. He sat on the end of the bed. So . . . it was unlikely that Coventry would be anywhere near this rendezvous. It would be a trap. A place to eliminate him while at the same time retrieving the crucial data. Yet, he could not afford to ignore the chance, however slight, that Coventry might be near. Failing that, he might have the opportunity to force one of them to tell him where she was being kept. Besides, although he was certain they wanted Coventry alive, these were dangerous and desperate people. He could not afford to jeopardize her well-being by ignoring the summons. He closed his eyes, inexplicably terrified that, despite his conscious belief that her life was not in danger, Coventry was in serious peril. But he could not help her by allowing worry to impede his senses, so he resolutely banished the anxiety to a distant corner of his mind.

It was now mid-afternoon. Some of his *Sotah* brothers should arrive before the rendezvous with Coventry's captors. Together they would plan to influence the outcome of the meeting behind the Warrior's Inn somewhat. Not for the first time in his life, Tiern wished that utilization of the power of *Sotah* did not take such intense concentration. The deadly potential of the force was negated in hand to hand combat because there was seldom time to draw upon it unless the opponent had already been disarmed. Still, the *Sotah* warriors were the most disciplined and formidable of all the warrior societies. They were trained to have lightning reflexes and astute, discriminating minds. Tiern wished to be nothing else.

Now, he must prepare himself for the evening. Pulling the bellcord, he ordered a meal. Knowing that it would take at least fifteen minutes for the food to arrive, he decided to cleanse himself in the mineral bath while he waited. The procedure would be more symbolic than necessary, but perhaps the ritual would ease his tension.

An hour later, his ritual cleansing and meal complete, Tiern retrieved the case that had contained his uniform and moved to the area of the chamber that provided the most space. Naked, save for the loose-fitting trousers and the characteristic red band about his forehead, he knelt and extracted his *Sotah* broadsword from the false bottom. Reverently he began to assemble it. The polished yellow metal, unique to Thadonia, gleamed. As each segment of the weapon clicked into place, the gleam intensified, taking on an unnatural brightness. It was a special blade—a sentient being, psychic in nature and imbued with the power of the *Sotah*. Achieving a bond with a weapon such as this was the final test of a *Sotah* warrior. The swords were as individualistic as the warriors they adopted. No one, other than the reclusive priests of *Sotah*, knew how the unique weapons were constructed. And they guarded their secrets jealously.

Standing, Tiern held the sword respectfully

before his face, point heavenward, and intoned the ritual chant.

Slumbering.
In the sunrise we are born.
Consciousness.
In the light of the Silver moon we are blessed.
Awaken.
Convergence begins in the light of morn.
Together.
We are one; we are light; we begin the quest.
We are Sotah.

As Tiern stood, eyes closed, intent on the refrain, rainbow-hued bands of light spiraled in a loving caress down the surface of the blade until they reached the pommel. Then, the colors divided, separating into glittering strands of incandescent light that wept down onto the hands of the warrior and began to weave sinuously up his arms. Tiern threw back his head with a muffled groan, clenching his teeth against the searing torment of the rapturous fusion. Gradually as the filaments of anatomized light disappeared, assimilated by the flesh of his body, the symbiotic psychic bond was reestablished. The sword became virtually weightless. He opened his eyes.

He felt revitalized. Studying the radiant broadsword, so much more than a mere weapon, he intoned the name he had given it so long ago: *Ven-Jikan*, Forever Friend. He sensed the subtle vibration of its response, and smiled. He felt invulnerable, capable of anything. But he knew that the sensation was merely a side effect of the reunion. The dangerous tendency to overconfidence would dissipate slowly over the next hours, leaving Tiern with a sense of wholeness and vitality which would last as long as he carried the sentient blade.

He began the drill. The noise of humanity in the streets of ReiDalgo faded away. He leapt, executing a perfect aerial somersault. He landed, the sound imperceptible to untrained human ears. Ven-Jikan spun out of his hand, revolving on its hilt up one arm and down the other, dancing its pleasure, singing its woe, as only a *Sotah* sword can do. Catching the weapon in his hand once more, Tiern continued. The only sounds to penetrate his concentration were the nearly inaudible sound of his bare feet striking the floor as he completed each leap, and the faint whisper of Ven-Jikan carving the air.

He had almost completed his exercises when his newly honed senses detected a presence approaching in the hall. A brother. They had begun to arrive. Because he had been summoned and was therefore expected, Tiern knew he would not knock. He turned as the door opened and a woman stepped into the room. She was unknown to him. Her black uniform was decorated with the blue bands of the *Sotah* in Rafat, the neighboring empire.

"Brother." Tiern nodded his head in welcome.

"Brother," she acknowledged him. "I am Singai. Am I the first?"

"I am Rainon. And, yes, you are the first."

"Then I will sleep a time while we wait for the others."

Tiern nodded as he watched her choose a corner of the room and recline on the floor. Until she knew the situation, she would not allow her senses to be lulled by comfort. He studied her briefly as she closed her eyes, and then turned back to complete his drill. As a *Sotah* brother, she was sexless to him. He had evaluated her form with the critical eye of a brother who would rely on her strengths and compensate for her weaknesses. She was sinewy and slight, not physically strong as he was; but she would be quicker and more agile than himself. A perfect complement in a battle. Still, he knew she must have strength too. The achievement of *Sotah* required the fulfillment of rigorous tests of endurance and strength.

Mid-eve arrived. The large red Quester's moon hung low in the sky while the smaller Silver moon glowed with ethereal effulgence overhead. Only the Wandering moon had yet to rise. Tiern secured his dyre and entered the alley behind the Warrior's Inn. His senses detected and marked the positions where his four brothers had concealed themselves. He had been slightly disappointed to discover no scanners among them, but he knew he should not have been. Scanners among the *Sotah* were as rare as true telepaths. But he had hoped. A scanner would have been able to pluck the information he sought concerning Coventry from the minds of his enemies without them even being aware of it.

Progressing slowly down the alley, he smelled his adversaries before he saw them. It was not because they were particularly unclean, but rather that they had no training in suppressing body odors. They smelled of perspiration and battle-lust. Tiern halted and held up a small packet which contained precisely nothing, for the disk was still safely concealed in his boot heel. "I have the disk. Bring out the girl."

He waited. Silence. Then, from the shadows, he saw a dyre move forward. A slender figure, cloaked and hooded, sat upon it. He knew instantly that, although the form was that of a woman, it was not Coventry. He turned, looking again to the shadows where the men hid. "Where is she?" he demanded.

Suddenly Ven-Jikan sang a warning. Tiern pivoted. The woman attacked. Her sword flashed, cold and chalky in the darkness as Tiern jumped aside, extracting Ven-Jikan from the baldric on his back. She wore the distinctive, indigo garb of a *Dalig*. His mind registered the shock of that discovery even as he sprang to meet her next attack.

The *Dalig* did not exist! The guild had been vanquished to the point of extinction almost half a century ago. Always diametrically opposed to the *Sotah* and everything they stood for, the *Dalig* had instigated the largest and most devastating battle Thadonia had ever seen. And, though it had cost the *Sotah* greatly, in the end, they had triumphed. So, from where had this woman come?

Their weapons clashed. A rain of scintillating sparks flew from the point of contact. They circled each other. Absolute silence reigned. Tiern studied his opponent in the moonlight. She was tall, lithe and graceful, but strong. He could not discern her features; her eyes were mere dark cavities in the nebulous whiteness of her face. And she was skilled, very skilled. He dismissed all thought of the men in the shadows, counting on his brothers to ensure a fair battle.

Suddenly she leapt high into the air. Sailing over Tiern's head, she brought her weapon down. The maneuver would have split his skull had he still been there. She turned to face him. This time it was he who leapt, but she jumped to meet him. They clashed in midair. Glowing golden blade grated against cool white, showering coruscating embers onto the combatants. And again they separated to evaluate. The sounds of other weapons clashing in battle reached Tiern's ears. He focused. Ven-Jikan vibrated in his hand. She was stalling, drawing on the *Dalig* force within her. He must attack quickly before the force achieved full strength.

There! A weakness. He attacked. She parried, struck his shoulder and released a bloodcurdling shriek. A bolt of icy white energy streaked toward him. His shield flared protectively, but he was briefly destabilized. She lashed out with her weapon. Her power-imbued broadsword penetrated his flesh. A bellow of agony escaped Tiern's tense lips as the malignant blade seared his flesh. Ven-Jikan sang. Psychic force raced through Tiern's body, blocking the pain, healing the wound.

Tiern watched her as he, too, began to draw on the power within him. Would he have time? She vaulted through the air, each of her feet striking at his face in quick succession, seeking to knock him from his feet. He dodged the maneuver, releasing the energy, still diverse and deficient, that he had drawn upon. It shot toward his enemy, a wide bolt of blazing puissance. Her shielding sensed its approach and fortified the point of contact. Even so, it was enough to knock her off her feet. Tiern pounced. Ven-Jikan pierced her heart. The woman screamed; her weapon wailed discordantly. She stared at him. Her eyes, visible now in the moonlight, glared hatred until gradually life's light was extinguished and the *Dalig* died.

A brother approached from behind. "Who was she?"

Tiern glanced up. Juste was a man of average height and build whom Tiern had worked with occasionally in the past. "I do not know."

"Do you think the priests know that the *Dalig* have reorganized their guild?"

Tiern shook his head. "They would have informed us."

Juste nodded. Together they turned to survey the carnage littering the alley. "There were six men in hiding. Had they stayed there, they would still be alive but, as you suspected, they were not honorable men. Someone wants you dead."

Singai came forward to stare down at the body of the woman. Squatting down, she grasped the high collar encircling the woman's throat and tugged it down. There, stretching from the base of the ear to the uppermost curve of the shoulder, glowing aberrantly in the faint light of the moons, was the *Dalig* tattoo. The depiction was that of a pregnant woman; her round belly was portrayed as the Thadonian world. From between her thighs, she birthed an army wielding swords. Singai growled in disgust. Leaning forward, she reached to retrieve the *Dalig* weapon.

Juste's iron grip on her forearm halted her. "Do not touch it."

"Why?"

"The consciousness within it may not be completely dead yet. And we do not know what effect it could have."

Singai nodded. Tiern nudged the weapon with his boot until it was hidden in the shadows at the edge of the alley. He looked at his four brothers. "Is there any information concerning the whereabouts of the woman, Coventry?"

"No." It was Loran who responded. A tall, blond man, he and Tiern had spent much time together in their youth, but had seen each other little since. "Not even to bargain for their lives would they speak."

Tiern nodded. Extracting a handful of the small red squares of cloth from his pocket, he began dropping them onto the bodies littering the alley. When he reached the *Dalig* woman, he bent and removed the pale headband encircling her forehead. Perhaps, if it became necessary and he was lucky, he would be able to obtain the services of a clairvoyant. In the aftermath of the battle, he found he was once again charged with desperate energy. Find Coventry! The thought echoed and reechoed in his mind.

Together, he and his brothers left the alley. They would separate now, for a time, each using their contacts within the city to attempt to discover where Coventry was being detained. As they approached their waiting dyre, Tiern noted the presence of a child in gray.

"Imnen," the boy called as he approached. "I have information for you."

Tiern's heart skipped as he reached into his pouch for funds. He placed them into the boy's hand. "Where is she?"

"The information is not absolutely certain," the boy cautioned him and Tiern nodded impatiently. "We believe she is being held at the old fortress south of here."

Chapter Fourteen

Tiern and his companions viewed the fortress from the security of a boulder-strewn rise. The stronghold towered bleak and forbidding against the star-studded night sky. They could discern no movement, yet they could not simply move in. Loran stood guard while the other four, Singai, Rainon, Juste and Modoc, sat to direct their minds on a mission of discovery. Reconnaissance *Sotah* style, Tiern thought wryly remembering how much more difficult the same objective had been in his guise on Earth.

The technique called *resa* was one of the most difficult for new disciples of *Sotah* to master. Instinctive fears had to be overcome before the subconscious would allow the spirit to leave the body. And even then, care must be taken not to wander too far afield lest the body perish, trapping the spirit forever between planes of existence.

The four *Sotah*, having each agreed upon an advance probe of a particular quadrant of the fortress, lay down on the spongy, dry sea grass in the lea of a jumble of stones. Tiern breathed deeply, inducing the obligatory level of relaxation. Slowly, he projected. He paused to look down on his body and those of his companions before moving in the direction of the southeast section of the stronghold.

There were no entrances. He penetrated the thick stone, moving inside. Walls of dismal, grayish rock, coated with moss due to the moistness of the sea air, enclosed a chamber barren of humanity. He moved on. More gray stone walls. A partially eaten meal littered the surface of three enormous, scarred, wooden tables. There was no sign of Coventry. A single, male guardsman sat on a cushion, resting on his forearms as he slept at one of the tables.

Voices. Tiern traced the sound. He entered a large room full of young men and women wearing the garb of the *Dalig*. How could there be so many? If the guild had been re-forming, should not some word of its activities have leaked? He counted the inhabitants—thirty-four!—before moving to the next chamber.

The room was large and, in comparison to the others, sumptuous. Golden draperies obscured the walls. A huge bed, draped in gold fabric, rested near the center of the far wall. A man, wearing the robes of a *Dalig* commander—deep indigo inscribed with runes of golden thread—sat writing at a desk. Abruptly, he looked up, checking over his shoulder. A jolt of recognition rocked Tiern. He had seen this man before. But where? The *Dalig* rose, walked to the door and inspected the corridor. Then, closing the door, he studied his chamber with narrowed eyes. Suddenly, just as he felt he was about to identify the occupant, Tiern's perceptions were blocked. The chamber acquired a shroud of blackness deeper than night. Swiftly, heedless of his psychic blindness, Tiern propelled himself back toward the safety of his body, allowing the bond between soul and spirit to guide him.

Singai, unable to find a trace of the woman Rainon sought, returned to the chamber that contained the only humanity in the entire southwest section of the fortress. The two men were *Dalig* junior commanders, and they were drinking heavily. They were both burly men, dark-haired and swarthy, but one was taller than the other.

"Zared, where do you want to be on the big day?"

The tall man grasped a new bottle of spirits and turned to view the shorter. "What big day?"

"You know. The day the Earthers find out we're not as ignorant and primitive as we allow them to believe. The day we take control of their spaceports and seize control of the galaxy. The day the *Dalig* rule."

"Oh. *That* day," Zared said with a smirk as he returned to sit at the scarred table opposite his companion. "Well, if we are lucky enough to reach *that* day without losing our lives, I want to be on Earth with our brethren to see the faces of the bureaucrats when they realize they are powerless." He laughed unpleasantly. "What about you, Gearr?"

Gearr nodded. "Me, too. But if that is not possible, then I at least want to live long enough to see the *Dalig* control Thadonia. Once our power base here is secure, it will only be a matter of a few short years until the *Dalig* move beyond the boundaries of a single world. And I will be able to content myself with having seen the end of the *Sotah*." He spat the last word distastefully.

Singai could not believe what she was hearing. She stayed, listening to their dreams of lust and glory and power, until she could stand no more. Then, exiting suddenly, she returned to her body so quickly that she experienced a moment of disorientation. Her own form had never felt more welcome. It felt pure, wholesome, and cleansing to a spirit soiled by the atmosphere of corruption and depravity from which she had come.

Tiern awoke. Juste and Singai were also just awakening. "Any movement?" Tiern asked Loran.

"Nothing." Loran shook his head.

Singai rose immediately, joining Loran on watch. Tiern and Juste sat quietly awaiting Modoc. Tiern had just begun to get concerned about him, in view of his own experience, when Modoc blinked and rose to a sitting position. "Are you all right?" Tiern asked.

"Yes." Modoc nodded, but his response was subdued.

Singai rejoined them, and they began to discuss the situation quietly. "There are nineteen *Dalig* and ten guardsmen," said Juste. He had been inspecting the northwest quadrant. "The entrance to the fortress from the seaside is busy. Much busier than it should be." He frowned. "I would like to know what is going on."

"Yes," Tiern responded with a frown before going on to tell them what he had discovered. He described the man whom he felt certain he knew, but none of the others recognized the verbal portrait he painted. "Singai?" Tiern prompted her for her report, signaling the end of his own.

She sighed. "The southwest section contains one large exterior entrance—well-guarded. But there were only two *Dalig* men, junior commanders, inside that quadrant. They spoke at length. What I heard leads me to believe that the plot you

271

uncovered on Earth, Rainon, is only a small part of a much larger conspiracy." She fell silent, her expression pained.

"Tell us," Tiern prompted.

"They said that with the help of the Earthers, the *Dalig* will soon achieve mastery of Thadonia. Once their power base here is assured, they will mobilize their counterparts on Earth and seize control of that world's space vessels." Singai continued, staring intently at the sole of her boot as she recounted everything she had heard. Suddenly, she looked at Tiern. "Rainon, they plan to seize control of the entire galaxy. To spread their poison from world to world. And to destroy Thadonia in the process." She leaned forward communicating her urgency. "I have been thinking. Perhaps it was the *Dalig*, through an agent, who somehow convinced the council of Emperors to conceal the true nature of the *Sotah* from Earthers. In doing so, the Emperors also concealed the capabilities of the *Dalig*, something absolutely essential to the success of their plan."

Tiern contemplated Singai. So . . . the details he carried outlined only a portion of the overall scheme, the segment pertaining to and devised by the Earthers. Men who did not dream they were merely being used as tools toward the achievement of a much greater and more menacing goal. The thought that there might already be *Dalig* on Earth alarmed him. How would the Earthers defend themselves against men who could kill with a thought? They had no natural shielding against psychic attack. The Earthers would never even perceive the source of the weapon used against them. A blaster could kill a *Dalig* or, for that matter, a *Sotah*. But how would the Earthers know against whom the weapon should be directed when the assassination of their most prominent leaders could take place from the distance and anonymity of a crowd?

His gaze swept his brothers. "Comments?"

Loran spoke first, from his position on guard. "I think we must attempt to commune with the priests. We need guidance. Also, at this point we are five against—" He shrugged. "—dozens, perhaps a hundred. If we are killed, the knowledge dies with us. We must pass it on before—" He looked to the fortress. "Before we enter their stronghold."

Tiern nodded. It was the same conclusion he had arrived at earlier, concerning the data disk, when he had decided to call on his brothers. He could understand Loran's reasoning. Yet, he had to struggle to suppress his anxiety at the delay communication would cause. *Zyk!* They had come here to seek and rescue Coventry. So far no one had reported discovering her whereabouts. And only Modoc had yet to speak. Tiern wanted to retrieve Coventry, not to . . . to become a guardian of the galaxy. Immediately, he quelled the callous thought. He was *Sotah*. As such, his duty *always* lay clearly before him. Protect the innocent. He nodded again. "We will hear from Modoc. Then, we will find a secure spot from which to commune."

Modoc nodded and began. "I saw only ten *Dalig* and, perhaps, eight or ten guardsmen. The northeast section has one exterior entrance, a single door, but it is guarded. It also contains access to the isolation compounds." He looked to Tiern. "I did find a woman I believe is the one you described among those imprisoned. She is blonde and wearing burgundy as you described. She—"

Modoc looked down avoiding Tiern's eyes. "She does not look well."

Tiern frowned as apprehension clutched at his stomach. "What do you mean?"

Modoc swallowed and raised his gaze to meet Tiern's. "I think she is . . . mad. She stares at the wall and . . . chants strange words."

"Where is she being kept?" Tiern had not meant to bark the words so demandingly, but his concern stripped him, momentarily, of his restraint.

"She is in a small cellar chamber."

"*Zyk!*"

"What is it?" Singai asked.

"Coventry has a fear of the underground. An unreasoning terror of such places."

Singai studied him compassionately. "Well then, we had best find a place from which we can safely communicate with the priests as quickly as possible." She looked to Loran. "Could we not use the area where the dyre are concealed? They will serve well as guards."

Loran nodded acquiescence. "I have no argument." The others rose and cautiously followed him as he led the way down the hill.

They entered the thick copse of brush in which they had concealed their dyre. The communication method they were about to attempt was similar to, but much more potent than, that employed by Tiern in summoning the help of his brothers. It also required more stamina to achieve when it was not initiated by the priests. Perhaps the increased difficulty was due to the fact that the priests resided so far away, in the seclusion of the mountains to the east. Tiern did not know. Perhaps they merely needed more practice. Only once each year—on the night that the Silver moon rose directly over the summit of Kalos

Mountain and the new *Sotah* were invested—was communication with the priests mandated. And then, the communication was a universal one, linking all *Sotah*, creating brotherhood.

Tiern knelt, forming a circle with his brothers, within the enclosing solitude of the brush. Taking a series of cleansing breaths, he centered, wiping all thought, all concerns, from his mind. Slowly, a glimmering blue phosphorescence rose from his body and gravitated toward the radiant illuminations beginning to rise from the kneeling forms of his brothers. Glimmering blue blended with the luminous green mounting from Singai. Transformed. Twined and merged with Modoc's blazing copper energy. Changed. Intertwined simultaneously with the shimmering force ascending from Loran and Juste. Incandescent embers of light danced within the unique fusion of energies.

Suddenly, like the blazing tail of a comet, the scintillating force sped eastward, invisible to all save those five of whom it was a part. The five brothers continued to kneel, to concentrate as they guided the communication to the mountains, and the priests of the *Sotah*. Long minutes they waited. A whispery touch. Had contact been established? Tiern reached. Yes. The touch became more tangible. He opened his mind, allowing the distant priests access to the information it carried. He sensed shock, questioning, determination. And then came the directive.

Retrieve the girl. Seek Emperor Rion and reveal the conspiracy. Then, initiate contact again. Tiern opened his eyes and looked at his brothers. Had they all received the same counsel?

"So, now we go to the fortress?" Modoc queried, echoing Tiern's silent question.

The others nodded their agreement and rose. Juste removed the red band from about his forehead, separating the seam. A thin black mask fell from the folds and he pulled it over his head. "I think we must conceal our identities and blend with the night if we are to enter the *Dalig* lair . . . and survive." In complete agreement, the others followed his example. Two minutes later, followed by the dyre which they now would conceal closer to the fortress, they once again ascended the hill overlooking the seaside fortress—five black figures at one with the shadowy landscape.

Tiern externalized his aura and subdued its radiance, to lend his form a shifting, vague aspect. Then, hugging the building, he approached the lone figure guarding the door on the northeast corner of the structure.

The *Dalig* guard was bored and projected only passive shields against psychic attack. Still, if he sensed a threat, they could flare in an instant, deflecting any blow. It would be best to be certain. Tiern drew Ven-Jikan. The guard leaned against the recessed doorway and stared at the night sky with a cryptic half-smile on his face. A mere three feet away now, Tiern knew he must strike quickly before the guard sensed his presence. He gripped Ven-Jikan more firmly, felt the blade vibrate in his hand. A step forward. He swung; Ven-Jikan sang through the air. The guard turned startled eyes toward him, but it was too late. In a single blow, the razor-sharp blade almost completely severed his head from his neck.

Quickly, Tiern bent to drag the body around the corner of the building. Straightening up, he saw his companions approaching. Returning to the door, he quietly lifted the latch and opened it a crack to peer into the corridor. Empty. Modoc moved ahead of him to lead the way.

The dimly lit corridor smelled of stale wood smoke and unperfumed lumo gel—the substance that was burned to provide light. Tiern, trailed by Juste, Singai, and Loran, followed Modoc as he moved silently along. Perhaps halfway down the corridor, Modoc halted and peered around a corner before darting past the opening and halting on the other side. Tiern glided to the edge of the passage, carefully looking into it. Immediately before him was a narrow flight of steps. Voices floated up from the lighted chamber below, but he could see no one.

He and Modoc moved simultaneously to slip down opposite sides of the stairwell. Loran crept across the opening to follow Modoc, while Juste and Singai shadowed Tiern. Not a whisper of sound betrayed their presence as they descended. Slowly, the room below came more fully into view. Tiern halted. He saw only one *Dalig,* a junior commander. Five guardsmen sat on low stools at a table under the *Dalig*'s watchful eye.

Were there others present? Concealed in the corners out of sight? Using hand signals, he swiftly acquainted his companions with the details of the scene. Modoc indicated the presence of another guardsman to Tiern's left. Six guardsmen and one *Dalig* . . . for certain. Perhaps one or two others in the corners. But it simply was not safe to use *Sotah* senses to determine the entire situation. The *Dalig* would have to be taken first, before he could contact his brothers. Modoc signaled that he would confront the *Dalig*. Abandoning the muted auras that had helped to camouflage their forms, they swiftly and silently vaulted down the remaining stairs.

The *Dalig*'s senses were honed. Although his back had been to the stairs and there had been no sound to betray them, he drew his weapon and turned to meet Modoc's attack. *Zyk!* They would have to move quickly or they would be trapped by *Dalig*. Ven-Jikan pierced the chest of a guardsman, and Tiern turned to meet another. Modoc uttered a stifled scream as the *Dalig*'s malevolent blade pierced his flesh, but he fought on. Singai, facing two guardsmen, muffled a groan of pain as her shielding failed her when they attacked simultaneously and a weapon grazed her side. Juste dispatched his opponent and turned to aid her. The *Dalig* cried out as Modoc's blade sliced his neck and blood sprayed from the wound. For an instant it seemed that he would fight on. But the healing power of his sword was inadequate for such a massive injury and he fell.

Loran, having bested his adversary, raced along the long wall of the cellar removing bars from the thick wooden cell doors. The release of the captives would help to mask their own departure and, with luck, perhaps some of them would escape the *Dalig*.

Tiern grasped Modoc's shoulder as the man sagged. "Will you make it?"

He drew a trembling breath. "Yes."

"Which chamber, Modoc?"

Modoc indicated one of the wooden doors lining the opposite wall. It was still secured with a thick bar; Loran had not reached it yet. Tiern released the bar and entered the chamber. Coventry lay huddled on a narrow cot, half-covered by matted animal pelts. *Magar!* She looked . . . completely drained. Blocking the rage that threatened to overwhelm his trained senses, he scooped her into his arms. She did not rouse. He hurried from the chamber into the guardroom that now churned with desperate humanity . . . the released prisoners.

"Leave. Now," Loran shouted as he placed a supporting arm around Modoc. Singai and Juste raced for the stairs with Tiern hot on their heels. He could hear Modoc panting slightly behind him as he labored up the stairs with Loran. A milling crowd followed them.

As they neared the corridor above, they could hear a small army approaching. Guardsmen. But how many silent *Dalig* were with them? Juste and Singai halted their flight, glancing cautiously into the corridor. Then, flinging themselves forward, they raced for the exit. Tiern, the sounds of pursuit spurring him on, sprinted after them. They had to escape the confines of the fortress. The *Dalig* outnumbered them drastically. If they were caught, they would die.

Juste flung open the outer door and almost ran head-on into a *Dalig*. Both taken by surprise, they froze for a microsecond, staring at each other. Singai acted. Jumping forward, she shoved Juste aside, simultaneously thrusting the point of her weapon into the *Dalig*'s throat. Then, vaulting his still twitching body, she ran into the night. Tiern, hard on Juste's heals, bounded over the body and veered toward the large jumble of boulders in which they had concealed their dyre. Modoc cursed behind him. Singai uttered a single piercing whistle. Abruptly, five of the shadowy boulders moved. Singai had summoned the dyre.

As Tiern mounted Faolan, still clutching Coventry's unconscious form to him, he looked over his shoulder. He saw perhaps twenty figures racing for freedom, and behind them, emerging from the fortress . . . guardsmen, their numbers liberally peppered with *Dalig*. Singai and Juste, astride their dyre, raced across the turf in the direction of ReiDalgo. "Go!" Tiern shouted to Loran and Modoc. He goaded Faolan into motion, keeping pace with his brothers. A bolt of energy arced behind them, striking the ground. And then they moved beyond the crest of the hill and beyond the range of the *Dalig*.

As Faolan's feet pounded along the trail to ReiDalgo, Tiern looked down at the woman he held protectively in his arms. She lay limply in his grasp, her face pallid in the moonlight. But it was her eyes that disturbed him. Her pupils were fixed and unfocused. His guts churned with guilt. He had promised her that he would look after her. But he had failed her. And he did not know what to do for her. He wanted nothing more than to undo the past hours, to protect her from pain and fear, to shelter her in his arms forever. Forever? He frowned. For some reason the thought of forever, with Coventry, did not generate the horror it always had in the past. His heart skipped. *Magar!* He did love her. Despite all his plans, his denial, it had happened. It was a different love than that he had felt for Aneire, but it was love. Hell! He looked down at the delicate features of the woman who had captured his heart without him even realizing it. What was he going to do now?

He and his companions slowed their mounts to enter the city gates. "Where is the nearest physician?"

It was Juste who responded. "In Tendina Square. That way." He pointed to their right.

*   *   *

With a low growl of impatience, Tiern rose to pace the outer chamber again. What was taking so long? Almost an hour ago, he had carried Coventry into the inner sanctum of the physician's infirmary while his *Sotah* brothers had gone to retrieve their belongings before leaving ReiDalgo for the emperor's summer estate. Tiern had been able to persuade Singai to retrieve his and Coventry's possessions from their chambers. They were all to meet at the inn across the street.

Tiern's hands clenched into fists as he stared from the window. Concern for Coventry and the need for haste warred within him. He watched as Singai rode up to the inn and leapt from her dyre. Only Juste had yet to return. Modoc and Loran had arrived together ten minutes ago.

Tiern whirled as a door opened behind him and the physician emerged. "Well? What is wrong with her?"

The man, a frown fixed firmly between his shaggy white brows, shook his silver-haired head and walked across the room to sit at his desk. "Physically, nothing. I ran an entire series of tests, including those most recently obtained from Earth. She was slightly dehydrated; I took care of that. And she has not eaten recently, but—" He trailed off. "You say that she has a terror of underground areas."

"That is correct."

"And she was below the surface for a number of hours?"

"Yes." Tiern could see that the man desired an explanation, but he could not provide him with one.

"Hmmm. I have heard of cases like this, but I have never seen one. I believe that she has withdrawn from reality, gone inside herself, so to speak. Medically, there is nothing I can do." He shrugged. "When her subconscious senses that she is safe, she will probably come out of it herself. It could be detrimental to the child if she stays in this condition for too long. She must eat well and regain her strength, or she could miscarry. I suggest that you speak to her. Tell her repeatedly that she is safe. Let her hear your voice."

His mind whirling, Tiern sank bonelessly onto a stool. "Did . . . did you say 'miscarry'?"

"Yes, it is possible if she remains as she is for too long."

"You must be mistaken."

The physician frowned. "Mistaken about what?"

"About a child!" The tempest of emotion building inside him was betrayed by the desperation of his voice. "Coventry is an Earther. Earth women habitually use pregnancy inhibitors to prevent conception."

"No mistake." The man shook his head firmly. "She *is* pregnant. Three or four weeks, I would say. Although it is perfectly possible that she is unaware of it as yet."

Tiern's emotions swayed between panic and elation. How was it possible? It was his own fault, he realized. He had assumed too much based on the information he had received concerning Earth habits. He had simply assumed that Coventry used an inhibitor. Had he not made that assumption, he would have taken steps himself to ensure that pregnancy did not occur.

Time spun back. He remembered his delight when Aneire, struck with morning sickness, had been unable to conceal her pregnancy from him.

He remembered the horror and anguish of discovering that she had murdered their child in an attempt to preserve her own unmarred beauty. He remembered holding her in his arms as her life's blood drained from her body. And, he remembered the guilt he had felt when he had been unable to grant the forgiveness she sought. *Magar!* He never wanted to feel such misery again. He had promised himself that he would never marry again, never sire another child to be sacrificed on the altar of a woman's vanity. He had failed in another promise. This one to himself.

"Are you all right?" The doctor's voice drew him back from the past.

Abruptly, he squared his shoulders. "Yes. Yes, I am fine." He could not allow personal feelings to jeopardize his obligation to his emperor or the *Sotah.* He looked at the kindly, yet somewhat stern-faced physician. "Can Coventry be moved out of the city?"

The man shrugged. "I do not see why not. She must be kept reasonably comfortable, and if she has not awakened by morning I would recommend that you try to induce her to swallow some liquid. But, I believe she will come to herself before too long. I do not think you have any need to worry overmuch at this point. If her condition has not improved in, say, forty-eight hours, then I would begin to get concerned."

After retrieving an outfit of clothing for Coventry from the pack on the dyre, Tiern entered the examining room. A woman, the physician's aide, moved away from the table on which Coventry lay and began to putter with some instruments on a counter. Tiern moved to

Coventry's side and stood staring down at her. She lay so still. Her eyes were closed now. The blood had been cleaned from her hands and the dampness of the hair surrounding her face testified to the fact that she had been bathed. The thin white gown in which she had been dressed rose slightly with each shallow breath she took. Yet, even though she was ghostly pale, she appeared beautiful to him.

Was Coventry like Aneire, or different? She was undeniably beautiful, but she had said she wanted children. Had she been sincere? Could he gamble the life of his child on her honesty? No! He would take no chances. He could not. He would not allow her out of his sight until the child was born. *Zyk!* He ran an agitated hand through his hair. She planned on returning to Earth at the end of a year. Tiern's throat tightened. He would not allow it. The thought of never seeing Coventry again tormented him as much as the thought of losing his child to another world. Coventry was on Thadonia now. If he had to, as the father of her child, he would use the law to keep her here.

His eyes fell on the faint line beneath her eye— the scar she had received when she had been attacked aboard the *Payload*. The slight disfigurement did not seem to bother her. Was he being unfair? Plotting to circumvent her actions before he even knew what her intentions would be? *Magar!* He did not know what to think or do.

Raking agitated fingers through his hair, he turned to the physician's aide. "Could you clothe her in these?" He indicated the blouse and leather skirt he had brought in. Without waiting for a response, he returned to the outer chamber to pace his turmoil away as he tried to think. But his brain refused to cooperate and his thoughts became a meaningless jumble.

"She is ready." The aide spoke from the doorway of the examination room.

Tiern reentered the chamber and stood looking down at her. He noted absently that the pale peach hue of the blouse became her. He picked her up, cradling her in his arms. What was he to do? Suddenly the solution came to him. He would marry her! He had already discovered that he loved her. And, she carried his child, so his reason for avoiding a union had been negated. Marriage—it was the only reasonable solution. Coventry would simply have to adapt to Thadonian life. He frowned as he strode toward the door. But he did not have the faintest idea how he would go about accomplishing the alliance. Not even on Thadonia could you force an unwilling woman to marry. What would he do if Coventry was adamantly opposed to the idea? He looked down at her as the doctor opened the exterior door for him and he stepped outside. She had stated once, immediately following a session of lovemaking that she had considered *fantastic*, that she thought she was falling in love with him. Although she had said immediately afterward that it had been a simple comment and that she planned on returning to Earth at the end of a year, the sentiment was a definite beginning. Perhaps through numerous sessions of *fantastic* lovemaking, he could convince her that she belonged on Thadonia . . . with him. He smiled slightly. He certainly was not averse to trying it when she felt better.

Suddenly the sound of pounding feet distracted him from his musings. Juste rode recklessly down the street toward him. Simultaneously, Modoc, Singai, and Loran emerged from the inn and raced for their dyre. Without knowing its cause, Tiern was gripped by urgency. "Faolan, kneel." He scrambled astride the waiting dyre, settling Coventry onto his lap just as Juste came abreast.

"The *Dalig*," Juste gasped. "They have entered the south gate."

Chapter Fifteen

As a small army of *Dalig* fanned out through the streets of ReiDalgo in search of the five *Sotah* who had dared to enter their fortress, Tiern and his companions left the city by its eastern gate. Tiern's eyes scanned the line of the horizon where the blackness of the landscape met the glowing night sky. Clouds flitted across the ancient faces of the three luminous moons. He hoped it would not rain, for they would ride through the night. As his companions headed their mounts swiftly in a southeasterly direction, he directed Faolan to bring up the rear. They left the high coastal plains and descended the grassy slopes, moving inland through rapidly changing terrain. The boulders which peppered the coastal area became larger, looming like sentinels over those who passed by. Trees, although still sparse, grew more massive as though warring for supremacy with the immense black stones. And the grasses, sheltered from the coastal winds, grew taller.

Tiern listened to the pounding feet of the dyre and the rustling of the grasses as Faolan forged through them. He looked down at the woman resting in his arms. "Well, Coventry," he said, mindful of the physician's instructions to speak to her, "what would you like to hear?" Her eyes fluttered open, and for an instant he thought she had returned to herself. But her pupils remained unfocused. Yet he felt she must have responded to his voice on some level. Heartened, he launched into a discourse on the country through which they traveled.

Dawn had begun to lighten the horizon. "We should rest here for a couple of hours." Tiern, still bringing up the rear, barely caught Loran's words. He looked around. They were on a slight rise. Below, in a small gully, a stream wound its way toward the ocean. It was a good place to rest and, as much as he hated to admit it, he was tired.

"I agree," Juste said, answering for them all as he headed down into the gully.

Tiern guided Faolan down to the stream and directed him to kneel. After dismounting and placing Coventry comfortably in the lea of a boulder, he removed the packs and saddle from Faolan to allow the beast an opportunity to roll in the grass. It was a calculated risk. If the *Dalig* were near, the move could be costly. Yet Faolan, too, needed respite and he would not rest as comfortably burdened by a saddle and supplies.

Returning to Coventry's side, Tiern removed his baldric and lay Ven-Jikan down at his side. Resting his hand on his weapon, knowing that the broadsword would warn him of an enemy's approach, Tiern studied Coventry. Her eyes were once again closed, her lashes dark smudges against her pale flesh. Despite the fact that the physician had not thought there was any need for worry, Tiern was concerned. He hoped she would emerge from her trance soon. Settling beside her, cradling her in the crook of his arm so that her head rested against his shoulder, he closed his eyes and slept.

The sound of conversation roused him. At the stream, Juste and Singai spoke in hushed tones. The two hours must be nearly past. He looked at the woman at his side. "It is time to go, Coventry." He began to shift himself from beneath her.

Coventry's mind swam up from the depths of unconsciousness. She sensed a presence near. It was comforting, somehow sheltering. She shifted, seeking to hold it to her.

"Coventry?" The voice was deep, familiar and warm.

"Hmmm?" She moaned, reluctant to cast off the sensations surrounding her.

"Coventry!"

She drew her brows together in a small frown of annoyance. "Wha–at?" She opened her eyes but discovered that they refused to focus properly. Trace. It was Trace who had spoken. She focused blearily on him.

He smiled widely. "You're awake!"

Her frown deepened. "Of course I'm awake. You woke me up." She pushed herself into a sitting position and rubbed her forehead with a groan. "Oh, hell!"

"What is it?" Tiern brushed the hair out of her face with his fingers.

"Headache," she muttered in explanation.

"Oh. Here, let me help."

As he began to move behind her, Coventry glanced into his face and realized he was grinning broadly. "Thanks so much for the sympathy," she said caustically. Trace tried, without much success, to wipe the smile from his lips. Then, as he completed moving behind her, her eyes widened. A copse of tall trees surrounded them. She looked down. She was sitting on grass! "Where are we?"

Her frown deepened. "How did we get here?" She rubbed furiously at her forehead. "Damn this headache!"

"Shush. I will explain everything soon. Do not worry." Threading his fingers into her hair, he began to massage her scalp. "How is that?"

"Mmmm. Nice."

"Good. I do sympathize, you know. I have occasionally suffered the affliction myself."

"Then why were you grinning like an idiot?"

"I was not grinning like an *idiot*. I was merely smiling because I was happy that you—" He halted abruptly.

Coventry bowed her head forward as his kneading fingers moved down the column of her neck. "Happy that I what?"

"Rainon, it is time to go." Coventry jumped and raised her head. A woman, dressed in the same type of black attire that Trace wore, stood before them. She was tall and very slender with short, wavy, auburn hair and brilliant blue eyes. Coventry couldn't help staring at her as Trace rose, donned his baldric, and aided Coventry to her feet. The woman's gaze was open, friendly and compassionate. She was completely feminine, and yet she radiated confidence in a way no other woman of Coventry's acquaintance ever had.

"Coventry, I would like you to meet one of my *Sotah* brothers, Singai." He looked to the woman. "Singai, this is Coventry."

Coventry nodded to the woman. "I am pleased to make your acquaintance, Singai."

Singai bowed her head in a formal gesture. "As I am yours, Lady Coventry." Before Coventry could recommend that she drop the "Lady" and simply call her "Coventry," Singai turned and strode away.

"Come, you must meet the others."

Coventry followed Trace's gaze to where three men stood in the shade of a large tree. Why did she have no recollection of having seen these people previously? Everything was moving too quickly. "Wait. Please!" She grasped Trace's arm. When had they met with these men? How had they gotten here? She rubbed her head in an attempt to banish the sense of disorientation. "I remember . . . being kidnapped. When I woke up I was locked in a small room. It was," she swallowed, "underground." She paused, looking up into Trace's face. "I know I did not handle that discovery very well. But . . . I cannot remember how we got here. Why?"

Compassion shone from Trace's eyes as he met her gaze. "You were unconscious when we found you. These men," he nodded in the direction of the three, "and Singai helped me to liberate you."

Coventry's face mirrored confusion. "But why was I unconscious?"

"I will explain everything as we ride. We do not have the time now. Come. Let me introduce you to my brothers of the *Sotah*." He led her forward. "This is Juste."

Juste nodded his head respectfully. "Lady Coventry."

"And this is Modoc," Tiern continued down the line, "and Loran."

"I am pleased to meet you all," Coventry responded with ingrained courtesy although disorientation still gripped her.

They rode through a cool, dim forest of monstrous trees. Yet Coventry was only peripherally aware of the strange beauty surrounding her. Her mind was full of all that Trace had told her. Even on Thadonia her life was in danger. And now, those on Earth appeared to have reassessed her value, judging her useful as a tool against Dalton. Yet, they themselves were merely tools, expendable to the *Dalig* whose plot was even more far-reaching than was known by their accomplices on Earth. Coventry shook her aching head in perplexity. She understood the *Dalig* scheme; she understood the details of Earth's part in the conspiracy. But, she would never understand the motivation behind either one. What could possibly be so important to these people that they would jeopardize the lives of thousands and, perhaps, the very existence of a planet to achieve it? It just didn't make sense to her.

They emerged from the shade of the forest onto a grassy meadow. Beyond the meadow, more of the black monolithic stones rose, towering threateningly in an almost impenetrable wall. A single gorge cut into the rock barrier like a jagged wound. Coventry shuddered. She didn't like those stones.

"Let us eat here," Trace said as he and Coventry caught up to his companions.

With silent nods of agreement, they dismounted. Everyone appeared to carry their own food stocks, Coventry noted. They each removed supplies from their dyre before freeing the animals to graze. Then, seating themselves in silence, they ate. The *Sotah* certainly were not a particularly gregarious group. Coventry had yet to hear them say anything that was not absolutely necessary communication. A Thadonian trait, or training? she wondered. She had always assumed fighters and soldiers to be loud, boisterous people prone to braggadocio.

Trace, too, remained silent, his eyes fixed broodingly on the horizon as he ate. What was on his mind? Instinct told her it was something more than the *Dalig* situation. She had caught him looking at her appraisingly a couple of times. Why? She took another bite of the salty dried meat that Trace had given her. It was almost as if he . . . knew something about her. Oh, God! Did he suspect her pregnancy? Had she perhaps said something when she was unconscious?

Tiern stiffened as he felt Ven-Jikan vibrate in the baldric against his back. *Friend, we are watched*, the telepathic communication came from the sentient sword.

Where? He had no need to speak verbally with Ven-Jikan. Only with his broadsword was true telepathy possible for Tiern.

There was a slight hesitation. *Uncertain. They are screening.*

Dalig then.

Almost certainly.

Casually, Tiern scoured the surroundings with his gaze. There were so many places for concealment among the black stones. He looked toward the canyon through which they must pass. Stones littered its floor, formed its walls, and fell from its ridges. He looked to his brothers, noted that they, too, scanned the area. Singai had extended her hand over her shoulder to touch her weapon, letting the contact sharpen the psychic communication. So far, none of them looked prepared to offer any suggestions.

An eerie high-pitched shriek rent the air. Tiern raised his eyes, saw the form of the large predatory bird circling overhead. *Ven-Jikan, can you*

use the eyes of the Lintue to see our enemies?
The metal of his sword possessed consciousness, awareness and psychic senses, but it had neither eyes nor ears, no ordinary senses beyond the vicarious ones of its symbiotic companion. And, at this moment, Tiern's senses were not enough.

Perhaps. But if they are screening psychically, it is possible they are also shielding physically. I will try.

Tiern waited. He looked at Coventry. She continued to eat, unaware of the undertones that bothered her companions. Somehow, in some way he had to ensure that her life and the life of his child were protected. The thought of how much he had at stake at this moment terrified him. Mechanically, Tiern took another bite of his jerky as he watched the bird overhead. There was no overt sign that it sensed an alien presence in its mind. Deliberately, he tore his eyes away. He did not want to give the enemy who watched any indication that the Lintue was important in any way.

His brothers had finished their meals and begun to resaddle their mounts when Ven-Jikan spoke again. *I saw nothing, my friend. They are well shielded.*

Tiern called Faolan to him. *Then, we have no choice but to continue as planned. We cannot remain here. At least we have the advantage of knowing that there will be an attack.* "Come." He held out his hand to Coventry and helped her into the saddle. Turning to look at his brothers, he read their eyes. They were aware of the situation. Their *Sotah* blades must have perceived Ven-Jikan's attempt to espy the enemy. *Zyk!* The *Dalig* had chosen the site for the ambush well. The canyon was the only route through the wall of rock that stretched from the mountains in the east to the coast on the west. There were trails over it, in places where the ascent was not so steep, but the nearest was at least five days distant. The *Sotah* had to proceed and hope that the *Dalig* did not outnumber them too badly.

Tiern turned to view the woman whose life meant so much to him. He could not proceed without providing her with some warning of what was to come. "Coventry—?"

"Yes?" She looked at him with her large, doe-soft eyes and he wanted nothing more than to take her in his arms and run from this place. But he could not.

He brushed a strand of hair away from her cheek. "There is danger ahead, probably in the canyon. You must not be surprised by anything you see me or my brothers do. We have . . . talents of which I have not told you. You must keep your wits about you."

"The *Dalig*?"

"Yes." Tiern looked into her eyes expecting to see fear, and it was there. But there was something more, something he did not quite recognize. Determination? Tenacity, perhaps?

"How many?"

He hesitated. "We have no way of knowing."

She nodded, understanding. "Could you pass me my knapsack please?"

Tiern hesitated, then reached to release the bag from its tether on Faolan's side. Handing it to Coventry, he waited, expecting her to remove something from it. But she merely hugged it to her. "Did you want something from it?" he asked finally.

"No." She looked at him and smiled. "I just want to hold it. It makes me feel secure."

"It will be much more awkward to carry that way."

"I do not mind," she responded in the Thadonian tongue.

Shrugging, Tiern mounted Faolan, settling Coventry comfortably on his lap. With all that had happened, he never had gotten her a mount of her own as he had promised. Yet, at this moment, he was glad of that fact. He wanted her close to him. Looking to his right, he observed Singai, mounted on her dyre, her eyes closed in concentration. Slowly, she externalized her aura, subduing it to a dark grayish tint, until it became a wavering camouflage that continued to expand until it shielded even her mount. Glancing further back, Tiern saw that Juste, Loran and Modoc, too, were cloaking themselves behind the fluctuating protection of their auras. It was a dubious concealment, for the enemy had no doubt observed the transformation. Yet, as the *Sotah* moved they would make difficult targets, harmonizing with the landscape like shimmering mirages.

Tiern faced forward. Had it not been for the gravity of the situation they now faced, he would have smiled at the expression he glimpsed on Coventry's wide-eyed profile as she sat before him. Tiern closed his eyes, concentrating on creating the wavering facade which he hoped would make them less plausible marks. The auras took quite a bit of energy to generate, but once in place they could be maintained by subliminal attention. The task completed, he and his companions moved forward, into the gorge, into the jaws of the trap.

Coventry hugged the knapsack to her chest. She didn't have a clue what Trace's friends had done to make themselves into rippling shadows. She assumed that she and Trace, too, appeared no more substantial than heat-waves, but she noticed no appreciable difference in her outlook, and she wasn't going to attempt to resolve that particular puzzle right now. She was more concerned with how she was going to manage to extricate the illegal blaster from its concealment in her luggage if she needed it. She considered simply withdrawing the weapon openly, but suspecting that Trace's loyalty to Thadonian law would compel him to confiscate it, she abandoned the idea. Surreptitiously, she ran her hands over the bag, attempting to discern the placement of the weapon. There! At least she knew where it was.

She studied her surroundings. Beneath the feet of the dyre, the grass of the meadow had given way to pinkish sand. She turned her eyes to the jagged sloping walls of rock that rose on each side of them. She couldn't see anyone. Yet, if Trace thought they were in danger, she was certain they were. A chill ran up her spine. She hadn't liked the appearance of this stone barrier from the instant she'd laid eyes on it.

Suddenly, what appeared to be a brilliant ball of light exploded in front of them. The dyre reared in fright. The shimmering shadows that had cloaked the *Sotah* dissipated. Before Coventry could do more than gasp, men began to drop from the rocks on either side of them, some of them jumping almost thirty feet without apparent injury to themselves. How could they do that? She felt herself grasped from behind as Trace swung her from the saddle and deposited her in the shelter of an enormous boulder.

"Stay out of sight," he ordered. And then, weapon in hand, he was gone.

Coventry didn't waste time. She had seen the *Dalig* descend on them. She knew that her companions were drastically outnumbered. Probably by as much as six to one. Recklessly throwing the contents of the knapsack onto the ground, she removed the blaster and ripped it from its protective wrapping. Triggering the switch to activate it, she raised herself onto her knees and peered over the top of the boulder.

A melee of human forms confronted her, yet the scene seemed eerily hushed. The only sound was the ringing clash of blades meeting blades, for neither the *Dalig* nor the *Sotah* were vocal in their attacks. She hesitated, racked by indecision as she tried to differentiate the deep purplish-blue *Dalig* clothing from the black worn by the *Sotah*. The shadowed canyon made the task difficult. Hell! She studied the chaotic scene, trying to separate friend from enemy. There had to be a means of identifying them. The bands! The *Sotah* wore either red or, in Singai's case, blue bands about their foreheads. But the *Dalig*'s headbands were white.

A scream of terrible agony ripped the air. Fear clenched Coventry's heart in its icy grip. Someone wearing the attire of the *Sotah* had fallen. Trace? The ranks of the Dalig parted fleetingly and she saw Trace fighting on, his back to a large boulder as he faced six sword-wielding warriors. She had to help him! Raising the blaster, she aimed it at one of the *Dalig*.

Suddenly, her field of vision was blocked. She lifted her gaze. A *Dalig* stood on the boulder in front of her, his sword raised over his head as he fixed gleaming eyes on her. He was so close. In the next instant, she would die. Instinctively, she shifted the aim of the blaster slightly and pulled the trigger. Light flashed, blinding her. Something warm and sticky sprayed her face. She blinked, trying to clear spots of light from her vision. The *Dalig* was gone. She closed her mind to the sight of the blood and fragments of flesh that clung to the surface of the boulder. She couldn't fall apart. Not yet. They needed her. Trace needed her.

She focused on the ongoing battle. Without thought, she concentrated her gaze on a *Dalig* fighter, aimed her weapon and pulled the trigger. Although her eyes saw the carnage as the small light-grenade reached its target and exploded into thousands of cutting laser-like beams, the image did not trigger any emotion. One thought occupied her mind. Survive! There was no room for emotion.

Mechanically, she aimed at another *Dalig* and repeated the operation. Again and again. Distrustful of the blaster's force and sizable area of effect, she always focused on the *Dalig* furthest away from her *Sotah* companions. She glimpsed Singai fighting valiantly, her back to the wall of the canyon. In the next instant, she reduced the number of Singai's combatants by one.

Suddenly another scream rent the air. Her eyes raked the confusion, seeking its source. A *Dalig* fell. She caught a flicker of motion out of the corner of her eye. Three *Dalig* approached her from the left. She shifted her position and fired. One blast eliminated two of them who had moved much too closely together. One died, the other was incapacitated. The third launched his weapon. There was something strange about the way the sword flew. It seemed almost to correct its trajectory slightly. Reacting on instinct, Coventry fired at it. The center of force missed the smaller target, leaving it whole, but the residual energy propelled the weapon away. The man who'd thrown the weapon was almost upon her. She scrambled back, distancing herself from his grasping hands even as she fired the blaster again. A scarlet starburst of bloody matter rained in all directions. She backed away as the man fell. The sight and smell of his death penetrated the shell shielding her emotions. Bile rose in her throat and she choked it back, swinging away from the horrible spectacle. Her breath came harshly in her ears as she once again sought Trace.

For an instant she couldn't see him. Panic clawed at her stomach. A collection of *Dalig* fighters parted momentarily and she glimpsed Trace in their midst. But even as her eyes found him, she saw his weapon fly from his hand. He screamed agonizingly and slumped from sight.

"No-o." Even as she wailed denial, fear and boldness, hate and love took possession of her and she ran toward the band of warriors, firing indiscriminately into their midst. Once again her mind avoided awareness of the slaughter inflicted by her alien weapon. She had only one thought. Trace. And she shrieked his name over and over as she ran toward the spot where he'd fallen.

As she neared, she saw him lying motionless on the ground. "Oh, God. Trace?" He didn't respond. She tripped over the sprawling remains of a *Dalig* as she scrambled to his side. Blood. There was so much blood. Blood, thick and warm and slick, coated her hand as she placed it on his chest. Bright, red, frothy blood coated his lips as he exhaled. A wave of dizziness struck her with the force of a hammer as the ground upon which she knelt seemed to ripple with instability. The world began to spin. She couldn't faint now! She wouldn't! Squeezing her eyes closed, she took a deep trembling breath. The dizziness receded. She opened her eyes.

"Trace?" He lay still. Panic clawed at her. Then suddenly she saw him draw a breath. She didn't know what to do. She felt helpless. Tears rolled unchecked down her cheeks as she cradled his head on her lap. "Don't you die. You hear me. Don't die." The words became a litany of prayer.

Another howl of pain split the air. Coventry turned tear-filled eyes on the battle still being waged. Three *Sotah* remained; still fighting dauntlessly against four to one odds. Damn the *Dalig!* Damn them to hell! Drawing strength from her grief and hate, Coventry raised the blaster once more and sighted through tear-blurred eyes at the *Dalig* warriors furthest from the *Sotah* she wanted to aid. She missed two shots, shooting the rocks beyond the fighters. Furious with herself for her failure when the weapon she used had such a scattering effect that missing should have been virtually impossible, she rubbed the wetness from her eyes, took a deep breath, and aimed more carefully. She didn't miss.

Finally it was over. The word retreat was apparently beyond the code of the *Dalig* society, for they had continued to fight and die down to the last man and woman. Juste had taken the final life, his sword piercing the heart of a man who would admit defeat only through death. The sound of his scream of agony as it echoed from the towering rock walls was one that would stay with Coventry for a long time. Now, Singai and Modoc knelt with her at Trace's side. Dazed, Coventry did not notice that the numerous superficial wounds they had suffered continued to close and heal before her eyes. Her thoughts were all for Trace. She lay the blaster aside and waited silently, as directed, but impatiently as Singai and Modoc each laid their hands upon Trace and closed their eyes.

Trace moaned and opened his eyes, fixing his gaze on Coventry. Singai and Modoc did not move, did not acknowledge the improvement. He murmured something.

"What?" she whispered, not wanting to disturb whatever it was the two *Sotah* were doing to help him. She brushed the hair back from his brow.

"Ven-Jikan." His words were barely audible and they didn't make any sense. Forever friend? Was he telling her he was dying?

She hastened to reassure him, although she was none too certain herself. "You are going to be all right."

"My sword. Bring me my sword. Quickly."

Not understanding, but sensing his urgency and wanting to console him, Coventry rose. She had only seen the weapon a couple of times, and never closely. She remembered that it had looked as though it had been crafted of gold. There were many weapons scattered about, but they all appeared to be silver. How was she to find it? She scanned the area, moving slowly in a widening circle around the area. Abruptly, off to her right she noticed a golden glitter. That must be it!

Hastening toward the spot, she discovered the weapon she thought must be Trace's, but it appeared to be firmly wedged into a crevice between two stones. She grasped the handle. Immediately a sensation she had never felt assailed her, disorienting her. It was as though she was being touched, a contact that was not physical. Gritting her teeth to control the strange light-headedness, she tugged on the weapon. It wouldn't budge. The boulder must have shifted onto it after it had fallen. Sitting down, she braced her feet against the stone, pushing it as she simultaneously pulled on the sword. With a scrape of metal against stone, it came loose.

You are Coventry. I have seen you in Rainon's thoughts. How is he? The words blazed in Coventry's mind more clearly than the spoken word ever could, and yet her senses tried to reject them as impossible, to rationalize them. There was no one near who could have spoken. Oh, God! She was hallucinating. Stress had unhinged her mind. She felt as though the sword was talking to her.

I am talking to you. And you are not hallucinating. How is Rainon? In instant response, the picture of Trace as she had seen him scant minutes ago flashed in her mind. *Take me to him quickly, or he will die. His brothers will not be able to give him enough strength to heal such an injury.*

Though comprehension eluded her, Coventry moved hastily back toward where Trace lay flanked by the kneeling forms of his *Sotah* companions. How could the sword possibly save Trace's life? It didn't make sense.

I am not a simple sword as you think of me. I, like all the blades of the Sotah and, unfortunately, the Dalig, am an intelligent being. We are constructed from sentient metal. In your terms, I would be called an alien life-form. Non-human but intelligent. Our existence is based upon the communication of thought and the manipulation of essence. On your world, I believe the term is psychic. One of the abilities we possess is the capability of healing.

Although the telepathic communication took place almost instantly, much more swiftly than a verbal conversation, Coventry had almost completed the few yards to return to Trace's side. The sword was a psychic healer? Why then had Singai and Modoc not searched for it rather than . . . doing whatever it was they were doing?

They are Sotah. Unused to her thoughts being received and responded to, Coventry jumped. *The Sotah have a mental bond with their weapon/companions. Touching a weapon that is bonded to another can disrupt the link with one's own blade.* Coventry knelt at Trace's side, saw the bright red blood still frothing at his lips with each exhalation. *Put me in direct contact with the flesh of his chest. Quickly.*

Panic once again threatened to overwhelm Coventry as she sensed the sword's urgency. With the sight of Trace's ashen face compounding her fear, she tore at the fastenings on his shirt until it opened. Only when she had laid the weapon on his chest did Singai and Modoc open their eyes.

Singai looked at Coventry. "He will live, I think. Stay with him. We must aid Juste with Loran's rites of passage."

Coventry, with nothing to do but wait, found herself surveying the scene of the battle. There were *Dalig* bodies everywhere, and she was responsible for the death of half of them. Yet she felt no remorse for killing them, merely horror that it had been necessary. She was not the person she had thought herself to be. That frightened her a little. Did that make her a bad person? Was she less principled than she believed herself to be? She sighed and closed her eyes to the sight, focusing her thoughts instead on the man she loved. If her will alone could help him survive, then he most definitely would, for at this moment there was nothing in the universe she wanted more.

Chapter Sixteen

Trace, grasping the sword he called Ven-Jikan in his hand, had allowed Coventry to help him to a more comfortable spot. His breathing was still shallow, but not labored. As he reclined, weak and pale, against the smooth face of a boulder, continuing to recuperate with the help of Ven-Jikan, Coventry sponged the worst of the blood from his body with water from a strangely shaped canteen she'd found on the dyre. When she had completed the task to the best of her ability, she cleansed herself, scrubbing vigorously until all hint of gore was gone. Yet she still felt soiled. Her body was racked by uncontrollable tremors and she wanted nothing more than to curl into a ball and cry. But she couldn't. Trace needed her now and she had to be strong. Battling her errant emotions, she settled herself once more at his side.

Although no longer fearful for his life, she nevertheless kept a concerned eye on him. He had always seemed so strong and vital, almost indomitable. To see him now so weak was a frightening and sobering experience. Somehow, Trace had become part of her. And she knew, without a doubt, that she *did* love him—with a love as certain and as indestructible as that her parents had shared. She didn't know precisely where this knowledge came from. It simply *was*. And whether her future was on Earth or Thadonia, she would be less without him.

Love was a strange emotion, she reflected. It made you whole, a more complete person, while at the same time creating a dependency on another human being that was almost paralyzing in its intensity. She had never seen herself as a particularly strong person, but she had always prided herself on her self-reliance. Now, this need for Trace, the sense that he had become essential to her life, made her feel as though she was balanced on the edge of a precipice. She was terrified. There were so many unanswered questions still surrounding their relationship.

The sound of muted conversation attracted her attention, and she raised her eyes to observe the three *Sotah* who remained hale. No one had said anything to her concerning her use of the illegal blaster, yet she felt certain they discussed it now. Juste glanced at her several times while examining the bodies of a number of *Dalig*, but he was too far away for her to perceive the expression on his face. He spoke to his companions, gesturing with his head in Coventry's direction. What were they saying? For the first time, Coventry thought to wonder what the Thadonian punishment for breaking the law might be. The *Sotah* were, after all, a law enforcement body.

One of the dyre tethered nearby made a noise in its throat and she glanced at the beasts before automatically returning her gaze to the three on the opposite side of the gorge. Juste, Singai and Modoc spoke together for a time, and then began to collect the bodies of their enemies, placing them near the base of the stone wall. Coventry felt that she should offer to help them with the task, but when she looked toward two of the bodies which hadn't yet been collected her stomach heaved and she had to close her eyes, drawing deep breaths in order to settle it again. She couldn't do it. She just *couldn't*. Now that the insulating factors of adrenaline and survival instinct had been removed from the equation, fortitude had abandoned her.

Feeling guilty, Coventry settled back. She looked instead toward the body the *Sotah* had laid out with such reverence in a shady area on this side of the gorge. Loran—he seemed so young. She hadn't even had the opportunity to get to know him. His death was an obscenity that offended her sense of propriety. Although she couldn't mourn for him as a person she knew and cared about, she grieved for the unfairness of a situation that had demanded he give up his life.

A shadow fell across her, making her jump even as she looked up and identified the owner as Modoc. He cleared his throat uncomfortably as though uncertain as to how to begin. "There are . . . twenty-eight dead."

Coventry nodded, watching him expectantly. "We cannot cover them by hand," he continued. "It would take too much time. Yet *Sotah* regulations forbid us to leave any body, even that of an enemy, to be desecrated by scavengers except in extreme circumstances." He paused expectantly, but Coventry still had no idea what he was getting at.

"Go on," she said.

He cleared his throat again. "We were wondering if it would be possible for you to use your . . . weapon on the wall of stone . . . to cause a rock slide which would protect the bodies."

"Oh." Could the blaster perform the task he wanted? Probably. "Of course. I will try." After checking Trace to ensure that he slept soundly and comfortably, Coventry rose to retrieve the blaster and follow Modoc.

Uncertain as to exactly what effect the blaster would have when fired consistently at stone, Coventry positioned herself at quite a distance from the wall. As she checked the charge on the weapon, she could sense the presence of the *Sotah* behind her. Although the power level had been dangerously low, the solar collector had recharged the weapon to almost half-strength while it had been idle. Deliberately keeping her gaze focused on the wall before her and not the bodies at its base, Coventry raised the weapon and fired. A small avalanche of fragmented rock resulted, but it was not nearly large enough to perform the task required. She hesitated. At this rate, there wouldn't be enough stored power to accomplish a rock slide.

She studied the black face of the stone wall. More than thirty feet above, perched on the edge of the gorge, some large boulders looked as if they would fall into the canyon with the slightest encouragement. The wall was slightly sloped. If she managed to dislodge the boulders, they would almost certainly roll down the slight incline and cause the desired effect. But did the blaster have enough range to hit them? She wouldn't know until she tried. Backing up a little further for safety's sake, she aimed the weapon at the base of the precarious boulders and fired.

For an instant nothing happened. Then a small clatter of stone rained down, and slowly one of the large boulders began to totter, gradually tipping. Suddenly it fell. Coventry's eyes widened and she swallowed. Stars above, what had she done? The stone was enormous, much larger than it had seemed from below when perched reasonably securely above. She turned. "Run," she yelled at her three companions. Hastily following her own advice, she followed them as they raced for the opposite side of the canyon, leaping over obstructions as they ran.

The noise became almost deafening. She tripped. The blaster flew from her grip as she caught herself, but she couldn't risk scrambling after it. Reaching Trace, Coventry knelt over him, shielding him with her body as well as possible while she wrapped her arms about her head and cringed. Dust choked her as the din gradually abated. Slowly, she raised her head.

The air was filled with clouds of choking dust and sand. The three *Sotah* stood, backs to her, staring across the gorge. Coventry rose to join them. There was no longer any sign of the *Dalig*. "Is . . . is everyone all right?"

Modoc turned to face her. Had the situation not been so serious, she might have laughed at his expression. His mouth open wide, he stared at her with wide disbelieving eyes. "*Kwoa?*"

"Is everyone all right? The dyre?"

"Yes . . . Yes. Everyone is fine. The dyre are uninjured."

"What manner of weapon is that?" Singai asked. Her appearance was only marginally less incredulous than Modoc's.

"It is called a blaster."

"And you brought it from Earth?"

Coventry shifted uncomfortably. "Well . . . yes." She felt compelled to explain. "It was concealed in my luggage without my knowledge."

"May I examine it?" Juste asked.

"I . . . I am afraid I dropped it while we were running. It must be around somewhere." She scanned the area, but so much dust had settled that, even had the blaster been lying in plain sight, she wouldn't have been able to discern it from the sandy surface.

"*Magar!*" Singai stared at her. "We must find it. If such a weapon fell into the hands of the *Dalig*—" She trailed off, leaving the balance of the sentence unspoken. Yet, no one present had any difficulty deducing her meaning.

For fully half an hour, they searched. The newly fallen stone littering the area made the task difficult. Finally, Juste called, "I have found it."

The others hurried to his side, joining him as he stared down. It was the blaster, all right. What was left of it. Apparently one of the boulders had fallen or rolled directly over it, for the weapon was now in a number of distinctly misshapen pieces. They stared at it silently for a moment. Eventually Modoc spoke. "I guess we do not have to worry about the *Dalig* finding it."

"It would seem not," Singai agreed. A moment later she sighed and turned away. "We must attend to Loran."

Singai knelt, head bowed, at Loran's side. Opposite her, Juste and Modoc mirrored her position. The dyre had been set to guard. It was time to begin the rites of passage. They would officially confirm Loran's death to the priests; and the whole of the *Sotah* would mourn for the loss of a brother and his symbiotic companion, the blade he had christened Tanac-kin, Gold-Dancer.

Singai heard the deep cleansing breaths taken by her companions and forced herself to focus on the difficult task at hand. She took a deep breath and purged all disruptive thought from her mind on the exhalation. Slowly, she focused inward, centering on the peace and serenity within herself. Visualizing the process as she had been taught, she gradually managed to summon the energy she needed. Luminous green, it rose wraithlike from her body to blend with Modoc's blazing copper and Juste's muted violet. As the separate energies twined and twisted, becoming one form, one distinct color, the *Sotah* became one in purpose.

The force became elongated, extending over the inert body of their dead companion. Pulsing with life, it hovered, luring the residue of spirit to it. Another energy began to rise from Loran's body. Sluggish and lethargic, colorless without Loran's conscious control, it merged with the energies blanketing his physical form. Singai sighed mentally. The major part of the task was done. Now, were a *Dalig* to discover Loran's body, there was nothing, absolutely nothing, they could learn from it. Loran's spirit was free to seek its rest.

The *Sotah* focused on the far distant Kalos Mountain. The transmuted force rose from the body and streaked away guided by the instinct of the *Sotah*. Endless minutes passed. Suddenly a delicate butterfly touch caressed her mind. She opened her mind, granting knowledge of all that had occurred to the priests, knowing that her companions did the same. Almost immediately, she sensed their grief and compassion, rage and disbelief. *The brotherhood will unite in their sorrow.* Singai heard the expected directive. It was always so. Whenever a brother of the *Sotah* died, the priests would sense his death. They would wait a time for confirmation of their knowledge, but if it did not come they would know that the brother had died alone. Then it was the priests who would initiate the rites of passage, and someone would be sent to retrieve the body so that it could be properly prepared and the residual guardian-spirit freed.

Singai waited. Gradually she sensed the sphere of contact expanding. Others had joined the nexus, nebulous and unidentifiable, but tangible. She looked to Rainon. Would the priests bring him into the connection? He did not yet have the strength to maintain contact on his own; the priests would have to do it for him. Yes, she was certain the priests would aid him. The sharing of distress was important. Grief must be confronted and dealt with. Even now she sensed the lessening of her own burden.

Coventry watched the *Sotah*. They had been sitting motionless for well over an hour. What were they doing? It was late afternoon. Would they camp here tonight? She looked at Trace. He wouldn't be able to travel far in any case, but the thought of spending the night here in the canyon unsettled her. The shadows lengthened. The tint of the violet sky deepened. Shuddering, Coventry purposefully turned her thoughts to other things.

She wondered how Dalton was doing. She missed him terribly, which seemed strange in view of the fact that they had hardly seen each other when they lived in the same city. But at that time, she had known that she could contact him at any opportunity. Now, she had to face the fact that she might never see her brother again. The thought hurt. Yet she knew that Dalton was where he wanted to be . . . on Earth among the Fringers he'd always felt an affinity for. And she . . . she was where she wanted to be too. Thadonia had already begun to become home; it was where Trace was.

Half an hour later, the *Sotah* rose from their vigilant positions around Loran's body and began to cover it with loose rocks. After checking on Trace once more—he slept soundly and comfortably—Coventry moved to aid them in their task. They worked silently, companionably. When the duty was done, Coventry swept her long braid back over her shoulder, dusted her hands off, and turned to face the others. "It will be dark soon. Are we . . . That is, where are we going to camp?"

Juste responded. "Once we are through the canyon, there is a meadow not too far distant. We will try to reach it before full darkness."

"What about Tra . . . um, Rainon?" Coventry stuttered over her error in Trace's Thadonian identity. "Will he be able to ride?"

"He should have regained much of his strength by now," Singai responded. "If we help him onto the dyre, you should be able to support him with little difficulty."

"Oh." Coventry frowned thoughtfully. In order to support Trace in the manner Singai suggested, she would have to sit behind him. Trace was tall and broad; she wouldn't be able to see a thing. Even if she managed to determine how to guide Faolan, how would she accomplish the task when she couldn't see? She voiced her doubts.

"The dyre is not difficult to guide. We can show you," Modoc said. "But I think Rainon must sit behind you as before. If he has not the strength to maintain his seat, we will secure him in some way."

Coventry nodded.

"Let us make haste then," Juste remarked, moving toward the dyre.

They had descended a rocky escarpment and snaked their way through a small forest of trees to reach the meadow. Now in the lengthening shadows of early evening, Coventry stared at the meadow in dismay. It was occupied. Fully occupied. There didn't appear to be an inch of ground to spare.

"It is a Vaileun caravan," Trace said from behind her. His voice sounded husky with weariness. "They will allow us to camp among them."

"Are you certain?" The questioner was Modoc.

Coventry sensed Trace's nod behind her. "They come this way often. I know them. We must ride in slowly to give the camp guard plenty of time to assess us."

Hesitantly, the *Sotah* nudged their mounts forward. As they neared the camp, they were met by a guard of six armed men. "What do you seek?" a tall brawny man asked.

"Fresh water and a place to camp," Juste responded.

The spokesman observed them suspiciously.

"Balar, do you not know me?" Trace asked from his position behind Coventry. "Has that poison you are so fond of swilling finally begun to rot your brain?"

Coventry stiffened. She certainly hoped Balar remembered him because she couldn't see a man forgiving such an inflammatory comment from anyone but a friend. The man squinted at them in the gathering gloom. "Rainon? Is that you?" He strode boldly forward. "It is you. *Magar!* What happened to you? You look like my brother-by-marriage at festival's end."

"That good?"

The man laughed boisterously and slapped

Trace on the back so solidly that Coventry felt him jar against her. "That *bad*. Come." He expanded his gaze to the other *Sotah*. "Come, all of you. You are welcome."

"You are too kind." Trace's voice sounded a trifle more labored despite the obvious wryness of his statement. Balar laughed uproariously in response, oblivious to the pain behind the comment. Coventry felt a strong desire to clout the thick-skulled dolt over the head. Couldn't he see that the friendly blow he'd administered had caused Trace discomfort?

Balar led them to another area of the camp, near the periphery. At his shouted order, a large tentlike structure was hastily vacated for the use of the *Sotah* guests. Within moments, with the aid of enthusiastic Vaileun boys, the dyre were tethered, relieved of their burdens, and watered. Balar excused himself to return to his duties and Singai, Modoc, and Juste took themselves off, intent upon whatever personal tasks demanded their attention.

Trace, gaining strength by the moment now, disdained the suggestion that he rest in the tent. Coventry helped him settle himself on the ground where he could observe the camp activities. Although she felt in desperate need of a wash and a change of clothing, she didn't want to leave Trace alone just yet. Sitting companionably at his side, she observed the Vaileun people. They appeared to be a naturally raucous people capable of extracting tremendous enjoyment from the simplest things in life. Many of the women wore colorful skirts and blouses similar to the outfit Trace had purchased and identified as being of Vaileun origin.

Shortly, two young men appeared around the

315

side of the tent carrying buckets. They deposited the pails near the entrance. "We thought to provide you with water for washing, Imnana," one of them said to Coventry.

Coventry rose; her lips curled into a delighted smile as she considered the allure of bathing. "Thank you very much." In reaction to her expression of warm appreciation the young man flushed and backed away. His friend clapped him heartily on the back and said something Coventry couldn't hear. Then, laughing, they raced off between the tents, shoving and pushing each other in youthful exuberance.

"I think you have stolen a heart," Trace observed with twinkling eyes.

Coventry sighed. "If I remember correctly, young love is often fickle. By nightfall, no doubt, his heart will be in his eyes as he stares at some beautiful, young Vaileun enchantress."

Trace laughed. "You are probably right."

"I think I will take advantage of the water they so thoughtfully provided though. I'd like to change." She picked up their packs and entered the tent. With surprise she realized that the interior of the transient structure was actually divided into five chambers. Four curtained doorways opened off of the central area which stretched from the entrance to the rear of the tent. Each of the four openings revealed a private chamber equipped with a large thick mattress. The central chamber contained a low table burdened by a variety of containers and flanked by numerous colorful cushions. The accommodations looked very comfortable.

Choosing one of the chambers, Coventry deposited the packs and went back out to retrieve one of the buckets. Then, after finding a large, shallow, claylike container in the main area that she thought would serve admirably as a washbasin, she secured the curtained flap and set about rejuvenating herself.

Against the backdrop of the velvety night sky, the moons glowed, their luminous radiance competing with the brilliance of the firelight. Shortly after dusk, the entire Vaileun populace had gravitated toward the large central area of the camp for the evening meal. Following Trace's lead, Coventry and the others had availed themselves of the generous Vaileun hospitality and partaken of a delicious meal. Now, the meal finished and the bowls collected for cleaning, people sat back to converse and relax. Coventry smoothed the beautiful red fabric of the Vaileun skirt she had donned as she watched the children run freely through the camp. Their high-pitched squeals and boisterous activity seemed to be not merely tolerated, but welcomed by the adults who looked on their antics with indulgent, and sometimes wistful, eyes.

Suddenly a hoard of energetic young people approached Trace. "Will you sing for us, Rainon?" one little girl of perhaps six or seven years asked, her voice shrill in order to be heard over the chatter of her companions.

"Tell us a story please?" a young man appealed. He appeared to be the oldest of the group, probably about eleven years.

The babble of demands and requests escalated. Sing? Story? Play? Coventry stared at Trace in amazement. These children did not fear him in the least. Despite the fact that they obviously knew him, she had expected the Vaileun children to be wary of him. After all, his stony countenance and unapproachable mien had terrified her in the beginning. She observed him as he smiled and tweaked the well-fed belly of a young boy. Suddenly she saw him with new eyes. This was not the same man who had introduced himself as Trace all those weeks ago on Earth. His manner had changed. He was more relaxed and open than Trace had been. He smiled more readily. Looking back, she realized that his disposition had begun to improve the moment they set down on Thadonia; it was then that she'd first heard him laugh. The man she watched now, teasing the Vaileun children, was Rainon. The name Trace no longer suited him for Trace was only a component of the personality of the man. Yet neither could Coventry bring herself to think of him as Rainon. Rainon, too, was only a part of him, the societal element. Rainon was the face he showed to the world outside his circle of loved ones. To Coventry, he was Tiern, as he had been initially all those long weeks ago on Earth before she'd even known the significance of the Thadonian birth-name. And now, she was beginning to see aspects of his personality that she had not noted before.

Coventry could only stare as Rainon settled two children on his lap and organized the others around him in a semicircle on the ground as he prepared to satisfy their demands for a story. Regarding him now, she wondered how she ever could have doubted that he would want his child. This man loved children. But the new knowledge only served to deepen her confusion. She instinctively felt that, if he learned of the child she carried, he would want it no matter how he felt about her. Yet, loving him, Coventry wanted his love. Somehow, she would have to prevent him from discovering the existence of the child until she could be certain of his feelings for *her*. She frowned, suddenly remembering the appraising gaze she had intercepted earlier. Did Tiern already know of the child? Oh, hell! She still didn't know what to think or do.

Absorbed by her thoughts, Coventry did not notice the passage of time or the gradually escalating noise level until a roll of drumbeats and a vociferous cheer attracted her attention. Standing in the cleared section which had been the cooking area just a short time ago, a Vaileun man juggled six spherical objects. Looking around, Coventry was startled to discover that the children had gone. She, Tiern, and the *Sotah* now sat at the forefront of a large circle of people surrounding the juggler. Every inch of available ground, to a depth of several people, was occupied.

"The Vaileun people are renowned for the quality of their entertainment," Tiern said quietly near her ear. "Watch." He nudged her and Coventry switched her gaze back to the performer. The Vaileun juggler had begun to perform some quite amazing feats of acrobatics without losing control of a single airborne item.

As the juggler left the improvised arena, the entertainment continued without pause, the space immediately filled with twelve men wearing colorful costumes. The tempo of the drums increased and was joined by the vibrant sound of stringed instruments. Coventry stared as the men began to dance. She had never seen anything quite like it. She was entranced by their energetic and agile movements. Primitive! That was the word that came to mind to describe the sight. And yet, it was more, so much more. The combination of sound, color and movement, blended so skillfully, told a story of pain, suffering, and the resilience of the human spirit. In the end, as the beat of the drums and the tempo of the music intensified, the entire audience was drawn into the triumphant moment of victory. Although she had no idea what history the dance had reenacted, there were tears in Coventry's eyes as it came to a finale and she heartily echoed the roar of appreciation from the viewers.

The next performer was a magician who performed some quite amazing sleight-of-hand feats. Then, a group of young men, whose dance included whirling, flaming brands like batons, entered the area. Next, a chorus of young women who sang a beautiful, haunting melody of love and loss. Finally, there was a pause.

Coventry turned to Tiern. "Do they perform like this all the time?"

He nodded. "Very often. The Vaileun caravans do a lot of trading for goods in the cities, but much of their income is the result of their reputation as outstanding performers. What we are seeing tonight is one of their rehearsals."

A group of women wearing colorful, flowing skirts and dainty sandals entered the circle. Slow, lilting music suffused the night and the women danced. Bangles on their arms and ankles clicked rhythmically in time to their graceful movements. Subtly the tempo of the music began to increase. Arms arched over their heads, long hair flowing around them like banners, the women leapt, twirled and bent like reeds in a current. Coventry watched them enviously. For the first time since she had left Earth, she truly missed performing. Although dancing had been only a part of her career, she had always loved it. Unconsciously, her feet began to tap in time to the music.

Abruptly the synchronization of the dancers' movements was abandoned. They separated. Moving to the edge of the circle, the women began to interpret the music individually for the audience. One of them danced not three feet away. Midnight hair flowed around her lithe form like a veil, concealing and revealing the subtle movements of her body at precisely the right moments. She took the music and made it her own, communicating her interpretation of the melody so well that Coventry could feel each emotion.

The tempo of the music altered again, becoming an intensely primal expression of life and passion. The dancer moved closer. Her gaze, radiant with excitement, met Coventry's. She looked at Coventry's tapping feet and smiled as she extended her hand. "Come," she mouthed.

Coventry hesitated. Was she being invited to join the dance? Oh, she wanted to. She ached to lose herself in the music. But would it be acceptable? She looked at Tiern. He smiled and made a shooing motion. It was all the encouragement she needed. Rising, she joined the dancer and eagerly observed the basic steps of the dance. It had been so long since she'd danced and the music was so alien that for the initial few moments she felt gauche next to the incredibly lissome and graceful Vaileun. And then, the feeling that had prompted her to become a performer in the first place came to her rescue. It was indescribable. Her entire body tingled and the music became a visual experience. A tropical storm raged in her blood; the surf pounded in her ears and the swaying palms became her limbs. Coventry danced.

*   *   *

The indulgent pride Tiern had felt as Coventry first joined the dancers gradually transformed to amazement. He had never seen her perform on Earth, but based on the extremely automated type of entertainment he had seen provided there, he expected whatever natural talent she might have had to be suppressed beneath rigid training. At best, he had anticipated her performance tonight to be a perfect emulation of that of the Vaileun woman. But, after the initial minutes of the dance in which she had learned the basic steps of the dance, Coventry's body had begun its own rendition of the music. Tiern could not take his eyes from her.

Her fair loveliness, highlighted by luminous moonlight and the flickering brilliance of the fires, shone conspicuously among the dusky Vaileun beauties. A product of her dissimilar culture, her performance was unique, but it lacked for nothing in expression. In fact, it communicated a sensuality and provocative enticement rarely found in a Vaileun performance. Her swirling golden hair, ignited by the firelight, seemed almost to become lashing tongues of flame as she moved toward him. Her gaze caught his, holding it captive, and he knew she danced for him. Suddenly, she threw her head back in a gesture of abandon and Tiern was reminded poignantly of the first time he had seen her make that gesture. She had ridden him with the same passionate wildness she portrayed in her dance. And suddenly he understood why Coventry, untrained in Vaileun dance, had drawn all eyes. She made love to the music. Just watching her, the caress of the music became an almost tangible touch. Yet, her dance was neither lewd nor obscene, merely subtly suggestive of eroticism.

He doubted that Coventry was even aware of the sexual nature of her interpretation of the music. But he was. He was hard and hot with wanting her and he was suddenly impatient for the evening's entertainment to draw to a close.

Minutes later, the music stopped and the women left the central arena. Coventry, smiling with exhilaration, rejoined him. Tiern noticed the appreciative gazes of several men lingering on her and placed a proprietary arm about her shoulders. The need within him to make it known that Coventry was not available surprised him. It seemed that, where Coventry was concerned, he was developing some very monogamous tendencies of his own. The thought of sharing her, with *anyone,* made his gut seethe with jealousy. She was unique; more vigorous and alive than any woman he had ever known. She had stolen his heart and he could never let her go. She was *his.* Coventry leaned back against him as a chorus of singers began to perform and, concealed by the shadows of the night, he tenderly nuzzled her ear. *Magar!* He loved her more each day. How was such a thing possible?

Finally the entertainment provided by their Vaileun hosts came to an end and people began to leave. "Come," he said to Coventry as he rose and helped her to her feet. His arm about her waist, he led her off. So great was his need to possess her that he had already decided upon a location for their lovemaking. He had concluded that the tent would be unsuitable. The presence of his *Sotah* companions just beyond the thin fabric walls would stifle their ardor. But, the small clearing just inside the forest that ringed the meadow would be perfect.

They passed beyond the periphery of the camp.

"Where are we going?" Coventry asked.

"Into the forest."

He sensed her sudden alarm as she looked at him. "Why? Are there not wild animals there at night?"

"Some; but few of them are large enough to be harmful and fewer still are actually dangerous. You need not fear."

"But why—?" She cringed against him as they entered the thick undergrowth and passed beneath the first of the large trees.

He stopped and looked down into the pale oval of her face. "Because I want you."

"You want . . . ? Oh. Could we not . . . I mean, what about the tent?"

"The tent is occupied by our traveling companions. Come." Grasping her firmly about the wrist, he moved on without giving her any further opportunity to object.

A faint rustling in the undergrowth attracted Coventry's attention and she had to clench her teeth to suppress an inclination to moan. Hell! She wanted him too. She only had to look at him to want him. But somehow, the dark unknown quantity of the forest detracted from the mood. Her damnable imagination was running wild. As far as she was concerned, if he didn't want to make love to her with his companions nearby, she could wait.

"Rainon—?"

"What?" He sounded distinctly impatient.

Coventry sighed. If there was anything to be really concerned about, he would know it, wouldn't he? "Nothing." Her voice was barely audible as she stared at the ominous black shadows. Suddenly he halted.

"Here. Just as I remembered it."

Coventry looked beyond him to the small clearing bathed in silvery moonlight. It didn't look that bad. The celestial light dispelled the eerie shadows of the forest. In fact it looked rather inviting. Still, Coventry found herself facing a moment of awkwardness. This was the first time in their relationship that she and Tiern had actually planned to make love. Always before, their encounters had begun as passionate confrontations. The newness of the situation and the strangeness of the setting had combined to make her feel slightly off balance. She discovered that she didn't know quite how to begin.

Tiern left her side to walk across the small clearing. Turning to face her, he began unfastening his shirt. His dark countenance appeared almost sinister in the indistinct illumination of the moons. His dark eyes, glittering with desire and purpose, mesmerized her. Her breath quickened in anticipation as she observed him. Whisking off his shirt, he bent to spread it carefully on the ground and then straightened to face her once more.

"Come here, Coventry." His husky baritone sent shivers up her spine and her legs moved instinctively toward him. She stared at his wide, muscular chest with its covering of silky, black hair. Stars, but he was the handsomest man she had ever seen. She was vaguely aware that somewhere along the line her opinion of his appearance had altered, but she was too overpowered by the passion-charged atmosphere to care.

She reached him and, looking up into that glittering gaze, automatically ran her palms over his magnificent chest. In the next instant, his arms were crushing her against him as he bent his head to envelop her lips in a devouring kiss. The electricity arching between them ignited into a roaring blaze and Coventry matched the fury of Tiern's desire with a feral avarice of her own. She grappled frantically with the fastenings on Tiern's trousers as he, more expertly, dealt with the encumbrance of her clothing. As each article of her apparel left her body, she struggled to press every inch of exposed flesh against the fiery heat of his body. She already ached to feel him inside her and he'd done nothing more than kiss her.

He was lifting her, lowering her onto the shirt he'd spread on the ground and falling over her. She gloried in the sensation of his body crushing hers. She was conscious of the slight prickle of grass against her thighs and the cool breath of the night air against skin left exposed by the heat of his body. She had no need of preliminaries tonight, and she tried to communicate her need as she twisted and turned in his arms, pulling him more tightly to her, wrapping her legs about his narrow hips as she urged him on. The only sounds she heard in the night were those of their breathing, harsh and gasping as they sought release. His hands were on her breasts teasing the already taut nipples until they ached. She felt him, hot and eager, against her and her hips surged upward in welcome. In the instant of their joining, he reclaimed her lips and Coventry gasped anew at the pleasure that rocked through her. Her fingers clenched on his buttocks as she urged him to a frenzy to match her own.

Coventry lay in the crook of Tiern's arm as they stared contentedly at the night sky. "Tiern?"

"Hmmm?"

"What is a Chayah?" The question had been bothering her ever since that morning in the warehouse when he had accused her of acting like one, but embarrassment had prevented her from asking.

"A Chayah is a mammal similar to one of Earth's canines. Why?"

His response hadn't told her a damn thing, and now, in order to discover more, she would have to remind Tiern of that humiliating morning. She wished she hadn't brought it up. She felt him shift to observe her.

"Why?" he repeated.

Coventry felt herself flushing and was thankful for the darkness. "Why do they rub themselves against stones?"

He stared at her uncomprehendingly for a moment and then slowly she saw the flash of his teeth in the moonlight as he smiled. "Oh, that. When the female Chayah is in season, she rubs herself against stones in her territory. Her scent is a powerful attraction to roving males and signifies her readiness to reproduce."

"Oh." Coventry frowned. "That is not a very flattering comparison."

Tiern shrugged. "Depends on your point of view, I suppose." They fell silent for a time, simply enjoying the night music of Thadonia's nocturnal creatures and the panorama of its night sky.

"Coventry?"

"Mmhmm?"

"I think we should marry soon."

Coventry's heart leapt in her breast. He wanted to marry her! And then the wording of his statement penetrated the thin fog of euphoria. He hadn't said he *wanted* to marry her. He hadn't even said he loved her. "Why?" Coventry asked hesitantly, already suspecting that his reply would seriously scar her heart.

He paused a moment before responding. "There

is something you may not know. Something the doctor I took you to in ReiDalgo discovered when he examined you."

Coventry's heart sank. "What is that?"

"You are pregnant, Coventry. You carry my child."

"And it is because of this that you have decided that we *should* marry?" She tried to keep her tone noncommittal but he must have sensed something for he took a long time to respond.

"Yes." His response was simple and to the point.

"And you think having a child together is a sufficient bond to unite two people in a marriage that should last the rest of their lives?" She was no longer able to keep the hurt and accusation from her voice. "Forget it!" She leapt to her feet and began jerking her clothing on.

Chapter Seventeen

Tiern stared at Coventry's livid stance in dismay. He had chosen to speak of marriage in regard to the child because he had thought that would be the approach most likely to sway her. He had assumed that, like any Thadonian woman, she would prefer to raise her child in a family unit. Sensing something awry as the conversation progressed, he had remembered that Earth families often consisted of a single parent, a child or children, and a hired caretaker. But the recollection had come too late for him to alter the course of the conversation. *Zyk!* He was furious with himself and with Coventry for being so damned difficult to understand. Jumping to his feet, he too began to don his clothing. Now he would have to devise a completely new plan of attack, and he didn't even know what it was that Coventry was looking for. Perhaps if he replayed the discourse in his mind once he had calmed down he would find a clue.

Finished dressing, he glanced at Coventry to see if she was ready to leave and was startled to see a sheen of tears wetting her cheeks. He went to her, automatically wrapping his arms around her to comfort her. "Why are you crying?"

She jerked her head back to look up at him with large angry eyes. "You really are an insensitive dolt, aren't you?" In her anger, she had reverted to English. Freeing herself from his embrace, she stalked in the direction of the camp. "Why don't you just . . . just . . . go to hell!" When she reached the boundary of the brush, she hesitated, apparently looking for a path. When no obvious choice presented itself, she turned with distinct impatience and waited for Tiern to take the lead.

Coventry's back was rigid with tension as she lay beside him. Only a few inches separated them, but the gap could just as easily have been a mile. Tiern still had no idea what had upset her. He had replayed their interchange numerous times to no avail. She had called him *insensitive,* but all that told him was that she thought he should know the reason for her ire. It was ironic that after years of avoiding another marriage, the woman he had finally chosen had turned him down. Yet, she had left him with the definite impression that the fault lay with him, that had he only said or done something differently she would have reacted differently. *Magar!* This was driving him insane. Perhaps he needed another opinion.

Reaching out, he grasped the hilt of Ven-Jikan. *I have a problem, Ven-Jikan. I would appreciate it if you would attempt to grant me some insight.*

Of course. What is the source of your difficulty?

Tiern paused. With the Iyi'Sefir, the species to which Ven-Jikan belonged, it was always important to be as specific as possible. *Coventry, the woman I brought from Earth . . . are you aware of her?*

I am aware of her. We contacted while you were injured.

Tiern frowned. He vaguely remembered asking Coventry to retrieve his blade for him. When

330

Ven-Jikan had failed to answer his summons, he had known that, in some way, the sword was trapped, unable to free itself telekinetically. Because his *Sotah* companions could not risk jeopardizing their own bond, Coventry had been his only hope of recovering his weapon. But "contact" in Ven-Jikan's terminology meant "mental communication," and that surprised him.

Coventry had said nothing about an experience which, for her, must have been unique if not even a little frightening. And also, the Iyi'Sefir rarely spoke to anyone other than their own kind and their symbiotic human companions. When physical contact with unbonded humans was occasionally necessary, they normally shielded themselves from mental communication because the experience was said to be extremely distressing unless a bond had been previously forged.

What is your difficulty, Rainon? Ven-Jikan prompted.

Tiern pulled his thoughts back to his present dilemma. *Coventry carries my child. I want to unite with her in marriage, but she refused. I need to understand the reason for her unwillingness.*

There was a brief pause. *Yes. I see the scene in your mind. Marriage is the name for the bonding of humans together. Correct?*

Yes.

I do not understand your ways in these matters well. What is the reason for this bonding?

Tiern sighed mentally. *Usually the people care for each other very much. They wish to share their lives and have children together.*

I sense a strong emotion, and the word "love" is in your mind, when you think of her. This is the word that describes the caring between people who . . . marry?

331

Usually . . . yes.

There was a pause as Ven-Jikan considered. *You did not mention this word to Coventry tonight. After telling her that she carried your child you told her that you thought you "should" marry. If "love" is important to these human unions, why did you not use the word?*

I did not think it would sway her. She once said she thought she was falling in love with me. When I told her not to . . . Tiern frowned, trying to remember the exact nature of that interchange. *When I told her not to love me, she said she had merely made an observation and that no matter how she felt, she would be returning to Earth.*

Why did you tell her not to love you?

Tiern grimaced. Sometimes talking to Ven-Jikan was almost as painful as simply working out a problem alone. *I did not love her at that time.*

There was a pause. Tiern sensed confusion in Ven-Jikan. *So you did not wish to marry her . . . then, but you do now. And now, you want her to love you.*

Magar! Yes, he wanted her love. He hadn't realized quite how much until just this instant. *Yes.*

I do not understand your problem, Rainon.

Zyk! Maybe he should have talked to someone else. Perhaps another woman could have aided him in understanding Coventry's reaction.

Do not be impatient, Rainon. I am trying.

Tiern sighed. *I know you are, Ven-Jikan. All right then. My problem is this. I want Coventry to agree to marriage instead of returning to Earth. And, I want . . . I want her love. I want us to raise our child together.*

I still do not understand, Rainon. When I contacted Coventry, she did not plan to return to Earth. She suspected the presence of a child and her thoughts were of raising it on Thadonia. Also, the word "love" was already in her mind when she thought of you. So, I do not know why she refused marriage. Unless . . . you are not a particularly sensitive species. If this "love" is to be felt by both parties in a union, perhaps she does not know that you feel "love" for her.

Coventry did not want to return to Earth? She knew of the child? She loved him! His pulse quickened. *If you knew these things, why did you not tell me at the beginning of this conversation?*

Tiern sensed that Ven-Jikan was affronted. *You did not ask me.*

I apologize. You are right. I cannot expect you to tell me something I did not ask.

There was no worded response, but he sensed a relaxation in his companion. *When you contacted, did you learn anything else from Coventry that I should know?*

I cannot answer that. There was nothing in her mind that represented a physical danger to you. Therefore, I do not know what information you should know.

Of course. Let me be more specific. He paused in an attempt to ensure that the wording of his query would leave nothing out. *Did Coventry mention . . .* He paused, frowning slightly. Would Coventry have told Ven-Jikan these things? Somehow he did not believe she would have. And Ven-Jikan's response was . . . unusual. He had said "there was nothing in her mind that represented a physical danger." Did Ven-Jikan, then, have knowledge of everything that had been in Coventry's thoughts. Tiern reworded his query. *Were there any thoughts in Coventry's mind pertaining to myself or the child, or to love and marriage, that you have not yet told me?*

Yes.

What were they, Ven-Jikan?

She did not want you to know of the child.

Startled by that revelation, Tiern looked at Coventry. The muscles in her back had relaxed; she had fallen asleep. The thought that she sought to deny him knowledge of his child pained him. *Why did she not want me to know?*

I cannot interpret her thoughts skillfully. She wanted to be with you, but she thought that if you knew of the child you would keep her with you only for the sake of the child, not for herself. Do you understand this?

Yes. Magar! In an attempt to hold her, he had used the very tactic most certain to drive her away. He had forgotten how proud and independent she was.

Do you now know why she refused to marry?

Yes. And now, it was too late to tell her of his love. She would not believe him. Tiern rubbed his brow in frustration. But, she would not escape him. He would think of something.

Then, I succeeded in aiding you with your problem.

Tiern sensed Ven-Jikan's pride and he smiled slightly despite his gloom. *Yes, Ven-Jikan. Thank you.* There was no response and he retreated into his thoughts. His brow puckered as he considered the contact between Coventry and Ven-Jikan. If the ability was a newly acquired talent, it might eventually come in very useful. *Ven-Jikan, how is it possible that you were able to "contact" Coventry? I was under the impression that you suffered ill effects if this was done without bonding. And how did you happen to learn so much from her mind? You do not know everything that is in my mind.*

Tiern hesitated as he considered the ramifications if this was no longer so. *Do you?*

No. As it has always been, I am unaware of much that is in your mind.

So, why were you able to receive so much from Coventry? She did not tell you these things, did she?

No. She did not tell me. Tiern sensed hesitation. *Your mind is . . . compartmentalized, your thoughts hidden in separate chambers. Although I can sense the emotions you feel in regard to your thoughts, I receive only those thoughts you do not . . . conceal. Coventry's mind is very different. There are no compartments. Her mind is . . . open, the thoughts exposed.*

Tiern frowned. He did not like the ramifications. *Why do you think this is?*

I do not know. She is from an alien world. Perhaps her kind have never experienced telepathic threat as have the people of Thadonia. They would then have had no need to develop any natural safeguards.

The theory made sense. Yet, if Coventry was to live safely on Thadonia, she would need to acquire some type of thought concealment capabilities. *Do you think she could learn to develop these . . . compartments?*

I do not know. She is too unfamiliar to me. But, if you wish for her to acquire these safeguards, I believe her best chance for doing so would be under the guidance of one of the Fehera.

Tiern resolved to make arrangements for her to meet a Feheran telepath as soon as possible. He shuddered to think of how easily the *Dalig* could have stolen information from her mind while she was in their hands. They could know absolutely everything about her. His mind turned back to his conversation with Ven-Jikan. *How was it that you suffered no ill effects from "contact" when there was no bonding in place?*

There was a bond. It is called a secondary link. I am bonded to you, and Coventry is bonded to you. Therefore, "contact" with her was merely a . . . detached connection to you. Do you understand?

No. My bond to you was brought about through a special ceremony conducted by the priests of Sotah. Coventry and I have not participated in any bonding ritual.

A major part of bonding consists of . . . caring, an emotional tie, a likeness of being. The link between you and Coventry was forged by your feelings for each other.

Tiern concentrated, trying to understand and weigh all the possibilities. *Do you mean that anyone to whom I am emotionally bonded is also linked, vicariously, to you?*

No, not anyone, and it is even possible that I will never again be able to achieve a contact with Coventry. Emotional bonds are less certain than the one you and I share. Perhaps the only reason I was able to achieve contact, without severe discomfort, was because her emotional state was so intense at the time. She was very worried about you. In essence, at that moment, she was so closely linked with you that she was almost part of you.

Tiern nodded thoughtfully. Ven-Jikan had not developed a new talent then. He would be unable to serve as a mind reader through contact with others. Oh well, although the talent would have proved useful, he had lived without it so far. He allowed his mind to drift as he sought sleep. Suddenly, another thought occurred to him. *Ven-Jikan?*

Yes?

You have never explained what it is about contact with others that you find so . . . discomfiting. Can you tell me?

Tiern sensed a mental sigh. *In our natural state many Iyi'Sefir . . . hibernate for many hundreds of years at a time, existing only in a dream-state. The reason for this is because we are . . . highly empathic. Too much conscious contact with creatures to whom we have no bond results in the loss of our identity. Yet because we are naturally symbiotic creatures who seek companionship, if we remain conscious we are relentlessly drawn to make contact . . . even without bonding.*

During contact we must rigorously guard our own identities, our own emotions. Because we are naturally empathic, this is very difficult to do. It is very stressful. Prolonged contact often results in . . . a form of insanity and ultimately death.

Tiern felt Ven-Jikan's anguish. He was sorry he had asked. And yet, now that he was aware of the precise nature of the danger, he knew that he could never ask Ven-Jikan to make "contact"— for any reason. *Good-night, Ven-Jikan.* Rolling on his side, he draped an arm over Coventry's waist and sought sleep.

The interior of the tent was gray with predawn illumination when Tiern opened his eyes. A familiar tickling in the back of his mind called him to wakefulness. The priests of the *Sotah* sought to commune with him. Moving carefully to avoid disturbing Coventry, he rose and left the chamber. His traveling companions met him wordlessly in the central chamber. Silently, they left the tent and the camp, seeking solitude in the forest.

Seating themselves in a clearing very similar to

337

the one where he had taken Coventry last night, they waited for renewed contact from the priests. Finally it came and Tiern closed his eyes to concentrate more fully.

Brothers of the Sotah, we call upon you to unite. Even as the words entered his mind, Tiern felt the presence of thousands of intellects as they joined the nexus. *The Dalig are invading in vast numbers. They have landed upon the shores of many countries. As it has always been with the Dalig, they enslave all those who are unprotected as they advance. However, this time they appear to be avoiding all cities save those which house the emperors or their chief administrators. We believe that they plan to eradicate Thadonia's rulership at the onset of their campaign. Those of you who are in a position to do so must attempt to discover how such a large scheme, with such far-reaching consequences, remained concealed. We must ensure it does not occur again. All other Brothers of the Sotah are to proceed to the sides of the emperors and chief administrators you have sworn to protect in each territory of each empire. There, you will await the call to meet the Dalig in battle.*

There was a pause, and Tiern assumed the communication ended. However, just as he opened his eyes, the message continued.

Brothers, a dark day is on the horizon. The Dalig have awakened the Fena'Gece. We must now awaken the Iyi'Sefır or face certain annihilation. The telekinetic forces unleashed will be tremendous. We ourselves must leave our mountain home. The battle to come will not be an easy one. It will mean the end of many lives, and we say farewell to those Brothers now. You will not be forgotten.

Tiern opened his eyes and studied the grim expressions on the faces of his companions.

There were no words to communicate the depth of their feelings so, as silently as they had come, they returned to camp. None of them had been born at the time of the last battle between the *Dalig* and the *Sotah*. Yet, the horror of it lived on in their history, unforgotten. Would any of them live to see another year? No one knew.

Reentering their private area within the tent, Tiern found Coventry already awake. She looked at him questioningly, but he was unable to decide what he should tell her . . . or even *if* he should tell her any of what he had learned. "We journey to the emperor's immediately. Ready yourself. I will see to Faolan."

Coventry cast another glance at her companions. What was the matter? They were all so . . . solemn this morning. She had thought, at first, that Tiern's grave, brooding manner might be a result of their argument, but after seeing virtually identical expressions mirrored on the faces of the other *Sotah*, she had revised her assumption. Something else was bothering them. Something serious. And that knowledge frightened her.

The sun had barely pulled itself over the horizon. The almost treeless prairie landscape through which they now rode was bathed in a beautiful golden glow. But there was no time to admire the scene properly for they rode the dyre as though pursued by Death himself. Coventry noted the bleak expression on Singai's face and shuddered. Perhaps Death in one of his myriad guises did stalk them.

Suddenly Tiern pointed to their left and shouted something Coventry couldn't catch over the drumming feet of the dyre. But Juste must have heard him for his gaze followed the direction of Tiern's finger. Nodding, he headed his mount in that direction while the others continued on. Coventry followed him with her eyes, trying to see beyond him to decipher what had caught Tiern's attention. Gradually she perceived some dark figures moving, hardly more than specks on the horizon. Who were they? But before they got close enough for her to see them clearly, Faolan descended into a small gully and they were lost from view. Why had Juste apparently gone to meet them? Determined to try to learn at least something of their predicament, Coventry looked over her shoulder at Tiern. One glance at his forbidding countenance stopped her. He looked positively savage.

Within an hour, Juste rejoined them. With him rode six more people who wore the attire of the *Sotah*. They rode without pause as the morning passed. Unfamiliar muscles in Coventry's body had begun to protest such prolonged, rigorous use. Yet, the stony faces of the *Sotah* deterred any protest. Thirty or more *Sotah* had joined them, gradually, in bands ranging from three to ten riders. And Coventry could see more in the distance, all journeying in the same direction; most seemed to gravitate slowly toward other bands, forming larger groups.

By mid-afternoon, the entire landscape seethed with racing dyre and their riders, all evidently *Sotah* although a few wore armbands of different colors as did Singai. When Coventry managed a glance to their rear, she could no longer see an end to the people riding behind them. Their own gathering appeared to have swollen to more than a hundred. Yet, the only sound was the muted roar of the dyre's three-toed feet pounding the prairie soil into dust. No one spoke. No one glanced to left or right. And every face she looked into, whether familiar or unfamiliar, registered the same expression of grim determination. It was positively . . . eerie.

Suddenly, Coventry sensed Faolan slowing. Peering ahead, she tried to see through the gaps of a group of riders who had fallen in in front of them. She caught a glimpse of an enormous stone edifice. As they drew nearer, she could see that the building itself was surrounded by a thick stone wall. Along the base of this wall, hundreds of milling *Sotah* had taken up position. And still, there was virtually no conversation. Silent, grim-faced men and women glanced at them as they passed and then returned to whatever they had been doing. Gradually, most of those who had ridden with them through the day broke off and spread out at the base of the wall, joining those already in position. By the time Tiern goaded Faolan through the open gate in the wall, only about twenty riders followed them through.

Tiern directed Faolan up a steep, paved drive lined with trees. However, instead of approaching the enormous building that Coventry had assumed was their destination, he followed a narrower trail around it and approached a long, low structure that Coventry recognized as a stable. Halting before it, he leapt from Faolan's broad back without bothering to have him kneel and held up his arms to Coventry. "Come," he said. The expression on his face still did not invite conversation. Placing her hands on his shoulders, Coventry allowed him to help her from the dyre. He automatically steadied her as her legs, weakened by hours in the saddle, wavered shakily. Once certain that she was securely on her feet, he left her, without comment, to lead Faolan into the stable.

Christine Michels

* * *

After a surprisingly brief wait during which Coventry still received no enlightenment, she, Tiern and their companions were ushered into the presence of Emperor Rion. Coventry observed the emperor and his four counselors—two of whom appeared to be Feheran—in fascination. The emperor, clad in a scarlet Thadonian robe similar in style to the one Ambassador Kalare had worn, appeared quite advanced in age though he was by no means feeble. His hair was as snowy white as that of his Feheran aides. Yet, his shorter stature and heavier body made it obvious that he was not of that race.

Coventry observed the interaction carefully, watching for indications of whatever protocol might be expected of her. She had never encountered a powerful personage quite as . . . gregarious as the ruler of Sulaiv. The moment they had been ushered into his presence, he had begun treating her *Sotah* companions like highly regarded . . . family. To her surprise he had greeted Juste, Modoc and Rainon by name, grasping their forearms in a masculine handshake accompanied by an earnest bright-eyed gaze that Coventry was unable to decipher. He then turned to Singai, welcoming her to his country and expressing his appreciation for her surrogate services—since her own emperor was too far distant to aid—in such trying times. Now, he looked at Coventry as she stood at Tiern's side.

"And you are Coventry Pearce," he said. "We received word of your arrival on our world and have been anxiously awaiting the opportunity to meet you. I only wish the circumstances could have been less . . . complicated."

Coventry looked into the emperor's bright blue eyes and sensed his sincerity. She smiled; although uncertain as to the exact nature of the circumstances of which he spoke, she would have to have been a stone not to detect the urgency of the situation. "Thank you for your kind welcome, Chazak'Imnen." She remembered from her language lessons that the emperors were always addressed as either Chazak, exalted one, or Chazak'Imnen, exalted lord.

He returned her smile, but the gesture seemed strained. "Come. Let us be seated." He included the entire party in his expansive gesture. "My Feheran colleagues inform me that we have much to discuss." He led the way to a long table in the center of the large chamber.

The table was higher than most that Coventry had encountered on Thadonia and, rather than cushions, numerous stools ringed it. After the emperor and his counselors had seated themselves, Tiern directed Coventry to one of the stools and sat next to her.

"Now then," Emperor Rion began, "I understand the first knowledge regarding our current situation originated on Earth. Would you like to begin, Rainon?"

Tiern bowed his head briefly in acknowledgment. "While stationed on Earth, I was contacted by an employee of the Global Intelligence Network. His name was Dalton Pearce." Tiern went on to describe every detail of what had transpired following his initial meeting with Dalton, with the exception of certain personal information that applied only to his relationship with Coventry. As he completed his account, he bent to move the heel of his boot to one side and extract the computer disk. "Based on the additional information

343

we now have, the disk may now be almost super-fluous. But, perhaps, you may learn something from it." He passed it to one of the counselors who then handed it to Emperor Rion.

The emperor nodded and spoke to a dark-haired counselor. "Taqir, do we have one of the Earth computers available?"

The man, Taqir, nodded. "Yes, Chazak."

"Good. Take this" —he deposited the disk in Taqir's hand— "and have it studied carefully."

Taqir nodded and left the chamber. Emperor Rion directed his gaze to those still assembled. "Who was it who discovered the *Dalig* link in this?"

"It was I, Chazak'Imnen," Singai responded. She went on to describe the conversation she had overheard while infiltrating the fortress in search of Coventry, and her assumptions based on what she had heard.

When she had finished, the emperor nodded gravely. "Most of the information you have given me was passed on to my Feheran friends by the priests of your society. However, it is always best to hear the reports first hand. I wish to commend you all for your sound judgment when you were unable to reach me. It was entirely due to your timely warning that the *Sotah* priests began monitoring Thadonian space. Mere hours ago, two unauthorized Earth ships were detected. With the aid of the Iyi'Sefir, they were . . . convinced that landing on Thadonia at this time would not be in their best interests. We can therefore assume, I think, that the Earther aid the *Dalig* expected will not materialize. My counselors and I believe that the Earth-based conspiracy that Rainon uncovered is a plot within a plot. We theorize that, just as the *Dalig* planned

344

to use the Earthers to further their own ambitions, so the Earthers schemed to betray their *Dalig* conspirators in an attempt to achieve their own ends. If the Earthers persist in their . . . designs, the Iyi'Sefir are prepared to destroy their ships telekinetically, if necessary. Thus, we believe we can now concentrate fully on the *Dalig* crisis. Is there anything further any of you can add to aid us in our assessment of the current situation?"

There was a brief silence as those present considered Emperor Rion's words. Finally Juste responded. "While at the fortress, I noted a number of *Dalig* entering from the seaside. This morning we learned that the *Dalig* invasion appears to be coming primarily from the direction of the sea. Therefore, I would like to suggest that, since the Terebian empire has not been in *Dalig* control for almost fifty years, perhaps the *Dalig* have seized control of an island as their base. If they are in control of a largely unpopulated island, it would explain how they were able to rebuild their numbers without being detected."

The emperor stared at Juste thoughtfully. "Yes, it would." Suddenly he transferred his gaze to a Feheran aide. Although he made no verbal comment, the Feheran nodded, rose, and left the room. Coventry was reminded of the telepathic abilities Tiern had spoken of when she had asked about the unusually tall, white-haired race.

"Now" —Emperor Rion redirected his gaze to those remaining— "I will explain why I was not in ReiDalgo when you sought me." He paused, clearing his throat. Then, folding his hands together before him on the table he began. "For some time now, I have been receiving . . . intimidating missives. They began as veiled suggestions, messages insinuating my ultimate demise. Gradually these escalated to outright threats against myself, my family and household, and all those loyal to me. I have since learned that all the Thadonian emperors were thus plagued. However, at the time each of us thought we were the only ones receiving threats. And as is customary, we kept these disturbing occurrences to ourselves. No emperor wants to admit he has problems within his domain for fear such an admission will reveal weakness. We know from history that when an empire is weak, it is absorbed by another, more powerful one. Thus, in effect, we each suspected one of our neighbors as being the instigator of the difficulty."

He looked at Tiern. "Shortly before you arrived from Earth, an entire stable of my most prized dyre was poisoned. The handler disappeared. Whether he was killed, or was a traitor, is still unknown. Neither the Feheran nor the *Sotah* have been able to discover the slightest trace of him. At that time, I decided that the danger to my people was real enough to warrant action. Based on the fact that this residence has superior defense capabilities, we left ReiDalgo as quietly as possible, leaving only a skeleton staff in place."

He paused once more, staring sightlessly at a point over their heads. "I now surmise that, because the only stretch of coastline suitable for such an invasion of our territory is so near ReiDalgo, the threats may have been designed to remove me, and a goodly portion of my defense staff, from ReiDalgo during the *Dalig* incursion. However, as hindsight serves no purpose, we must now look to the future. We must determine the identity of the *Dalig* leader. He is obviously a man of some power. Only someone in a relatively key position would have the connections necessary to orchestrate the takeover of his world by a foreign power, even as a ruse. Had he not been an influential personality, the Earthers involved would never have been convinced of the validity of the scheme. Do any of you have suggestions as to where we should seek this person?"

Coventry had listened avidly to the entire discourse. The *Dalig* were invading en masse. No wonder everybody was so grim. All of Thadonia was on the verge of war. She was distracted from her thoughts by Singai.

"I would suggest, Chazak, that only one of the counselors could have affected such a scheme. Or, possibly, one of the chief administrators or emperors themselves."

The emperor nodded. "We are already considering the possibility that one of the counselors might be involved. However, I have almost dismissed the likelihood of the traitor being one of my brother emperors or their administrators, unless one of you can enlighten me as to how he would be able to conceal his shift in alliances from his *Sotah* guardians and their ever-present companions, the Iyi'Sefir."

His statement was met with silence. "Very well then. Let us consider the counselors. Do any of you know how we might narrow the prospects? Each emperor has anywhere from five to twelve advisers. We are dealing with eleven empires. If we assume an average number of counselors to be eight, we have eighty-eight suspects."

"Do you feel you can eliminate your own staff from the list of suspects, Chazak'Imnen?" Modoc asked.

"I would like to think so, naturally," Emperor Rion responded cautiously. "But I will not do so.

The situation we are facing is too serious to make such assumptions."

Tiern cleared his throat. "I had almost forgotten. After our first contact with a *Dalig*, I took this from her person." He extended the *Dalig* headband to the nearest counselor. "Perhaps a clairvoyant might glean some information from it. Also, while we were searching the fortress, an incident did occur that could possibly be of some help. It had slipped my mind until this moment." He went on to describe his encounter with a *Dalig* officer whom he thought he had recognized.

"I do not recognize the man you describe, but I agree with you. It could be important." Emperor Rion turned to his Feheran counselor. "Shorba, can you, perhaps, extract the likeness in his mind for further investigation?"

"I will try, Chazak." So saying, the Feheran, Shorba, rose and approached Tiern. Then, placing his hands on either side of Tiern's forehead, he said, "Think of this man you saw, Imnen. Let it fill your mind, blocking out all other images." He fell silent, a slight frown puckered the flesh between his chalky brows. The silence stretched into two minutes . . . three. "I have it, Chazak."

"Transfer it to me."

The Feheran bowed slightly from the waist in acknowledgment of the directive and then approached the emperor. Duplicating the position he had adopted with Tiern, he closed his eyes. Emperor Rion's features creased with strain. "Ah, yes. I, too, have seen this man before, but I do not remember his identity." He opened his eyes as the Feheran resumed his seat. "Perhaps he is a chancellor. In that position he would often serve as an aide to one of the counselors." He directed his gaze to his own advisers. "Find out what empire this man serves and perhaps we will have narrowed our list of suspects from eighty-eight to eight."

The Feheran nodded. The other counselor, an auburn-haired giant who had thus far remained silent, inclined his head and responded. "It will be done, Chazak'Imnen."

"Very well. I think we can consider this meeting at an end." He directed his gaze to Tiern and the other *Sotah*. "The barracks are overflowing. Should I wish to contact you to discuss something further, I do not want you camped outside the walls. Therefore, you will be assigned chambers and stay as my guests." He transferred his gaze to the auburn-haired counselor. "Delick, you will take care of the arrangements and provide refreshments for our guests."

"Certainly, Chazak."

Night pressed at the windows of the emperor's summer residence. Yet Tiern did not sleep. First he had been unable to exorcise the image of Coventry asleep in the chamber next to his, and then his mind had begun to churn with thoughts concerning the impending battle. Now, naked save for his trousers, he knelt in the center of the large chamber allotted him and prepared to execute the calming ritual of his *Sotah* exercises. But first he had to clear his mind of its troubling thoughts. *Ven-Jikan?*

I am aware, Rainon.

At one time the Fena'Gece and the Iyi'Sefir were of the same race, were they not?

From your point of view, yes.

We know they share a symbiotic relationship with the Dalig just as the Iyi'Sefir are the companions of the Sotah.

Ven-Jikan made no response, Tiern had merely put into words something that was fact. Tiern continued attempting to organize his thoughts. Something was bothering him. *You said that the Iyi'Sefir are empathic. Are the Fena'Gece also empaths?*

No. The Fena'Gece are . . . in most ways, diametrically opposed to the Iyi'Sefir. Where we are empathic, they are coercive. They seek bonding with individuals of . . . like personality, just as we do. But, if they do not find such a one, they can dominate and control almost any individual, save those of very strong mind, through force-bonding.

Tiern had never fully understood how the *Dalig* managed to enslave people to become *Dalig* warriors. How could someone be forced to battle on the side of their enemies? Now, for the first time, he began to understand more fully the history he had been taught. It was not the *Dalig* who enslaved. It was the Fena'Gece.

Are you aware of how the Dalig and the Sotah came into existence? Ven-Jikan asked.

Tiern thought. During training, the priests had taught the history of the *Sotah* only as it pertained to specific battles. None had ever mentioned the beginnings of either the *Sotah* or the *Dalig,* and Tiern had never thought to ask. *No.*

Then it is time you knew. It is always best to know as much as possible about one's enemies before a battle. Would you like to know now?

Yes. Continue.

The Iyi'Sefir and the Fena'Gece have been on this world since its birth. At that time, as you said, we were akin to a single race. Although our physical form was molecular, like metal, we had no capability to move. Our existence was based on pure thought. Our companionship was with each other. We did not know then of the human entity.

Eventually, humankind appeared. We sensed their presence, but it meant nothing to us. We were content with each other. You see . . . at one time, the Fena'Gece were the symbiotic companions of the Iyi'Sefir. There was a pause in the flow of words to his mind, but Tiern waited patiently, knowing that Ven-Jikan would resume when he was ready.

Eventually, the humans came to our mountains. They were interested in the unique properties of the stone they found there. Always, when they found a grayish stone, the Fena'Gece, it was . . . connected by means of intertwining metallic strands to a stone of a yellowish hue, the Iyi'Sefir. Although we shunned contact, they did not leave us in peace. Always, they were there, examining, studying. Before long they began severing the delicate filaments that bound us together. The pain was excruciating. Suddenly, there were those of our kind who were alone. They had no physical contact. We heard their cries of anguish and fear, we spoke to them, but we could not . . . touch them. We could not provide the connection they needed.

Once more Ven-Jikan fell silent for a time, and Tiern reviewed what he had heard, appalled by the insensitivity of his Thadonian ancestors. And yet, if the Iyi'Sefir and Fena'Gece had shunned contact, how could they have known?

Ven-Jikan resumed. *It was inevitable that one of these isolated beings, maddened by pain and anguish, should eventually reach out to his tormentor. It managed to extend its severed filaments into the flesh of a human. This being was a Fena'Gece. And it found the bond it established with the human much more to its liking than the bond it had previously experienced with the*

Iyi'Sefir. The human carried the stone to which it had been bound everywhere, thus the Fena'Gece acquired mobility. It also gained the ability to feel and see a much greater range of things through its relationship with the human. And it discovered human lust and greed. Eventually it had its human companion return it to the mountains where it revealed to the entire race what could be ours if we would simply . . . evolve and . . . use human companions.

Before long, the Fena'Gece began abandoning their relationship with the Iyi'Sefir in favor of the much more seductive one they could share with the human beings. Not all the Fena'Gece left, of course. Not enough humans could be brought to the mountains. But because they wanted to leave and the Iyi'Sefir felt that what the Fena'Gece chose to do was . . . immoral, our relationship changed. The Iyi'Sefir and Fena'Gece still share the same mountain range. Although our relationship in our natural form is still somewhat symbiotic in that it keeps us alive, we no longer communicate. But, in those long-ago times, because the Iyi'Sefir could not bring themselves to force bonding on humans as so many of the Fena'Gece did, those that had been abandoned began to die.

Eventually, we discovered that by putting ourselves in a dream-state, what your kind calls hibernation, we could forestall death almost indefinitely. This is what those of us who no longer had a companion chose to do. Years passed. I do not know how many because the Iyi'Sefir had very little concept of the passage of time.

One day, a human came again to our mountains. He had learned of the existence of the Iyi'Sefir and our refusal to enforce bonding on humans. He had come to seek our aid, but he did not know *how to contact us. Knowing that we were a race that communicated by thought but unable to do that himself, he sat on the mountain and called. Eventually, one of us heard his call and came out of hibernation. This being allowed the "contact" without bonding although it was extremely painful for him and difficult not to lose himself in the emotions of the man.* Once more Ven-Jikan halted in his tale. Tiern sat silently, stunned by all that he had heard.

The man sought our aid because . . . the Fena'Gece and their human companions had begun to oppress other humans . . . by very cruel means. The Fena'Gece had become obsessed with experiencing power in all its various forms. The humans did not have the means or the understanding of our kind that would enable them to successfully fight this oppression. After some thought, the being in contact with the man woke the other Iyi'Sefir from their hibernation and they discussed the problem. We could no longer hold ourselves away from humans. Perhaps it had been our very refusal to bond with humans which had allowed the Fena'Gece to evolve into such immoral creatures. At the man's request, the Iyi'Sefir being he had contacted bonded with him. He then left the mountain in search of honorable men and women who would willingly bond with the Iyi'Sefir in order to combat the Fena'Gece and their companions who were already becoming known as Dalig. That man was the founder of the Sotah.

Tiern considered all that he had heard. *Why is this part of our history not more widely known?*

These times predated your . . . recorded past.

Tiern's mind seethed with half-formed questions that he could not seem to focus on long enough to put into words. Finally, he managed to concentrate on one. *Neither the Dalig nor the Sotah carry our companions as stones. How did it come to be that you are in the form of a weapon?*

Just as the priests could not answer that question for you when you asked as a boy entering the Sotah, so too am I unable to respond. It was long ago agreed that such knowledge would never become . . . common.

Tiern nodded. He had suspected as much. He began to go over in his mind everything Ven-Jikan had told him. Was there some knowledge there that could aid them? He frowned as a thought occurred to him. *Ven-Jikan?*

Yes?

The bonding process between you and me did not involve the process of . . . intertwining metallic filaments into my body. He remembered the sensation of the bonding as fibrous strands of light wept from the blade, sinking into his flesh and disappearing, a feeling so exquisitely pleasurable it was agonizing. *How was our bond achieved?*

Both the Iyi'Sefir and the Fena'Gece have evolved since our first contact with humans. The metallic fibers were . . . inconvenient because we could never be physically separated from our companions without initiating hibernation. Over time, we developed an . . . energy that served in the same manner.

Tiern began to get excited. *Exactly the same manner? Can it be severed as was done long ago? Can the Fena'Gece be killed in this way without the necessity of killing those of their companions who were force-bonded?*

There was a long silence. Finally, Ven-Jikan spoke. *I do not know, Rainon. Perhaps there is a way to . . . disrupt or weaken the energy fibers. I will have to . . . consider.*

Slightly deflated, but hopeful nonetheless, Tiern nodded and moved into his ritual *Sotah* maneuvers. If Ven-Jikan could perceive a means of isolating the Fena'Gece, the knowledge could entirely alter the nature of the battle to come.

Chapter Eighteen

Coventry's thoughts churned as she lay in the unfamiliar bed. She missed Tiern's presence dreadfully. The man she loved, the father of her child, would go into battle against an enemy soon. He could die. She wanted to keep him from fighting, to protect him, but she knew the thought was a selfish one. He could no more turn his back on this situation than he could cut out his heart. And, had he been the kind of man to run from danger, she could not have loved him as she did. Tiern. The possibility of his death terrified her. If she never saw him again, . . . if he never held her in his arms again, . . . she didn't think she would be able to live with the pain. She closed her eyes and felt hot tears slip down her cheeks. Yet, it was she herself who was robbing them of these final hours before the battle. It was she who had placed her pride before her love. Did it matter that Tiern did not return her love? Yes, she admitted to herself, it did. But not as much as it had. To hell with pride!

Flinging back the bedcoverings, she rose and donned her robe. Staring at her reflection in the mirror, she splashed her face with tepid water in an attempt to erase the traces of her tears. Suddenly the faint line of the scar beneath her eye drew her attention and she explored it with trembling fingertips. She remembered Tiern's strange preoccupation with the slight disfigurement. Perhaps he was one of those people who was repulsed by the slightest flaw. She had heard of people like that.

She met her own gaze in the mirror. She still hated her eyes. Why couldn't she have had eyes like Dalton's? On impulse, she turned to her knapsack and withdrew the only item that had survived her flight from Earth: the case containing her collection of contact lenses.

Five minutes later, Coventry stood at Tiern's door determined to swallow her pride and salvage what she could of the hours left them. Wiping her palms nervously against the rich fabric of her robe, she closed her lids over sapphire eyes, took a deep breath and knocked. For the longest time, there was no response and her resolve began to waver. Perhaps he was already asleep. She would try once more before returning to her room. She had just raised her hand to knock again when the door opened. Tiern stood before her clad only in a pair of trousers. The expression on his face was stern and preoccupied, yet she found that she had grown so used to his forbidding countenance that it did not disturb her . . . much. She allowed her gaze to drop to his broad, muscular chest. Stars, he had the most magnificent body.

"Coventry?"

Startled, her eyes flew to his face. "I . . . I need to talk to you. Please?"

Wordlessly, he stepped back, opened the door wider and allowed her entry. She walked to the center of the room and turned to face him. He was leaning against the door, watching her with that strange, heated gaze that never failed to fluster her. Wiping her palms nervously against the fabric of her robe again, she tried to recall just what it was she had planned to say. Oh, yes. She had been determined to swallow her pride and admit to her feelings. Suddenly her pride had a death-grip on her larynx. She cleared her throat.

"I . . . I came here to tell you that I love you." The words left her mouth in a rush. There, she had said it. It was a relief to finally have the words in the open. But there was no response from Tiern. Her words hung uncomfortably in the air between them. Finally, she shifted her gaze back to him. He hadn't moved; his expression was unreadable. There was an air of expectancy about him.

Why didn't he say something? What did he want from her? Damn, this was harder than she had imagined it would be. She began to pace the room. "I know you don't love me." She abandoned the Thadonian tongue. It was too hard to express herself in an unfamiliar language. "I know that you find the scarring of my face . . . unattractive."

"Coventry—"

She held up her hand. "Don't stop me, or I will never get this out." She swallowed. "But despite the lack of love on your part, I think you care for me. We seem to complement each other. And I can find a means of concealing the scar. Maybe . . . maybe, if we have the time together, you'll grow to love me." Hell! This was not coming out well at all. Even to her own ears her words sounded stilted.

"Coventry—" He sounded sympathetic.

Oh God, she didn't want his sympathy. She was a fool to have come. "Well, I just wanted you to know. I . . . I'd better go." And all the time a part of her brain was begging him: *Don't let me leave.*

"Coventry." He gripped her shoulders as she approached the door, forcing her to look up at him. "Am I to understand that you have just changed your mind about becoming my consort?"

Coventry lowered her eyes. Was that what she had done? Yes. Yes, she had changed her mind. Having Tiern on unequal terms was better than not having him at all. Slowly, she nodded.

"Look at me, Coventry." When she didn't respond immediately, he placed one finger beneath her chin to raise it until her eyes once again met his. "I do love you, Coventry." Her skepticism must have been revealed in her eyes. "I am telling you the truth, Coventry. I love you." He emphasized each tiny word. "And I do not just say that because we are to be parents. I had fallen in love with you even before I knew of the child. I just did not want to admit it to myself . . . or to you. But, even had there been no child, I would eventually have asked you to marry me because I could not have allowed you to leave me."

As Coventry stared at his unconventionally handsome face, she felt the faint stirring of hope. Did she dare to believe him? Unconsciously she leaned her cheek against his palm as he raised his hand to stroke a finger over the narrow line on her cheek.

"I could never find you unattractive, Coventry. This tiny mark is all but invisible. Why would you think that I could dislike your appearance for such a reason?"

"When it happened, you were so . . . so obsessed with it."

"Coventry." He breathed her name as he pulled her into his embrace. She felt his chin against the top of her head. "I appeared . . . obsessed with your injury because of something that happened a long time ago. I will tell you."

Coventry listened with mounting horror to the halting, husky words as Tiern told her of his first wife and how she had died. How could Aneire have been so consumed with the need to retain her beauty that she would murder a child conceived in love rather than gain a few pounds or suffer a few stretch marks? The thought was inconceivable to Coventry. The woman must have been unbalanced.

There was so much pain in Tiern, even now. Yet she was incapable of erasing it. As he fell silent, Coventry felt a new tension in him, induced by the anguish of his memories. Was there anything she could say to help assuage his torment? Wrapping her arms tightly around him, she repeated the words she had said earlier. "I love you." At first she sensed no change in him. And then, slowly the tautness began to ease from his muscles and he clutched her to him convulsively. When the intensity of his hold eased and he lifted his head to look into her face, he smiled at her tenderly.

"We can have as many children as you want," she said, returning his smile as she pictured them as a family in the wide-open spaces of Thadonia. Unfortunately the vision in her mind depicted herself in a rather advanced state of pregnancy, and she decided to add a provision. "Provided that your affections do not stray when I am fat and ugly."

The smile disappeared from his face. "You forget, Coventry, this is Thadonia. I had thought we might ask one of those attractive Vaileun women to join our union."

Coventry tensed. "Like hell! If you want to

marry me, the marriage will be a monogamous one 'til . . . 'til death do us part. And if you can't live with that you'd better rescind your proposal right now because I haven't forgotten the rules of Thadonian marriage: you need my permission to bring another woman into the union."

Tiern stared at her and she was frustrated by her inability to read his expression. "Well?" she prompted.

"I am considering."

"You're—" Furious, she tried to free herself of his hold. "Let me go, you . . . you insufferable—" Her diatribe was cut off by his laughter.

"I am teasing you, you foolish woman. Our union will be monogamous. On *both* sides." He looked at her meaningfully. "And I will not look permissively upon straying affections either. You have fair warning."

Coventry slowly relaxed in his embrace. "Hmmm. So I have. Perhaps I should reconsider." She attempted to keep her face as expressionless as his had been.

"Too late. The agreement is made." He lowered his head to catch her lips in a searing kiss. When he had her senses thoroughly scrambled, he raised his head to look into her heavy-lidded eyes. "Why have you hidden your beautiful eyes beneath those pieces of colored plastic?"

Coventry stared at him uncomprehendingly until his words penetrated the fog surrounding her brain. "You . . . think my eyes are beautiful?"

"Incomparably," he assured her.

"Then I will never hide them again."

"Good." Bending his head to capture her lips once more, he lifted her in his arms. This was home. This was where she belonged. In the arms of the man she loved.

Later, much later, cuddled against the heated length of the magnificent body that she never tired of, Coventry remembered what had prompted her to throw her pride to the winds and speak of her love this night. "Tiern, I am afraid for you, . . . for us."

He didn't ask her why. Tightening his hold on her, he simply said, "Me too."

For a second, the fact that he had admitted to fear increased her own anxiety. But ultimately, when she thought about it, his admission calmed her. Fear would prompt caution; he would not take unnecessary risks. She knew that he would do his best to come back to her, and that was all she could ask of a man like Tiern.

Coventry opened her eyes to the grayness of predawn light. Tiern was not beside her. For an instant, fear clutched at her. He would not have gone to face the *Dalig* without saying good-bye, would he? She rose on one elbow as her eyes raked the room, and then she saw him. He sat in the center of the chamber in what appeared to be a meditative trance. Shifting nearer the edge of the bed, she settled back contentedly to observe him.

He was naked, his spine erect as he knelt, eyes closed, holding the weapon he called Ven-Jikan in his hands. She understood the name now that she knew the metal housed an intelligent being. Someday soon, she would ask Tiern to tell her about his unconventional friend and companion. Now, she allowed her eyes to roam Tiern at leisure, drinking in the sight of him. The tapered, masculine beauty of his smooth-skinned, bronzed back and the indentation of his backbone, ramrod straight, at its center. The thick black hair, combed straight back from his forehead to caress his shoulder blades, held in place by the *Sotah* headband. The too-strong line of his jaw with its ever-present bluish shadow of whiskers just beneath the surface. There was no doubt in her mind; he was the embodiment of male attractiveness.

Suddenly he rose and, unaware of her avid gaze, began to execute a series of smooth, flowing movements that Coventry couldn't quite label as either dance or exercise, but more a combination of the two. Her eyes widened in surprise as Ven-Jikan appeared to levitate for fully two minutes between Tiern's outstretched hands. She considered some of the things she had witnessed since coming to Thadonia. Things that should not have been possible. In retrospect, her credulity astonished her. And yet, things that would have seemed strange and frightening on Earth somehow seemed . . . fitting on Thadonia.

The time Tiern devoted to his exercises stretched into long minutes. Her eyelids began to grow heavy and she wished Tiern would return to bed. It was still so early. As she hazily admired the muscles flexing in his long hair-roughened legs, sleep reclaimed her.

Tiern looked down on Coventry's sleeping form. Like most people, she still slept. But he was too restless to stay in the room any longer. He needed to know what was happening. Brushing his lips lightly against her forehead, he left the room to seek the seers' chamber.

Ten minutes later, he located the room on the first floor. He entered quietly. Six Feheran sat in chairs specifically designed to be comfortable for hours at a time. Their eyes were closed as they maintained a continual telepathic link with others of their race. He wondered which was the communicator, but he dared not ask for fear of disrupting their concentration. The Feheran designated the communicator would sense his presence before long.

He did not have long to wait. A woman opened her eyes, focusing intently on him. "I am the communicator, Kyra. Is there something you require, *Sotah* Rainon?" Her voice was fluid and pleasant.

"Kyra." Tiern bowed his head slightly in acknowledgment of her introduction. "What is the current situation?"

"The battle is beginning. The *Dalig* and *Sotah* are at combat in many areas. The Fena'Gece and the Iyi'Sefir are, thus far, not engaged. But we do not believe that the threat of self-annihilation will forestall them indefinitely. The Fena'Gece's determination to expand their hold throughout the galaxy has increased their menace. The Iyi'Sefir are determined to stop them at any cost. When you feel tremors begin to rock our world, you will know that the mountains in which they reside have begun to collapse. We—" Her eyes slid away from his. "We have yet to determine what the repercussions may be."

Tiern swallowed uncomfortably. There was no further hope of averting the battle then. It had already begun. He considered Kyra's words. The mountain range, in which the Fena'Gece and the Iyi'Sefir existed, encircled the entire planet. What would the consequences for his world be if they destroyed themselves? Tiern had known for some time that the Iyi'Sefir had the capability of destroying the planet. It was a capability all had hoped they would never use. Yet, as *Sotah*, he understood that it could and would be used if the Iyi'Sefir had no other means of fulfilling their self-imposed roles as guardians of morality. Was planetary destruction on the horizon? A sense of fatalism invaded his soul. Whatever would be, would be. He could do nothing but his best. He looked at the communicator. "How far away are the *Dalig* from here?"

She shrugged, a gesture uncommon in the Feheran people that revealed the extent of her own stress. "Three hours possibly. Five at the most." Tiern nodded gravely and left without comment.

As he walked through the winding corridors of the first level, Tiern touched the hilt of his broadsword where it rested against his back. *Ven-Jikan?*

I am aware.

Have you considered the possibility of severing the Fena'Gece bonding?

Yes.

What conclusions have you reached?

The bonds are formed with energy. Only energy can disrupt energy.

So it is hopeless. Tiern's sense of fatalism grew.

I did not say that, my friend. Humans are incapable of using energy in such a manner, without the augmentation of specially designed devices, but . . . perhaps the Iyi'Sefir are not. I have consulted with my kind. We may be able to do something, but we are still . . . investigating the possibilities.

There is nothing I can do?

No, Rainon. You must rely on your Sotah training. With it, you are as well-prepared as it is possible to be.

Tiern had just decided to return to his room to await the now inevitable call to arms, when he encountered Emperor Rion and his two Feheran counselors. "Chazak." Tiern nodded his head in greeting.

"Ah, Rainon. You rise early. Come. Walk with me and I will bring you up to date on the Earth situation you uncovered." The emperor gestured for him to take a position at his side, and Tiern obediently fell into step. "The Earther ships remain in Thadonian orbit, but they have not attempted to land. As a precaution, I have had all shuttlecraft guidance systems at the spaceport suspended. If they attempt to touch down during the heat of the battle, it will be perilous for them."

Tiern nodded, without comment. He knew that, as head of the council of emperors which had been formed to deal with Earth contact, Emperor Rion must continue to monitor the threat, small though it might be at this point. But he found it difficult to consider the possible hazard the Earthers might still represent. Their presence was much less tangible than that of the *Dalig* and Fena'Gece. If the *Sotah* and Iyi'Sefir failed in the upcoming confrontation, there would be nothing left for the Earthers to seize in any case.

The emperor continued. "I have also been in contact with Earth's leaders. They say they have no knowledge of the plot. If they are telling the truth, the situation concurs with your assessment that the scheme was that of a dissident faction within the government." The emperor paused. "It is very strange when you think of it. The *Dalig* are, in effect, our dissidents. They plot to take control of Thadonia, Earth's spaceports and the galaxy. With the promise of riches, they bring into their scheme Earthers of similar ambition. The dissident Earthers then form a plot within the *Dalig* scheme to cut their *Dalig* coconspirators out of

the plan and seize control of Thadonia themselves. It is enough to make your head spin."

The emperor shrugged. "Ah, well. We will deal
with Thadonia's *Dalig*. The Earth leaders assure
us that they will deal with their own insurgents.
Soon, relations between Earth and Thadonia will
resume and we will each be a little wiser for our
troubles. Do you agree, Rainon?"

"Yes, Chazak-Imnen." Tiern suspected that beneath the emperor's show of optimism his awareness of what they faced was as perceptive as his
own.

"Ah, here we are." They had reached a door that
opened onto a large council chamber on their
right. "I have duties to which I must attend. I
believe the morning meal is about to be delivered to your chambers if you care to return now.
Thank you for your company."

Tiern bowed his head. "It was my pleasure,
Chazak." He turned to leave.

"Rainon—?"

Tiern turned back to face Emperor Rion.
"Yes?"

The emperor seemed momentarily at a loss for
words. "I wish you well." Without waiting for
a response, he turned and entered his council
chambers.

Tiern was just opening the door to his room
when the first tremor struck, knocking him
against the doorframe. He closed his eyes in
anguish, but the pain was not physical. The battle
had been joined. For the first time in Thadonian
history, the Iyi'Sefir and the Fena'Gece battled
each other directly. The telekinetic power the
Sotah priests had warned them of had been
unleashed. Opening his eyes, he took a deep

breath and concealed his concern before opening the door.

Coventry, seated on a cushion before a low table laden with breakfast dishes, turned to face him as he entered and closed the door. "What was that?"

"The battle has begun," he said simply as he joined her at the breakfast table. "But it is still some distance away."

"Oh." She studied him with a troubled expression on her face, and he wondered if he had concealed his own anxiety poorly. "I was worried when I awoke and you weren't here," she said. "I thought . . . I thought you might have left already."

"I will not leave without telling you."

"I'm glad," she said, watching him anxiously for another moment. Abruptly, she seemed to thrust whatever plagued her aside, for she smiled. "Well, let's eat."

Although Tiern felt little like eating, he knew he would have need of the nourishment, so he chose a couple of meat-stuffed pastries from the variety provided.

"Tiern?"

"Yes?"

"When this is over, tell me what our lives will be like . . . where we will live."

Another tremor shook them, but Tiern ignored it. "We will live on my estate about three days' journey from here. For the most part, our lives will center around it because it is the land that will provide our living. We grow crops that furnish food and fiber for clothing. The excess is sold or bartered for those things which we cannot provide for ourselves."

"It sounds very demanding."

Tiern shrugged. "The estate practically runs itself. I have employed very competent people. They are fully aware that the quality of life we all enjoy is directly linked to the prosperity of the estate."

"Oh." Coventry took another bite of her meal and regarded him thoughtfully. Finally, after swallowing, she lay down her fork with an air of decision. "How much time are you required to spend away from the estate fulfilling your duties as *Sotah*?"

Ah, so that is what had been bothering her. "The *Sotah* is an enormous organization. Accordingly, assignments are rotated. It is an unusual occurrence for more than one quarter of us to be activated at any one time. We all have our own lives, and this is understood. I will rarely be called upon more than twice in a year, and the average length of each service is seldom longer than three weeks." He studied Coventry, awaiting her reaction.

"So, this," she waved her hand expressively and he had no doubt she referred to the *Dalig* situation, "does not occur very often. But, I still don't understand what being *Sotah* requires of you. When you *are* called, is it usually as a soldier to fight a war, or as an investigator? If you are primarily an investigator, why don't the emperor's soldiers fight the wars?"

"My primary duty has always been to investigate in order to preserve and maintain peace. This usually involves the apprehension of criminals. Such is the function of the *Sotah*. But we have also sworn to protect our respective empires and emperors. If that demands that we function as warriors, or soldiers as you call them, then that is what we must do. The emperor's troops of warriors are . . . ineffective against the *Dalig;* they do not have the training. To pit them against *Dalig* without the aid of *Sotah* would be sending them to their deaths."

She considered his words thoughtfully. "So what would happen if one empire declared war on another? You have each sworn to protect your respective emperors. What then?"

"The *Sotah's* first loyalty is always to the *Sotah.* We are brothers. We do not war on each other." He considered her for a moment. "Do you understand?"

She nodded slowly. "I think so."

"And have I managed to appease some of your worry?"

"You will not often be in the kind of danger that . . . that you will soon face?"

"It is unlikely," he assured her.

"And you won't be going off for months at a time while I have no contact with you?"

"No."

"Then you have managed to appease my worry." She smiled.

They continued their meal in companionable silence, ignoring the frequent tremors that continued to be felt through the stone of the stronghold. Thoughts of the coming hours and what the future might hold occupied them. When Tiern had finished forcing himself to swallow as much as he could for the sake of energy stores, he rose, removed the baldric containing Ven-Jikan, and reclined on the bed for a time. He had slept little last night and he knew he would not sleep again until it was over. Nevertheless, simply relaxing his body would aid in providing it with stamina. He positioned his forearm over his eyes to block the bright daylight now flooding the apartment and emptied his mind of thought.

A few minutes later, Coventry joined him on the bed, stretching out beside him as she rested her head on his chest. He positioned his arm to hold her, enjoying the sensation of simply feeling her against him for a time. And then slowly, tenderly, he began to make love to her. She was a remarkable woman, and he did not think his assessment was entirely due to the involvement of his emotions.

Rainon?

Tiern raised his head slightly at Ven-Jikan's call. *Yes?*

It is time to move now to meet the Dalig. They are less than an hour away. You must stop at the armory and choose another sword for yourself. All Sotah must fight with two weapons wherever possible.

Why?

The Iyi'Sefir have devised a means which may accomplish the severing of the bond between the Fena'Gece and those of the Dalig who are forced companions. But the method is not certain. If it results in damage to ourselves, we do not want to endanger our companions.

How are you going to be able to tell who, among the Dalig, is an unwilling participant?

We know.

Tiern looked at Coventry's sleeping form as she lay in the circle of his arms. The lovemaking they had shared had been warmer and more caring than he would have thought possible. They had allowed their bodies to express the depth of the emotion they shared in a way that words never could. He reached to brush a strand of golden hair from her forehead. She looked so peaceful;

he hated to wake her. He allowed his eyes to roam her lovely face, drinking in the sight of her, memorizing each line and curve. "Coventry." Her eyes opened almost immediately. "I must go."

Her eyes reflected her anxiety, yet she merely nodded, observing him as he rose to prepare to leave. The air was thick with the emotion between them, yet the words had all been said. Trailing him to the door, she kissed him once more and he carried her final, husky words with him as he entered the corridor. "I will be waiting for you."

Chapter Nineteen

As Tiern joined his *Sotah* brothers on the field surrounding the emperor's fortress, he was immediately assailed by an atmosphere of expectancy. Over a thousand *Sotah* had congregated to protect their emperor, yet silence reigned, the product of discipline imparted long ago. There were no friendly greetings, no words of encouragement to nervous companions and no boisterous activities designed to instill false bravery. The *Sotah*, through their telepathic symbiotic companions, were focused on the approach of the *Dalig*. And not even the tremors that continued to rock the ground on which they stood hindered that focus. Like supple young trees, their bodies simply shifted automatically to regain stability.

Taking up a position among his brothers, Tiern joined the link. Immediately he felt the *Dalig* presence. They were near. He scanned the horizon. Dust, churned by hundreds of marching feet, hung in the still air. Very near. Not for the first time, he wished that the dyre could have been trained to accompany their owners into battle. But the scent of blood crazed the beasts and they were as likely to attack friend as foe, so any such attempt always had resulted in failure.

Suddenly there was a faint, disturbing ripple in the link he shared with his brother *Sotah*, and he knew that, somewhere, in some distant battle, a *Sotah* had died. A minute later there was another ripple, and another. Too many.

And then, the *Dalig* army rose over the horizon. As one body, the *Sotah* moved forward to engage the enemy. The instant they met, screams of agonizing pain rent the air. *Sotah* and *Dalig* alike began to fall. Tiern looked into the eyes of the nearest enemy, reading him. Malevolence struck him like a blow and he ran the last steps to engage this man, this creature, who by his very existence offered insult to the potential of humankind. In one blow, he managed to knock the sword from his enemy's hand. Having removed the *Dalig*'s shield, he struck with the telekinetic weapon he had once used against the man who had called himself Kys aboard the *Payload*. It was the only telekinetic capability taught to the *Sotah*, and some were incapable of mastering it, but when used it was highly effective. The *Dalig* dropped. Tiern turned to face another enemy. He raised Ven-Jikan.

No! He is coerced. Use the other sword.

In the blink of an eye, Tiern switched swords, carrying Ven-Jikan high in his left hand as he parried the blows of the Fena'Gece puppet, in the guise of a *Dalig* warrior, with the other. Immediately, he sensed a change in Ven-Jikan. Coruscating energy leapt from the tip of his companion-sword. The filaments of unfamiliar power, flickering with energized scintilla, snaked through the air toward the warrior. Yet they did not contact the man, but the *Dalig* blade he carried. The response was immediate. The warrior froze. Visible tendrils of energy withdrew from his body as the Fena'Gece sword prepared to combat the Iyi'Sefir's attack.

Now! Knock the weapon from his hand. Quickly, Rainon!

It required little effort to extricate the sword from the hand of an immobilized, entranced man. The instant the sword left the man's grasp, even before it struck the ground, Ven-Jikan withdrew the energized tentacles. The man's gaze took on awareness. Yet, he appeared too stunned to move. "Get to the rear, man. Quickly!" Tiern gave him an impatient shove to move him in that direction as he whirled to face his next opponent. Too late! He received a stunning blow to his left arm. His mind blocked the pain. He knew without examining the wound that Ven-Jikan had managed to shield him from the worst of it and that the pain was primarily the result of contact with the energy implanted in a *Dalig* weapon.

The battle raged on. Quaking terrain. Blood. Dust. The screams of the injured and dying. Fatigue. These became the elements of Tiern's world. He no longer knew how many men he had killed, nor how many he had helped free of *Dalig* control. Yet he had seen the other *Sotah* and their symbiotic weapons performing the same feat as had Ven-Jikan, and he felt certain the *Sotah* had saved a number of men who did not deserve to die this day. The sun had passed its zenith. How much time had passed? Two hours? Three? And still the *Dalig* came. How many were there?

He whirled to face another snarling countenance and . . . stopped dead. He faced his own estate manager, Varen. Only reflexes honed by years of rigorous training saved his life as he leapt from the path of the blade that sought to end his life. *Ven-Jikan?* He sought confirmation that Varen was indeed coerced and had not merely managed to conceal a proclivity toward corruption.

He is coerced. Switch blades. His companion's words had an urgent quality as they sounded in his mind, but Tiern did not have time to do more than take note of the fact as Varen attacked. He and Varen had been sparring partners for years. Despite the fact that he was not *Sotah,* the man was a master swordsman. Desperately, Tiern parried his friend's attack as he waited for Ven-Jikan to act. The coruscating energy seemed slower this time, not as vibrant, as it arched through the air to contact the weapon in Varen's hand. But the response was as immediate as it had been in all the previous instances. Varen was immobilized as the Fena'Gece strove to combat the direct attack. With split-second timing, Tiern knocked the malevolent blade from Varen's hand. Ven-Jikan withdrew the energy, but not as swiftly as before; his timing was off. With horror, Tiern saw that desperately flailing tentacles of a similar energy had snaked up from the Fena'Gece, following his companion. He sensed danger for Ven-Jikan.

Instinctively he leapt into the path of the lashing strands of energy. *No!* He heard the word in his mind even as he came into contact with the Fena'Gece. The energized filaments penetrated his abdominal flesh. Agony. Magnified a hundredfold. None of the pleasure he felt through bonding with Ven-Jikan. He was defiled, sullied by the contact to the point that his stomach heaved with sickness and bile rose in his throat. *Fight it!* He fought. He concentrated with every fiber of his being on purging this loathsome beast from his body. He hated it for being what it was. He pitied it for not understanding its own potential. He loved what it could have been. A scream of rage and pain sounded in his brain. And then he was free, collapsing to his knees as his strength failed him.

He stared at his shaking hands. The sword he had carried from the armory was gone. Had he dropped it? Suddenly he saw that, while he had struggled against the hold of the Fena'Gece, Varen had seized the weapon to protect him. *Ven-Jikan?*

I am here, friend.

Are you all right?

Yes. But I am weak. I do not have the strength for more direct contact. I do not even know how effectively I will be able to continue to shield you.

How are the other Iyi'Sefir? Do they tire also?

Those here, yes. Soon we will be forced to abandon the attempt to save the lives of the enslaved humans.

Tiern, breathing deeply, had begun to regain a measure of his strength. He looked at the battles being waged around him, saw Varen engaged in combat with a young *Dalig*. He was more than holding his own. Suddenly another tremor undulated through the earth beneath him, rippling the soil like a giant serpent. *What of the Iyi'Sefir in the mountains, Ven-Jikan? How goes the battle there?*

There was no response.

Ven-Jikan?

Many die. Most from telekinetic battle, but countless others as a result of the collapsing stone. The tremendous release of combative energy is destroying the mountain range.

I am sorry. Tiern rose slowly to his feet. His strength was returning. It was time to return to the fray.

377

Christine Michels

* * *

Twilight cloaked the landscape. Coventry had moved from the window of Tiern's apartment only twice all day. Once to answer the door and decline the invitation to join a number of women who, like herself, awaited men on the battlefield. Coventry preferred her solitary vigil from the vantage point of Tiern's apartment where she could see the battlefield beyond. And the second time, she had been forced to abandon her post by the demands of bodily functions.

Now, she looked down on the field littered with bodies. Only a few tight knots of warriors fought on. She had seen some figures retreating over the horizon and was reasonably certain that they could not be *Sotah*. Did that mean the *Sotah* had won? Did Tiern live? The waiting, the anxiety was driving her crazy. She fixed her gaze on the people still moving below, striving to recognize Tiern. Yet she knew the attempt was in vain. The distance was too great.

Suddenly a shudder greater than any that had rocked the fortress throughout the day struck with the force of a tidal wave, knocking Coventry to the floor. Plaster rained down from the ceiling. Furniture toppled. Somewhere nearby she heard the high-pitched scream of a woman. Yet one thought remained uppermost in Coventry's mind. She had to return to the window, to her vigil. The certainty that Tiern would die if she abandoned her post had settled deep within her. And, illogical though the certitude might be, she refused to give it up.

As she pulled herself back into the window seat to view the field beyond, her eyes widened in horror. An enormous fissure was snaking its way across the grassland, swallowing all in its path. People both dead and living toppled into it even as they scrambled to escape. Even those that still fought deserted the battlefield. Thankfully, most were on this side of the fracture, and they ran for the security of the walled fortress. A few, heading in the other direction, tried to leap the giant crack, but only succeeded in falling into it. *Dalig.* Within minutes there was no further movement. The quake had stopped as suddenly as it had begun. The only people left on the field lay unmoving. Darkness moved closer, attempting to cloak the scene of horror from eyes already strained. Reluctantly, Coventry turned from the window.

Tiern leaned against the inner wall of the fortress, observing the activity within the compound in an uncomprehending daze. He was beyond fatigue. Now that Ven-Jikan had withdrawn the bolstering strength that had been infusing his body throughout the battle, he was on the verge of complete exhaustion.

The battle is over, my friend. Here. Everywhere. The Fena'Gece and the Dalig have acknowledged defeat. Thadonia will survive.

Vaguely Tiern wondered why he felt no emotion. Where was the elation, the sense of victory? With deadened eyes, he watched the emperor's troops as they prepared to enter the battlefield to collect the bodies of the dead and injured. In the center of the compound, huge mugs of a thick, rich broth were being dispensed to the exhausted *Sotah.* He saw no one among his brothers whom he recognized. *Ven-Jikan?* It was an effort even to communicate mentally.

Yes?

What news of Modoc, Singai and Juste?

There was a brief pause. *I cannot contact*

Modoc's companion. Singai is alive. Juste is . . . grievously injured. His arm was severed during combat. Had he accepted his loss, his chances would have been better. But he demanded that it be replaced so that his companion could attempt to heal it. Now, . . . well, perhaps he will live.

Tiern winced. How many *Sotah* had been lost this day?

Only one in five Sotah survived. He was surprised by Ven-Jikan's reply for he had not directed his thought to him. Fatigue was interfering with his ability to compartmentalize his thoughts.

The Dalig? Tiern prompted Ven-Jikan for further information.

One in twelve survives, including their leader. Their defeat was not as complete as in the previous battle. This time, they retreated before their ranks were so completely decimated. They will be observed closely.

Has the Dalig leader been identified then?

Yes. The Feheran have uncovered his identity thanks to you. The Dalig leader was counselor to Emperor Kard in the Terebian Empire. He is called Ilden, Counselor Ilden.

I have met him. He concealed himself well. What of the Fena'Gece and Iyi'Sefir? How do they fare?

Of those in the mountains, the numbers are equal. One in thirty Fena'Gece and one in thirty Iyi'Sefir remain. It will take thousands of years of replication to reproduce the numbers lost. But we give thanks that our race survives. Of those who are human-bonded, the Iyi'Sefir fared better than the Fena'Gece as indicated by the success of the Sotah.

Tiern swayed dizzily as he tried to force his tired brain to absorb the figures Ven-Jikan spouted so readily. He needed to see Coventry; he needed rest; and, he needed a bath, in that order. But first, his raging thirst compelled him to consume a cup of the healing brew, so he made his way shakily toward the steaming cauldron.

Unable to await news of the battle, and of Tiern, Coventry went in search of news. The corridors on the upper level were deserted and she was forced to brave the milling, duty-bound throng on the main floor. But even there, her search almost failed for no one seemed to possess the knowledge she sought. Frantic with worry, she stumbled into a chamber occupied solely by tall white-haired Feheran. They reclined in chairs, their eyes closed, and Coventry stared at them in wonder. How could they sleep? Suddenly, as she was about to back from the room, a man opened his eyes and pinned her with his penetrating gaze.

"I am the communicator, Andac. What news do you seek, Coventry Pearce?"

Coventry stared at him. "How . . . how do you know my name?"

"We perceive the names of all who visit us. Your identity shines in your mind. What news do you seek?"

Still stunned, Coventry was nevertheless able to focus on the fact that this man was apparently able to provide her with answers. "Rainon . . . *Sotah* Rainon. Is he—?" She couldn't bear to voice her question. The mere vocalization opened the realm of a possibility she did not want to consider. But the Feheran seemed to understand her query. After closing his eyes briefly, he responded.

"*Sotah* Rainon is well."

She slumped back against the door with relief. "He must be very tired."

"All those who survive are tired, Coventry Pearce."

"Coventry. Just Coventry, please," she said absently. His statement brought to mind the picture of the field beyond the fortress with its tangle of bodies that only hours before had been living, breathing human beings. How much worse would the experience have been for Tiern who had seen his comrades fall? "How . . . how can I arrange for a bath and refreshment for his chamber?"

"I will make the arrangements." Once again, he closed his eyes. "It is done."

"Thank you, . . . Andac." She turned to leave the room and return to Tiern's apartment.

Tiern opened the door and stepped into the room, his eyes automatically seeking the solace of Coventry's presence. For a moment, as he closed the door behind him, he thought the chamber was empty. And then he saw her as she emerged from the bath chamber. Suddenly, she looked up and saw him in the doorway. Her lips curled in the most beautiful smile of welcome he had ever seen. In an instant, she closed the distance between them, wrapping her arms firmly about his waist as she rested her head against his chest.

"I was so afraid for you," she murmured.

He responded wordlessly, holding her tightly within his embrace as he brushed the top of her golden head with his lips. She felt so good in his arms. So good. He closed his eyes wearily.

"Come," Coventry said, raising her head to look up into his face. "I have arranged a bath for you."

"I am too tired to even raise the cloth to wash my face," he said. "I will bathe later."

"No." She shook her head as she stepped back

to grip his hand. "You will bathe now, while the water is hot enough to soothe your muscles. If you are too tired to wash yourself, then I will do it for you. You will rest more easily after a bath."

Intrigued by the thought of having Coventry wash him, Tiern allowed her to lead him to the bath despite his fatigue. As she began to remove his clothing, soothing aching muscles with caressing hands as she worked, he felt her love for him as tangibly as a spring breeze. The magnitude of the emotion he felt humbled him. What had he done to earn the love of a woman like Coventry? Her mind must be absolutely seething with questions about Thadonia, about things she had witnessed that she could not possibly understand. And yet, not once had she questioned him at inopportune times. Not once had she failed to grasp the magnitude of a situation and adapt. Not once had she failed him. Was it any wonder that she had so thoroughly ensnared his heart? He loved everything about her. Even her fiery temperament. *Especially* her temperament, he amended on reflection. For when he managed to transform her anger into passion, the latter rivaled the former in intensity. Yes, Coventry Pearce was the perfect woman. For him.

"Step in." Her words startled him from his thoughts, and he realized she was ready for him to enter the bath. He obliged and decided Coventry had been right; the warm water was pure bliss. With a sigh of contentment, he leaned back in the large tub and closed his eyes, relishing the dual caress of the warm water and Coventry's soapy hands on his aching limbs. Slowly, the tension eased from his muscles.

"Tiern. Wake up, Tiern." Distantly Coventry's

soft voice penetrated the fog of lassitude surrounding him and he opened his eyes. She
smiled tenderly. "Let me wash your hair and
then you can go to bed to sleep." He adjusted
his position as she directed and moments later
stepped from the tub as she toweled him dry. He
had not been bathed and dried with such tender
care since he was a child. And it felt good, really
good. Yet he wondered briefly in some distant
corner of his mind why his male ego wasn't
outraged at the necessity for such assistance.
Why wasn't he embarrassed? Because it was
Coventry, he realized. Were another woman to
provide such care to him, he would have been
thoroughly humiliated. With Coventry he could
be . . . himself.

"Come." He watched her as she led him to the
bed and folded back the bedding for him. When he
was settled, she crawled in next to him, wrapping
her arms around him. He wanted desperately to
make love to her, but he knew his body wasn't up
to it, so he contented himself with her comforting
presence. Coventry had been right about the bath,
he reflected. Now, instead of the bone-numbing
weariness that had afflicted him, his body felt as
though it drifted on a soft cloud. He slept.

The next day the rites of passage were performed for those *Sotah* who had given their lives
to preserve their world. Their bodies were laid to
rest in the very soil which had absorbed so much
of their blood, and a cairn of stone was erected
to remind the living of their debt to those that
lay there. It was a solemn occasion shared by the
priests of the *Sotah* and committed to the annals
of Thadonian history by archivists. But when it
was over, despite grief and pain and memories,

life resumed—as it must. And although laughter was rare, it was understood that in the days to come, even that would resume. For that is the reason so many had died. To preserve goodness and the right to happiness. To preserve the laughter.

Three hushed but peaceful days followed for Tiern and Coventry as they and the other *Sotah* enjoyed the hospitality of Emperor Rion. They had shared three nearly idyllic days of lovemaking and languorous, unhurried conversation, during which Tiern had finally been able to explain much of Thadonian life to Coventry. Now, the morning of the fourth day, it was time to go home. His estate manager, Varen, who had managed to survive the *Dalig* conflict, had warned him that much work would be required to repair the damage done to the estate by the invading *Dalig*. Yet, despite the destruction Varen had described, Tiern faced the future with optimism. He was alive. At his side stood a woman who loved him. And, he was to be a father. He was content with life.

Both Varen and Coventry would ride dyre provided by Emperor Rion. Varen had already mounted and sat waiting for the journey to begin. Tiern helped Coventry onto the smaller, more gentle female that had been furnished for her use. Then, he turned to face Emperor Rion who had honored him by appearing to bid him a personal farewell. "Chazak Imnen," he said, bowing his head. "I wish you a long and healthy life."

"And you, *Sotah* Rainon. And you. Remember, I expect to be invited to the ceremony of your union to your chosen consort. You have chosen well."

"Thank you, Chazak," Tiern said before turning to mount Faolan. "Farewell."

The emperor nodded in reply and the trio goaded their mounts toward the open gate. As they neared the portal, a man stepped from the sidelines. "Juste!" He was pale and leaned rather heavily on a man at his side. "I had heard that you remained in isolation."

"I convinced the physician that the chance of infection from so brief an outing was minimal. We have been through much together, you and I and Singai. I wanted to wish you farewell."

"I am glad you came. I saw Singai a short time ago. She is preparing to return to her own land. Have you seen her?"

Juste nodded. "Just a minute ago." He wavered slightly on his feet, forcing the man at his side to steady him, and Tiern realized he was much weaker than he wanted to let on. The physician would have been wiser to have allowed Tiern entry to the sickroom when he had asked to see Juste, he reflected with annoyance.

"We must go, Juste." The best thing he could do now, was to move on so that his *Sotah* brother could return to his convalescence. "Visit us when you are well. We will look forward to it."

"I will. Live long and healthy, Rainon."

"And you, Juste," Tiern said as he once again directed Faolan forward.

They had traveled more than half the distance to Tiern's estate. It was late afternoon and they were just entering an expanse of forest. Suddenly Ven-Jikan spoke. *Rainon, I sense something ahead.*

What?

I do not know. It could be nothing more than the weight of a storm in the air. But, it could be a human presence, screened to disguise itself.

Tiern looked at the sky surrounding them. It

was clear. He frowned and touched Ven-Jikan, making certain the weapon was loose in his baldric. Varen, who had observed the motion, sent him a questioning look. Tiern nodded in response and saw him check the positioning of his own weapon. Scanning forest shadows as they moved, they rode on.

Suddenly, perhaps three hundred yards into the dim forest, a single man rode from concealment, positioning himself directly in their path. Tiern recognized him immediately. It was Counselor Ilden, the *Dalig* leader. If hate had been a weapon Tiern would have been dead, for the emotion issued from the man's eyes like a projectile.

"*Sotah* Rainon," he growled. "I have come to challenge you, . . . and to kill you. You will pay for fifty years of planning that came to naught."

Knowing that there could be no avoiding the confrontation, Tiern nodded wordlessly. With a glance, he directed Varen to take Coventry and leave the small clearing. Coventry remained silent as she obediently turned her mount to follow Varen. Yet, as she looked at him, her eyes begged him to take care.

The two combatants sat a moment longer, taking each other's measure before dismounting. Tiern gave Faolan a swat, prompting him out of the area, and the *Dalig* did likewise. Tiern was under no illusions. The battle would not be an easy one. One who had managed to achieve *Dalig* leadership would possess capabilities surpassing Tiern's own. Yet, he refused to consider the possibility that he might lose. Life was too precious; he had too much to live for.

The *Dalig*'s attack was swift. Their weapons clashed, cold white against warm gold. Sparks flashed at the contact. They circled each other. The forest had grown silent. Neither the chirruping of insects nor the call of birds disturbed the stillness. Tiern focused on his opponent, reading each slight muscular movement in the cruel face and disciplined body. Suddenly Ilden leapt, attempting to disrupt Tiern's balance with a stunning blow to the head with his booted feet. Tiern dodged. Slashed at the legs sailing over his head. Connected. A sound, part rage and part pain, escaped his opponent's lips as he landed. Agile despite the injury, he turned to face Tiern once more.

Tiern attacked. The *Dalig* anticipated his move and blocked it. Once again swords from opposite ends of the spectrum of good and evil met. Coruscating embers of energy showered the combatants. The *Dalig* feinted to one side and pricked Tiern's shoulder with his weapon. A brief surge of agony raged through Tiern before Ven-Jikan managed to block it. Tiern gritted his teeth. Focused once more. The conflict dragged on. Ilden began to get the upper hand. Tiern suffered four wounds to his two. He had to act, do something. But what?

Without warning, he leapt, sailing over his opponent's head. His objective was not to incapacitate the *Dalig* physically, but to disarm him. The move surprised Ilden. Tiern slashed at his sword hand, connecting. The *Dalig* screamed in agony. But although the hand was almost severed from his wrist, somehow he maintained a grip on his weapon. In a move that Tiern would not have thought possible, Ilden transferred the sword to his left hand. But even in that, Tiern gained a slight advantage. Although highly skilled, the *Dalig* was not as proficient with his left hand.

Tiern pressed the advantage. They battled back

and forth across the small clearing. Slash. Parry. Leap. Strike. The *Dalig* was drawing heavily on the healing power of his weapon, even as he fought, for his right wrist showed little bleeding and seemed to be healing itself at a phenomenal speed. Tiern leapt, slashing at the left wrist. Connected. Again the weapon stayed within the *Dalig's* grasp. How? Again Tiern vaulted through the air, kicking at the weapon. Finally, it flew from Ilden's grasp, landing a short distance away. Almost immediately he saw it begin to levitate itself as it attempted to return to its companion. He acted instantly, instinctively, telekinetically attacking the vulnerable area in the *Dalig's* brain. For an instant he thought he would fail. Ilden seemed somehow to shield himself against it even without the presence of the Fena'Gece. And then, abruptly, the *Dalig's* eyes widened and he crumpled to the forest floor to stare sightlessly at the treetops overhead. Breathing heavily, Tiern looked down on his body. The *Dalig* leader was dead.

"Tiern." He turned at Coventry's call. She raced toward him from across the clearing. Tears of relief glistened in her eyes. Opening his arms wide, he caught her to him. *Now* it was over. *Now* they could begin their lives together. Heedless of Varen's presence at the edge of the clearing, he lowered his head to kiss the woman he loved, the woman who loved him, the woman who suited him above all others. Coventry.

Epilogue

It was late when he returned to the house. It had taken hard work, and a lot of it. But the estate was finally back in shape. The *Dalig* invasion only a fading memory. "Coventry," Tiern called as he entered the bedchamber. He was certain she would be waiting up for him. She always did. And then he spotted her and was struck by a sense of déjà vu so strong it left him speechless.

Coventry sat on the floor before the fireplace, her legs curled to one side. One hand rested on her stomach, now in an advanced state of pregnancy, the other held a paper that she read by the firelight. Her long golden hair tinged with flame, she looked up at him and smiled. "I have received a letter from Dalton."

Still too stunned by the picture she made, Tiern did not reply. Had he somehow known, subconsciously, all those months ago on Earth when he had first pictured her like this, that she would be his wife and bear his child? Fate or coincidence?

"Tiern?" Coventry was gazing at him with a worried expression.

He shook his head. "I am sorry. What did you say?"

"I said, I have received a letter from Dalton."

He smiled, happy for her. "What does it say?" He moved to sit beside her.

"He says that, as reward for his part in exposing the plot that could have ruined future relations with Thadonia, and as recompense for his treatment at the hands of G.I.N. personnel, he has been awarded the position of emissary for the Fringers. They have begun to be recognized, once again, as an element of Earth society that cannot be ignored." She looked up from the letter. "He sounds very passionate. I think he will make a good politician."

Tiern nodded. She was so beautiful in the flickering firelight that he found it difficult to concentrate on her words. But he was happy for Dalton. He was a good man. He deserved better treatment than he had received.

"Tiern, you are not listening."

"I am sorry. What did you say?"

"Dalton and LaReine are getting married."

"How do you feel about that?"

"I'm not sure. I did not particularly like her the first time we met, but," she shrugged, "perhaps circumstances played a part in that. As long as she makes Dalton happy, I will be content."

"Good." He put his arm around her so she could lean back against his chest. And then he placed his hand on her stomach so he could once again experience the wonder of feeling the movement of their child within her. "Now quit worrying about Dalton and his love, and worry about your own."

"Yes, Imnen," she said with mock meekness as she turned in his embrace. "What is your wish?"

"I wish you would remove my boots and massage my feet," he replied with a straight and solemn face. "I have worked very hard this day, and they ache."

"Go to hell," she responded without heat, in

English, as she leaned forward to brush her lips over his.

He smiled. "You are not so easily angered as you once were, my love." He had found he liked the endearments the English language afforded.

"That is because I come to understand you better every day, Tiern. I can almost always tell when you are teasing."

He frowned. "Then I will have to devise new methods."

Coventry reared back, staring into his face in surprise. "You like to have me angry with you?"

"No." He brushed her lips with a tender kiss.

"Then why—?" He placed a finger over her lips.

"Because soothing your anger is . . . extremely enjoyable." He lifted her breast, heavy with impending motherhood, in his palm, stroking the nipple with his thumb.

She placed her arms around his neck. "We have a lifetime ahead of us. I would venture to say that you will see me angry with you a few more times."

And then, the only sound in the room was the crackle of the fire, a cold comparison to the fire in the hearts of two lovers destined to find each other across a galaxy of stars.

TIMESWEPT ROMANCE

TIME OF THE ROSE
By Bonita Clifton

When the silver-haired cowboy brings Madison Calloway to his run-down ranch, she thinks for sure he is senile. Certain he'll bring harm to himself, Madison follows the man into a thunderstorm and back to the wild days of his youth in the Old West.

The dread of all his enemies and the desire of all the ladies, Colton Chase does not stand a chance against the spunky beauty who has tracked him through time. And after one passion-drenched night, Colt is ready to surrender his heart to the most tempting spitfire anywhere in time.

_51922-4 \qquad $4.99 US/$5.99 CAN

A FUTURISTIC ROMANCE

AWAKENINGS
By Saranne Dawson

Fearless and bold, Justan rules his domain with an iron hand, but nothing short of the Dammai's magic will bring his warring people peace. He claims he needs Rozlynd—a bewitching beauty and the last of the Dammai—for her sorcery alone, yet inside him stirs an unexpected yearning to savor the temptress's charms, to sample her sweet innocence. And as her silken spell ensnares him, Justan battles to vanquish a power whose like he has never encountered—the power of Rozlynd's love.

_51921-6 \qquad $4.99 US/$5.99 CAN

HISTORICAL ROMANCE
HUNTERS OF THE ICE AGE: YESTERDAY'S DAWN
By Theresa Scott

Named for the massive beast sacred to his people, Mamut has proven his strength and courage time and again. But when it comes to subduing one helpless captive female, he finds himself at a distinct disadvantage. Never has he realized the power of beguiling brown eyes, soft curves and berry-red lips to weaken a man's resolve. He has claimed he will make the stolen woman his slave, but he soon learns he will never enjoy her alluring body unless he can first win her elusive heart.

_51920-8 $4.99 US/$5.99 CAN

A CONTEMPORARY ROMANCE
HIGH VOLTAGE
By Lori Copeland

Laurel Henderson hadn't expected the burden of inheriting her father's farm to fall squarely on her shoulders. And if Sheriff Clay Kerwin can't catch the culprits who are sabotaging her best efforts, her hopes of selling it are dim. Struggling with this new responsibility, Laurel has no time to pursue anything, especially not love. The best she can hope for is an affair with no strings attached. And the virile law officer is the perfect man for the job—until Laurel's scheme backfires. Blind to Clay's feelings and her own, she never dreams their amorous arrangement will lead to the passion she wants to last for a lifetime.

_51923-2 $4.99 US/$5.99 CAN

LOVE SPELL
ATTN: Order Department
Dorchester Publishing Co., Inc.
276 5th Avenue, New York, NY 10001

Please add $1.50 for shipping and handling for the first book and $.35 for each book thereafter. PA., N.Y.S. and N.Y.C. residents, please add appropriate sales tax. No cash, stamps, or C.O.D.s All orders shipped within 6 weeks via postal service book rate. Canadian orders require $2.00 extra postage and must be paid in U.S. dollars through a U.S. banking facility.

Name _____

Address _____

City _____ State _____ Zip _____

I have enclosed $_____ in payment for the checked book(s).

Payment <u>must</u> accompany all orders. ☐ Please send a free catalog.

FROM LOVE SPELL
HISTORICAL ROMANCE
THE PASSIONATE REBEL
Helene Lehr

A beautiful American patriot, Gillian Winthrop is horrified to learn that her grandmother means her to wed a traitor to the American Revolution. Her body yearns for Philip Meredith's masterful touch, but she is determined not to give her hand—or any other part of herself—to the handsome Tory, until he convinces her that he too is a passionate rebel.

_51918-6 $4.99 US/$5.99 CAN

CONTEMPORARY ROMANCE
THE TAWNY GOLD MAN
Amii Lorin

Bestselling Author Of More Than 5 Million Books In Print!

Long ago, in a moment of wild, rioting ecstasy, Jud Cammeron vowed to love her always. Now, as Anne Moore looks at her stepbrother, she sees a total stranger, a man who plans to take control of his father's estate and everyone on it. Anne knows things are different—she is a grown woman with a fiance—but something tells her she still belongs to the tawny gold man.

_51919-4 $4.99 US/$5.99 CAN

LOVE SPELL
ATTN: Order Department
Dorchester Publishing Company, Inc.
276 5th Avenue, New York, NY 10001

Please add $1.50 for shipping and handling for the first book and $.35 for each book thereafter. PA., N.Y.S. and N.Y.C. residents, please add appropriate sales tax. No cash, stamps, or C.O.D.s. All orders shipped within 6 weeks via postal service book rate. Canadian orders require $2.00 extra postage and must be paid in U.S. dollars through a U.S. banking facility.

Name _____

Address _____

City _____ State _____ Zip _____

I have enclosed $_____ in payment for the checked book(s).
Payment <u>must</u> accompany all orders.☐ Please send a free catalog.

AN HISTORICAL ROMANCE
GILDED SPLENDOR
By Elizabeth Parker

Bound for the London stage, sheltered Amanda Prescott has no idea that fate has already cast her first role as a rakehell's true love. But while visiting Patrick Winter's country estate, she succumbs to the dashing peer's burning desire. Amid the glittering milieu of wealth and glamour, Amanda and Patrick banish forever their harsh past and make all their fantasies a passionate reality.

_51914-3 $4.99 US/$5.99 CAN

A CONTEMPORARY ROMANCE
MADE FOR EACH OTHER/RAVISHED
By Parris Afton Bonds
Bestselling Author of *The Captive*

In *Made for Each Other*, reporter Julie Dever thinks she knows everything about Senator Nicholas Raffer—until he rescues her from a car wreck and shares with her a passion she never dared hope for. And in *Ravished*, a Mexican vacation changes nurse Nelli Walzchak's life when she is kidnapped by a handsome stranger who needs more than her professional help.

_51915-1 $4.99 US/$5.99 CAN

LEISURE BOOKS
ATTN: Order Department
276 5th Avenue, New York, NY 10001

Please add $1.50 for shipping and handling for the first book and $.35 for each book thereafter. PA., N.Y.S. and N.Y.C. residents, please add appropriate sales tax. No cash, stamps, or C.O.D.s. All orders shipped within 6 weeks via postal service book rate. Canadian orders require $2.00 extra postage and must be paid in U.S. dollars through a U.S. banking facility.

Name _____

Address _____

City _____ State _____ Zip _____

I have enclosed $_____ in payment for the checked book(s). Payment <u>must</u> accompany all orders.☐ Please send a free catalog.

FUTURISTIC ROMANCE
FIRESTAR
Kathleen Morgan
Bestselling Author of *The Knowing Crystal*

From the moment Meriel lays eyes on the virile slave chosen to breed with her, the heir to the Tenuan throne is loath to perform her imperial duty and produce a child. Yet despite her resolve, Meriel soon succumbs to Gage Bardwin—the one man who can save her planet.

_0-505-51908-9 $4.99 US/$5.99 CAN

TIMESWEPT ROMANCE
ALL THE TIME WE NEED
Megan Daniel

Nearly drowned after trying to save a client, musical agent Charli Stewart wakes up in New Orleans's finest brothel—run by the mother of the city's most virile man—on the eve of the Civil War. Unsure if she'll ever return to her own era, Charli gambles her heart on a love that might end as quickly as it began.

_0-505-51909-7 $4.99 US/$5.99 CAN

LEISURE BOOKS
ATTN: Order Department
276 5th Avenue, New York, NY 10001

Please add $1.50 for shipping and handling for the first book and $.35 for each book thereafter. PA., N.Y.S. and N.Y.C. residents, please add appropriate sales tax. No cash, stamps, or C.O.D.s. All orders shipped within 6 weeks via postal service book rate. Canadian orders require $2.00 extra postage and must be paid in U.S. dollars through a U.S. banking facility.

Name_____
Address_____
City _____ State _____Zip_____
I have enclosed $_____in payment for the checked book(s).
Payment <u>must</u> accompany all orders.□ Please send a free catalog.